My Little Pony Holiday Memories

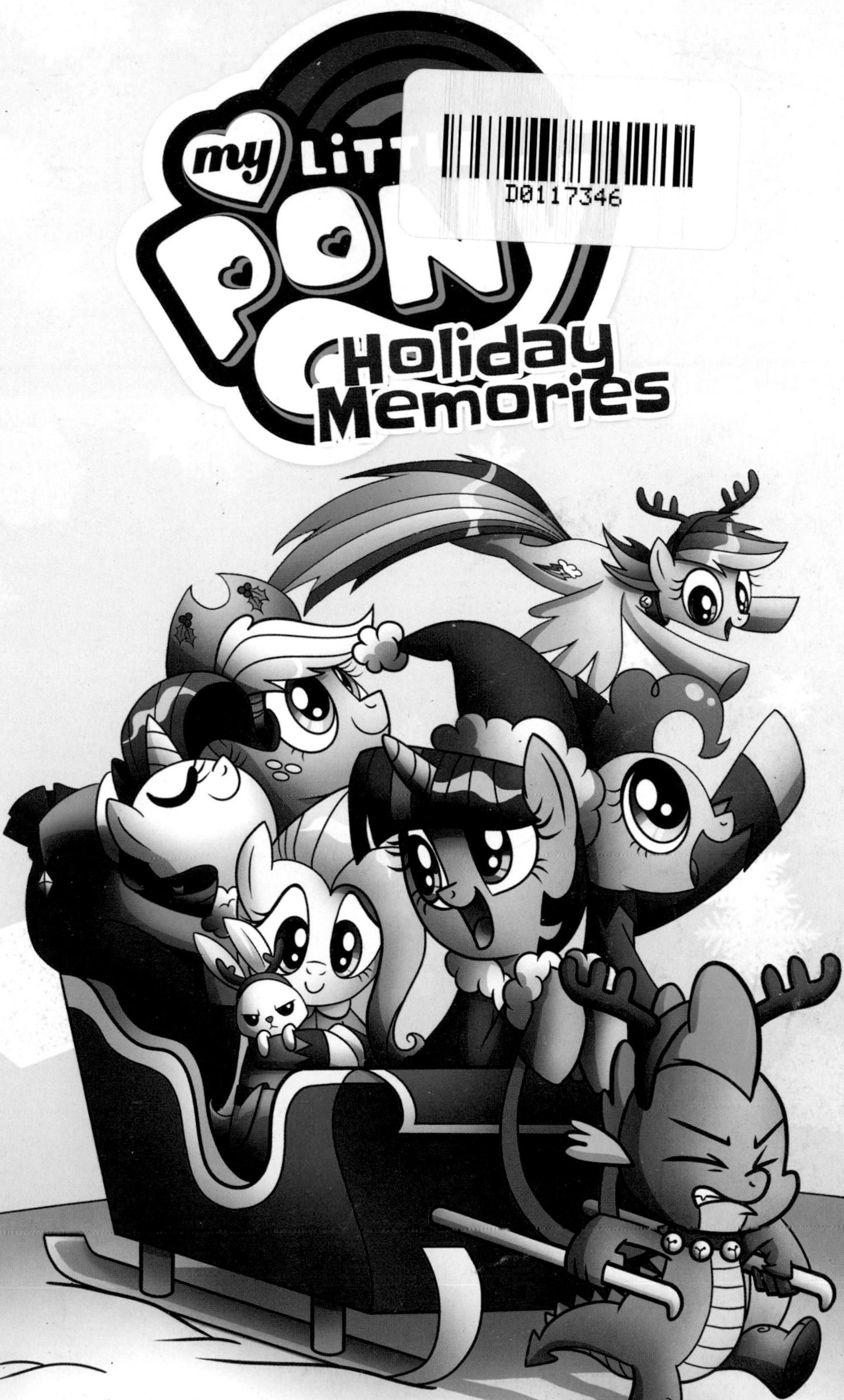

Facebook: **facebook.com/idwpublishing**
Twitter: **@idwpublishing**
YouTube: **youtube.com/idwpublishing**
Tumblr: **tumblr.idwpublishing.com**
Instagram: **instagram.com/idwpublishing**

www.IDWPUBLISHING.com

Licensed By:

Chris Ryall, President & Publisher/CCO
Cara Morrison, Chief Financial Officer
Matthew Ruzicka, Chief Accounting Officer
John Barber, Editor-in-Chief
Justin Eisinger, Editorial Director, Graphic Novels and Collections
Jerry Bennington, VP of New Product Development
Lorelei Bunjes, VP of Technology & Information Services
Anna Morrow, Marketing Director
Tara McCrillis, Director of Design & Production
Mike Ford, Director of Operations
Shauna Monteforte, Manufacturing Operations Director
Rebekah Cahalin, General Manager

Ted Adams and Robbie Robbins, IDW Founders

**COVER ARTIST
BRENDA HICKEY**

**LETTERER
NEIL UYETAKE**

**SERIES EDITORS
BOBBY CURNOW
AND MEGAN BROWN**

**COLLECTION EDITORS
ALONZO SIMON
AND ZAC BOONE**

**COLLECTION DESIGNER
CLAUDIA CHONG**

ISBN: 978-1-68405-721-4   23 22 21 20   1 2 3 4

Originally published as MY LITTLE PONY MICRO-SERIES #6: APPLEJACK, MY LITTLE PONY HOLIDAY SPECIAL 2015, MY LITTLE PONY HOLIDAY SPECIAL 2017, and MY LITTLE PONY HOLIDAY SPECIAL 2019.

Special thanks to Tayla Reo, Ed Lane, Beth Artale, and Michael Kelly.

For international rights, contact licensing@idwpublishing.com

My Little Pony: Holiday Memories

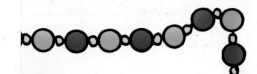

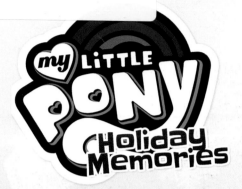

IN SEARCH OF... SASS SQUASH!

WRITTEN BY Bobby Curnow
ART & LYRICS BY Brenda Hickey
COLORS BY Heather Breckel

TALES OF HEARTH'S WARMING EVE

WRITTEN BY Katie Cook
ART BY Katie Cook, Brenda Hickey, Agnes Garbowska, and Andy Price
COLORS BY Heather Breckel

A FLIM FLAM HEARTH'S WARMING EVE

WRITTEN BY James Asmus
ART BY Brenda Hickey
COLORS BY Heather Breckel

HOLIDAY HASSLE

WRITTEN BY James Asmus
ART BY Andy Price
COLORS BY Heather Breckel

KRUMPLE HORN

WRITTEN BY James Asmus
ART BY Trish Forstner
COLORS BY Heather Breckel

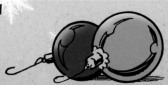

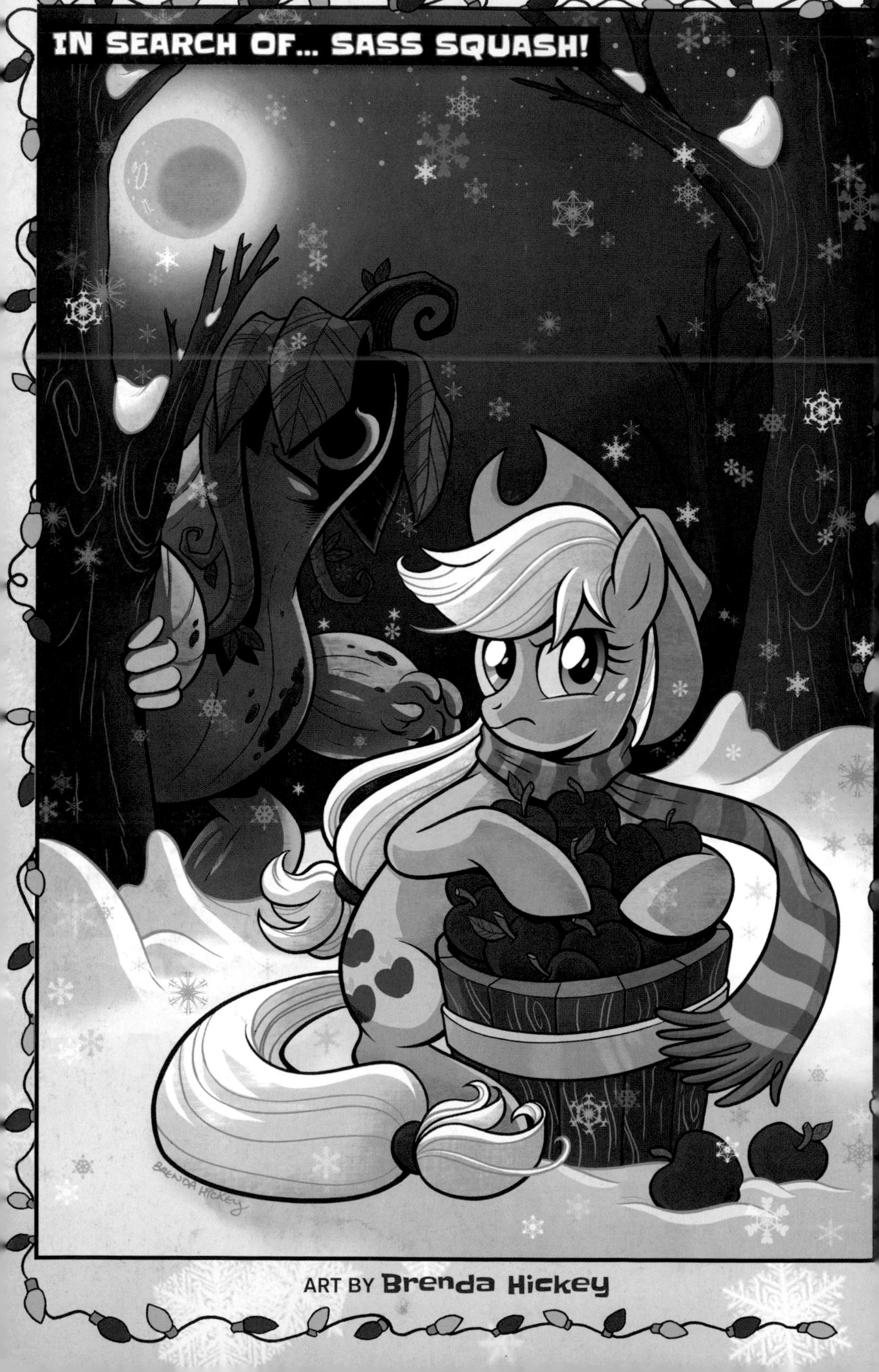
IN SEARCH OF... SASS SQUASH!
BRENDA HICKEY

ART BY Brenda Hickey

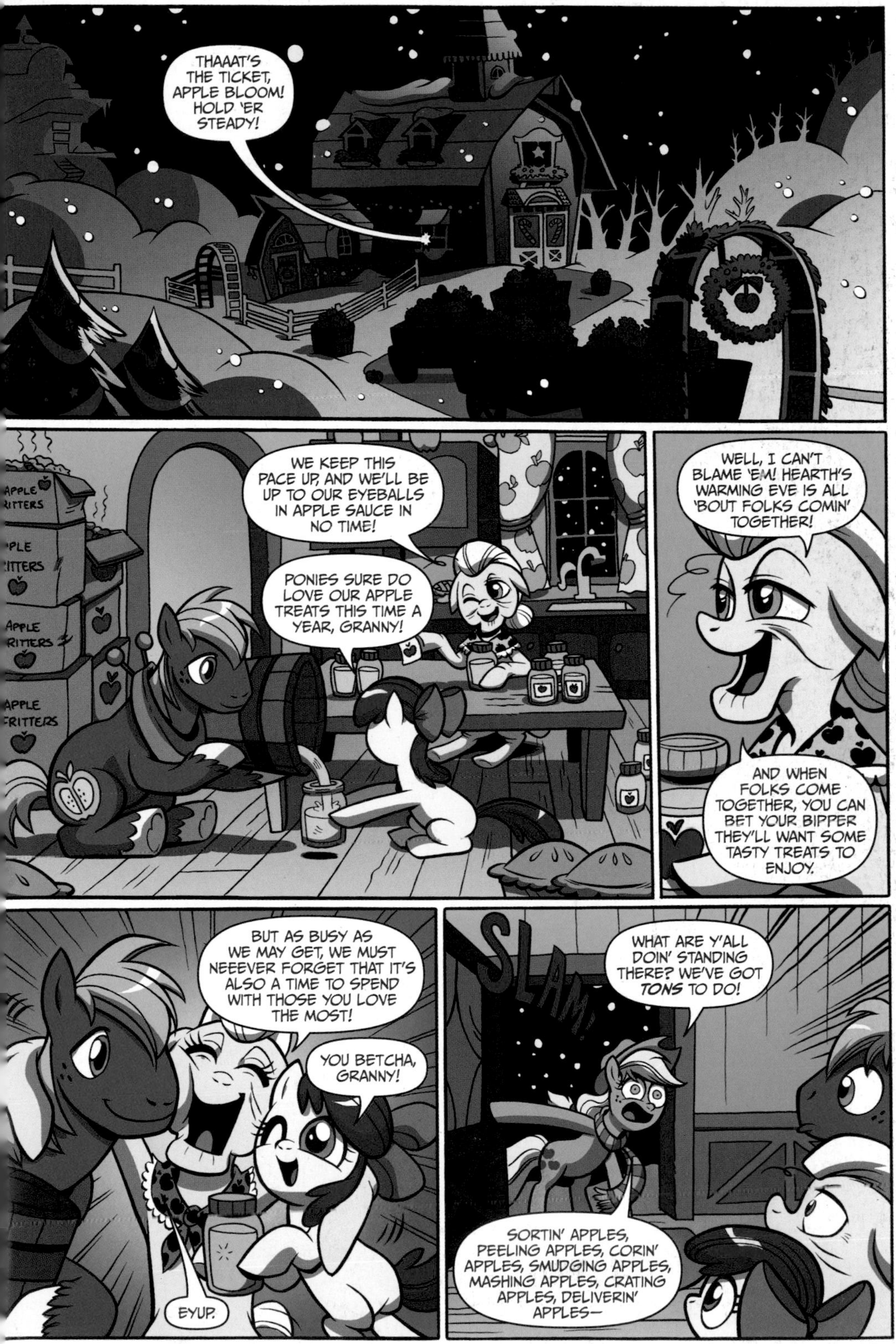
THAAAT'S THE TICKET, APPLE BLOOM! HOLD 'ER STEADY!
APPLE FRITTERS
APPLE FRITTERS
APPLE FRITTERS
APPLE FRITTERS
WE KEEP THIS PACE UP, AND WE'LL BE UP TO OUR EYEBALLS IN APPLE SAUCE IN NO TIME!
PONIES SURE DO LOVE OUR APPLE TREATS THIS TIME A YEAR, GRANNY!
WELL, I CAN'T BLAME 'EM! HEARTH'S WARMING EVE IS ALL 'BOUT FOLKS COMIN' TOGETHER!
AND WHEN FOLKS COME TOGETHER, YOU CAN BET YOUR BIPPER THEY'LL WANT SOME TASTY TREATS TO ENJOY.
BUT AS BUSY AS WE MAY GET, WE MUST NEEEVER FORGET THAT IT'S ALSO A TIME TO SPEND WITH THOSE YOU LOVE THE MOST!
YOU BETCHA, GRANNY!
EYUP.
SLAM!
WHAT ARE Y'ALL DOIN' STANDING THERE? WE'VE GOT *TONS* TO DO!
SORTIN' APPLES, PEELING APPLES, CORIN' APPLES, SMUDGING APPLES, MASHING APPLES, CRATING APPLES, DELIVERIN' APPLES—

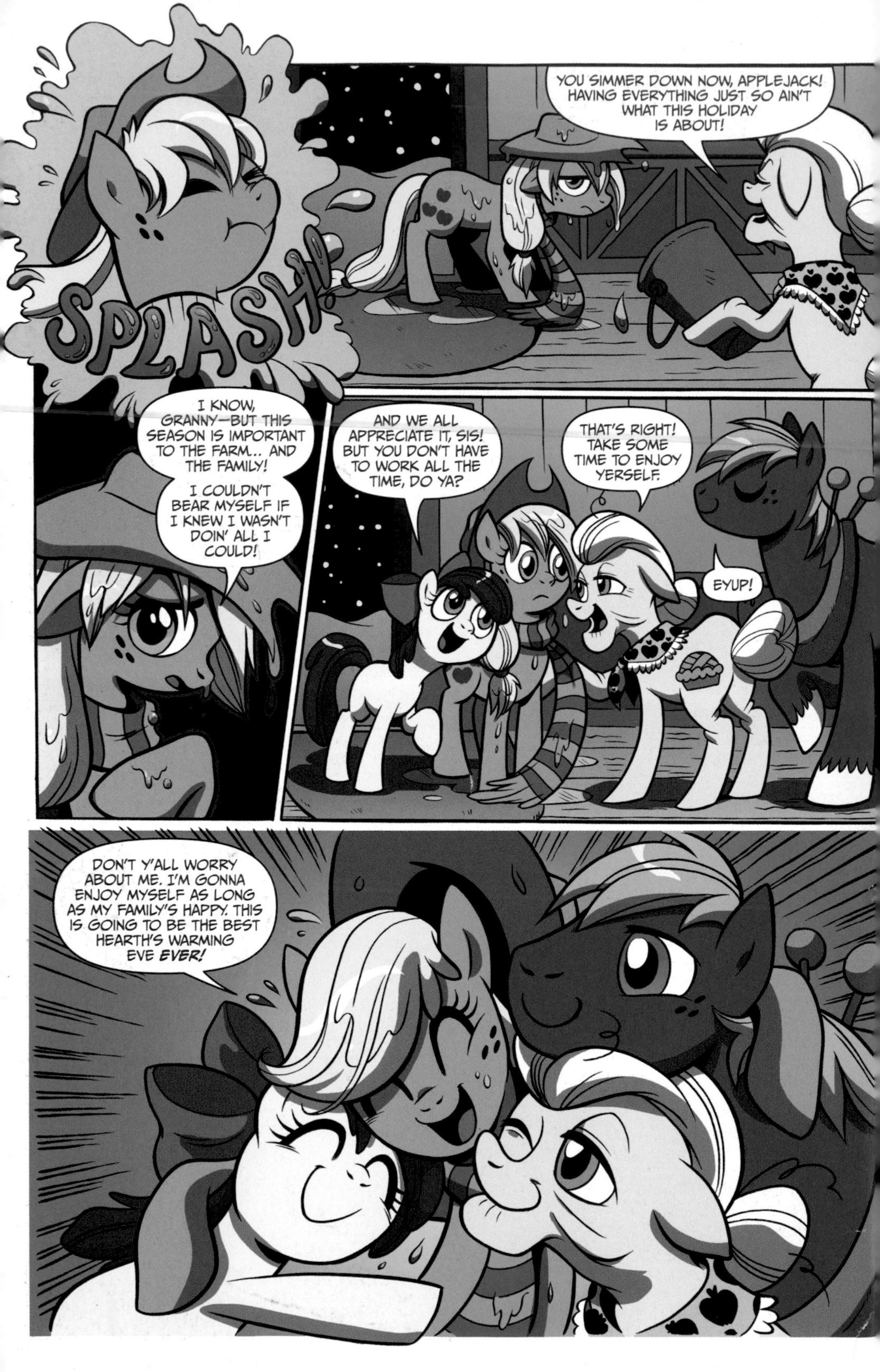
SPLASH!
YOU SIMMER DOWN NOW, APPLEJACK! HAVING EVERYTHING JUST SO AIN'T WHAT THIS HOLIDAY IS ABOUT!
I KNOW, GRANNY—BUT THIS SEASON IS IMPORTANT TO THE FARM... AND THE FAMILY!
I COULDN'T BEAR MYSELF IF I KNEW I WASN'T DOIN' ALL I COULD!
AND WE ALL APPRECIATE IT, SIS! BUT YOU DON'T HAVE TO WORK ALL THE TIME, DO YA?
THAT'S RIGHT! TAKE SOME TIME TO ENJOY YERSELF.
EYUP!
DON'T Y'ALL WORRY ABOUT ME. I'M GONNA ENJOY MYSELF AS LONG AS MY FAMILY'S HAPPY. THIS IS GOING TO BE THE BEST HEARTH'S WARMING EVE *EVER!*

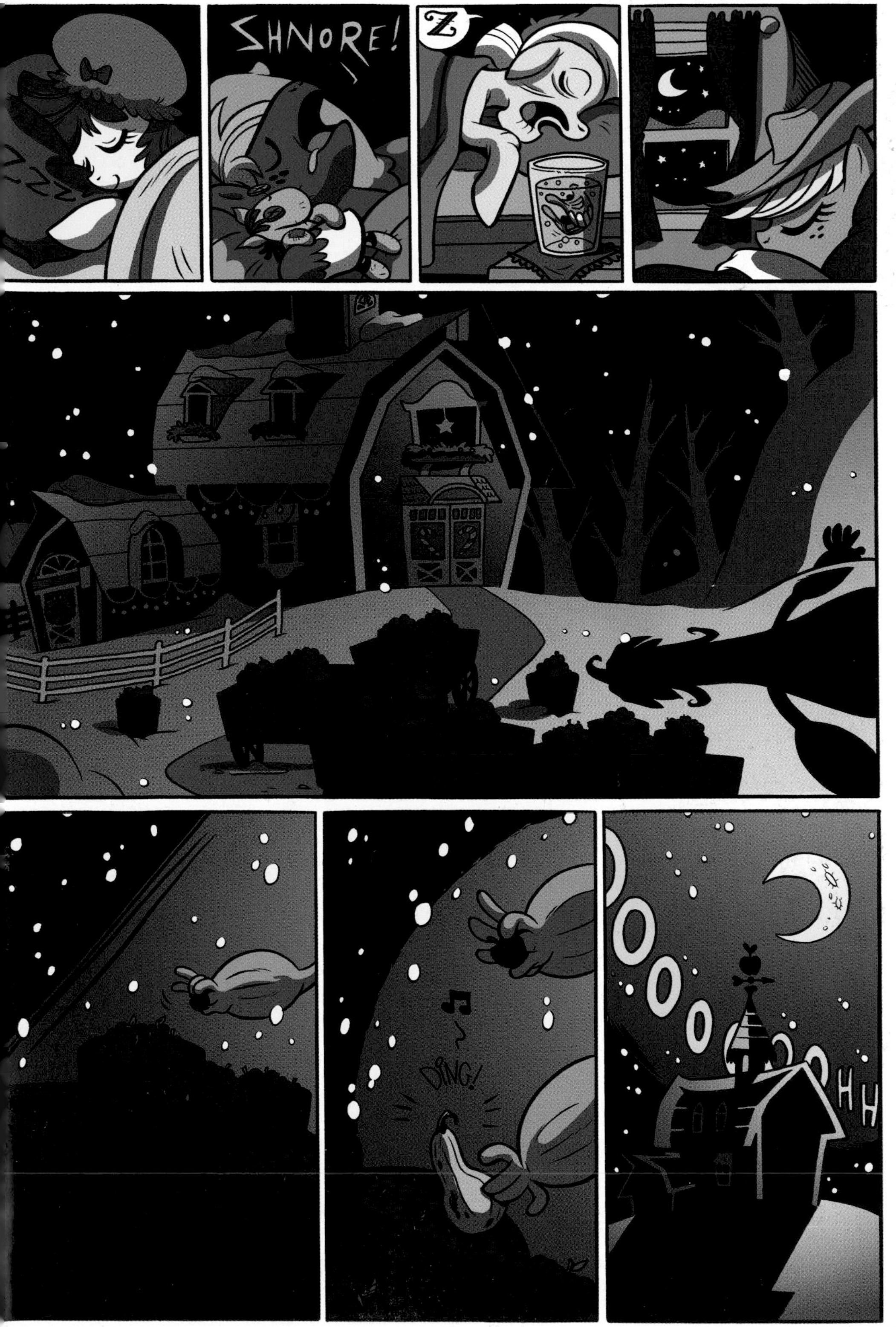
Z-ZZZ
SHNORE!
Z
DING!
OOOOOOOHH

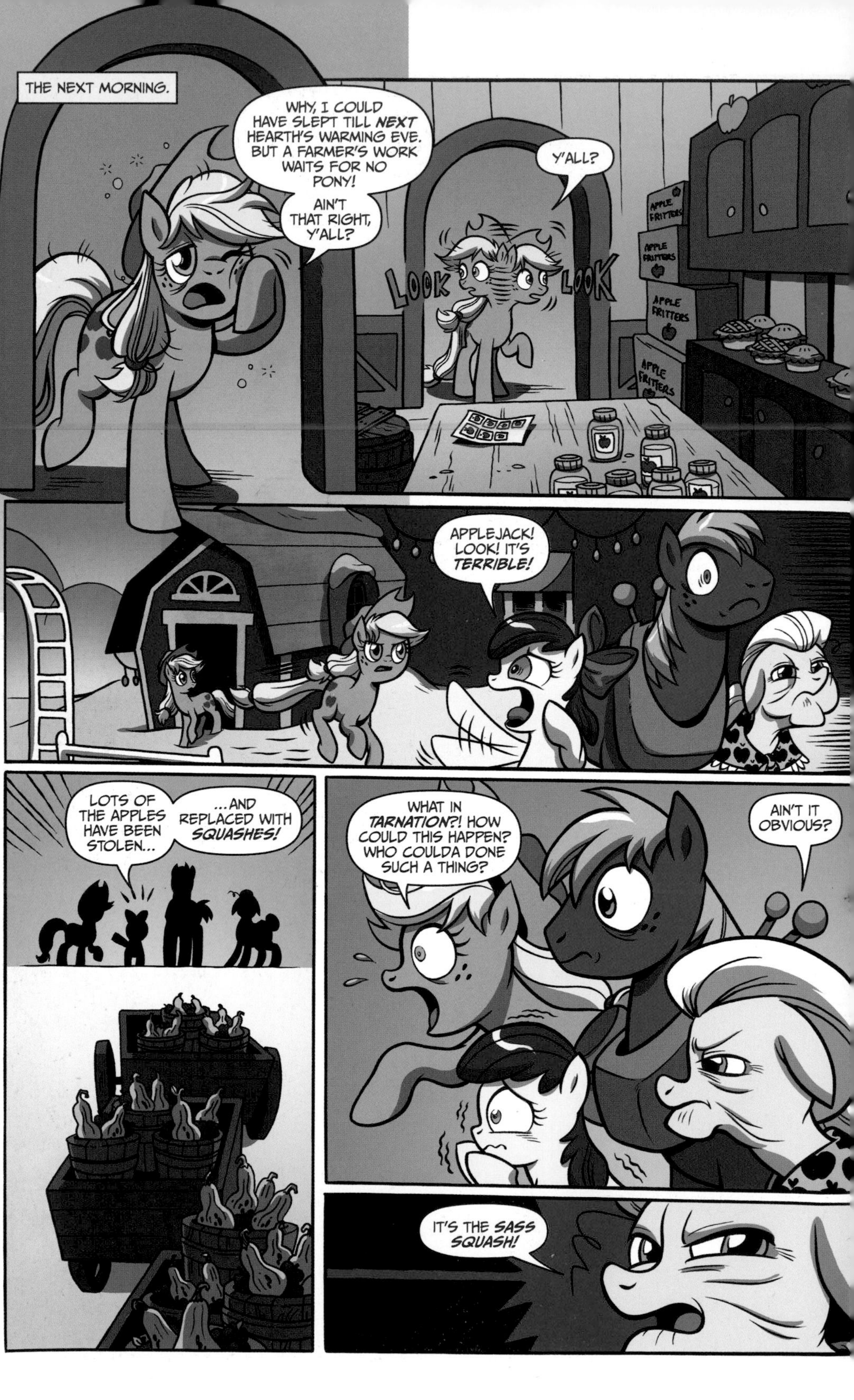
THE NEXT MORNING.
WHY, I COULD HAVE SLEPT TILL NEXT HEARTH'S WARMING EVE. BUT A FARMER'S WORK WAITS FOR NO PONY!
AIN'T THAT RIGHT, Y'ALL?
Y'ALL?
LOOK
LOOK
APPLE FRITTERS
APPLE FRITTERS
APPLE FRITTERS
APPLE FRITTERS
APPLEJACK! LOOK! IT'S TERRIBLE!
LOTS OF THE APPLES HAVE BEEN STOLEN...
...AND REPLACED WITH SQUASHES!
WHAT IN TARNATION?! HOW COULD THIS HAPPEN? WHO COULDA DONE SUCH A THING?
AIN'T IT OBVIOUS?
IT'S THE SASS SQUASH!

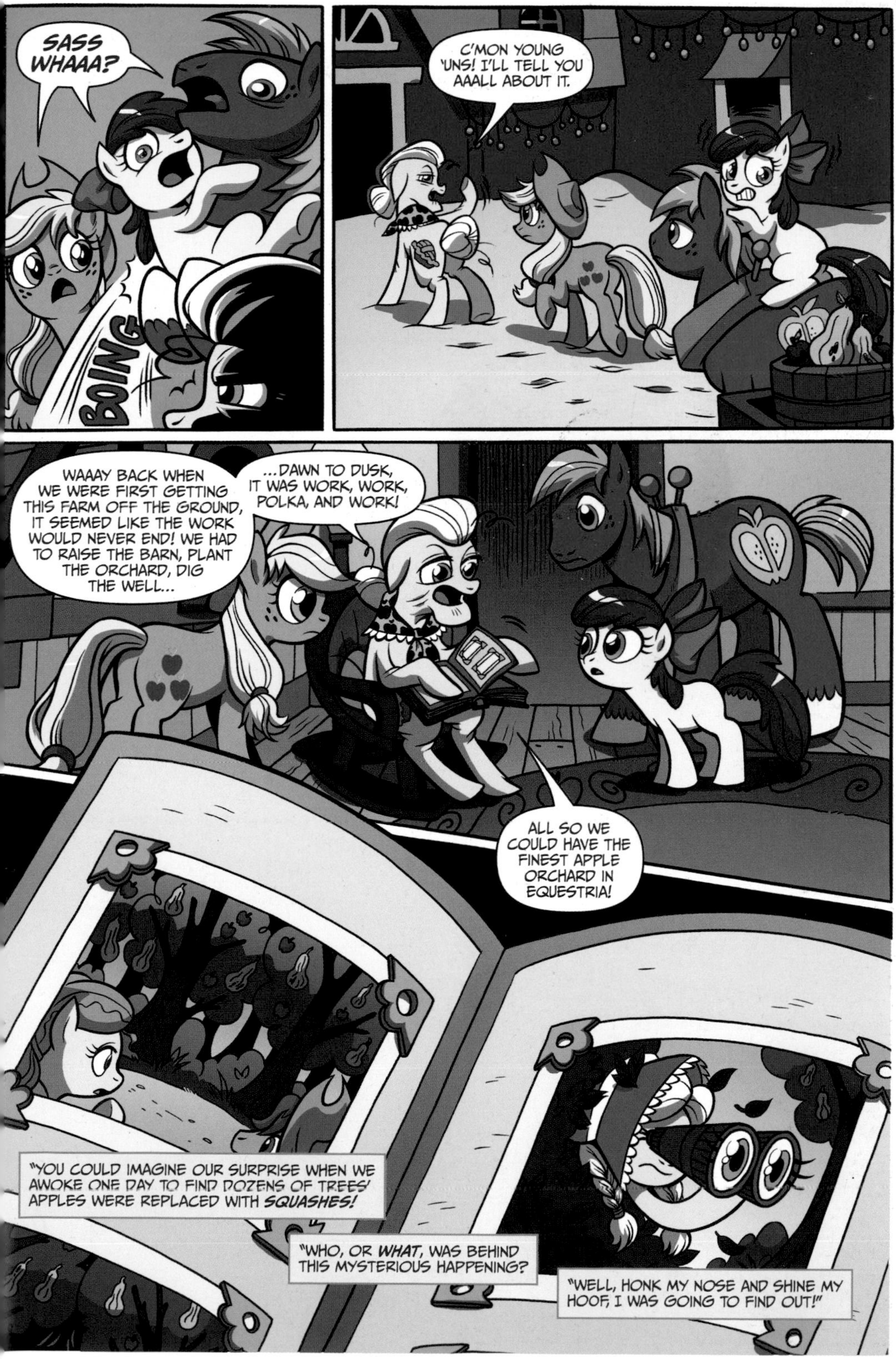
SASS WHAAA?
BOING
C'MON YOUNG 'UNS! I'LL TELL YOU AAALL ABOUT IT.
WAAAY BACK WHEN WE WERE FIRST GETTING THIS FARM OFF THE GROUND, IT SEEMED LIKE THE WORK WOULD NEVER END! WE HAD TO RAISE THE BARN, PLANT THE ORCHARD, DIG THE WELL...
...DAWN TO DUSK, IT WAS WORK, WORK, POLKA, AND WORK!
ALL SO WE COULD HAVE THE FINEST APPLE ORCHARD IN EQUESTRIA!
"YOU COULD IMAGINE OUR SURPRISE WHEN WE AWOKE ONE DAY TO FIND DOZENS OF TREES' APPLES WERE REPLACED WITH SQUASHES!
"WHO, OR WHAT, WAS BEHIND THIS MYSTERIOUS HAPPENING?
"WELL, HONK MY NOSE AND SHINE MY HOOF, I WAS GOING TO FIND OUT!"

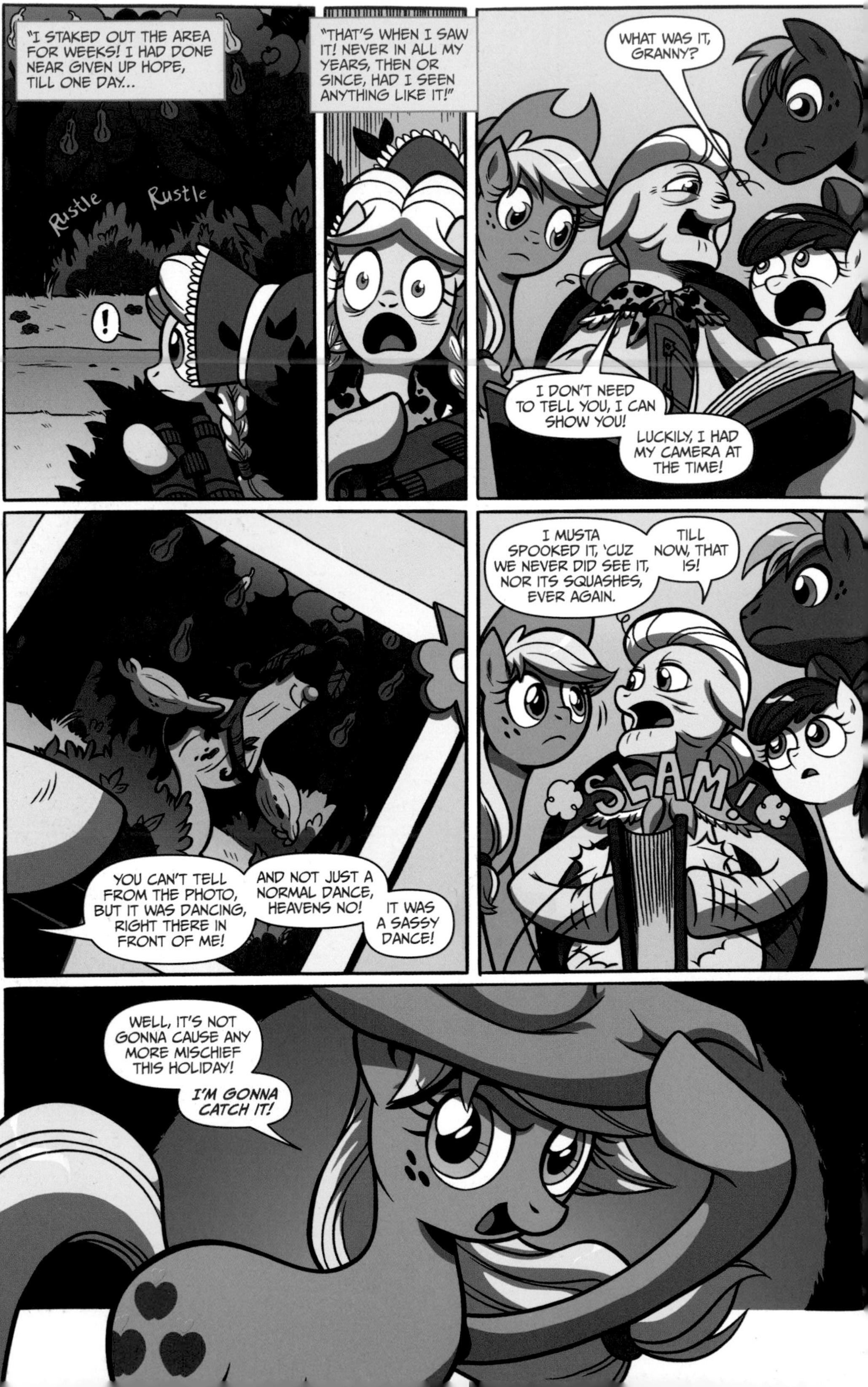
"I STAKED OUT THE AREA FOR WEEKS! I HAD DONE NEAR GIVEN UP HOPE, TILL ONE DAY...
Rustle
Rustle
!
"THAT'S WHEN I SAW IT! NEVER IN ALL MY YEARS, THEN OR SINCE, HAD I SEEN ANYTHING LIKE IT!"
WHAT WAS IT, GRANNY?
I DON'T NEED TO TELL YOU, I CAN SHOW YOU!
LUCKILY, I HAD MY CAMERA AT THE TIME!
YOU CAN'T TELL FROM THE PHOTO, BUT IT WAS DANCING, RIGHT THERE IN FRONT OF ME!
AND NOT JUST A NORMAL DANCE, HEAVENS NO!
IT WAS A SASSY DANCE!
I MUSTA SPOOKED IT, 'CUZ WE NEVER DID SEE IT, NOR ITS SQUASHES, EVER AGAIN.
TILL NOW, THAT IS!
SLAM!
WELL, IT'S NOT GONNA CAUSE ANY MORE MISCHIEF THIS HOLIDAY!
I'M GONNA CATCH IT!

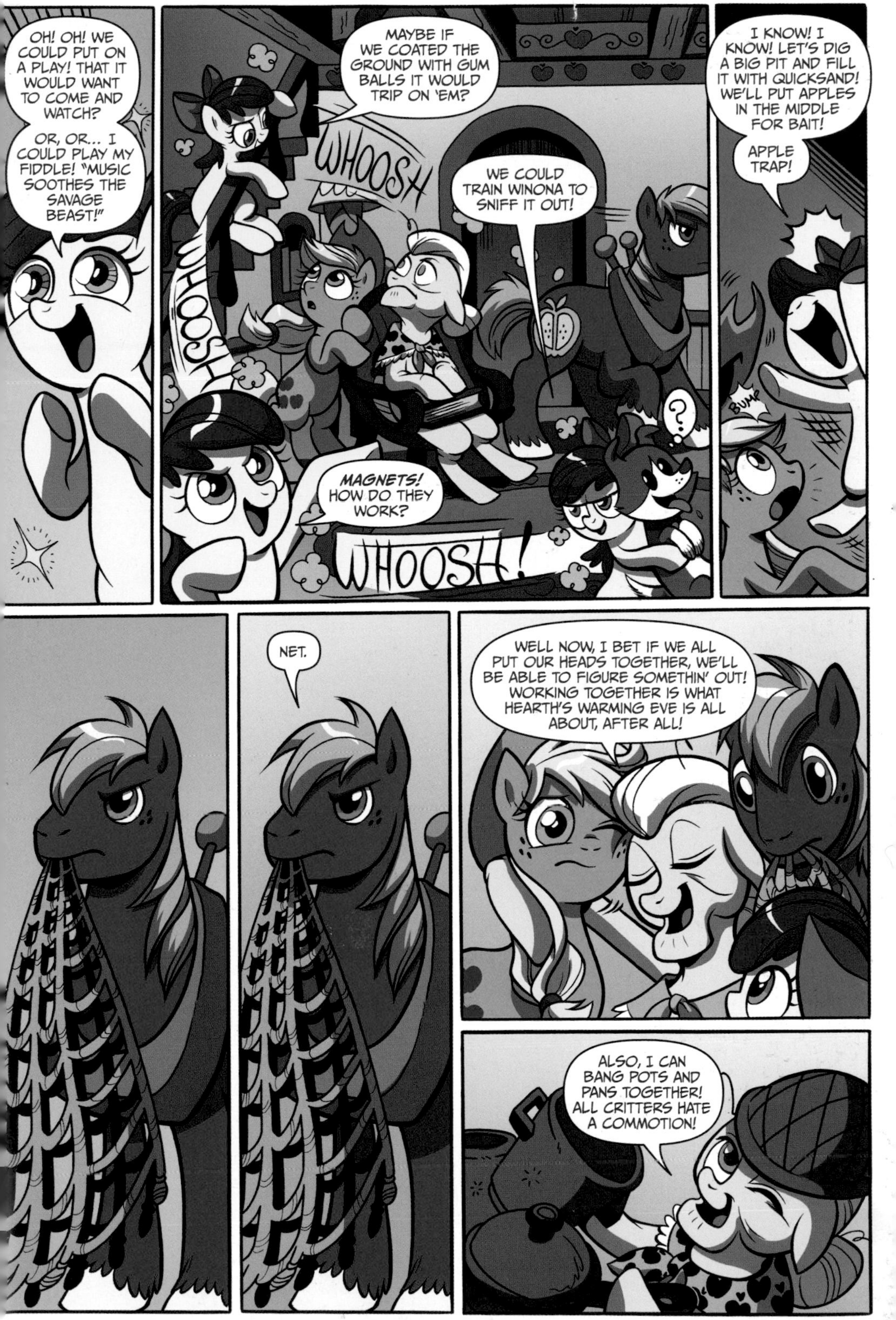
OH! OH! WE COULD PUT ON A PLAY! THAT IT WOULD WANT TO COME AND WATCH?
OR, OR... I COULD PLAY MY FIDDLE! "MUSIC SOOTHES THE SAVAGE BEAST!"
MAYBE IF WE COATED THE GROUND WITH GUM BALLS IT WOULD TRIP ON 'EM?
WHOOSH
WHOOSH
WE COULD TRAIN WINONA TO SNIFF IT OUT!
?
MAGNETS! HOW DO THEY WORK?
WHOOSH!
I KNOW! I KNOW! LET'S DIG A BIG PIT AND FILL IT WITH QUICKSAND! WE'LL PUT APPLES IN THE MIDDLE FOR BAIT!
APPLE TRAP!
BUMP
NET.
WELL NOW, I BET IF WE ALL PUT OUR HEADS TOGETHER, WE'LL BE ABLE TO FIGURE SOMETHIN' OUT! WORKING TOGETHER IS WHAT HEARTH'S WARMING EVE IS ALL ABOUT, AFTER ALL!
ALSO, I CAN BANG POTS AND PANS TOGETHER! ALL CRITTERS HATE A COMMOTION!

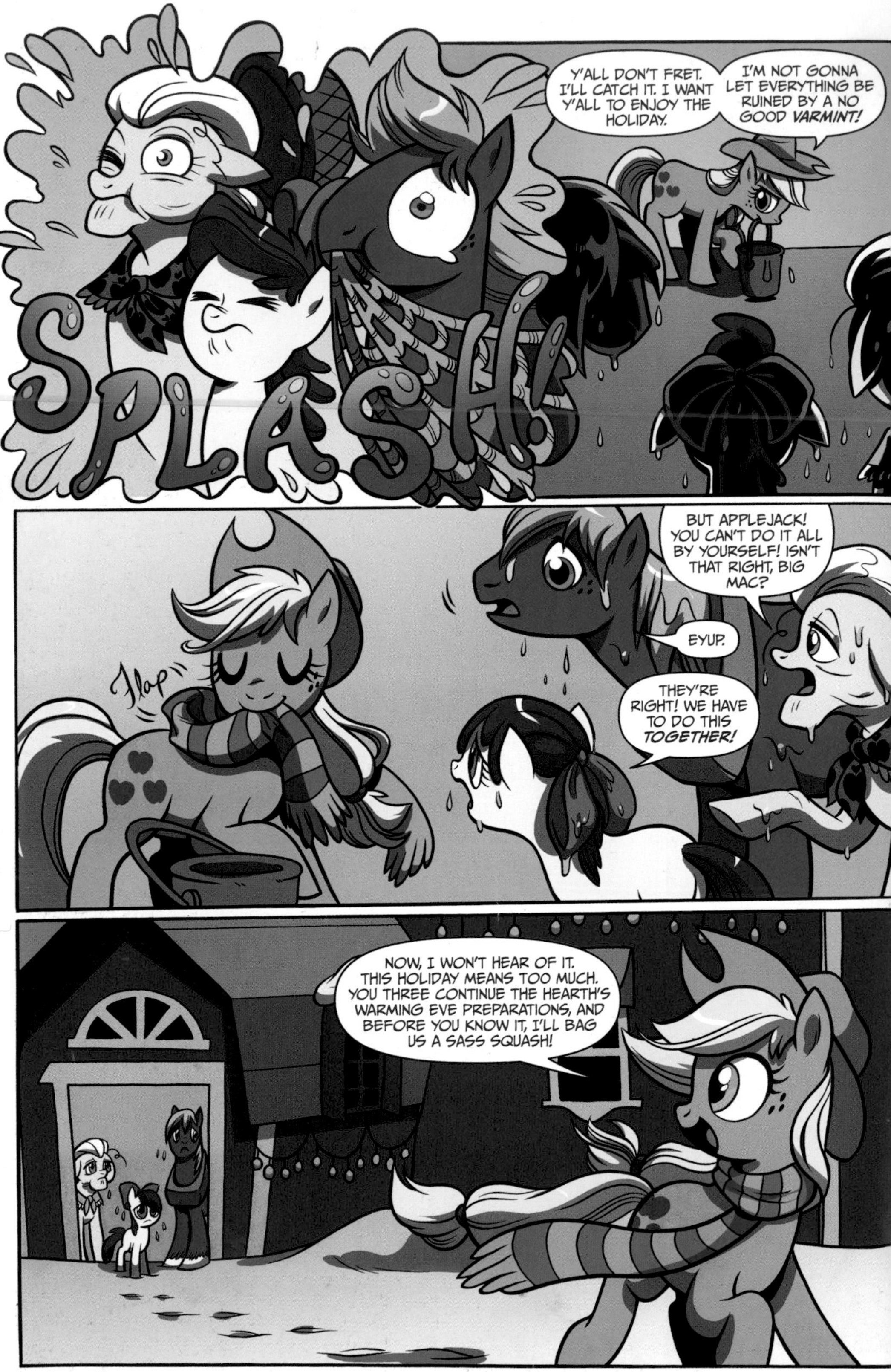
SPLASH!
Y'ALL DON'T FRET. I'LL CATCH IT. I WANT Y'ALL TO ENJOY THE HOLIDAY.
I'M NOT GONNA LET EVERYTHING BE RUINED BY A NO GOOD VARMINT!
BUT APPLEJACK! YOU CAN'T DO IT ALL BY YOURSELF! ISN'T THAT RIGHT, BIG MAC?
EYUP.
THEY'RE RIGHT! WE HAVE TO DO THIS TOGETHER!
Flap
NOW, I WON'T HEAR OF IT. THIS HOLIDAY MEANS TOO MUCH. YOU THREE CONTINUE THE HEARTH'S WARMING EVE PREPARATIONS, AND BEFORE YOU KNOW IT, I'LL BAG US A SASS SQUASH!

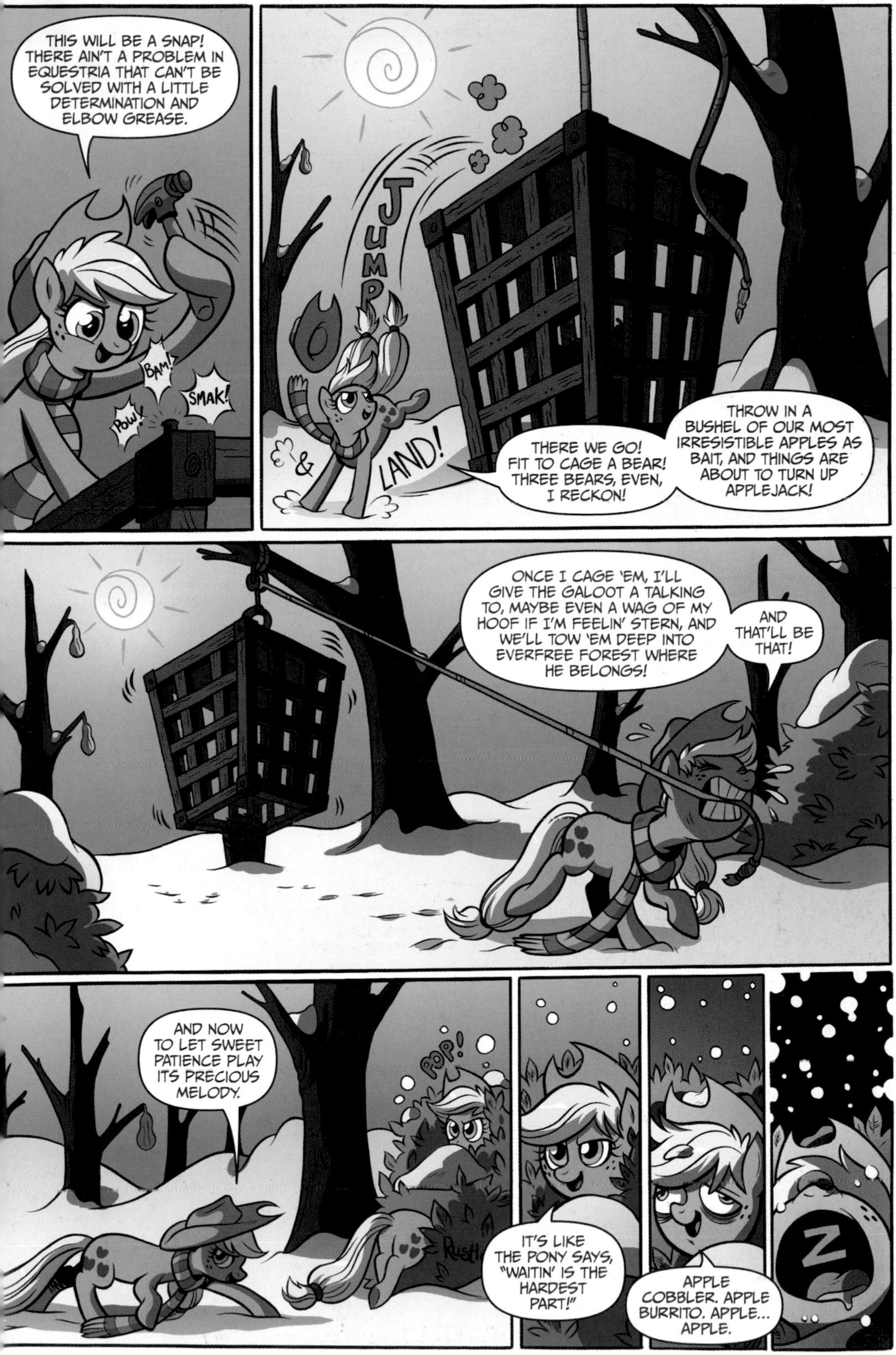
THIS WILL BE A SNAP! THERE AIN'T A PROBLEM IN EQUESTRIA THAT CAN'T BE SOLVED WITH A LITTLE DETERMINATION AND ELBOW GREASE.
BAM!
SMAK!
POW!
JUMP
&
LAND!
THERE WE GO! FIT TO CAGE A BEAR! THREE BEARS, EVEN, I RECKON!
THROW IN A BUSHEL OF OUR MOST IRRESISTIBLE APPLES AS BAIT, AND THINGS ARE ABOUT TO TURN UP APPLEJACK!
ONCE I CAGE 'EM, I'LL GIVE THE GALOOT A TALKING TO, MAYBE EVEN A WAG OF MY HOOF IF I'M FEELIN' STERN, AND WE'LL TOW 'EM DEEP INTO EVERFREE FOREST WHERE HE BELONGS!
AND THAT'LL BE THAT!
AND NOW TO LET SWEET PATIENCE PLAY ITS PRECIOUS MELODY.
POP!
RUSTLE
IT'S LIKE THE PONY SAYS, "WAITIN' IS THE HARDEST PART!"
APPLE COBBLER. APPLE BURRITO. APPLE... APPLE.
Z

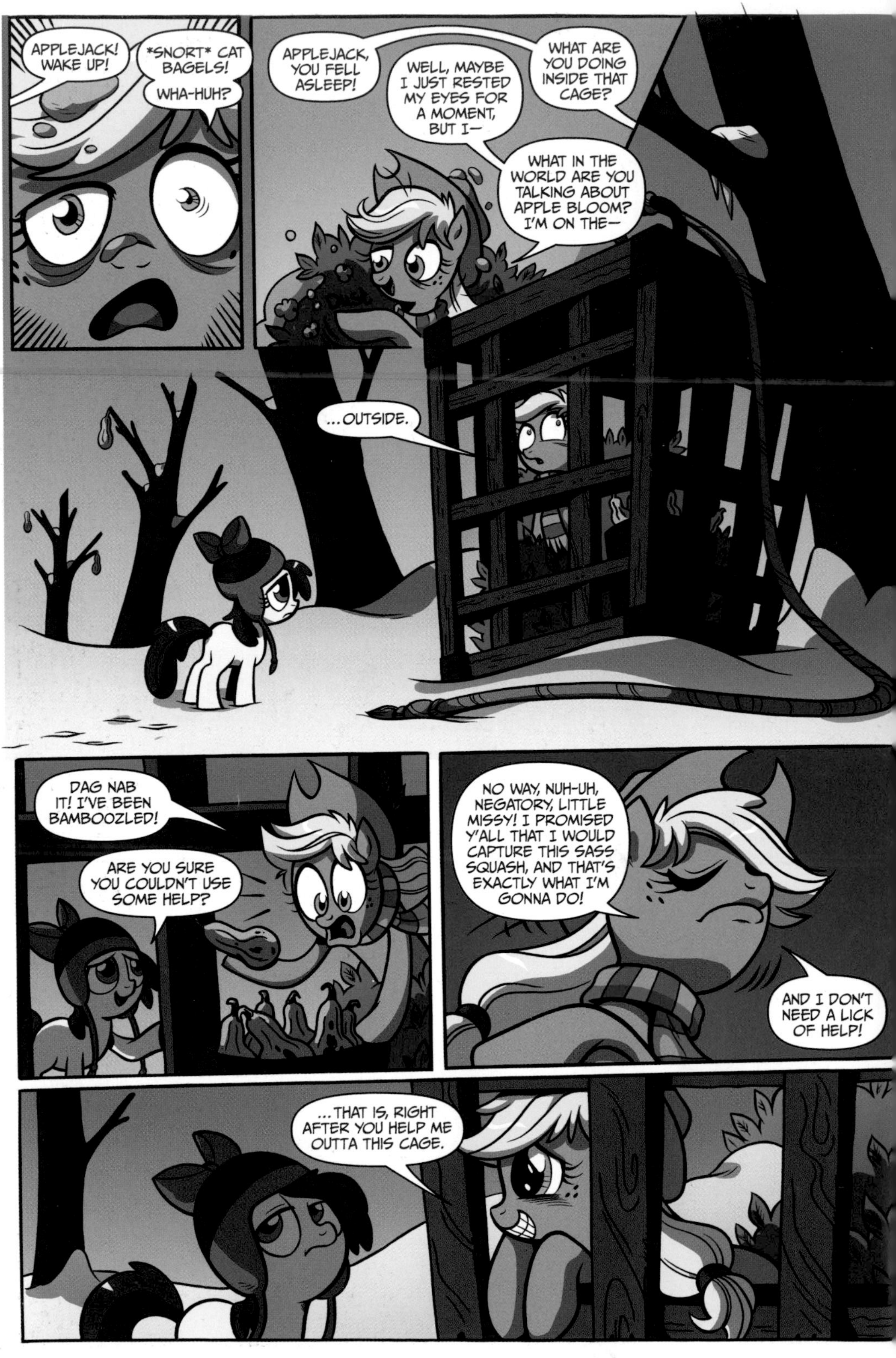
APPLEJACK! WAKE UP!
SNORT CAT BAGELS!
WHA-HUH?
APPLEJACK, YOU FELL ASLEEP!
WELL, MAYBE I JUST RESTED MY EYES FOR A MOMENT, BUT I—
WHAT ARE YOU DOING INSIDE THAT CAGE?
WHAT IN THE WORLD ARE YOU TALKING ABOUT APPLE BLOOM? I'M ON THE—
...OUTSIDE.
DAG NAB IT! I'VE BEEN BAMBOOZLED!
ARE YOU SURE YOU COULDN'T USE SOME HELP?
NO WAY, NUH-UH, NEGATORY, LITTLE MISSY! I PROMISED Y'ALL THAT I WOULD CAPTURE THIS SASS SQUASH, AND THAT'S EXACTLY WHAT I'M GONNA DO!
AND I DON'T NEED A LICK OF HELP!
...THAT IS, RIGHT AFTER YOU HELP ME OUTTA THIS CAGE.

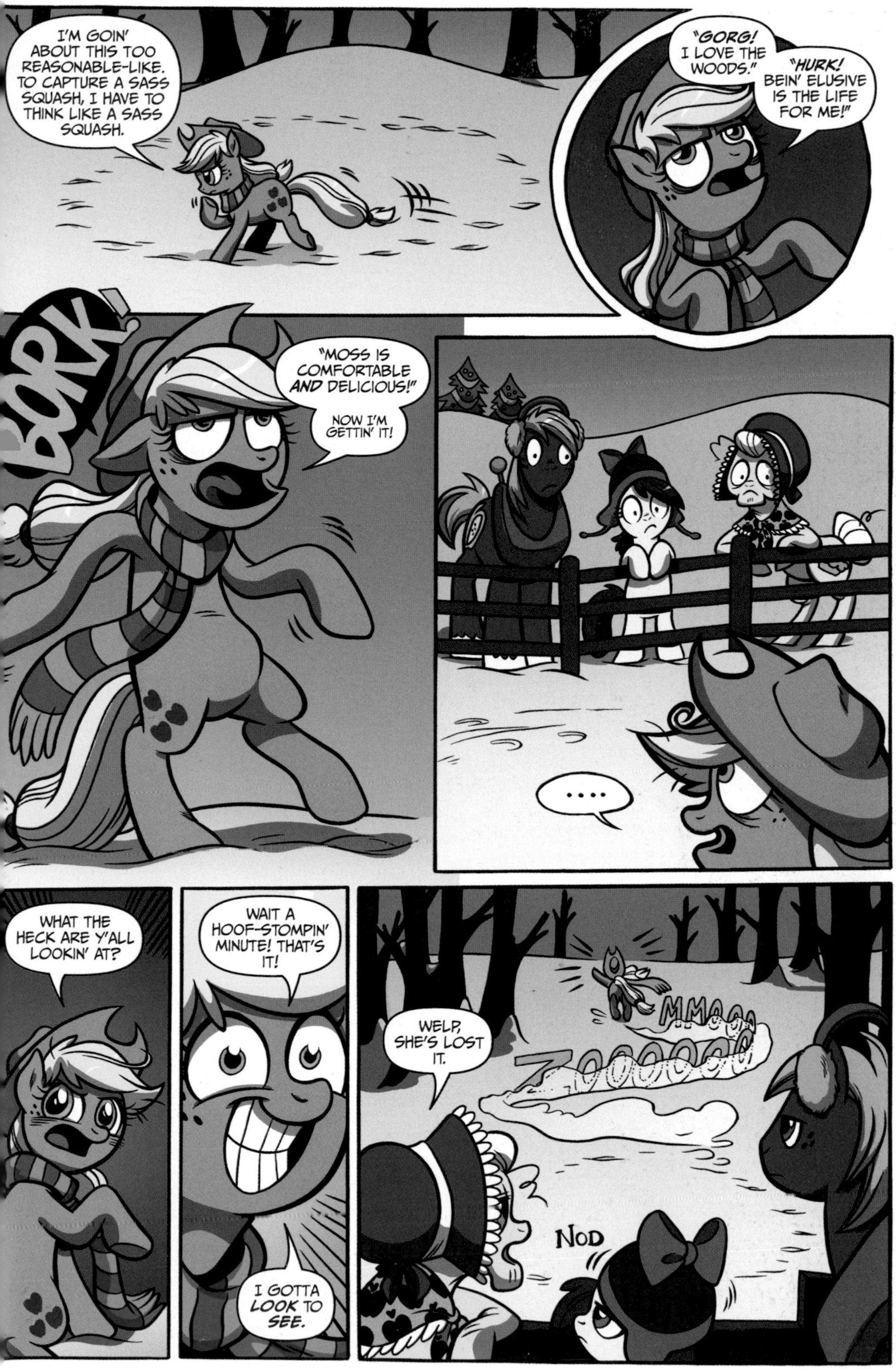
I'M GOIN' ABOUT THIS TOO REASONABLE-LIKE. TO CAPTURE A SASS SQUASH, I HAVE TO THINK LIKE A SASS SQUASH.
"GORG! I LOVE THE WOODS."
"HURK! BEIN' ELUSIVE IS THE LIFE FOR ME!"
BORK!
"MOSS IS COMFORTABLE AND DELICIOUS!"
NOW I'M GETTIN' IT!
....
WHAT THE HECK ARE Y'ALL LOOKIN' AT?
WAIT A HOOF-STOMPIN' MINUTE! THAT'S IT!
I GOTTA LOOK TO SEE.
WELP, SHE'S LOST IT.
MMOOOO
ZOOOOOOO
NOD

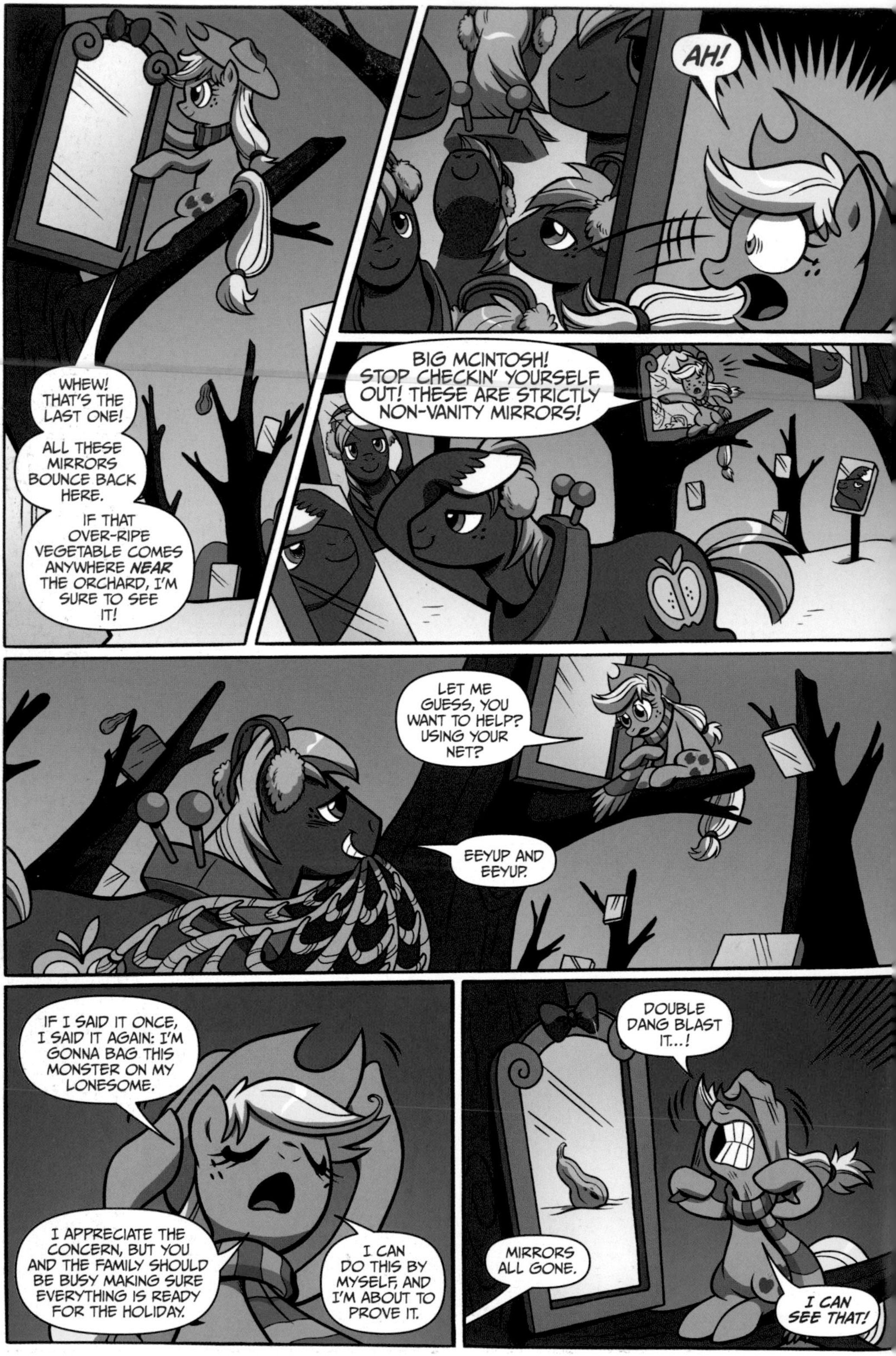
WHEW! THAT'S THE LAST ONE!
ALL THESE MIRRORS BOUNCE BACK HERE.
IF THAT OVER-RIPE VEGETABLE COMES ANYWHERE *NEAR* THE ORCHARD, I'M SURE TO SEE IT!
AH!
BIG MCINTOSH! STOP CHECKIN' YOURSELF OUT! THESE ARE STRICTLY NON-VANITY MIRRORS!
LET ME GUESS, YOU WANT TO HELP? USING YOUR NET?
EEYUP AND EEYUP.
IF I SAID IT ONCE, I SAID IT AGAIN: I'M GONNA BAG THIS MONSTER ON MY LONESOME.
I APPRECIATE THE CONCERN, BUT YOU AND THE FAMILY SHOULD BE BUSY MAKING SURE EVERYTHING IS READY FOR THE HOLIDAY.
I CAN DO THIS BY MYSELF, AND I'M ABOUT TO PROVE IT.
DOUBLE DANG BLAST IT...!
MIRRORS ALL GONE.
I CAN SEE THAT!

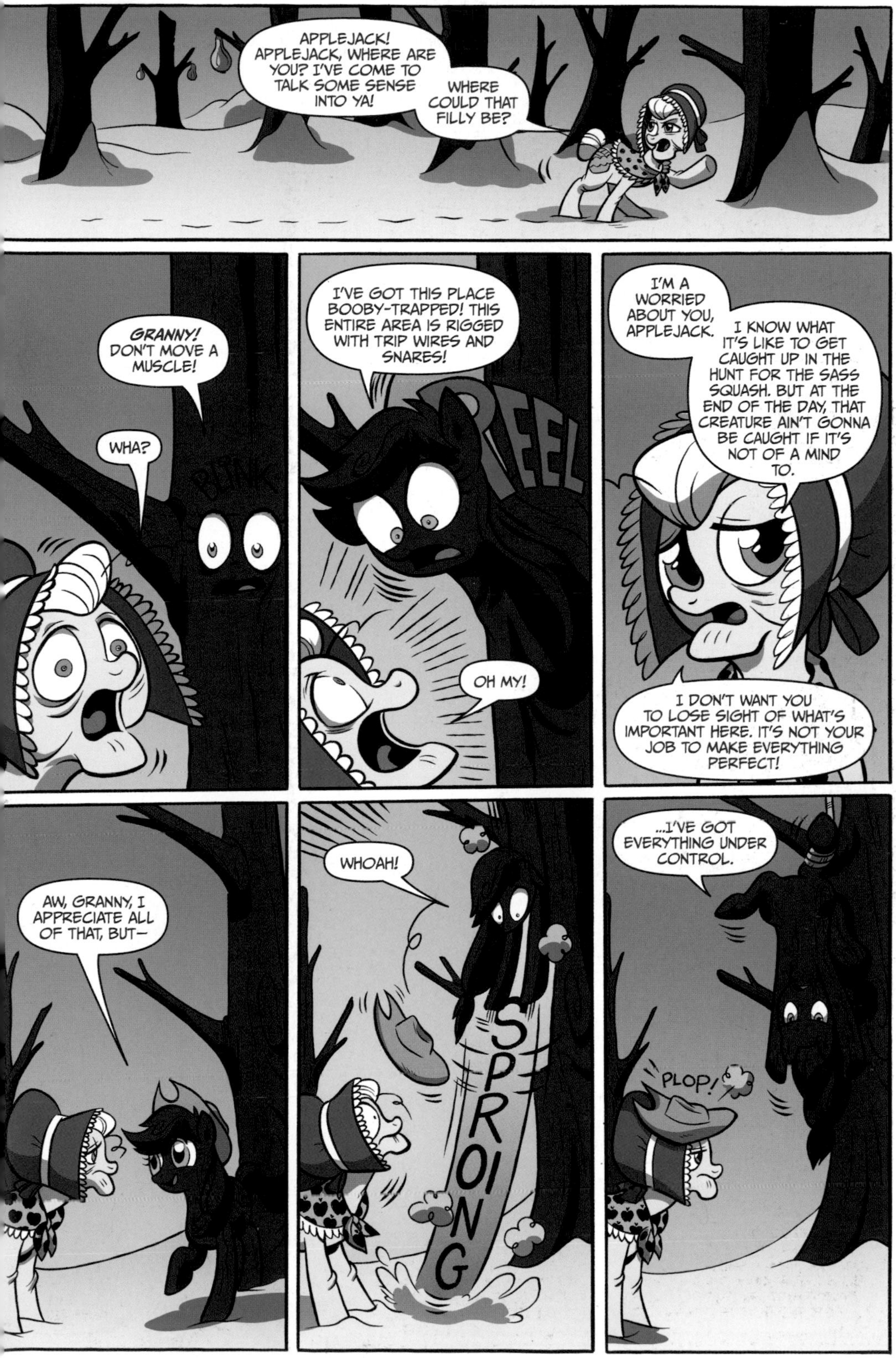
APPLEJACK! APPLEJACK, WHERE ARE YOU? I'VE COME TO TALK SOME SENSE INTO YA!
WHERE COULD THAT FILLY BE?
GRANNY! DON'T MOVE A MUSCLE!
WHA?
BLINK
I'VE GOT THIS PLACE BOOBY-TRAPPED! THIS ENTIRE AREA IS RIGGED WITH TRIP WIRES AND SNARES!
REEL
OH MY!
I'M A WORRIED ABOUT YOU, APPLEJACK.
I KNOW WHAT IT'S LIKE TO GET CAUGHT UP IN THE HUNT FOR THE SASS SQUASH. BUT AT THE END OF THE DAY, THAT CREATURE AIN'T GONNA BE CAUGHT IF IT'S NOT OF A MIND TO.
I DON'T WANT YOU TO LOSE SIGHT OF WHAT'S IMPORTANT HERE. IT'S NOT YOUR JOB TO MAKE EVERYTHING PERFECT!
AW, GRANNY, I APPRECIATE ALL OF THAT, BUT—
WHOAH!
SPROING
...I'VE GOT EVERYTHING UNDER CONTROL.
PLOP!

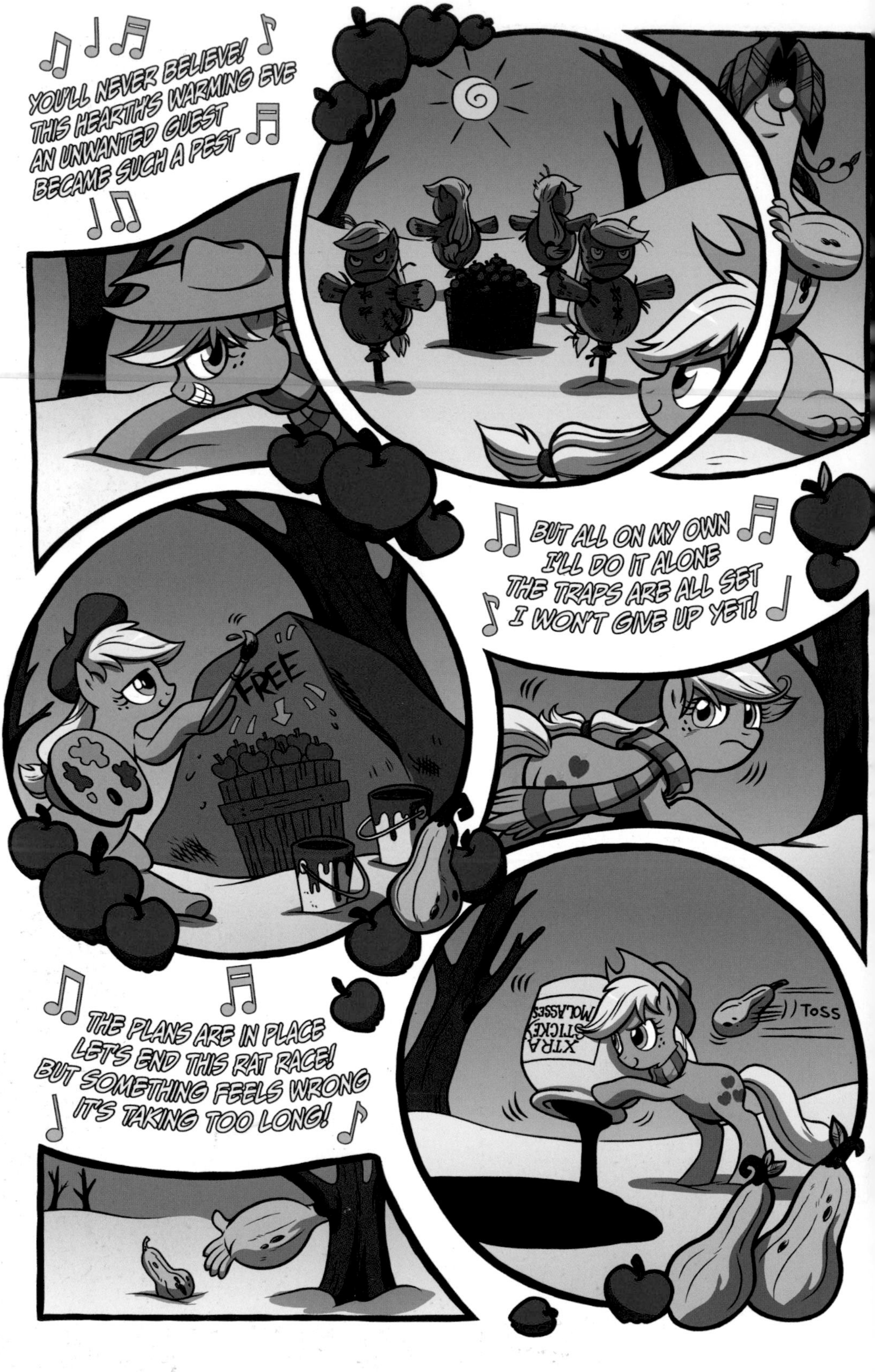
YOU'LL NEVER BELIEVE!
THIS HEARTH'S WARMING EVE
AN UNWANTED GUEST
BECAME SUCH A PEST
BUT ALL ON MY OWN
I'LL DO IT ALONE
THE TRAPS ARE ALL SET
I WON'T GIVE UP YET!
FREE
XTRA STICKEY MOLASSES
TOSS
THE PLANS ARE IN PLACE
LET'S END THIS RAT RACE!
BUT SOMETHING FEELS WRONG
IT'S TAKING TOO LONG!

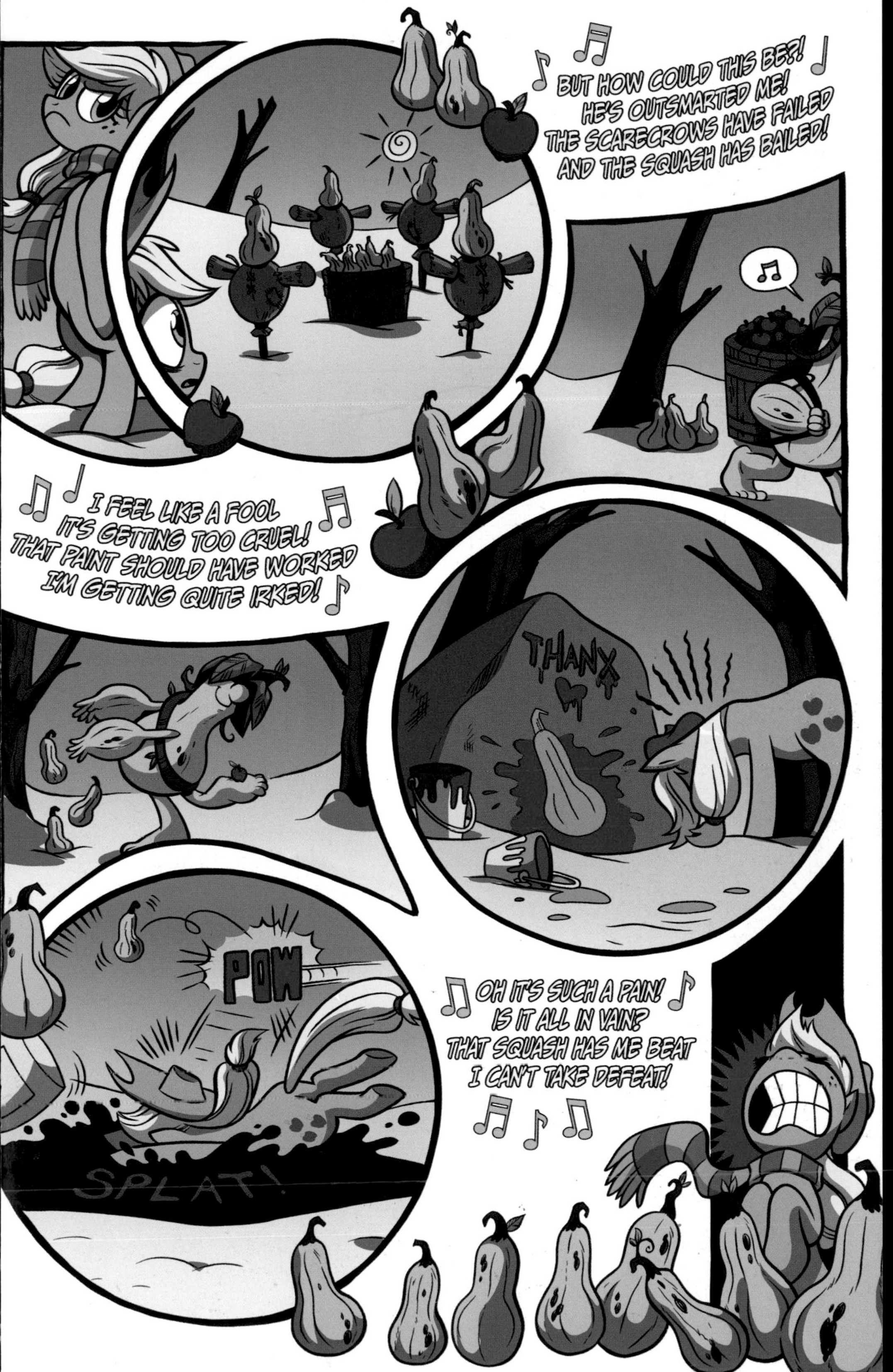
BUT HOW COULD THIS BE?! HE'S OUTSMARTED ME! THE SCARECROWS HAVE FAILED AND THE SQUASH HAS BAILED!
I FEEL LIKE A FOOL IT'S GETTING TOO CRUEL! THAT PAINT SHOULD HAVE WORKED I'M GETTING QUITE IRKED!
THANX
POW
SPLAT!
OH IT'S SUCH A PAIN! IS IT ALL IN VAIN? THAT SQUASH HAS ME BEAT I CAN'T TAKE DEFEAT!

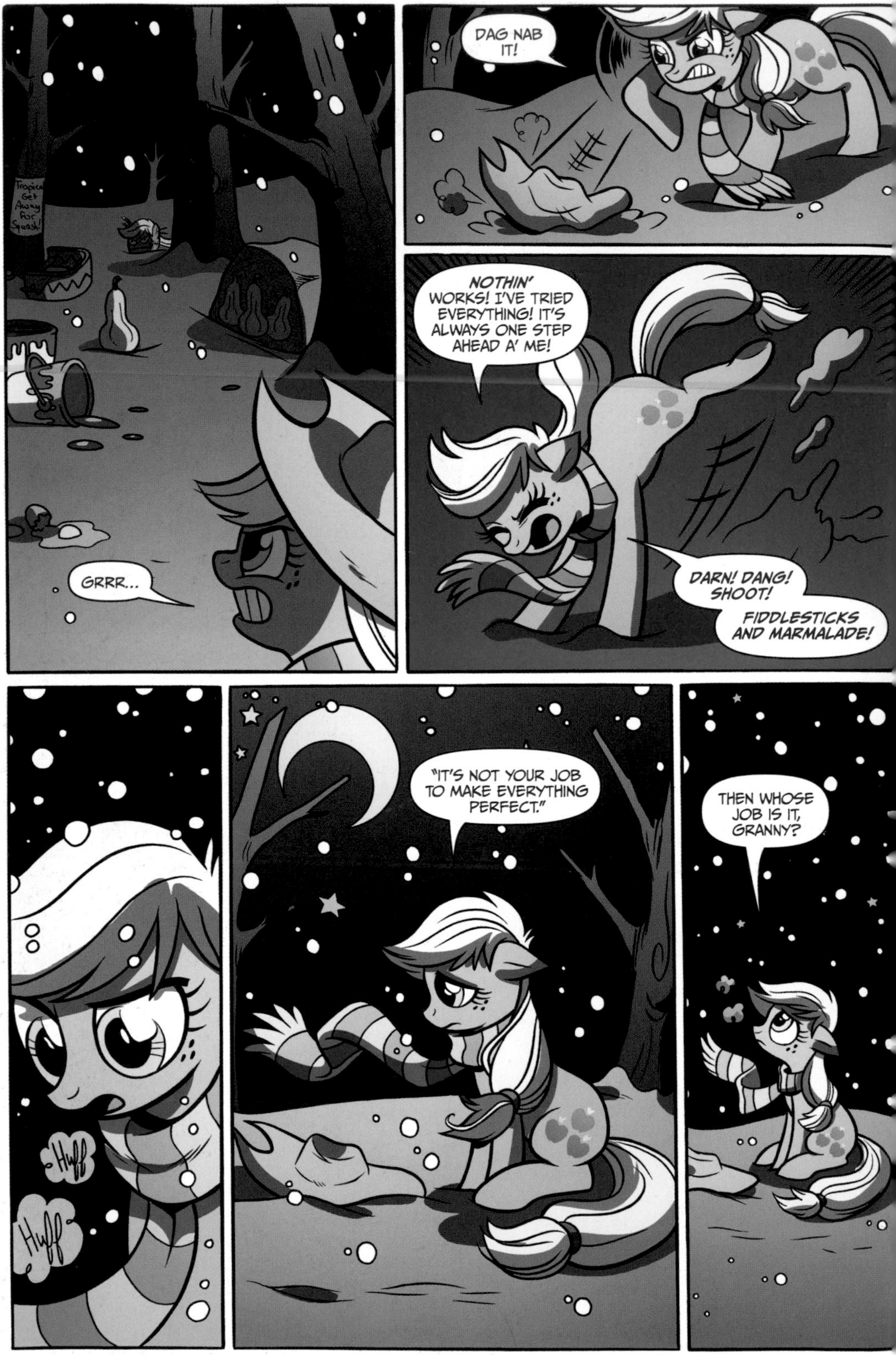
GRRR...
DAG NAB IT!
NOTHIN' WORKS! I'VE TRIED EVERYTHING! IT'S ALWAYS ONE STEP AHEAD A' ME!
DARN! DANG! SHOOT!
FIDDLESTICKS AND MARMALADE!
Huff
Huff
"IT'S NOT YOUR JOB TO MAKE EVERYTHING PERFECT."
THEN WHOSE JOB IS IT, GRANNY?

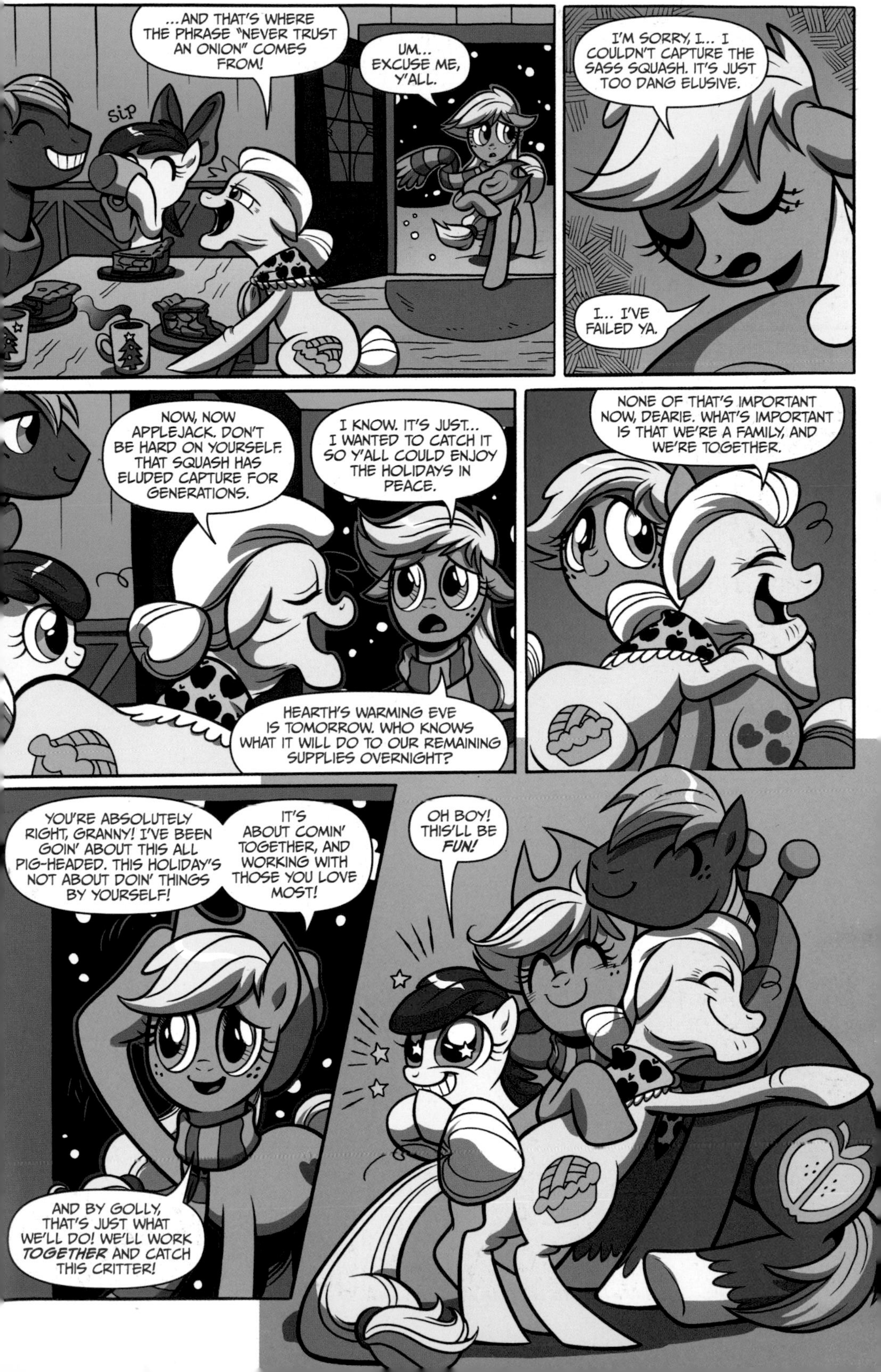
...AND THAT'S WHERE THE PHRASE "NEVER TRUST AN ONION" COMES FROM!
SIP
UM... EXCUSE ME, Y'ALL.
I'M SORRY, I... I COULDN'T CAPTURE THE SASS SQUASH. IT'S JUST TOO DANG ELUSIVE.
I... I'VE FAILED YA.
NOW, NOW APPLEJACK. DON'T BE HARD ON YOURSELF. THAT SQUASH HAS ELUDED CAPTURE FOR GENERATIONS.
I KNOW. IT'S JUST... I WANTED TO CATCH IT SO Y'ALL COULD ENJOY THE HOLIDAYS IN PEACE.
HEARTH'S WARMING EVE IS TOMORROW. WHO KNOWS WHAT IT WILL DO TO OUR REMAINING SUPPLIES OVERNIGHT?
NONE OF THAT'S IMPORTANT NOW, DEARIE. WHAT'S IMPORTANT IS THAT WE'RE A FAMILY, AND WE'RE TOGETHER.
YOU'RE ABSOLUTELY RIGHT, GRANNY! I'VE BEEN GOIN' ABOUT THIS ALL PIG-HEADED. THIS HOLIDAY'S NOT ABOUT DOIN' THINGS BY YOURSELF!
IT'S ABOUT COMIN' TOGETHER, AND WORKING WITH THOSE YOU LOVE MOST!
AND BY GOLLY, THAT'S JUST WHAT WE'LL DO! WE'LL WORK TOGETHER AND CATCH THIS CRITTER!
OH BOY! THIS'LL BE FUN!

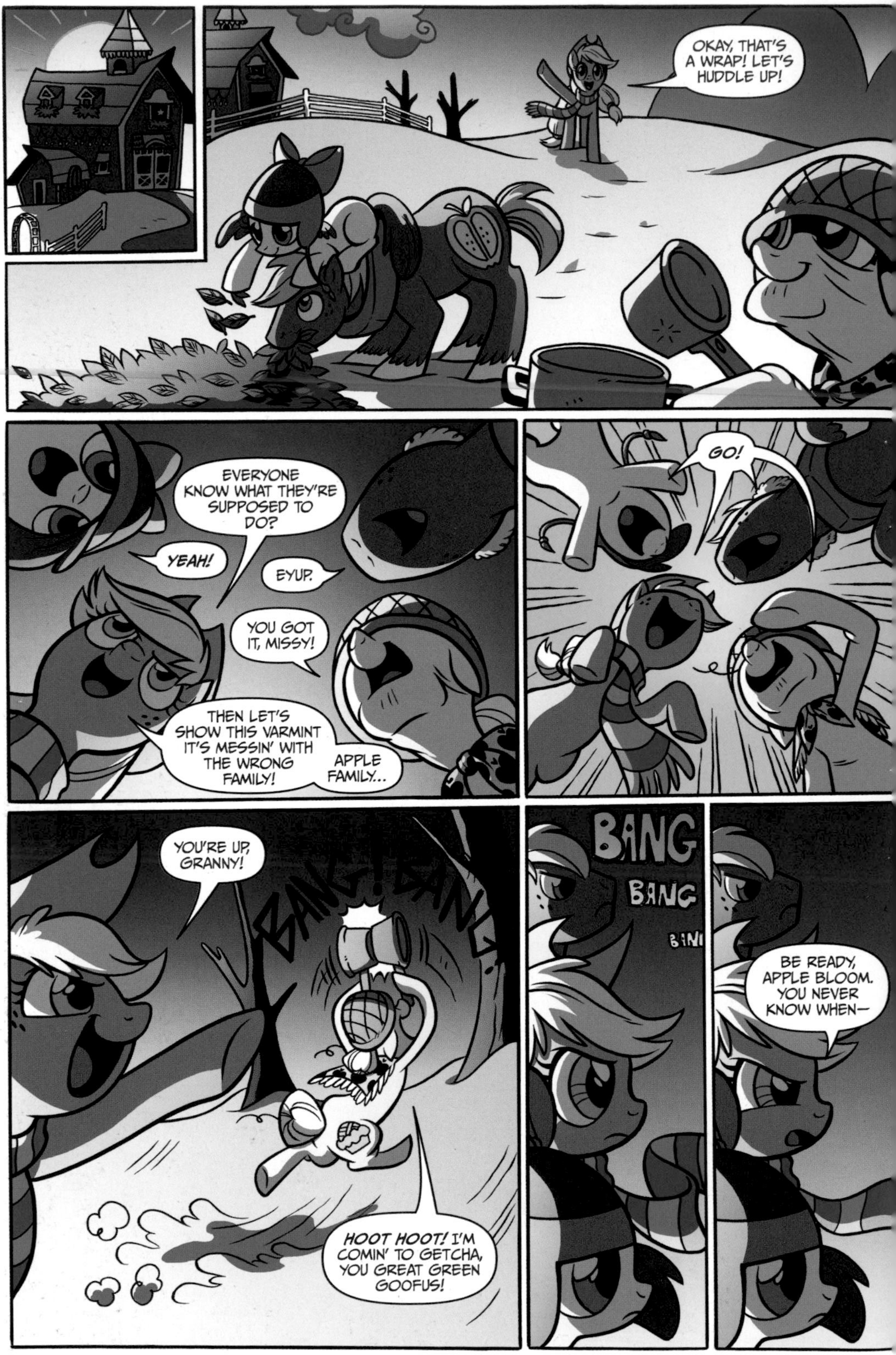
OKAY, THAT'S A WRAP! LET'S HUDDLE UP!
EVERYONE KNOW WHAT THEY'RE SUPPOSED TO DO?
YEAH!
EYUP.
YOU GOT IT, MISSY!
THEN LET'S SHOW THIS VARMINT IT'S MESSIN' WITH THE WRONG FAMILY!
APPLE FAMILY...
GO!
YOU'RE UP, GRANNY!
BANG! BANG!
HOOT HOOT! I'M COMIN' TO GETCHA, YOU GREAT GREEN GOOFUS!
BANG
BANG
BE READY, APPLE BLOOM. YOU NEVER KNOW WHEN—

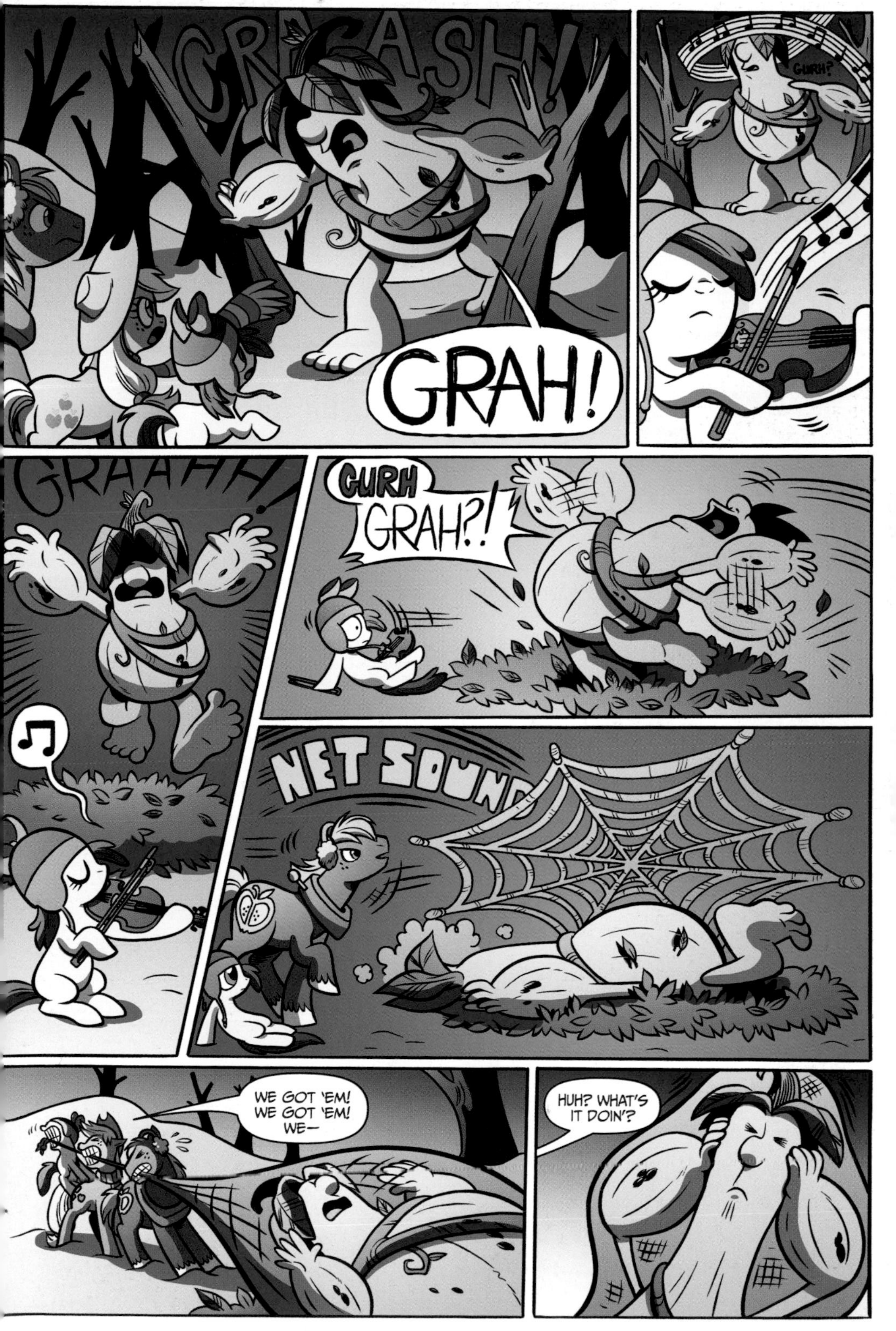
CRAASH!
GURH?
GRAH!
GRAAHH!
GURH GRAH?!
NET SOUN
WE GOT 'EM! WE GOT 'EM! WE—
HUH? WHAT'S IT DOIN'?

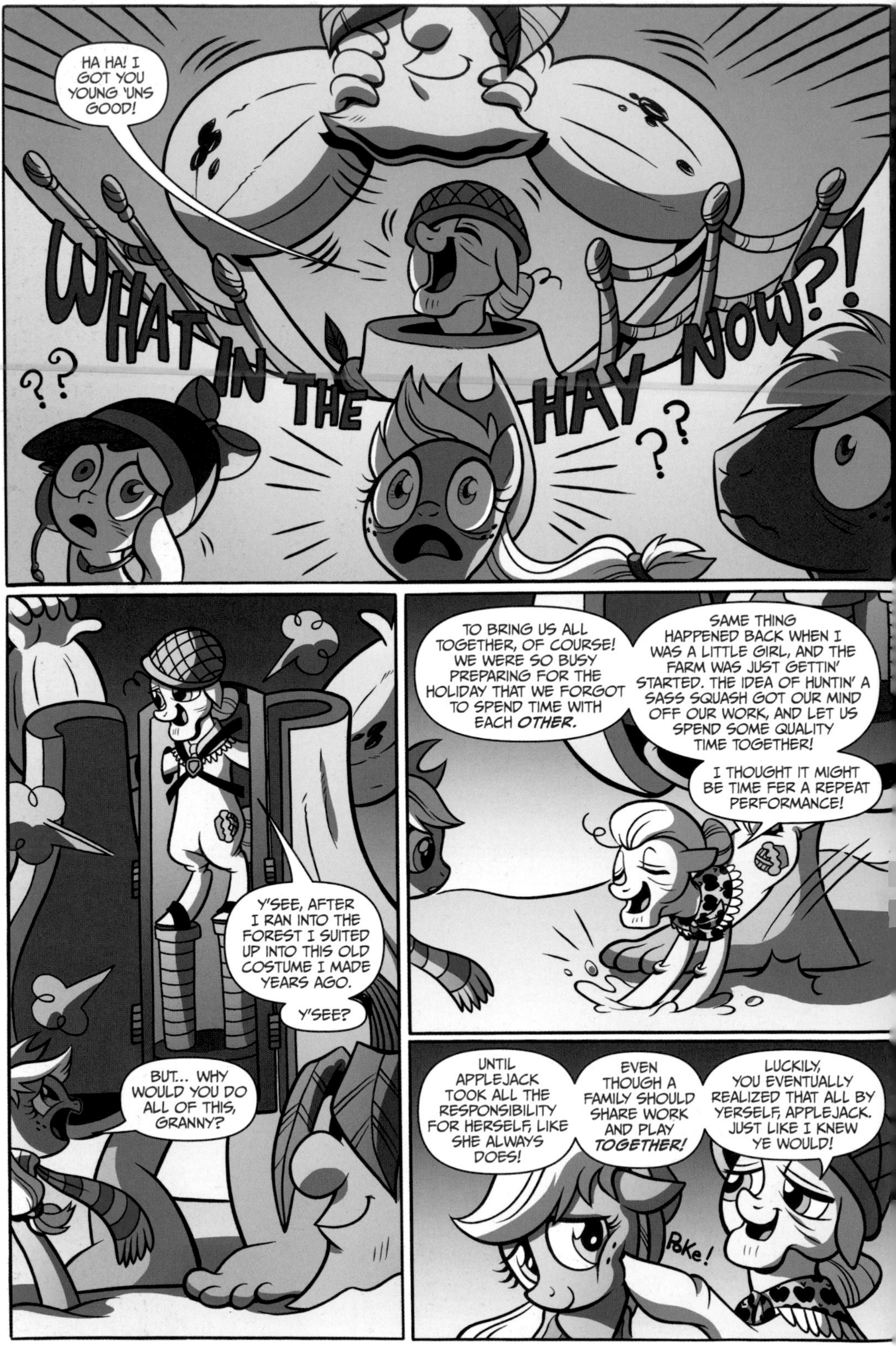
HA HA! I GOT YOU YOUNG 'UNS GOOD!
WHAT IN THE HAY NOW?!
Y'SEE, AFTER I RAN INTO THE FOREST I SUITED UP INTO THIS OLD COSTUME I MADE YEARS AGO.
Y'SEE?
BUT... WHY WOULD YOU DO ALL OF THIS, GRANNY?
TO BRING US ALL TOGETHER, OF COURSE! WE WERE SO BUSY PREPARING FOR THE HOLIDAY THAT WE FORGOT TO SPEND TIME WITH EACH OTHER.
SAME THING HAPPENED BACK WHEN I WAS A LITTLE GIRL, AND THE FARM WAS JUST GETTIN' STARTED. THE IDEA OF HUNTIN' A SASS SQUASH GOT OUR MIND OFF OUR WORK, AND LET US SPEND SOME QUALITY TIME TOGETHER!
I THOUGHT IT MIGHT BE TIME FER A REPEAT PERFORMANCE!
UNTIL APPLEJACK TOOK ALL THE RESPONSIBILITY FOR HERSELF, LIKE SHE ALWAYS DOES!
EVEN THOUGH A FAMILY SHOULD SHARE WORK AND PLAY TOGETHER!
LUCKILY, YOU EVENTUALLY REALIZED THAT ALL BY YERSELF, APPLEJACK. JUST LIKE I KNEW YE WOULD!
POKE!

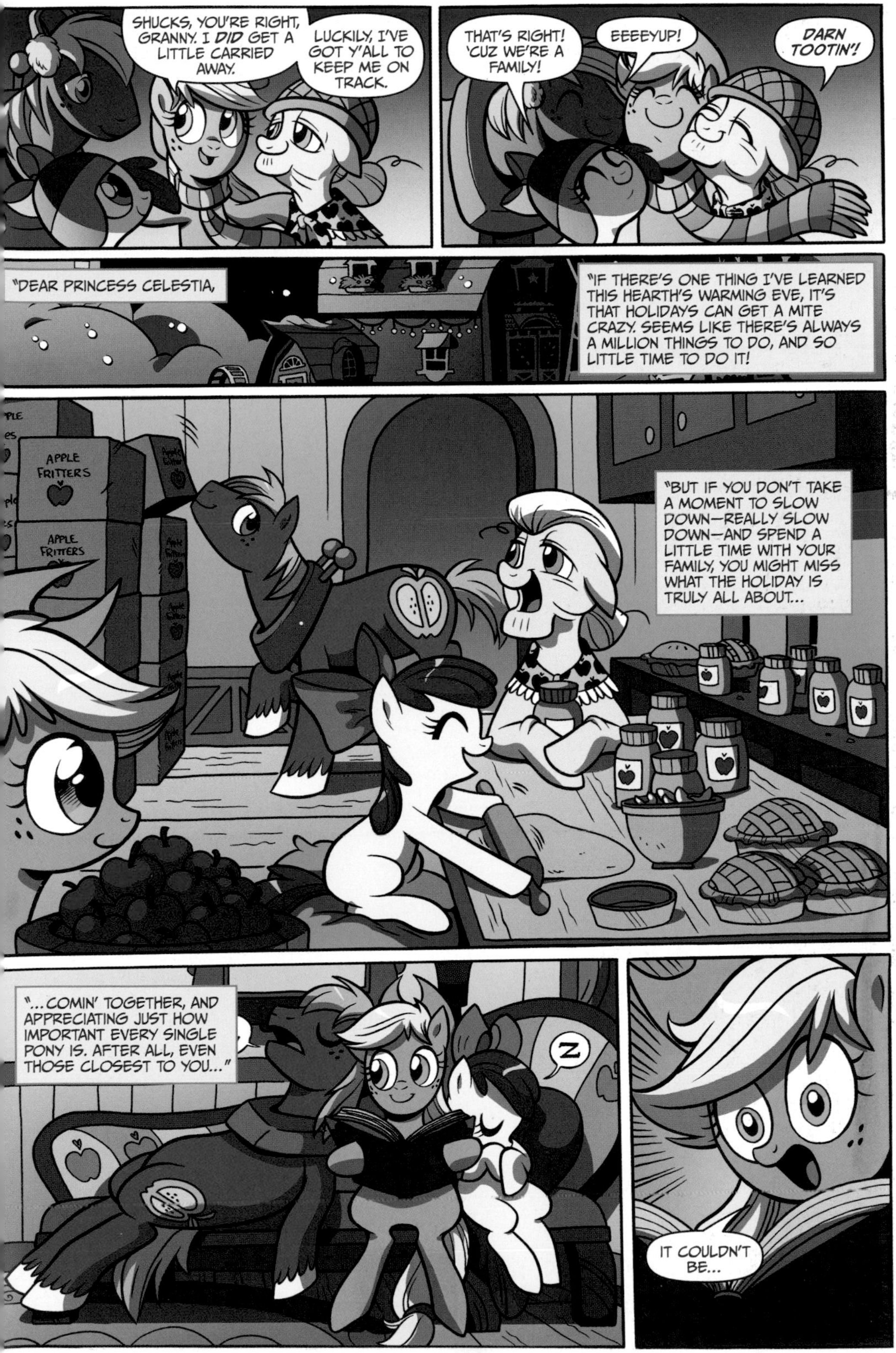
SHUCKS, YOU'RE RIGHT, GRANNY. I *DID* GET A LITTLE CARRIED AWAY.
LUCKILY, I'VE GOT Y'ALL TO KEEP ME ON TRACK.
THAT'S RIGHT! 'CUZ WE'RE A FAMILY!
EEEEYUP!
DARN TOOTIN'!
"DEAR PRINCESS CELESTIA,
"IF THERE'S ONE THING I'VE LEARNED THIS HEARTH'S WARMING EVE, IT'S THAT HOLIDAYS CAN GET A MITE CRAZY. SEEMS LIKE THERE'S ALWAYS A MILLION THINGS TO DO, AND SO LITTLE TIME TO DO IT!
APPLE FRITTERS
APPLE FRITTERS
"BUT IF YOU DON'T TAKE A MOMENT TO SLOW DOWN—REALLY SLOW DOWN—AND SPEND A LITTLE TIME WITH YOUR FAMILY, YOU MIGHT MISS WHAT THE HOLIDAY IS TRULY ALL ABOUT...
"...COMIN' TOGETHER, AND APPRECIATING JUST HOW IMPORTANT EVERY SINGLE PONY IS. AFTER ALL, EVEN THOSE CLOSEST TO YOU..."
Z
IT COULDN'T BE...

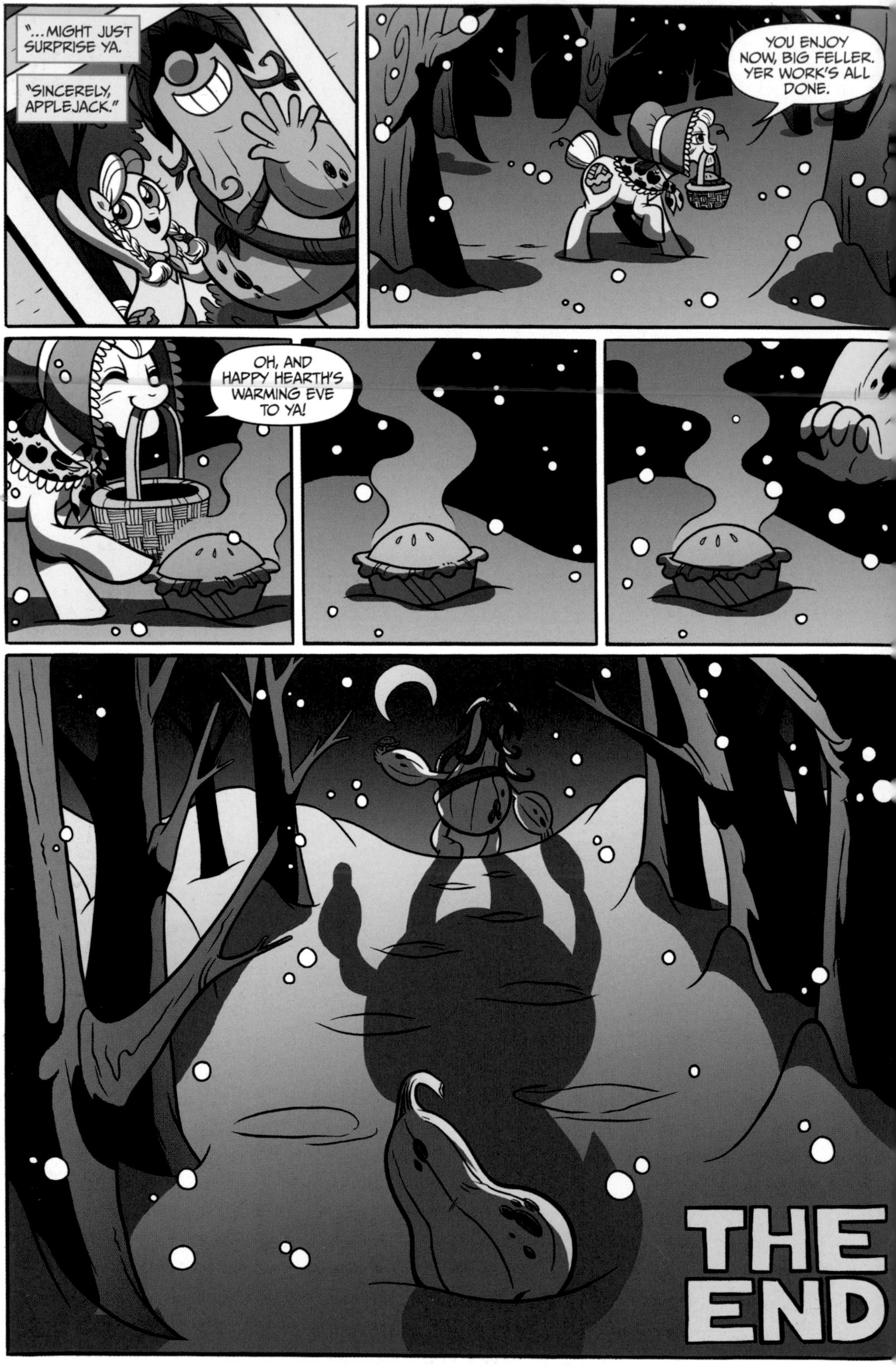
"...MIGHT JUST SURPRISE YA.
"SINCERELY, APPLEJACK."
YOU ENJOY NOW, BIG FELLER. YER WORK'S ALL DONE.
OH, AND HAPPY HEARTH'S WARMING EVE TO YA!
THE END

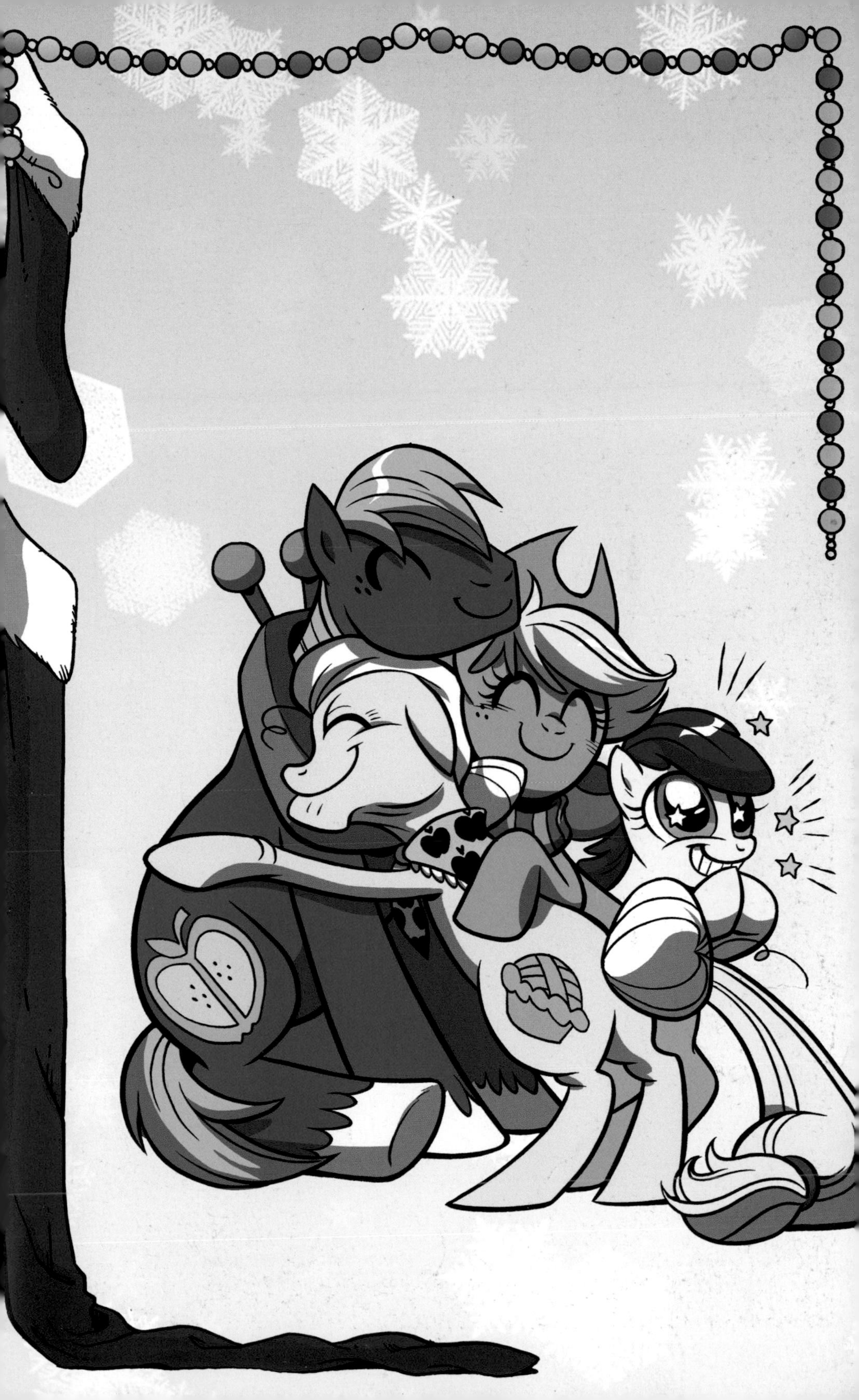

TALES OF HEARTH'S WARMING EVE

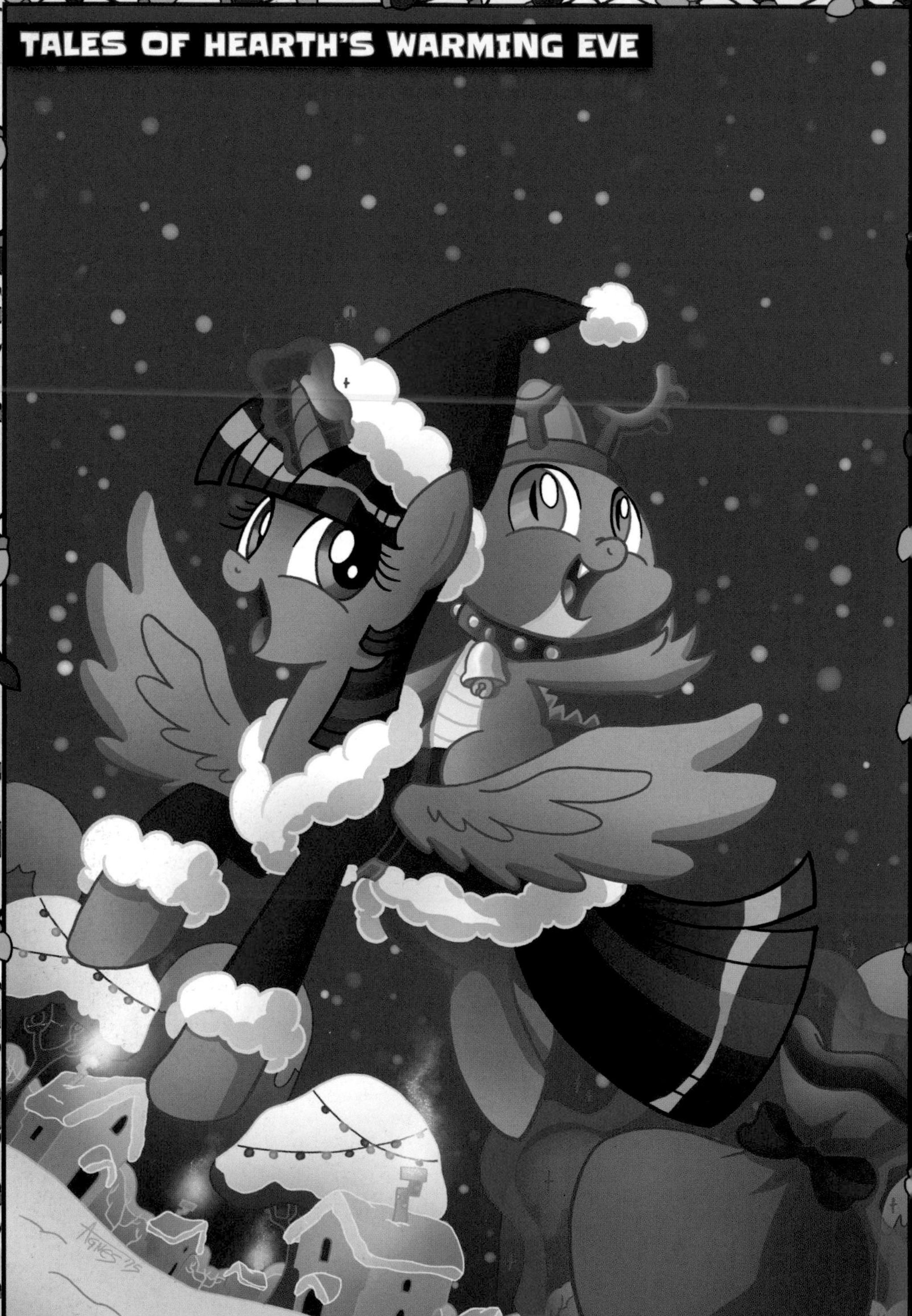

ART BY Agnes Garbowska

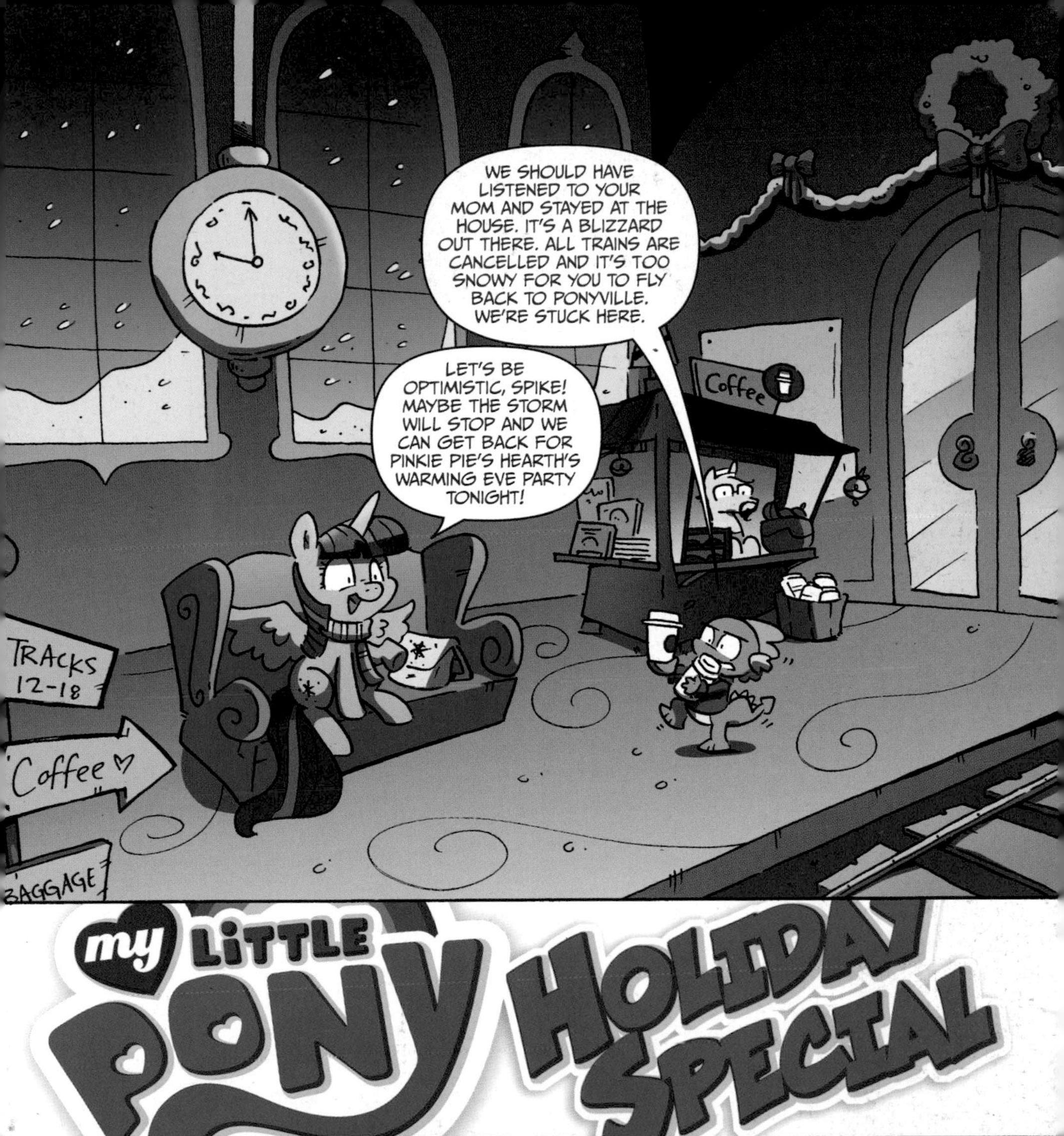
WE SHOULD HAVE LISTENED TO YOUR MOM AND STAYED AT THE HOUSE. IT'S A BLIZZARD OUT THERE. ALL TRAINS ARE CANCELLED AND IT'S TOO SNOWY FOR YOU TO FLY BACK TO PONYVILLE. WE'RE STUCK HERE.
LET'S BE OPTIMISTIC, SPIKE! MAYBE THE STORM WILL STOP AND WE CAN GET BACK FOR PINKIE PIE'S HEARTH'S WARMING EVE PARTY TONIGHT!
Coffee
TRACKS 12-18
Coffee
BAGGAGE

MY LITTLE PONY HOLIDAY SPECIAL

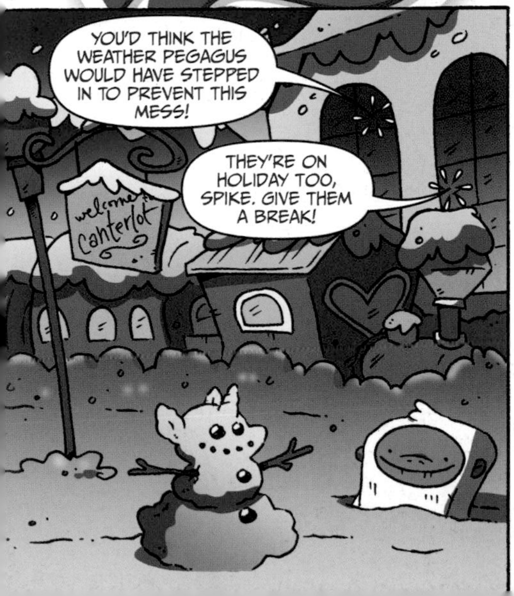
YOU'D THINK THE WEATHER PEGAGUS WOULD HAVE STEPPED IN TO PREVENT THIS MESS!
THEY'RE ON HOLIDAY TOO, SPIKE. GIVE THEM A BREAK!
welcome to Canterlot

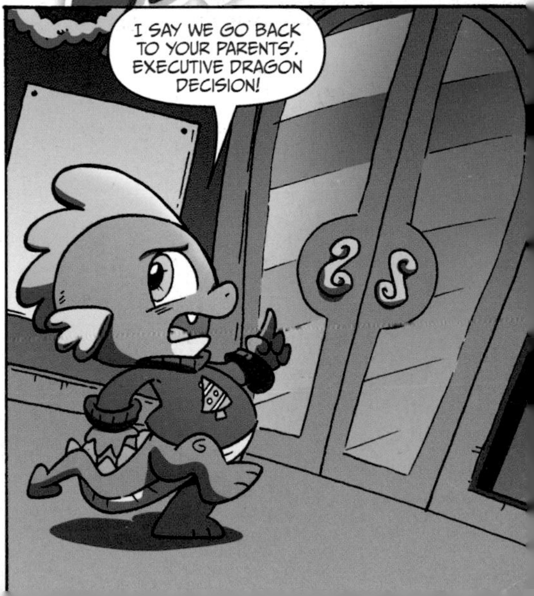
I SAY WE GO BACK TO YOUR PARENTS'. EXECUTIVE DRAGON DECISION!

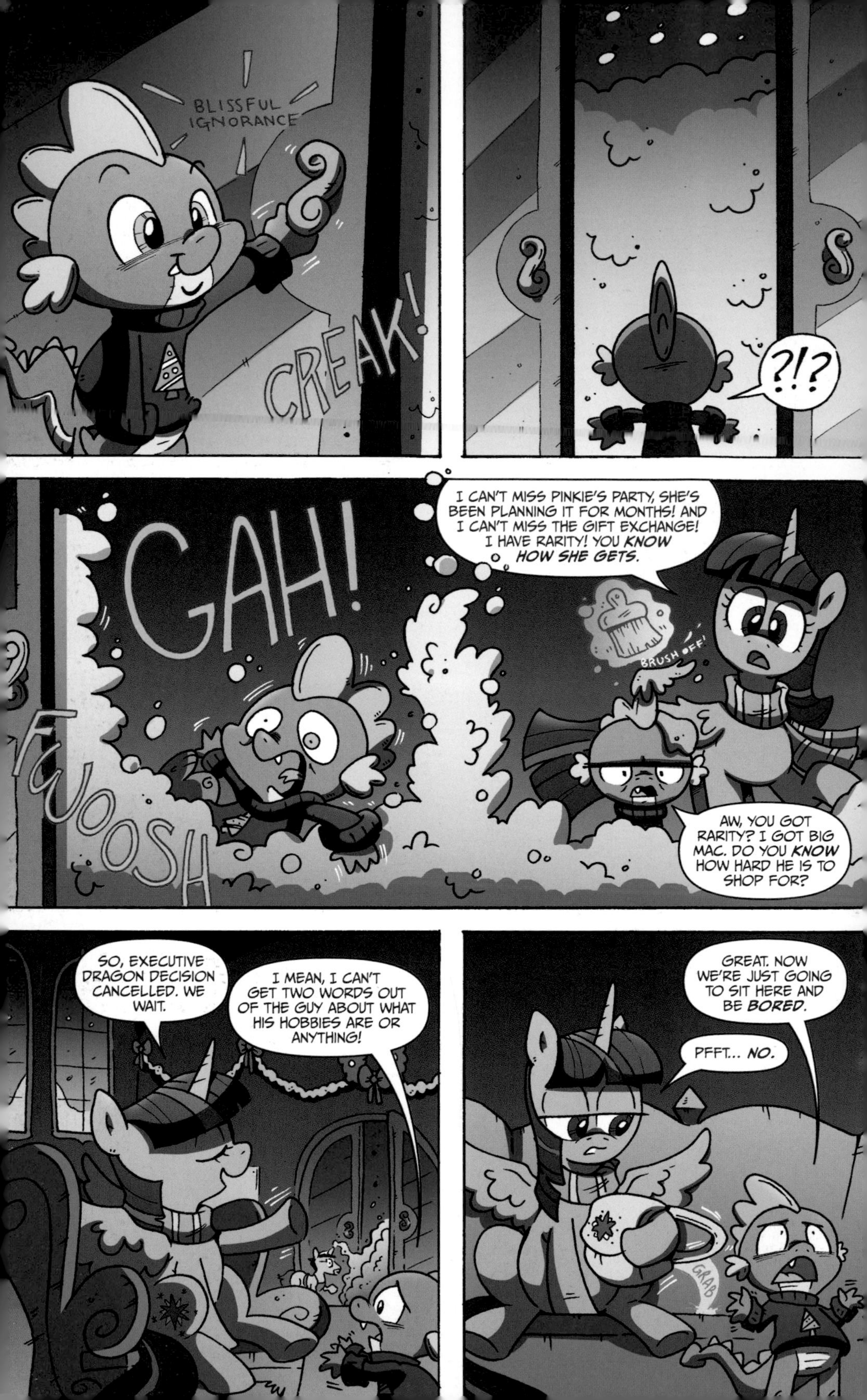
BLISSFUL IGNORANCE
CREAK!
?!?
GAH!
FWOOSH
I CAN'T MISS PINKIE'S PARTY, SHE'S BEEN PLANNING IT FOR MONTHS! AND I CAN'T MISS THE GIFT EXCHANGE! I HAVE RARITY! YOU KNOW HOW SHE GETS.
BRUSH OFF!
AW, YOU GOT RARITY? I GOT BIG MAC. DO YOU KNOW HOW HARD HE IS TO SHOP FOR?
SO, EXECUTIVE DRAGON DECISION CANCELLED. WE WAIT.
I MEAN, I CAN'T GET TWO WORDS OUT OF THE GUY ABOUT WHAT HIS HOBBIES ARE OR ANYTHING!
GREAT. NOW WE'RE JUST GOING TO SIT HERE AND BE BORED.
PFFT... NO.
GRAB

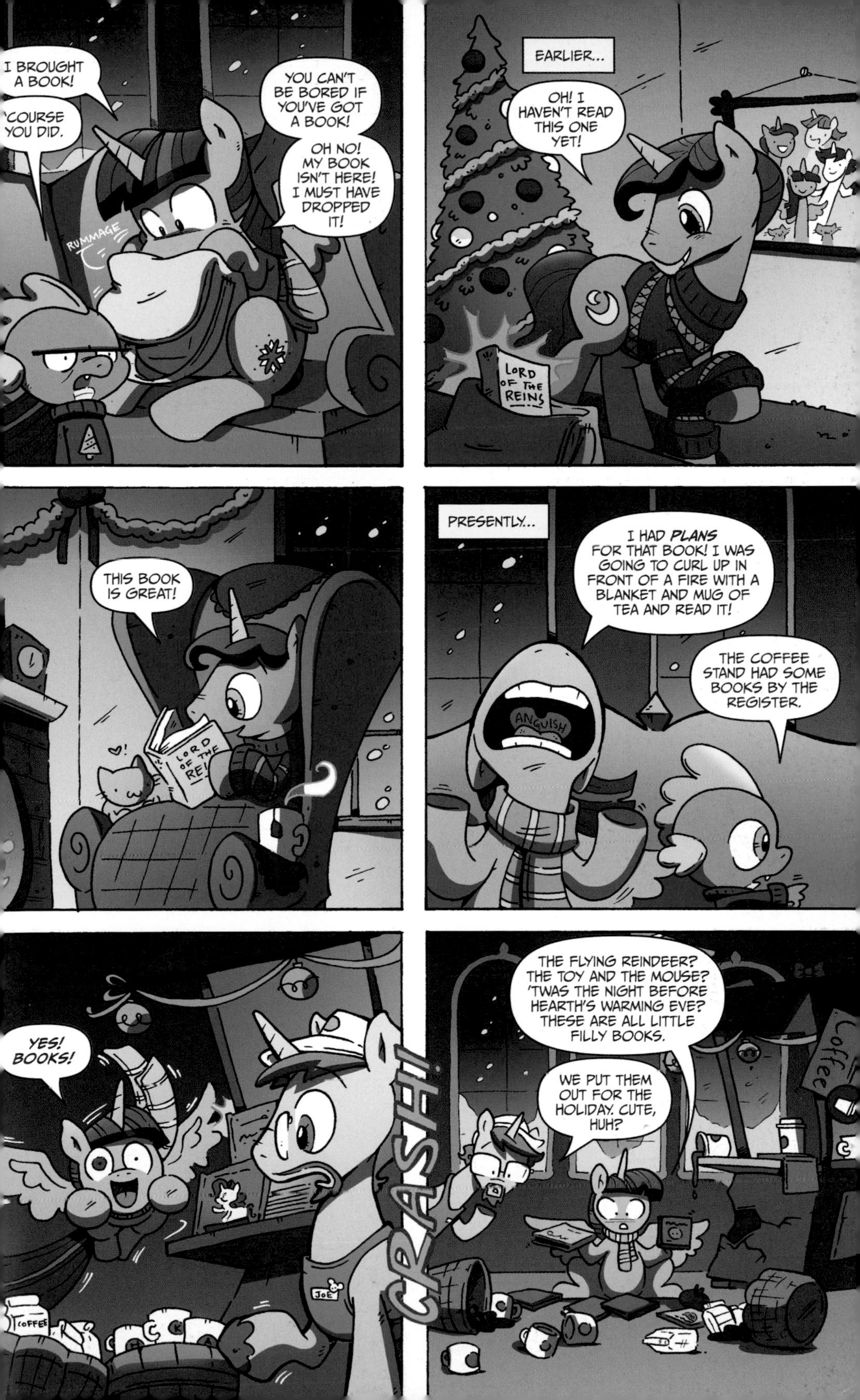
I BROUGHT A BOOK!
'COURSE YOU DID.
YOU CAN'T BE BORED IF YOU'VE GOT A BOOK!
OH NO! MY BOOK ISN'T HERE! I MUST HAVE DROPPED IT!
RUMMAGE
EARLIER...
OH! I HAVEN'T READ THIS ONE YET!
LORD OF THE REINS
THIS BOOK IS GREAT!
LORD OF THE RE
PRESENTLY...
I HAD ***PLANS*** FOR THAT BOOK! I WAS GOING TO CURL UP IN FRONT OF A FIRE WITH A BLANKET AND MUG OF TEA AND READ IT!
ANGUISH
THE COFFEE STAND HAD SOME BOOKS BY THE REGISTER.
YES! BOOKS!
CRASH!
JOE
COFFEE
THE FLYING REINDEER? THE TOY AND THE MOUSE? 'TWAS THE NIGHT BEFORE HEARTH'S WARMING EVE? THESE ARE ALL LITTLE FILLY BOOKS.
WE PUT THEM OUT FOR THE HOLIDAY. CUTE, HUH?
Coffee

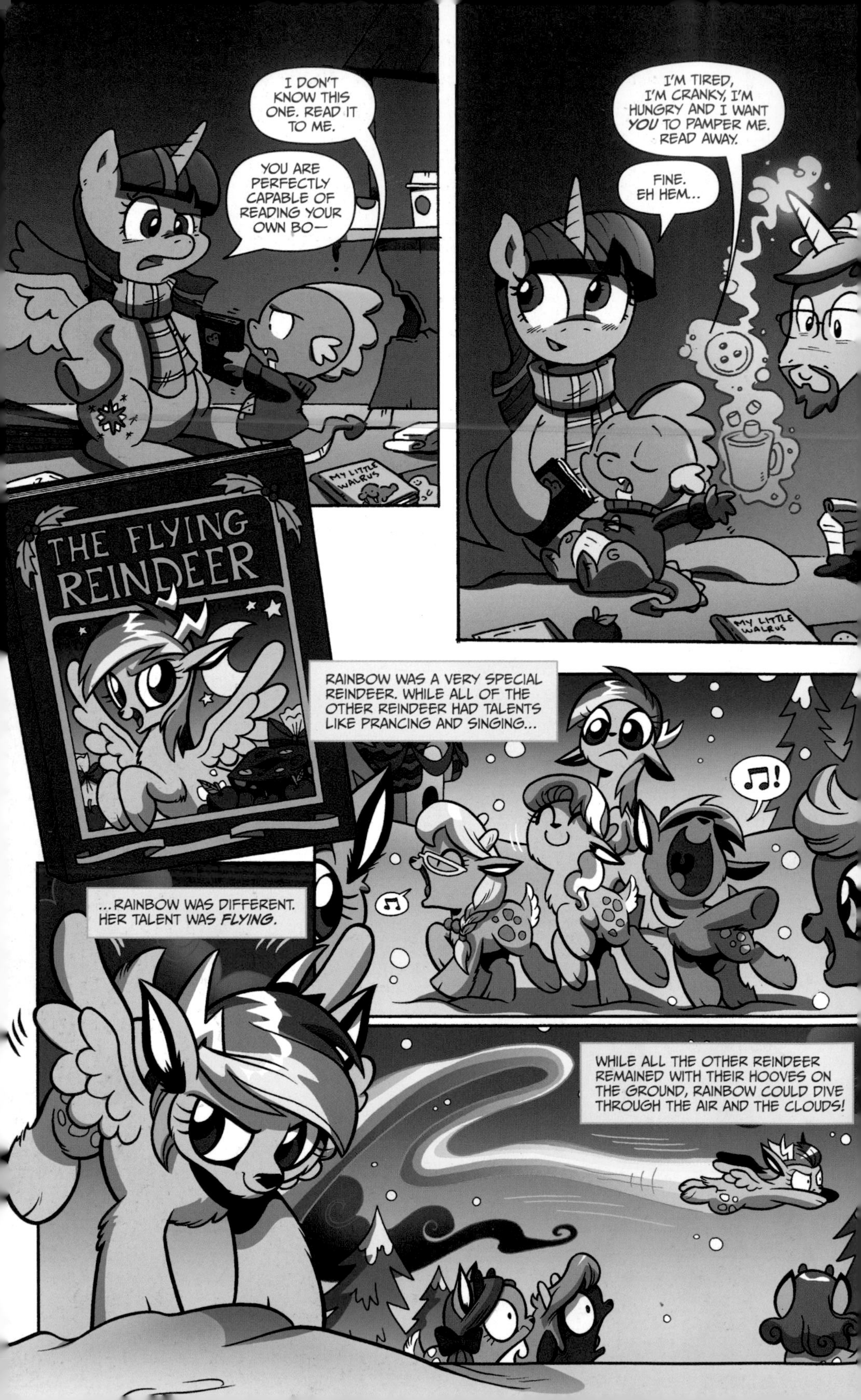

I DON'T KNOW THIS ONE. READ IT TO ME.
YOU ARE PERFECTLY CAPABLE OF READING YOUR OWN BO—
I'M TIRED, I'M CRANKY, I'M HUNGRY AND I WANT YOU TO PAMPER ME. READ AWAY.
FINE. EH HEM...
MY LITTLE WALRUS
THE FLYING REINDEER
MY LITTLE WALRUS
RAINBOW WAS A VERY SPECIAL REINDEER. WHILE ALL OF THE OTHER REINDEER HAD TALENTS LIKE PRANCING AND SINGING...
♫!
...RAINBOW WAS DIFFERENT. HER TALENT WAS FLYING.
WHILE ALL THE OTHER REINDEER REMAINED WITH THEIR HOOVES ON THE GROUND, RAINBOW COULD DIVE THROUGH THE AIR AND THE CLOUDS!

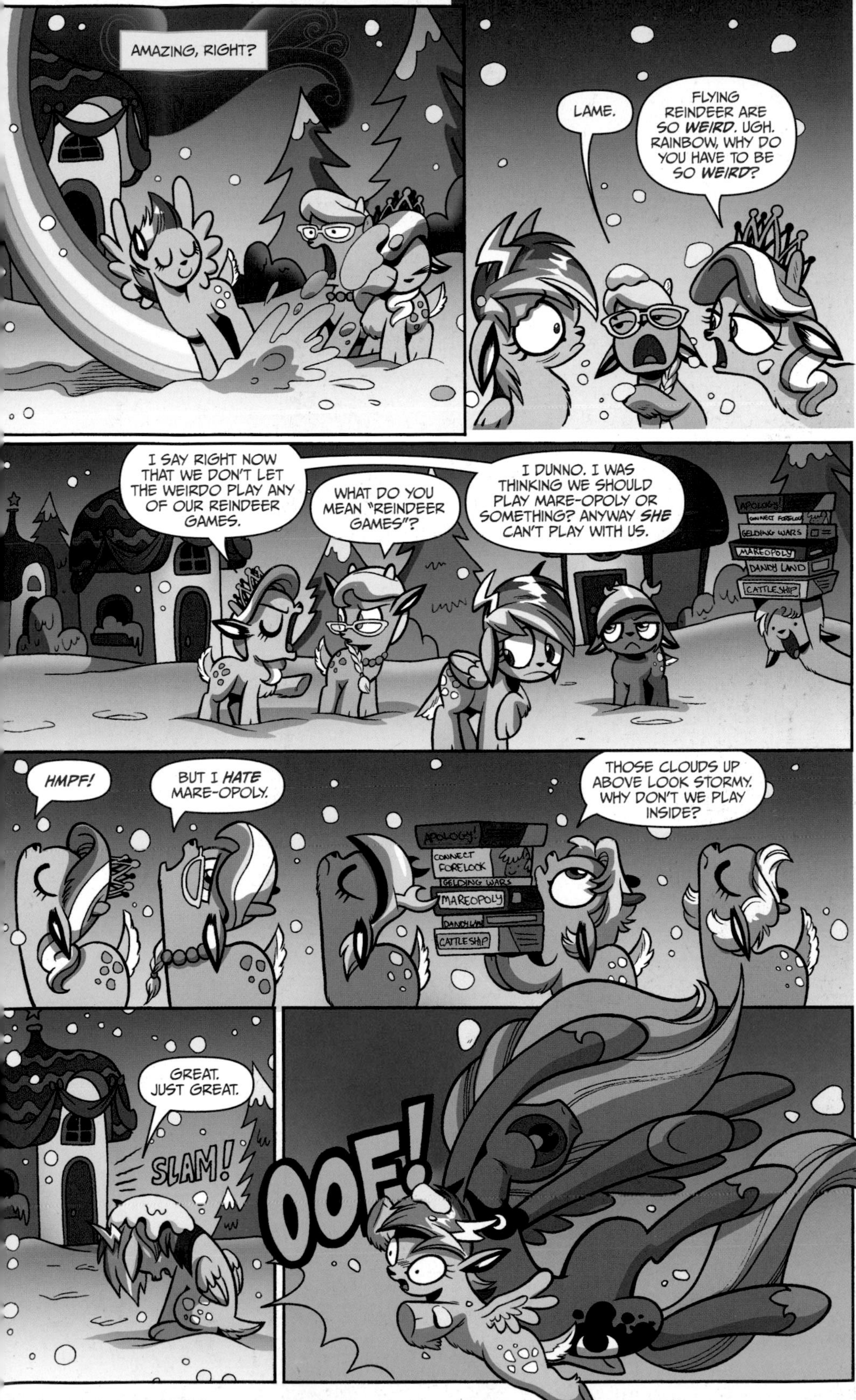
AMAZING, RIGHT?
LAME.
FLYING REINDEER ARE SO WEIRD. UGH. RAINBOW, WHY DO YOU HAVE TO BE SO WEIRD?
I SAY RIGHT NOW THAT WE DON'T LET THE WEIRDO PLAY ANY OF OUR REINDEER GAMES.
WHAT DO YOU MEAN "REINDEER GAMES"?
I DUNNO. I WAS THINKING WE SHOULD PLAY MARE-OPOLY OR SOMETHING? ANYWAY SHE CAN'T PLAY WITH US.
APOLOGY!
CONNECT FORELOCK
GELDING WARS
MAREOPOLY
DANDY LAND
CATTLESHIP
HMPF!
BUT I HATE MARE-OPOLY.
THOSE CLOUDS UP ABOVE LOOK STORMY. WHY DON'T WE PLAY INSIDE?
GREAT. JUST GREAT.
SLAM!
OOF!

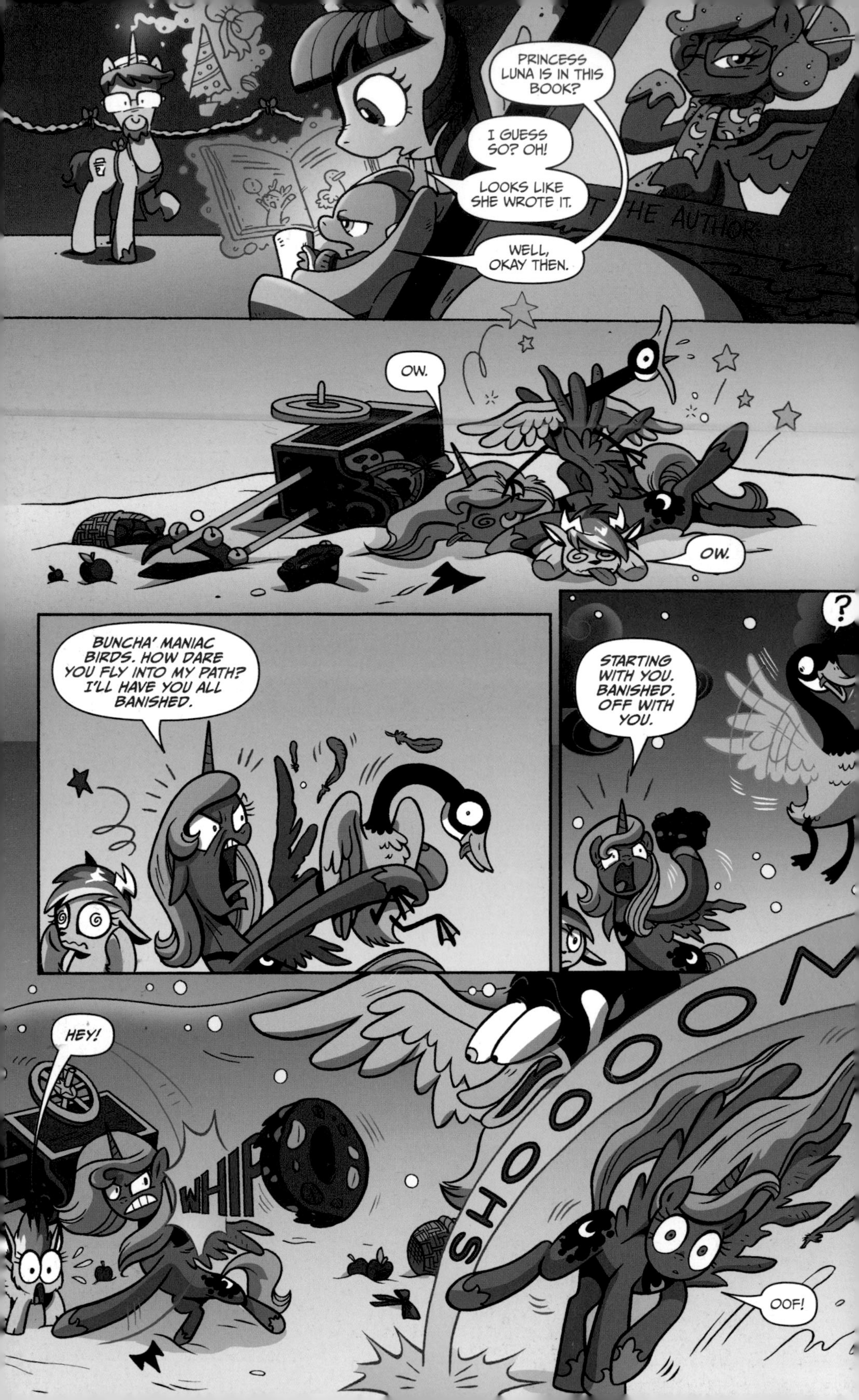
PRINCESS LUNA IS IN THIS BOOK?
I GUESS SO? OH!
LOOKS LIKE SHE WROTE IT.
WELL, OKAY THEN.
OW.
OW.
BUNCHA' MANIAC BIRDS. HOW DARE YOU FLY INTO MY PATH? I'LL HAVE YOU ALL BANISHED.
STARTING WITH YOU. BANISHED. OFF WITH YOU.
?
HEY!
WHIP
SHOOOOOM
OOF!

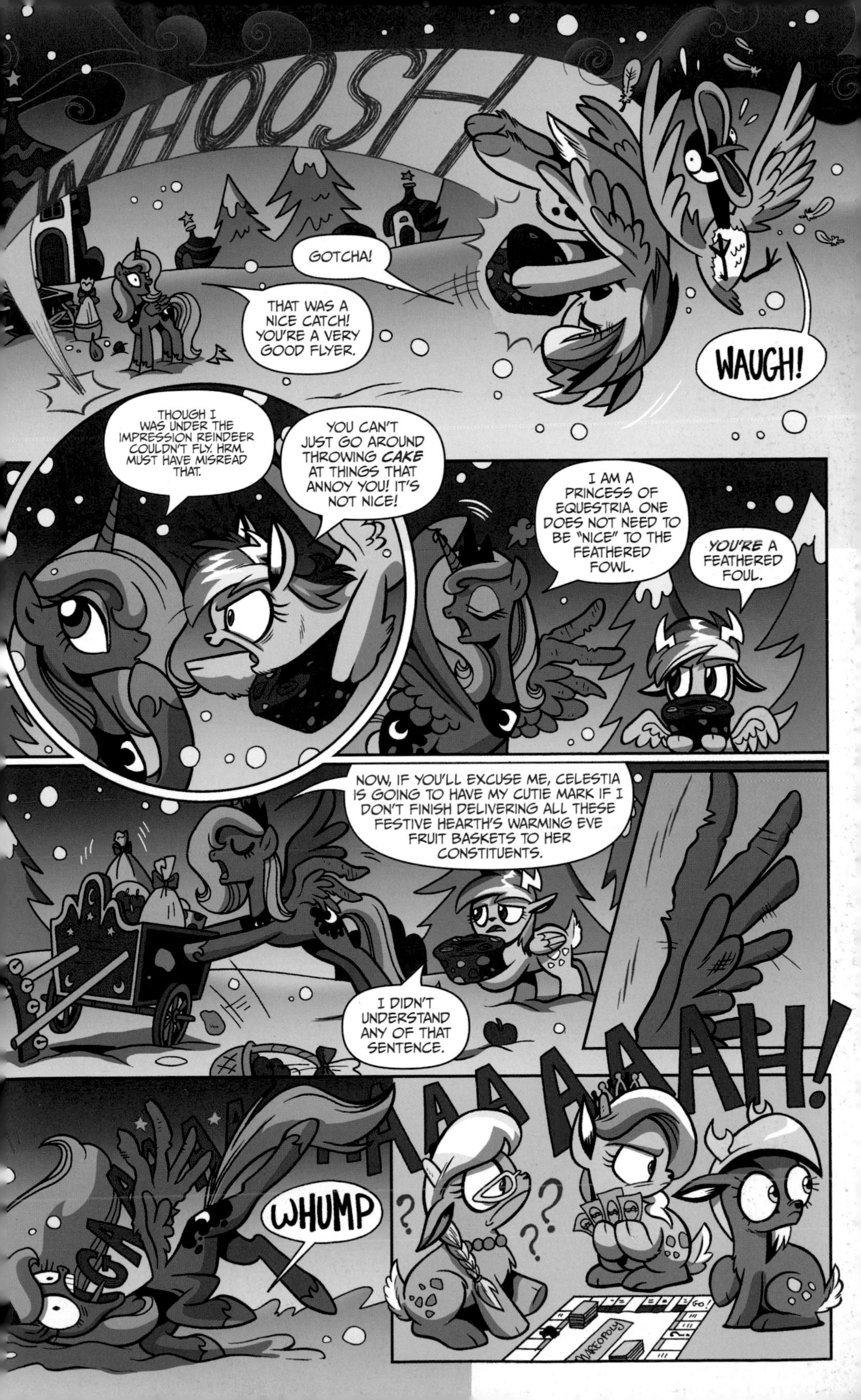
WHOOSH
GOTCHA!
THAT WAS A NICE CATCH! YOU'RE A VERY GOOD FLYER.
WAUGH!
THOUGH I WAS UNDER THE IMPRESSION REINDEER COULDN'T FLY. HRM. MUST HAVE MISREAD THAT.
YOU CAN'T JUST GO AROUND THROWING CAKE AT THINGS THAT ANNOY YOU! IT'S NOT NICE!
I AM A PRINCESS OF EQUESTRIA. ONE DOES NOT NEED TO BE "NICE" TO THE FEATHERED FOWL.
YOU'RE A FEATHERED FOUL.
NOW, IF YOU'LL EXCUSE ME, CELESTIA IS GOING TO HAVE MY CUTIE MARK IF I DON'T FINISH DELIVERING ALL THESE FESTIVE HEARTH'S WARMING EVE FRUIT BASKETS TO HER CONSTITUENTS.
I DIDN'T UNDERSTAND ANY OF THAT SENTENCE.
AAAAAAAH!
WHUMP
GO!
MAREOPOLY

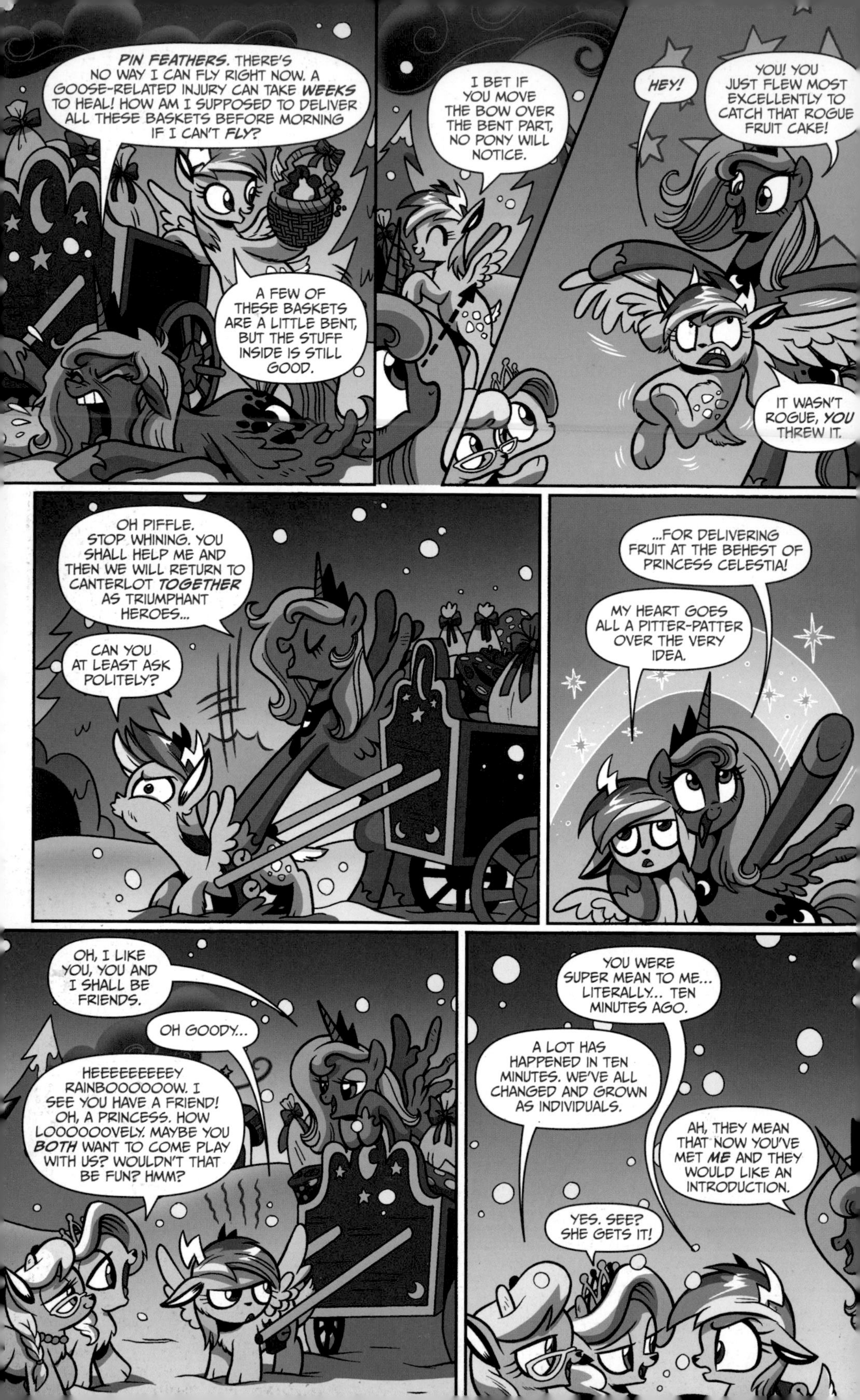
PIN FEATHERS. THERE'S NO WAY I CAN FLY RIGHT NOW. A GOOSE-RELATED INJURY CAN TAKE WEEKS TO HEAL! HOW AM I SUPPOSED TO DELIVER ALL THESE BASKETS BEFORE MORNING IF I CAN'T FLY?
A FEW OF THESE BASKETS ARE A LITTLE BENT, BUT THE STUFF INSIDE IS STILL GOOD.
I BET IF YOU MOVE THE BOW OVER THE BENT PART, NO PONY WILL NOTICE.
HEY!
YOU! YOU JUST FLEW MOST EXCELLENTLY TO CATCH THAT ROGUE FRUIT CAKE!
IT WASN'T ROGUE, YOU THREW IT.
OH PIFFLE. STOP WHINING. YOU SHALL HELP ME AND THEN WE WILL RETURN TO CANTERLOT TOGETHER AS TRIUMPHANT HEROES...
CAN YOU AT LEAST ASK POLITELY?
...FOR DELIVERING FRUIT AT THE BEHEST OF PRINCESS CELESTIA!
MY HEART GOES ALL A PITTER-PATTER OVER THE VERY IDEA.
OH, I LIKE YOU, YOU AND I SHALL BE FRIENDS.
OH GOODY...
HEEEEEEEEEY RAINBOOOOOOW. I SEE YOU HAVE A FRIEND! OH, A PRINCESS. HOW LOOOOOOVELY. MAYBE YOU BOTH WANT TO COME PLAY WITH US? WOULDN'T THAT BE FUN? HMM?
YOU WERE SUPER MEAN TO ME... LITERALLY... TEN MINUTES AGO.
A LOT HAS HAPPENED IN TEN MINUTES. WE'VE ALL CHANGED AND GROWN AS INDIVIDUALS.
AH, THEY MEAN THAT NOW YOU'VE MET ME AND THEY WOULD LIKE AN INTRODUCTION.
YES. SEE? SHE GETS IT!

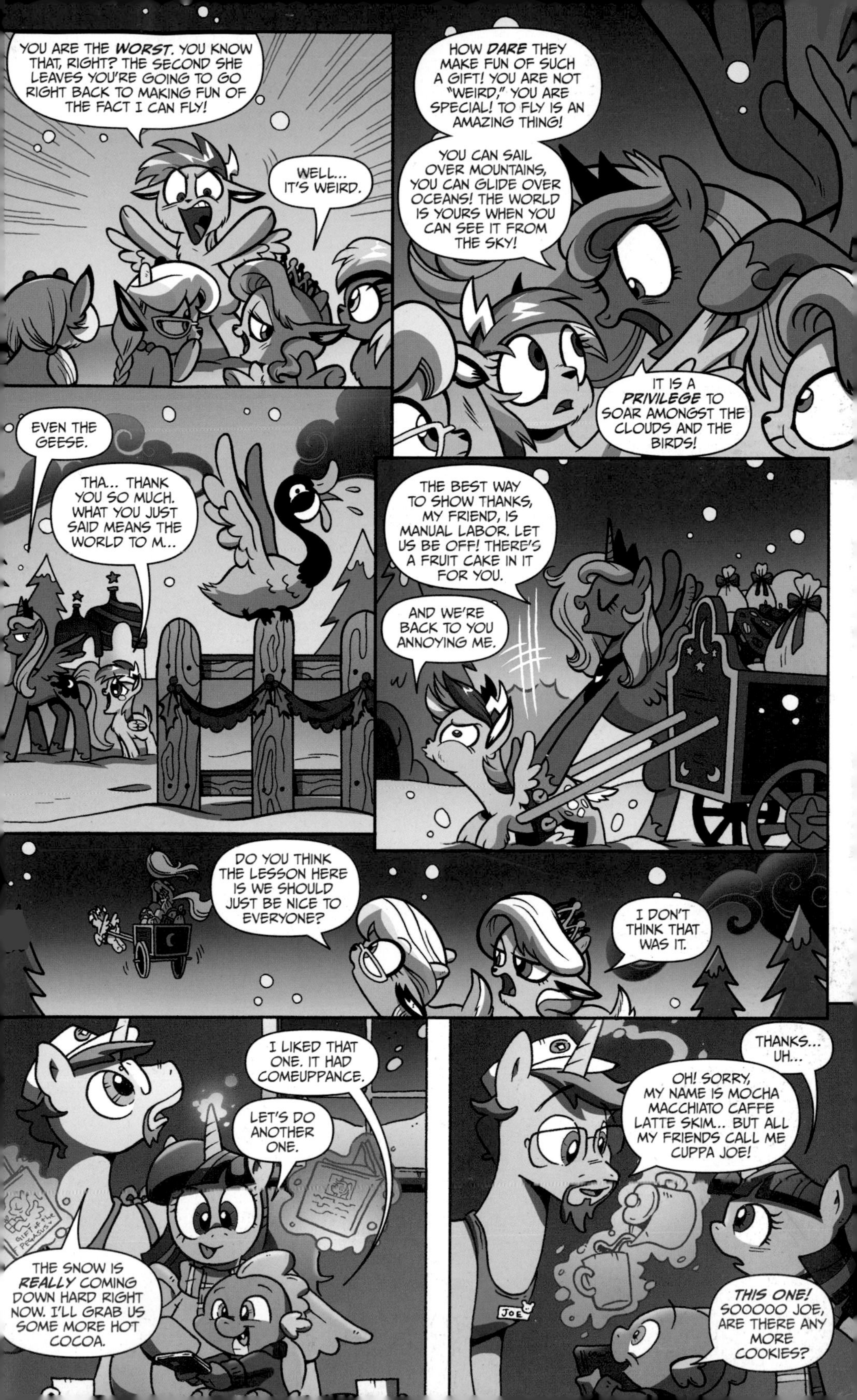
YOU ARE THE WORST. YOU KNOW THAT, RIGHT? THE SECOND SHE LEAVES YOU'RE GOING TO GO RIGHT BACK TO MAKING FUN OF THE FACT I CAN FLY!
WELL... IT'S WEIRD.
HOW DARE THEY MAKE FUN OF SUCH A GIFT! YOU ARE NOT "WEIRD," YOU ARE SPECIAL! TO FLY IS AN AMAZING THING!
YOU CAN SAIL OVER MOUNTAINS, YOU CAN GLIDE OVER OCEANS! THE WORLD IS YOURS WHEN YOU CAN SEE IT FROM THE SKY!
IT IS A PRIVILEGE TO SOAR AMONGST THE CLOUDS AND THE BIRDS!
EVEN THE GEESE.
THA... THANK YOU SO MUCH. WHAT YOU JUST SAID MEANS THE WORLD TO M...
THE BEST WAY TO SHOW THANKS, MY FRIEND, IS MANUAL LABOR. LET US BE OFF! THERE'S A FRUIT CAKE IN IT FOR YOU.
AND WE'RE BACK TO YOU ANNOYING ME.
DO YOU THINK THE LESSON HERE IS WE SHOULD JUST BE NICE TO EVERYONE?
I DON'T THINK THAT WAS IT.
I LIKED THAT ONE. IT HAD COMEUPPANCE.
LET'S DO ANOTHER ONE.
GIFT of the PEGASUS
THE SNOW IS REALLY COMING DOWN HARD RIGHT NOW. I'LL GRAB US SOME MORE HOT COCOA.
THANKS... UH...
OH! SORRY, MY NAME IS MOCHA MACCHIATO CAFFE LATTE SKIM... BUT ALL MY FRIENDS CALL ME CUPPA JOE!
JOE
THIS ONE! SOOOOO JOE, ARE THERE ANY MORE COOKIES?

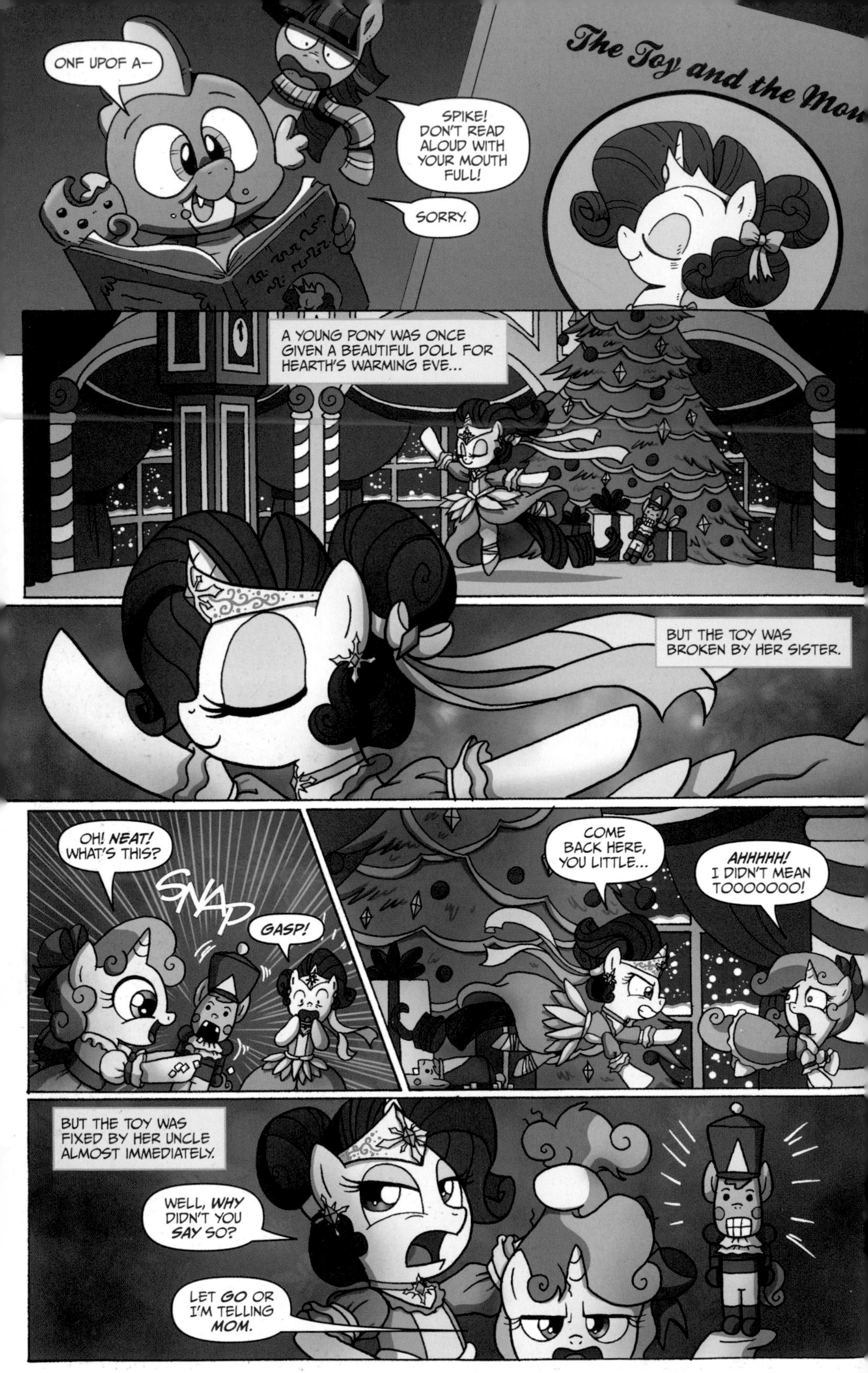

The Toy and the Mou
ONF UPOF A—
SPIKE! DON'T READ ALOUD WITH YOUR MOUTH FULL!
SORRY.
A YOUNG PONY WAS ONCE GIVEN A BEAUTIFUL DOLL FOR HEARTH'S WARMING EVE...
BUT THE TOY WAS BROKEN BY HER SISTER.
OH! NEAT! WHAT'S THIS?
SNAP
GASP!
COME BACK HERE, YOU LITTLE...
AHHHHH! I DIDN'T MEAN TOOOOOOO!
BUT THE TOY WAS FIXED BY HER UNCLE ALMOST IMMEDIATELY.
WELL, WHY DIDN'T YOU SAY SO?
LET GO OR I'M TELLING MOM.

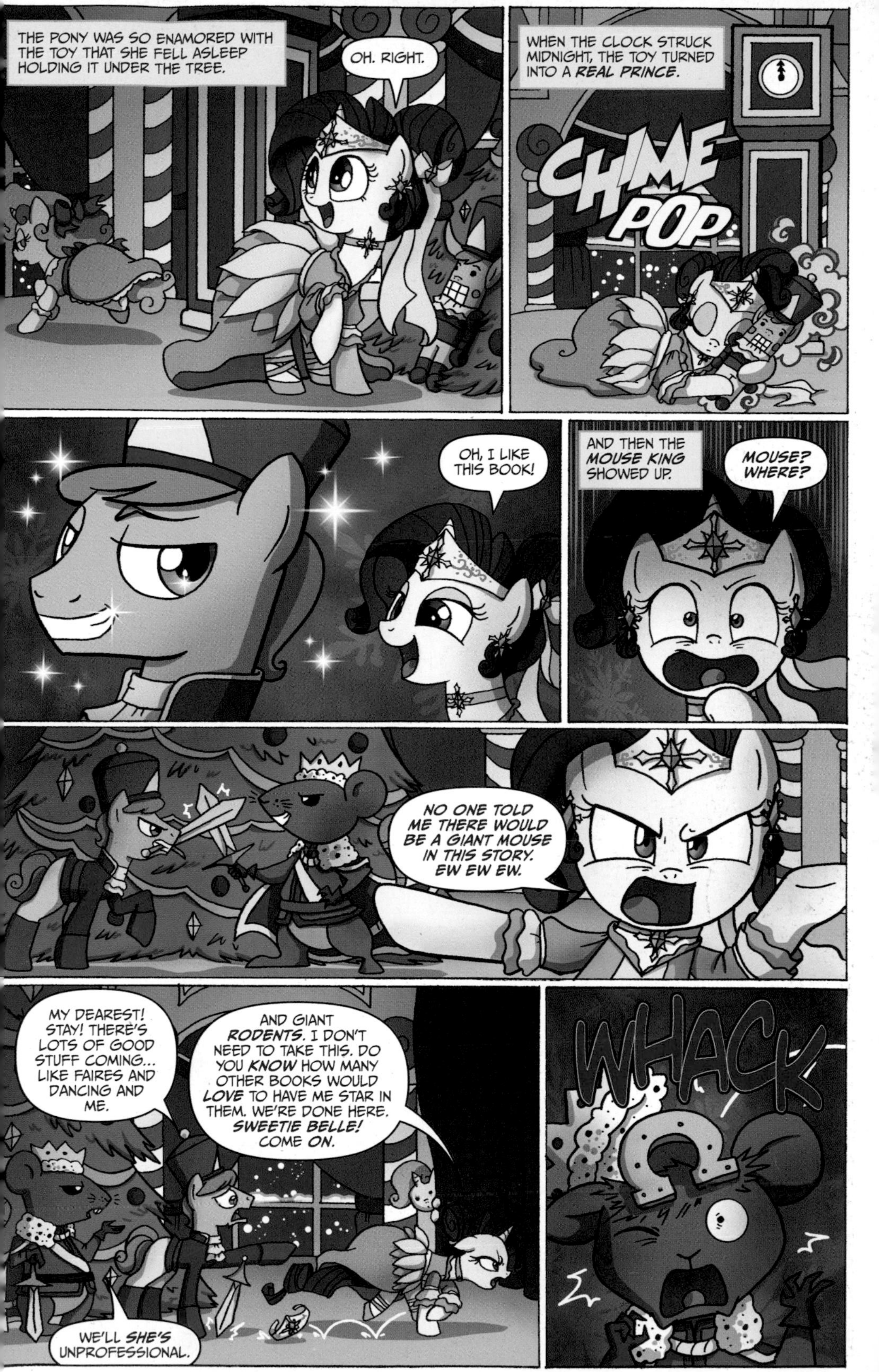

THE PONY WAS SO ENAMORED WITH THE TOY THAT SHE FELL ASLEEP HOLDING IT UNDER THE TREE.
OH. RIGHT.
WHEN THE CLOCK STRUCK MIDNIGHT, THE TOY TURNED INTO A REAL PRINCE.
CHIME
POP
OH, I LIKE THIS BOOK!
AND THEN THE MOUSE KING SHOWED UP.
MOUSE? WHERE?
NO ONE TOLD ME THERE WOULD BE A GIANT MOUSE IN THIS STORY. EW EW EW.
MY DEAREST! STAY! THERE'S LOTS OF GOOD STUFF COMING... LIKE FAIRES AND DANCING AND ME.
AND GIANT RODENTS. I DON'T NEED TO TAKE THIS. DO YOU KNOW HOW MANY OTHER BOOKS WOULD LOVE TO HAVE ME STAR IN THEM. WE'RE DONE HERE. SWEETIE BELLE! COME ON.
WE'LL SHE'S UNPROFESSIONAL.
WHACK

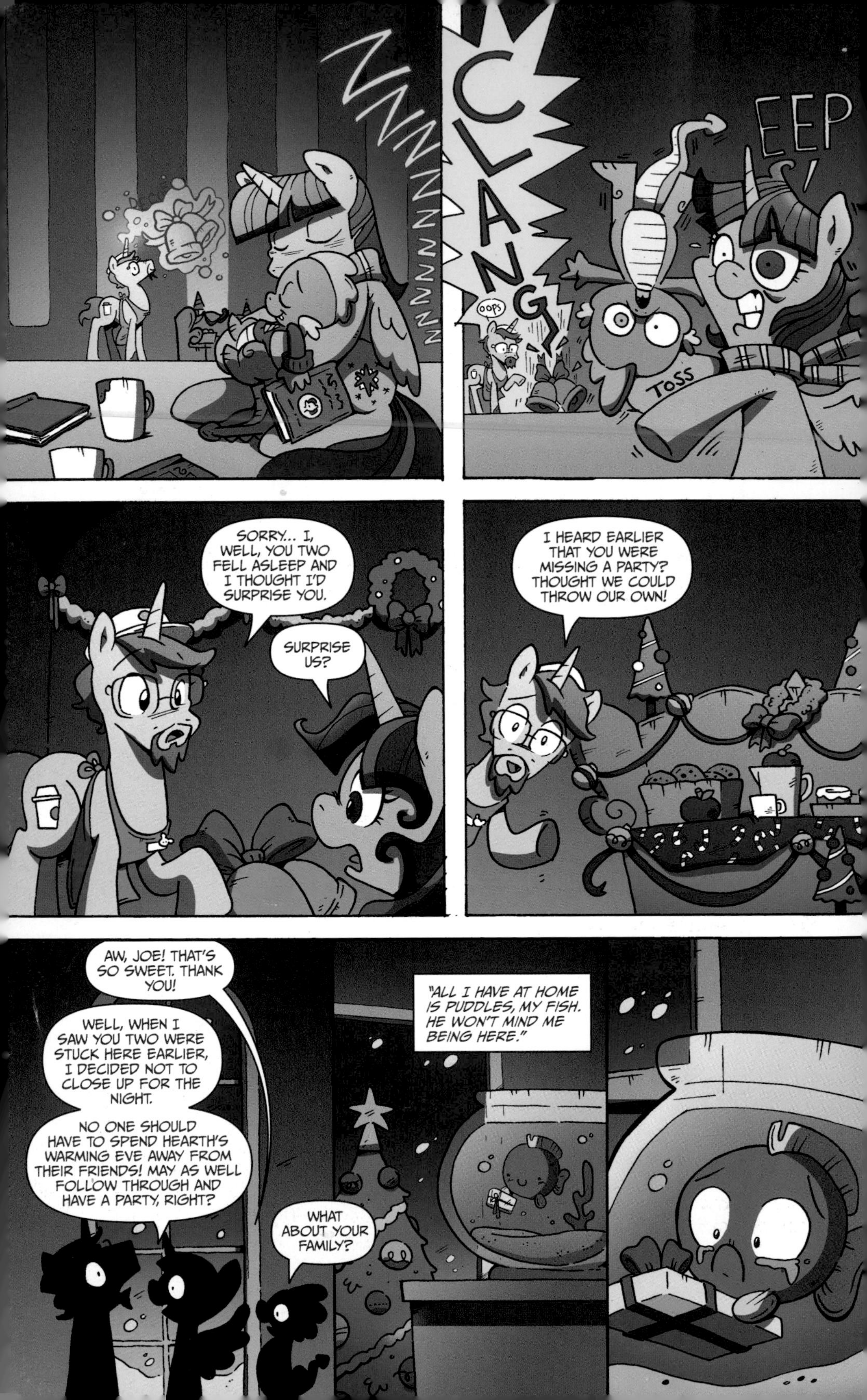
ZZZZZZZZZZZZ
CLANG
EEP
OOPS
TOSS
SORRY... I, WELL, YOU TWO FELL ASLEEP AND I THOUGHT I'D SURPRISE YOU.
SURPRISE US?
I HEARD EARLIER THAT YOU WERE MISSING A PARTY? THOUGHT WE COULD THROW OUR OWN!
AW, JOE! THAT'S SO SWEET. THANK YOU!
WELL, WHEN I SAW YOU TWO WERE STUCK HERE EARLIER, I DECIDED NOT TO CLOSE UP FOR THE NIGHT.
NO ONE SHOULD HAVE TO SPEND HEARTH'S WARMING EVE AWAY FROM THEIR FRIENDS! MAY AS WELL FOLLOW THROUGH AND HAVE A PARTY, RIGHT?
WHAT ABOUT YOUR FAMILY?
"ALL I HAVE AT HOME IS PUDDLES, MY FISH. HE WON'T MIND ME BEING HERE."

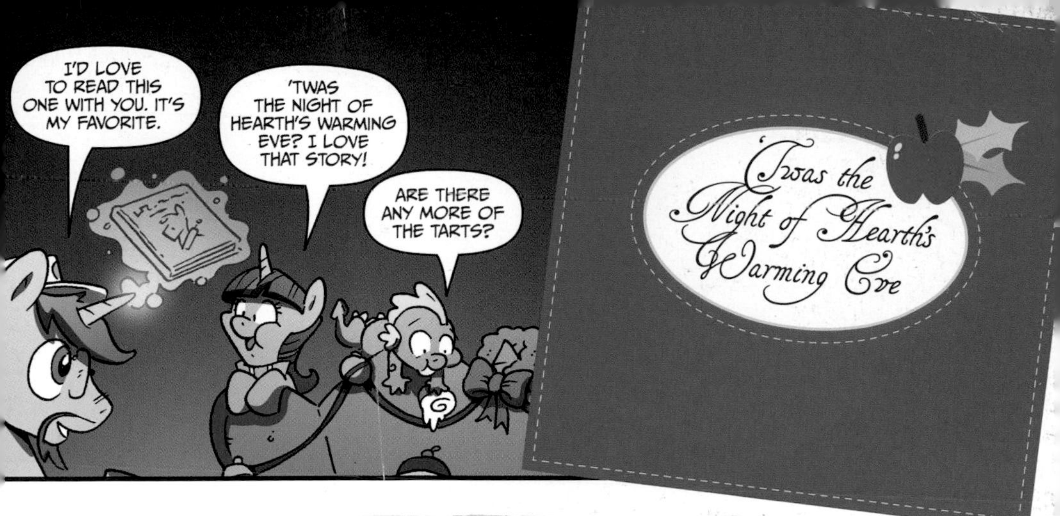
I'D LOVE TO READ THIS ONE WITH YOU. IT'S MY FAVORITE.
'TWAS THE NIGHT OF HEARTH'S WARMING EVE? I LOVE THAT STORY!
ARE THERE ANY MORE OF THE TARTS?
'Twas the Night of Hearth's Warming Eve

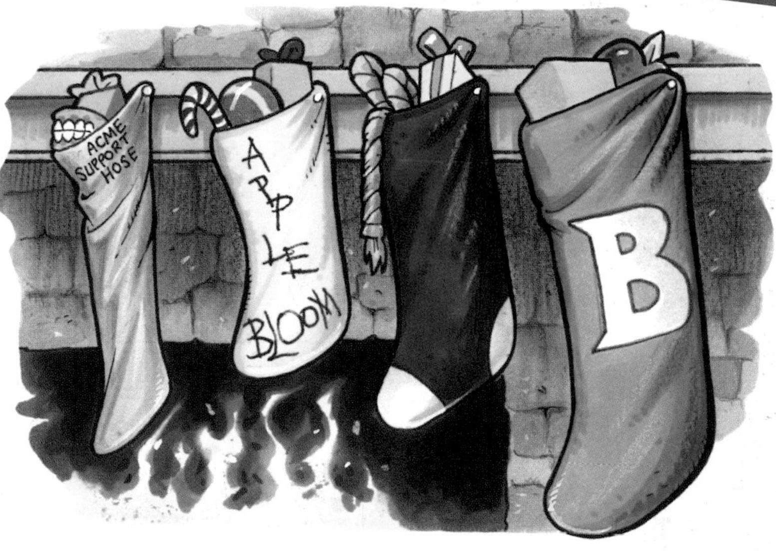
ACME SUPPORT HOSE
APPLE BLOOM
B

'Twas the night of Hearth's Warming Eve
And all through the home
Not a creature was stirring
Not even the cat (whose name was Jerome)
The stockings were hung by the chimney with care
Stuffed to the brim with bad gifts from last year that might go up in a flare

The fillies were nested all
snug in their beds
While visions of sugar plums
danced in their heads.
What's a sugar plum you say?
It's a candy. I looked it
up yesterday.

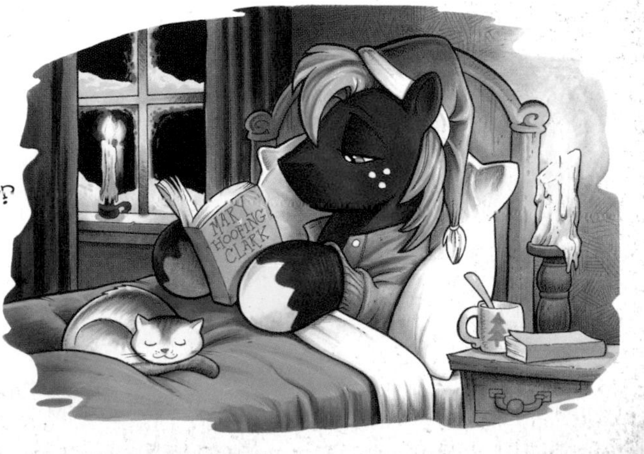
MARY HOOFING CLARK

In my pajamas, down to
the slipper like bunnies
Had just settled in after
reading the funnies.

Then out in the orchard there arose such a racket,
I sprang from my bed and grabbed for my jacket.

Away to the fields, I flew like a flash,
And into the snow I fell with a splash.

When what did my wondering eyes then see,
But my sisters trying to build a present... just for me.

Out in the barn, they secretly worked,
I had to sneak over, my interest was perked.

"One sister called out to the farm animals helping,
 Now Bessie, now Porkchop, now Clucky and you there that's yelping,
 Hand me that screwdriver and hold this right here,
 NO HOLD IT THERE. Did you seriously mishear?"

It's really her fault for having the livestock as aides,
did she expect a pig to be a jack of all trades?

Yeesh.

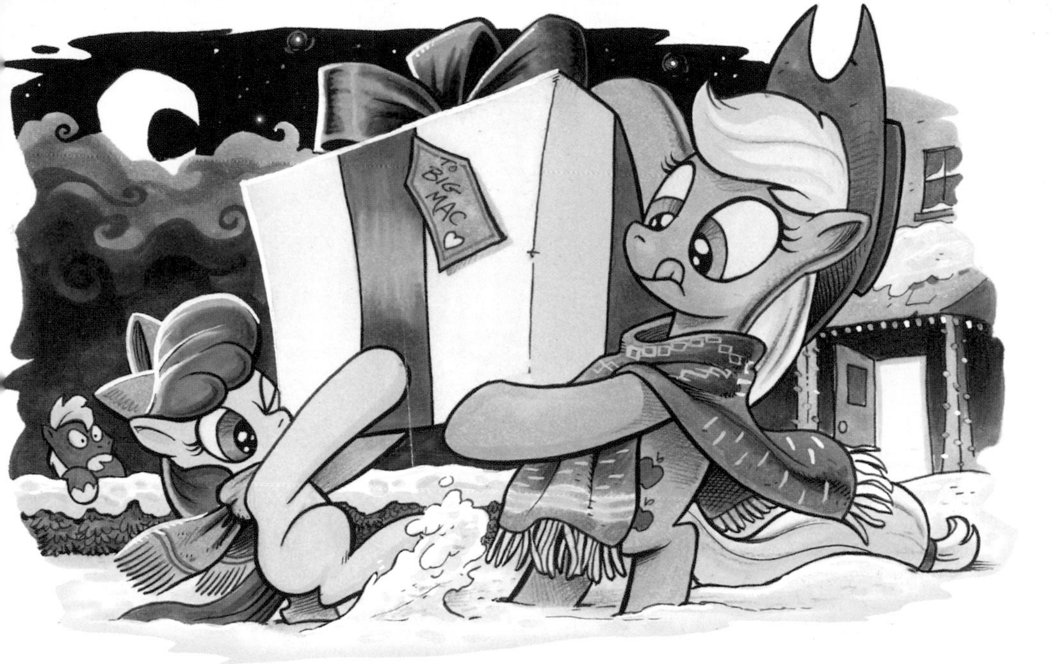
To BIG MAC

"To the top of the porch!" Cried a sister as they carried the gift,
The two of them, along with a cow, planted it in a snow drift.
"We can't go through the door, he'll see us!" One cried,
"You got a BETTER idea?" The other one chide.

"Down the chimney!" the little one barked!
"That's the dumbest idea..." the other tried to remark.
But too late is was, because she'd rushed up the roof.
The other one followed, lifting up the gift with an "OOF."

I chucked inside, watching them try,
Then had a brief start as I
looked to the sky.

Up at the chimney my
sisters were setting
my gift lower into
the...
"WAIT.
I THINK THERE'S
A FIRE IN THE
FIREPLACE."
I almost screamed
like a banshee.

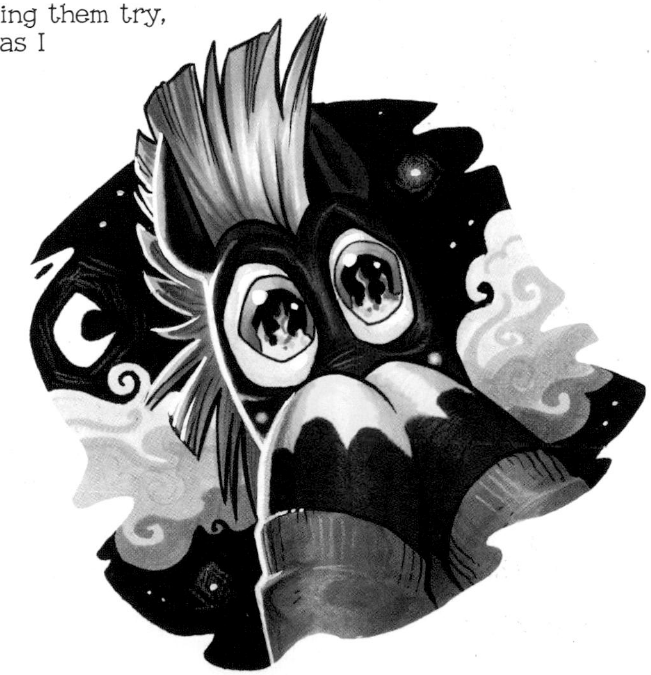

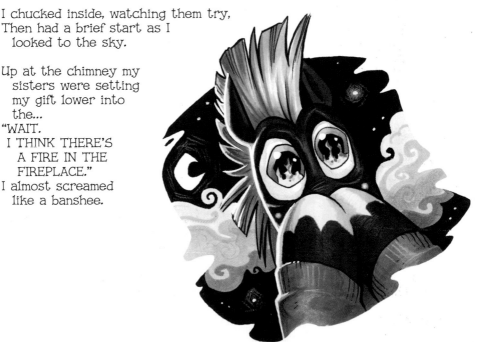

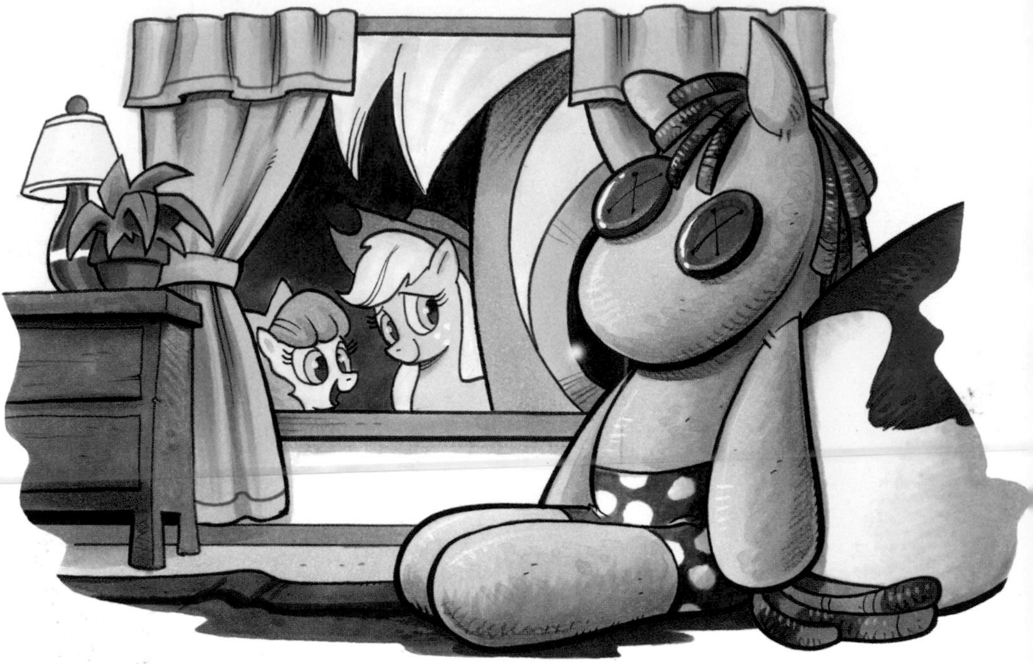

I ran into the house as quick as I could,
And grabbed up some cider to extinguish the wood.

WOOSH went the drink into the fire, dousing the log,
The sizzle and crackle of flames going out made deep fog.
I peered through the mess to see what I could,
And there on the wet log, my present stood.

I could finally see it, it was
completely ideal!
It was a little version of
our home, It hit me
right in the feels.

A home for
my action figure...
my beloved
Smarty Pants,
It even had replicas
of all of our plants.

"That's not an action figure,
it's a DOLL."

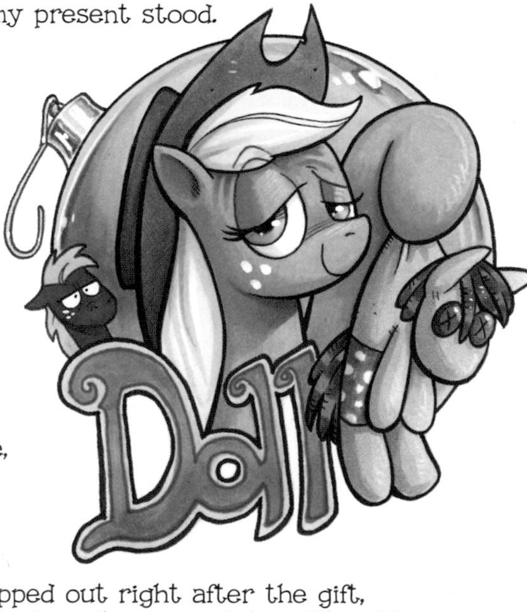
Doll

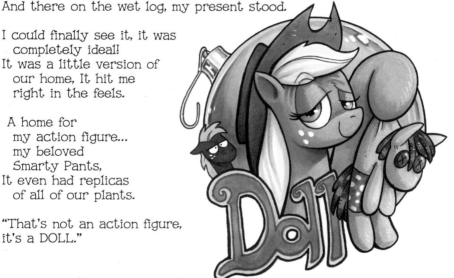

My sisters popped out right after the gift,
I pulled them in for a hug, complete with a lift.

"Love you, big bro!" they said as I ruffled their hair,
Hugging them close, I know how they care.

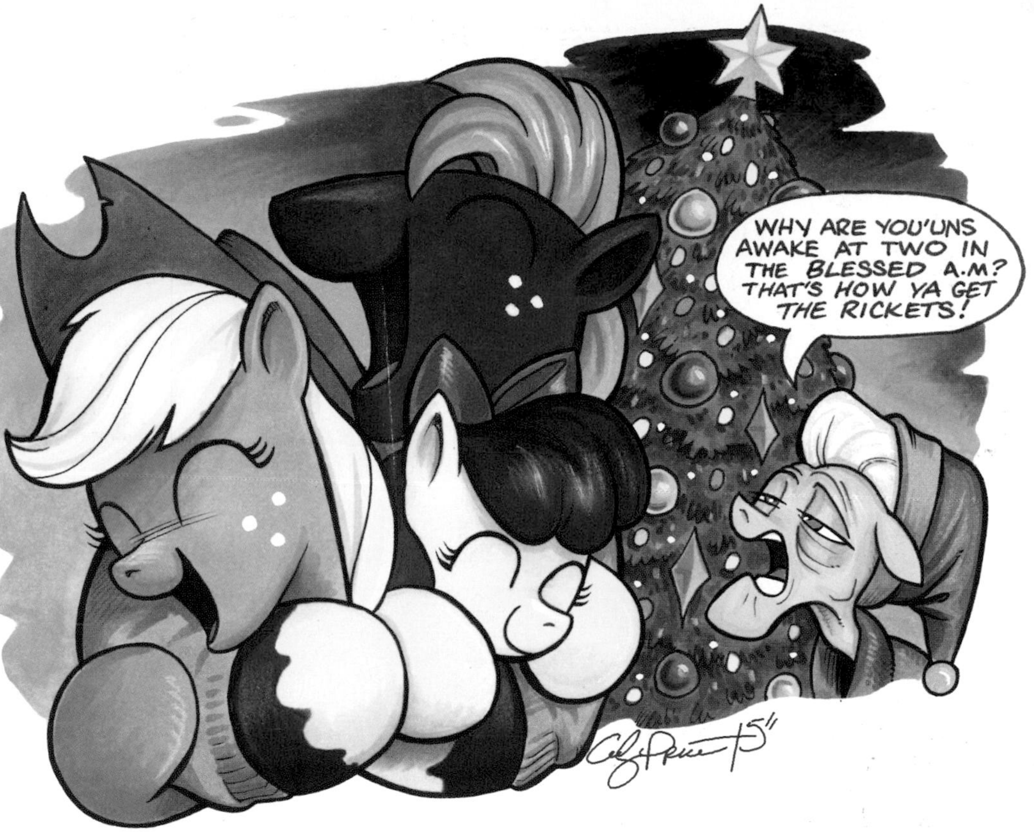
WHY ARE YOU'UNS AWAKE AT TWO IN THE BLESSED A.M? THAT'S HOW YA GET THE RICKETS!

The night ended with presents, family, and food,
We re-lit the fire, for the perfect holiday mood.

Settled in with my family, cozied up to the fire,
I knew there was no higher life to aspire.

I looked at my gift with my eyes shining bright,
Happy Hearth's Warming Eve to all, and to all a good night.

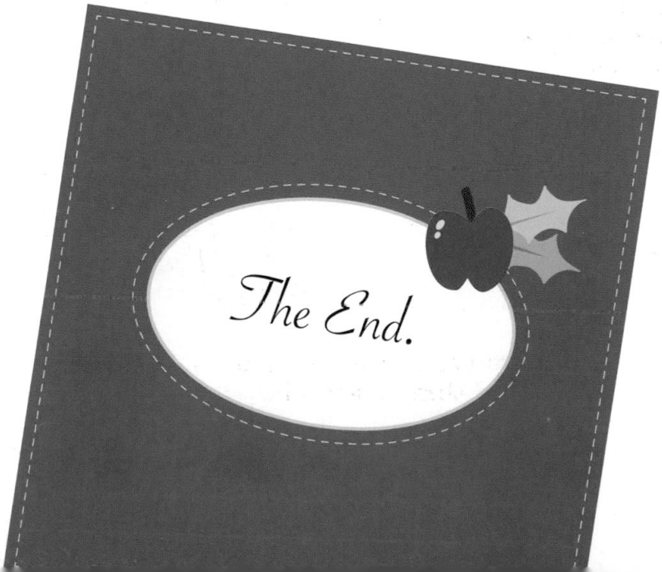
The End.

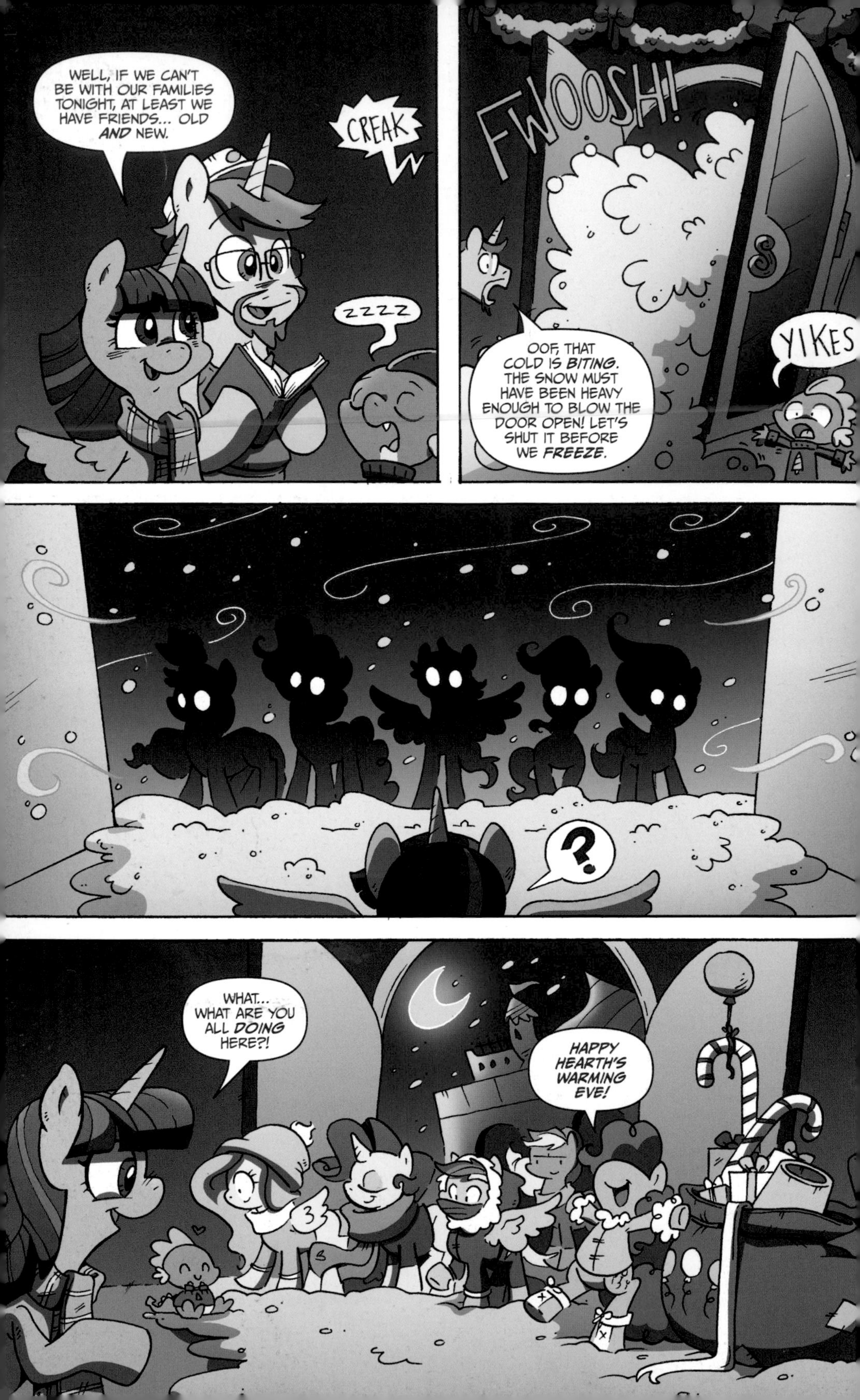
WELL, IF WE CAN'T BE WITH OUR FAMILIES TONIGHT, AT LEAST WE HAVE FRIENDS... OLD *AND* NEW.
CREAK
ZZZZ
FWOOSH!
OOF, THAT COLD IS *BITING*. THE SNOW MUST HAVE BEEN HEAVY ENOUGH TO BLOW THE DOOR OPEN! LET'S SHUT IT BEFORE WE *FREEZE*.
YIKES
?
WHAT... WHAT ARE YOU ALL *DOING* HERE?!
HAPPY HEARTH'S WARMING EVE!

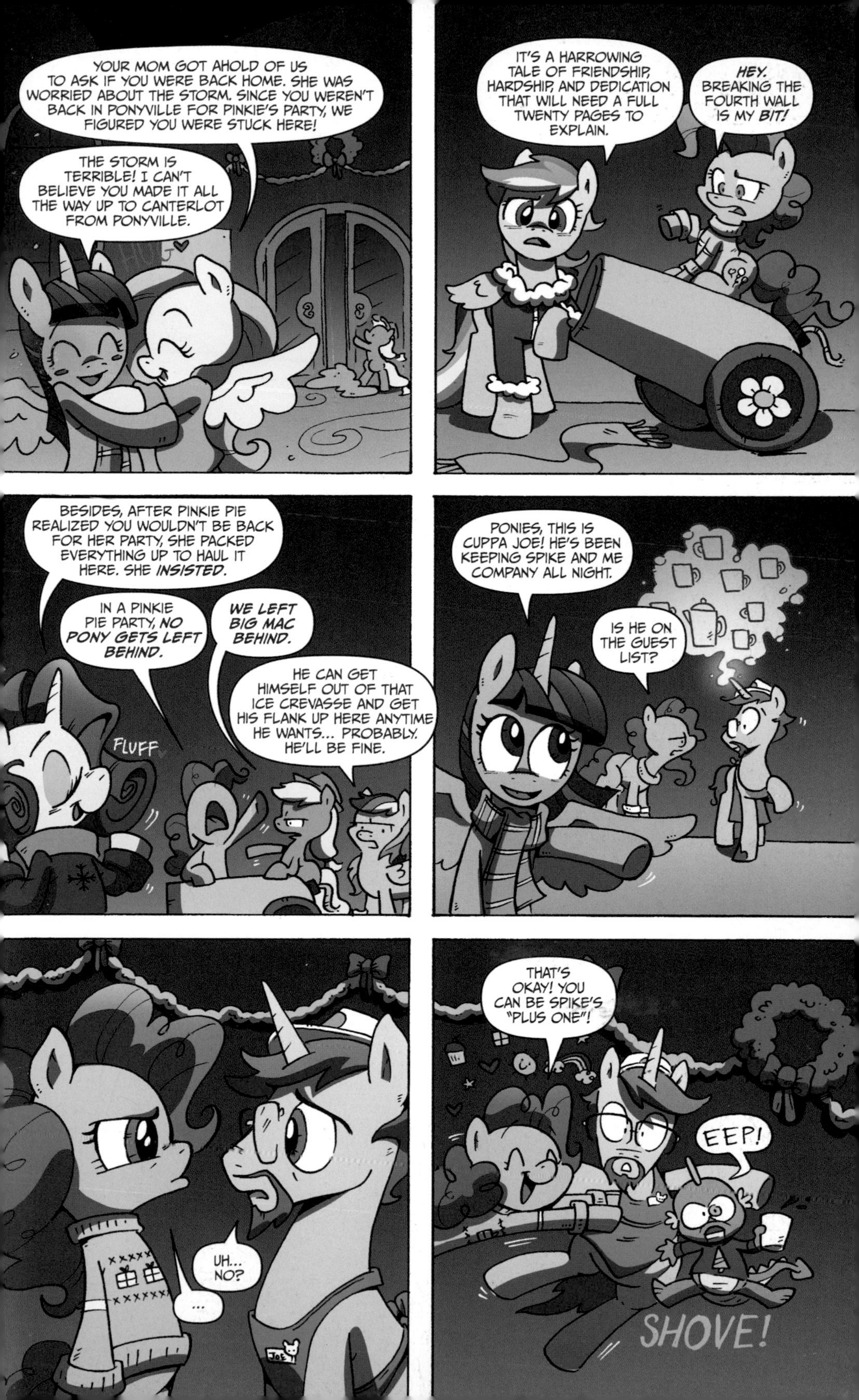
YOUR MOM GOT AHOLD OF US TO ASK IF YOU WERE BACK HOME. SHE WAS WORRIED ABOUT THE STORM. SINCE YOU WEREN'T BACK IN PONYVILLE FOR PINKIE'S PARTY, WE FIGURED YOU WERE STUCK HERE!
THE STORM IS TERRIBLE! I CAN'T BELIEVE YOU MADE IT ALL THE WAY UP TO CANTERLOT FROM PONYVILLE.
IT'S A HARROWING TALE OF FRIENDSHIP, HARDSHIP, AND DEDICATION THAT WILL NEED A FULL TWENTY PAGES TO EXPLAIN.
HEY. BREAKING THE FOURTH WALL IS MY BIT!
BESIDES, AFTER PINKIE PIE REALIZED YOU WOULDN'T BE BACK FOR HER PARTY, SHE PACKED EVERYTHING UP TO HAUL IT HERE. SHE INSISTED.
IN A PINKIE PIE PARTY, NO PONY GETS LEFT BEHIND.
WE LEFT BIG MAC BEHIND.
HE CAN GET HIMSELF OUT OF THAT ICE CREVASSE AND GET HIS FLANK UP HERE ANYTIME HE WANTS... PROBABLY. HE'LL BE FINE.
FLUFF
PONIES, THIS IS CUPPA JOE! HE'S BEEN KEEPING SPIKE AND ME COMPANY ALL NIGHT.
IS HE ON THE GUEST LIST?
UH... NO?
...
JOE
THAT'S OKAY! YOU CAN BE SPIKE'S "PLUS ONE"!
EEP!
SHOVE!

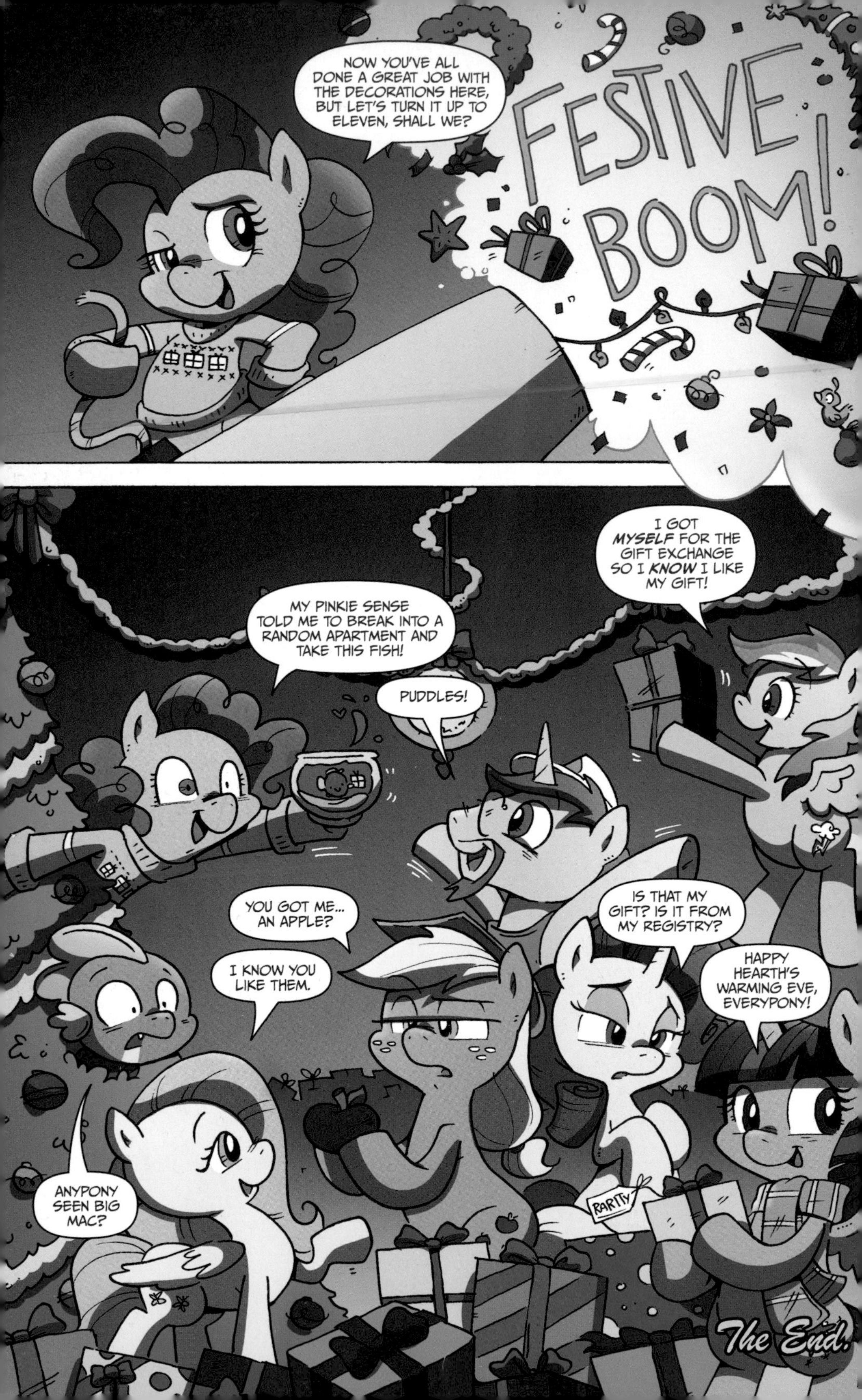
NOW YOU'VE ALL DONE A GREAT JOB WITH THE DECORATIONS HERE, BUT LET'S TURN IT UP TO ELEVEN, SHALL WE?
FESTIVE BOOM!
MY PINKIE SENSE TOLD ME TO BREAK INTO A RANDOM APARTMENT AND TAKE THIS FISH!
PUDDLES!
I GOT MYSELF FOR THE GIFT EXCHANGE SO I KNOW I LIKE MY GIFT!
YOU GOT ME... AN APPLE?
I KNOW YOU LIKE THEM.
IS THAT MY GIFT? IS IT FROM MY REGISTRY?
RARITY
HAPPY HEARTH'S WARMING EVE, EVERYPONY!
ANYPONY SEEN BIG MAC?
The End.

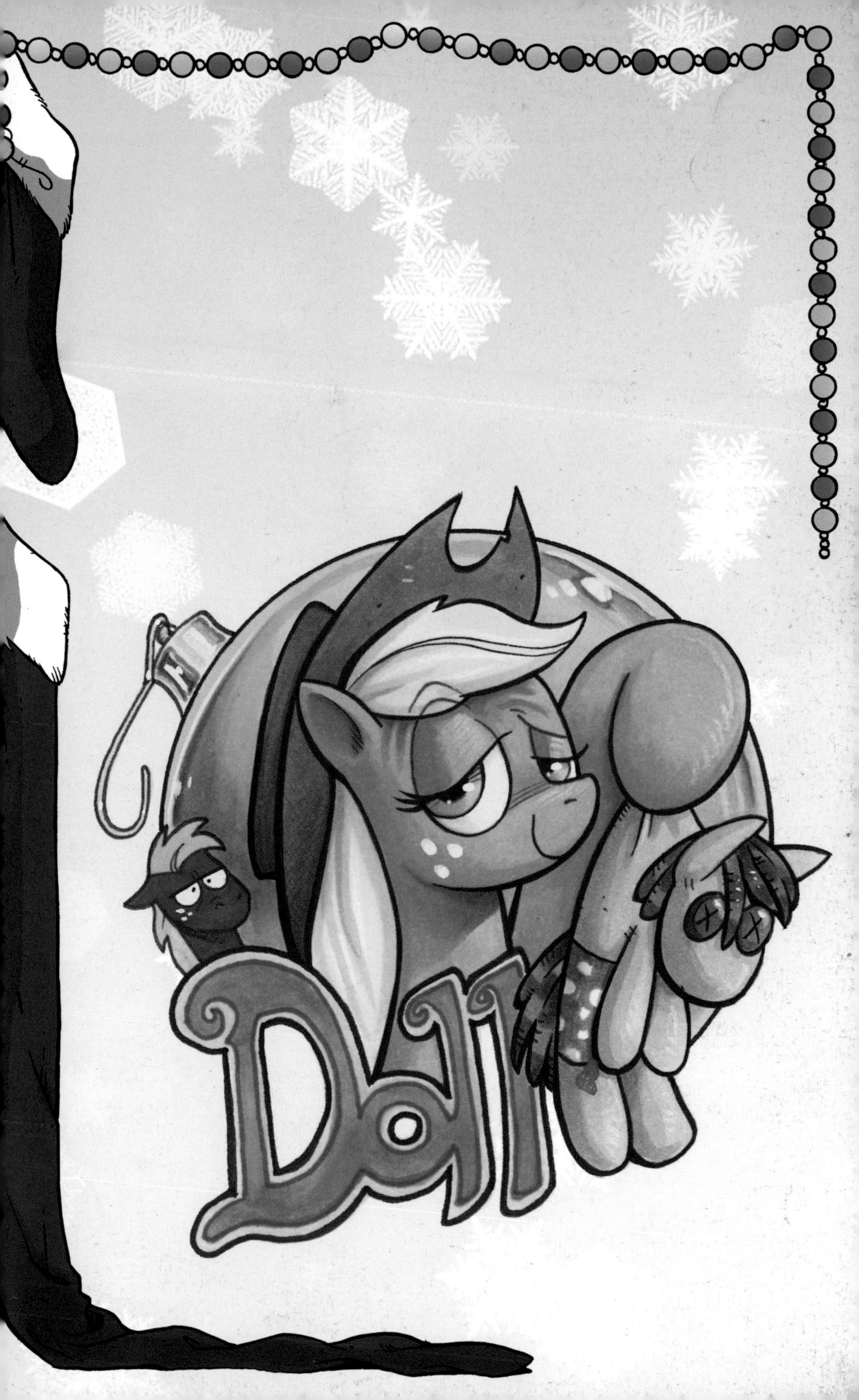

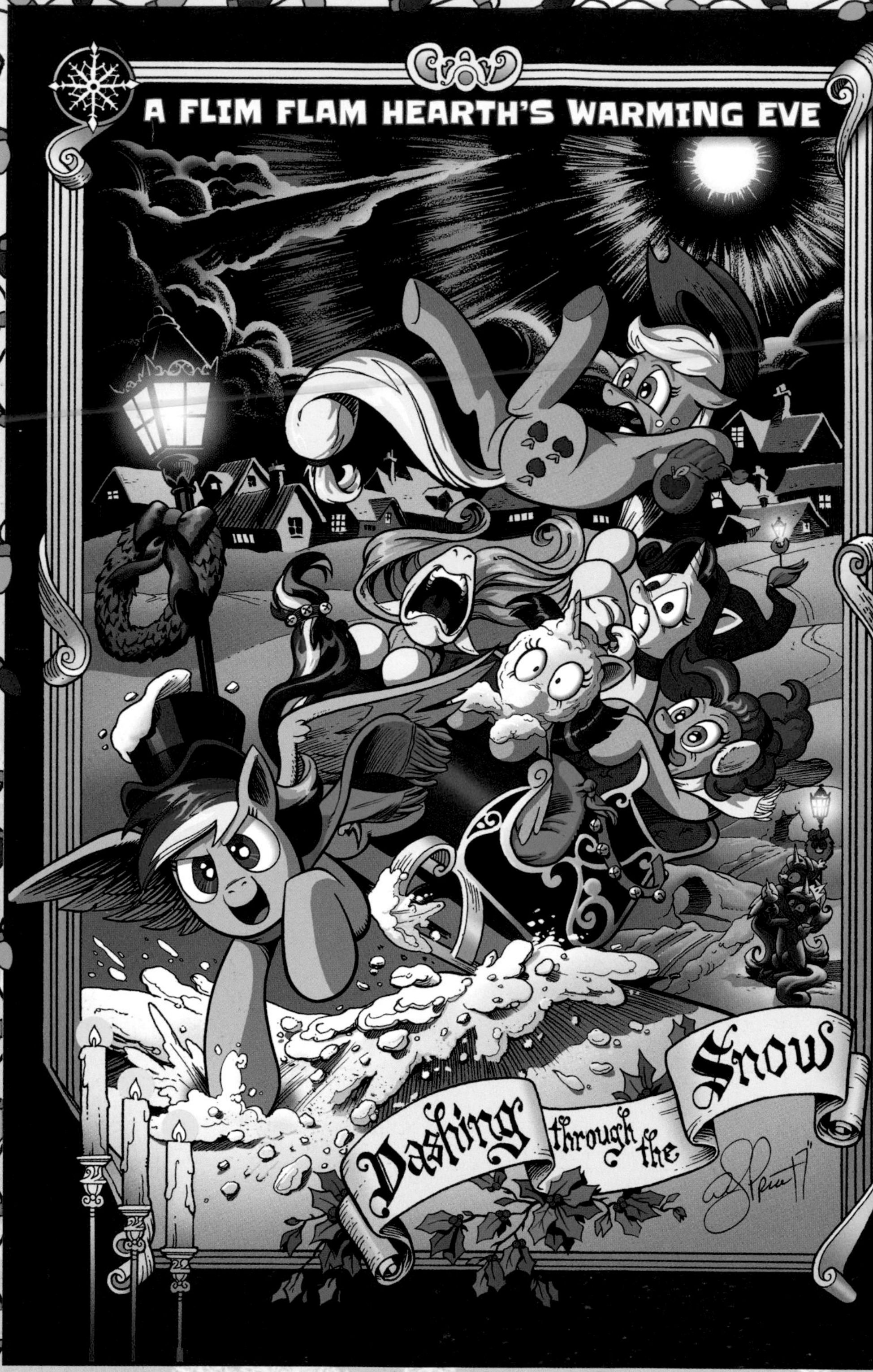
A FLIM FLAM HEARTH'S WARMING EVE
Dashing through the Snow

ART BY Andy Price

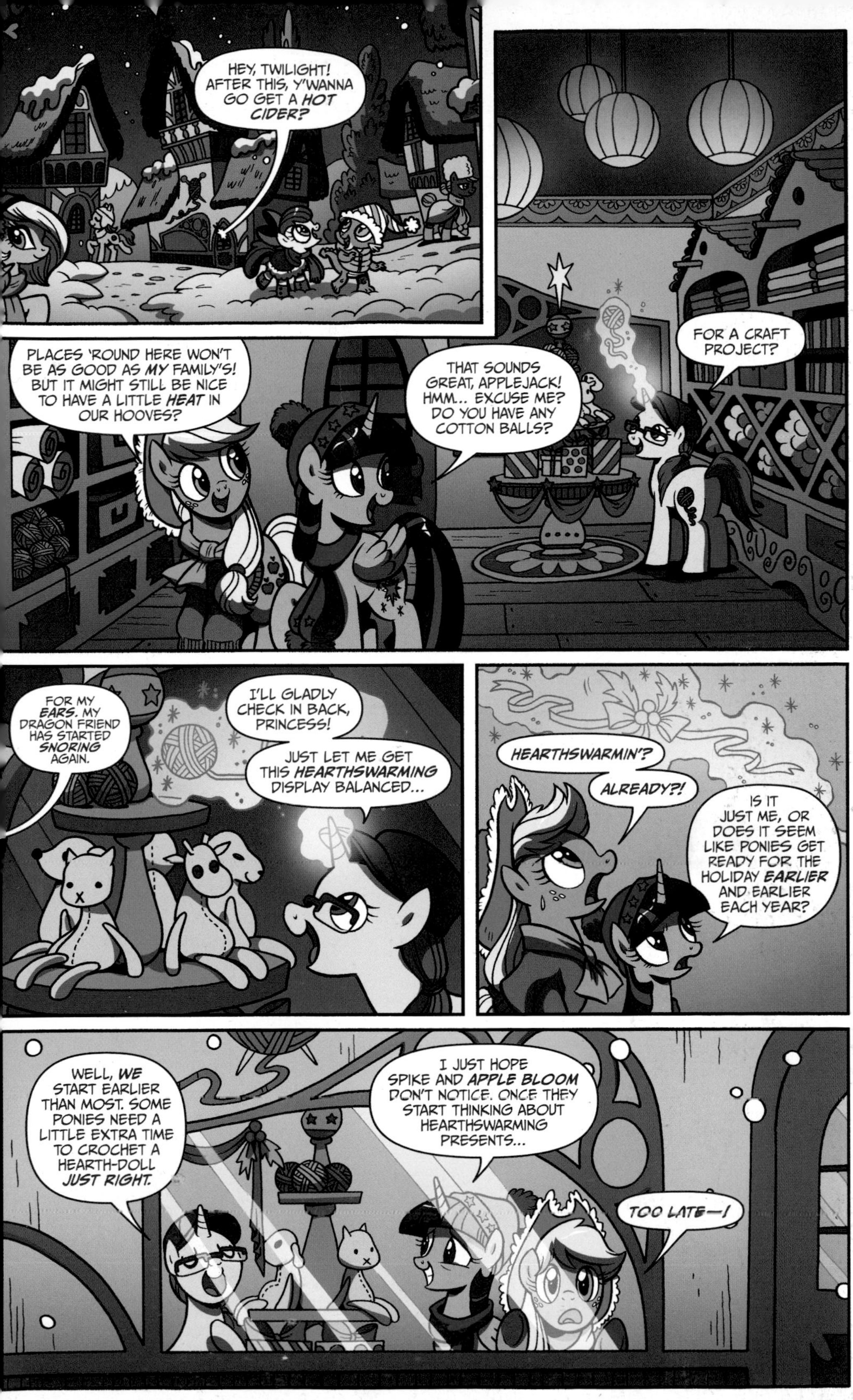
HEY, TWILIGHT! AFTER THIS, Y'WANNA GO GET A HOT CIDER?
PLACES 'ROUND HERE WON'T BE AS GOOD AS MY FAMILY'S! BUT IT MIGHT STILL BE NICE TO HAVE A LITTLE HEAT IN OUR HOOVES?
THAT SOUNDS GREAT, APPLEJACK! HMM... EXCUSE ME? DO YOU HAVE ANY COTTON BALLS?
FOR A CRAFT PROJECT?
FOR MY EARS. MY DRAGON FRIEND HAS STARTED SNORING AGAIN.
I'LL GLADLY CHECK IN BACK, PRINCESS!
JUST LET ME GET THIS HEARTHSWARMING DISPLAY BALANCED...
HEARTHSWARMIN'?
ALREADY?!
IS IT JUST ME, OR DOES IT SEEM LIKE PONIES GET READY FOR THE HOLIDAY EARLIER AND EARLIER EACH YEAR?
WELL, WE START EARLIER THAN MOST. SOME PONIES NEED A LITTLE EXTRA TIME TO CROCHET A HEARTH-DOLL JUST RIGHT.
I JUST HOPE SPIKE AND APPLE BLOOM DON'T NOTICE. ONCE THEY START THINKING ABOUT HEARTHSWARMING PRESENTS...
TOO LATE—!

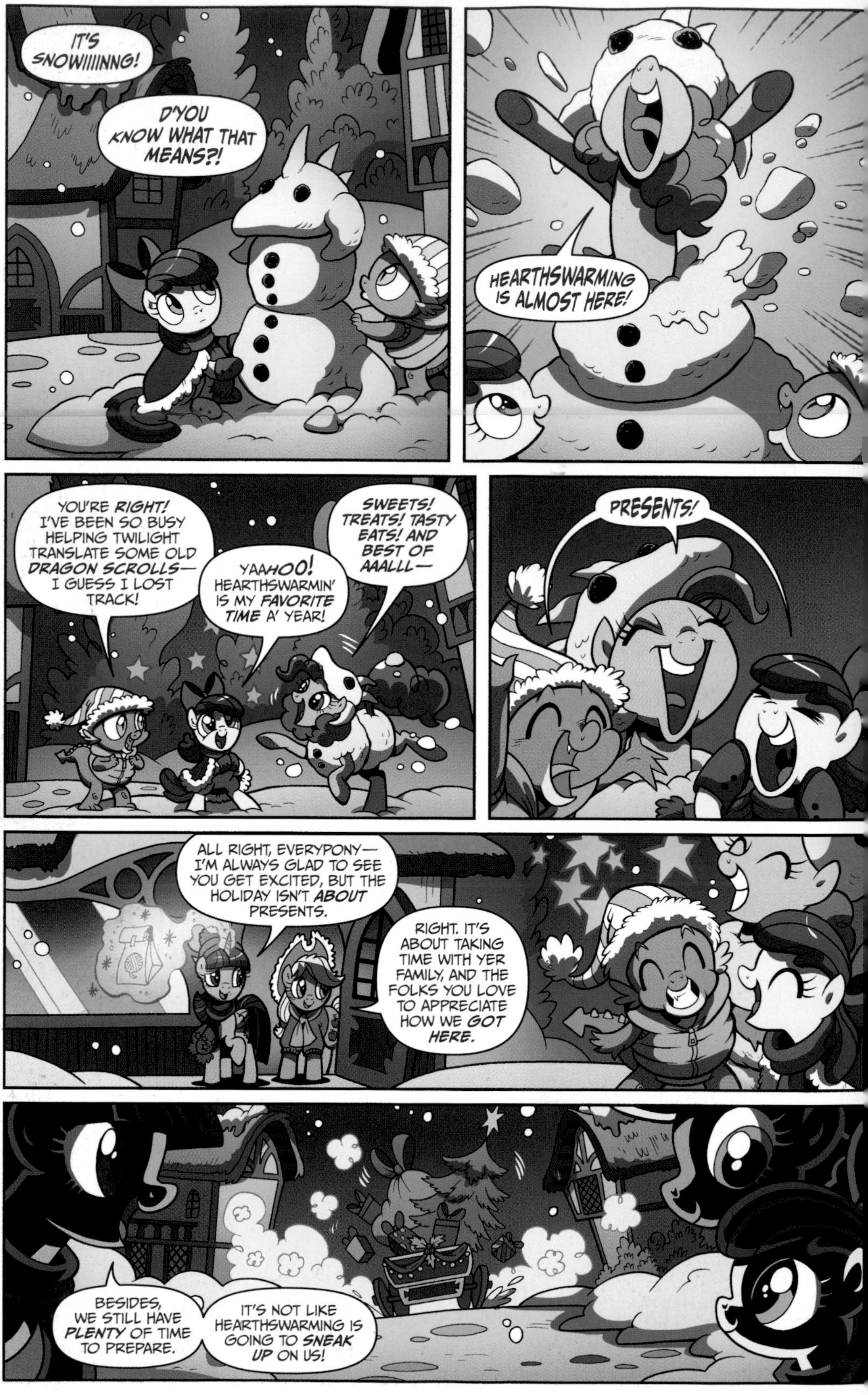
IT'S SNOWIIIINNG!
D'YOU KNOW WHAT THAT MEANS?!
HEARTHSWARMING IS ALMOST HERE!
YOU'RE RIGHT! I'VE BEEN SO BUSY HELPING TWILIGHT TRANSLATE SOME OLD DRAGON SCROLLS— I GUESS I LOST TRACK!
YAAHOO! HEARTHSWARMIN' IS MY FAVORITE TIME A' YEAR!
SWEETS! TREATS! TASTY EATS! AND BEST OF AAALLL—
PRESENTS!
ALL RIGHT, EVERYPONY— I'M ALWAYS GLAD TO SEE YOU GET EXCITED, BUT THE HOLIDAY ISN'T ABOUT PRESENTS.
RIGHT. IT'S ABOUT TAKING TIME WITH YER FAMILY, AND THE FOLKS YOU LOVE TO APPRECIATE HOW WE GOT HERE.
BESIDES, WE STILL HAVE PLENTY OF TIME TO PREPARE.
IT'S NOT LIKE HEARTHSWARMING IS GOING TO SNEAK UP ON US!

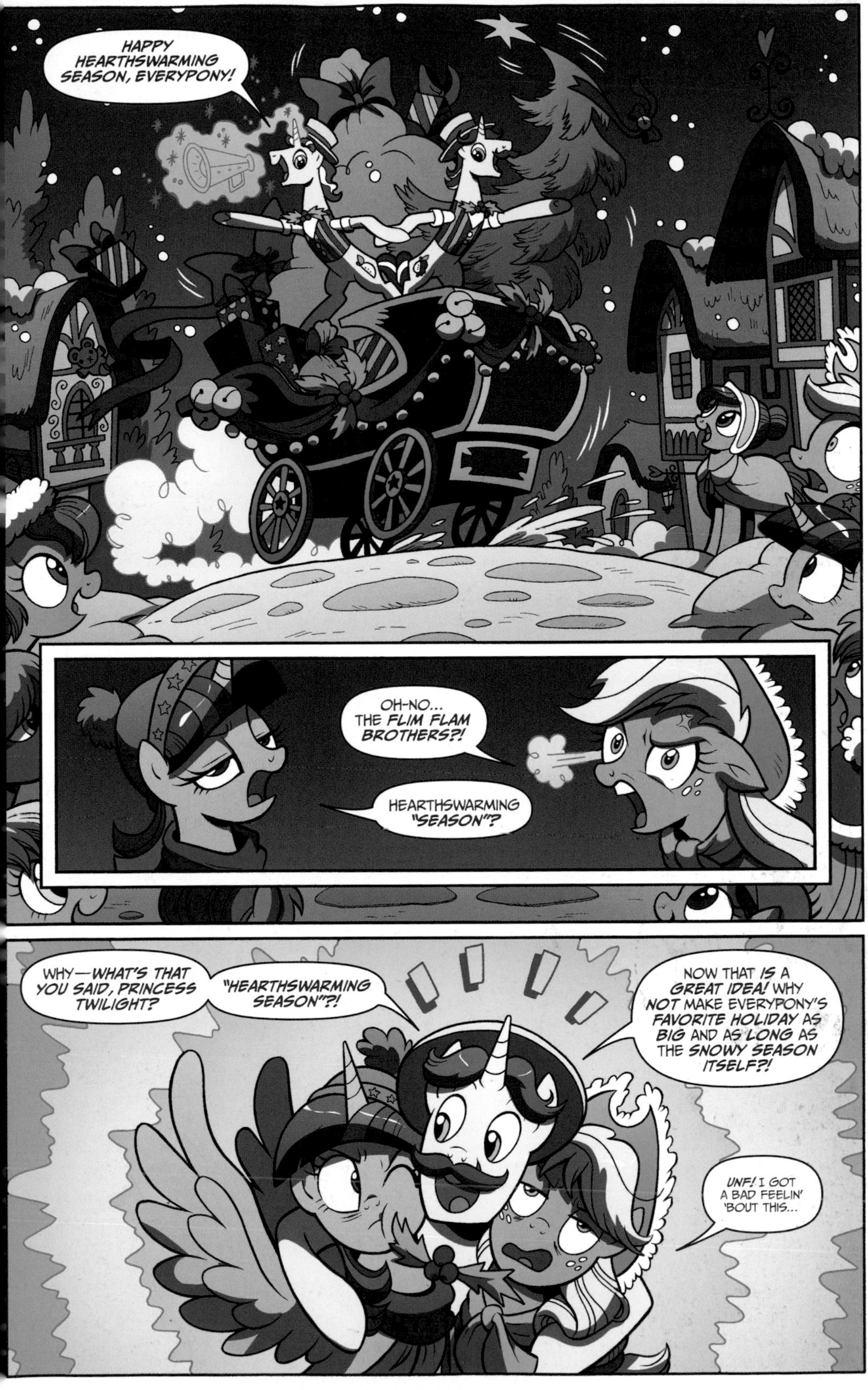
HAPPY HEARTHSWARMING SEASON, EVERYPONY!
OH-NO... THE FLIM FLAM BROTHERS?!
HEARTHSWARMING "SEASON"?
WHY—WHAT'S THAT YOU SAID, PRINCESS TWILIGHT?
"HEARTHSWARMING SEASON"?!
NOW THAT IS A GREAT IDEA! WHY NOT MAKE EVERYPONY'S FAVORITE HOLIDAY AS BIG AND AS LONG AS THE SNOWY SEASON ITSELF?!
UNF! I GOT A BAD FEELIN' 'BOUT THIS...

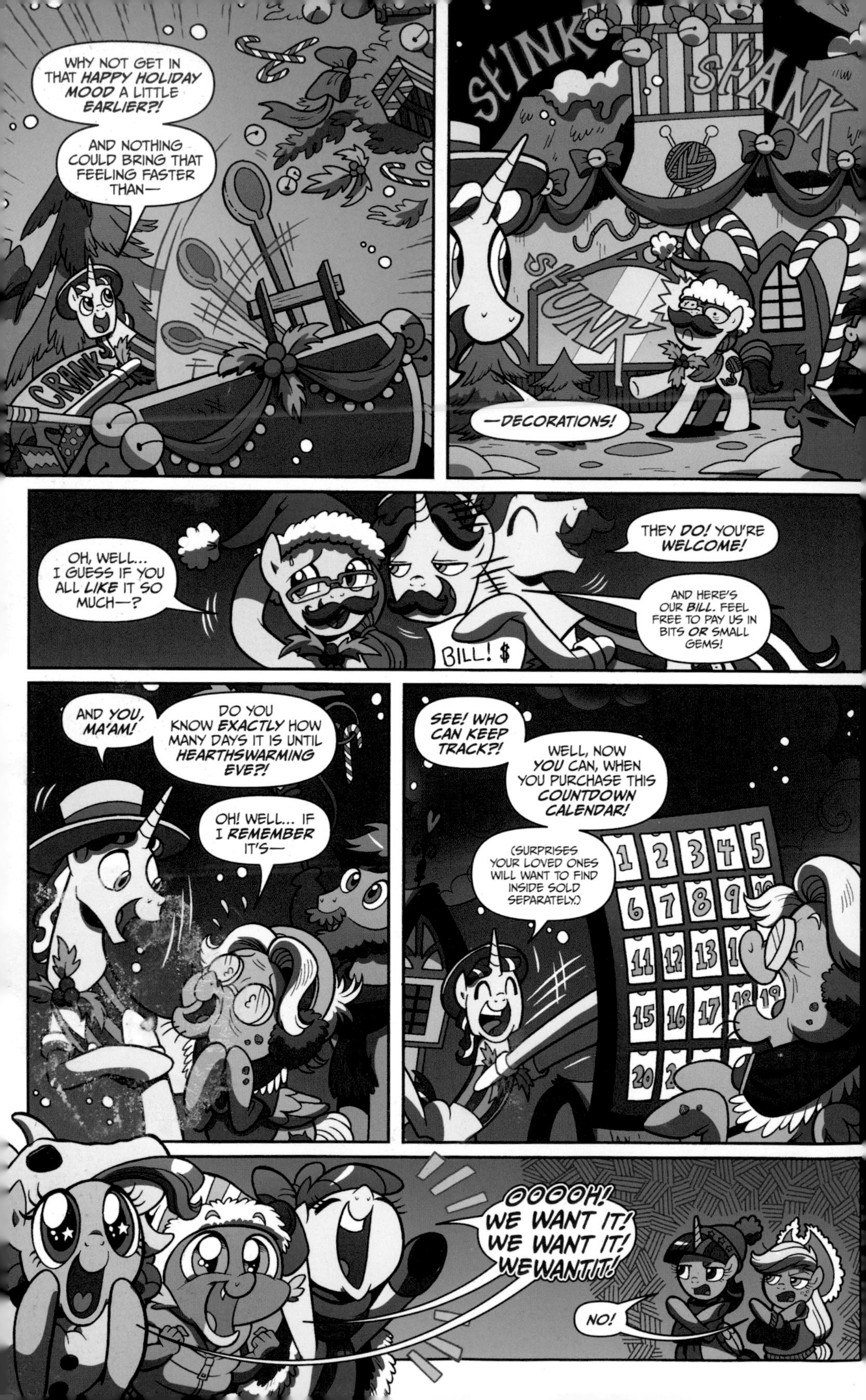

WHY NOT GET IN THAT HAPPY HOLIDAY MOOD A LITTLE EARLIER?!
AND NOTHING COULD BRING THAT FEELING FASTER THAN—
CRANK
SHINK
SHANK
SHUNK
—DECORATIONS!
OH, WELL... I GUESS IF YOU ALL LIKE IT SO MUCH—?
THEY DO! YOU'RE WELCOME!
AND HERE'S OUR BILL. FEEL FREE TO PAY US IN BITS OR SMALL GEMS!
BILL! $
AND YOU, MA'AM!
DO YOU KNOW EXACTLY HOW MANY DAYS IT IS UNTIL HEARTHSWARMING EVE?!
OH! WELL... IF I REMEMBER IT'S—
SEE! WHO CAN KEEP TRACK?!
WELL, NOW YOU CAN, WHEN YOU PURCHASE THIS COUNTDOWN CALENDAR!
(SURPRISES YOUR LOVED ONES WILL WANT TO FIND INSIDE SOLD SEPARATELY.)
OOOOH! WE WANT IT! WE WANT IT! WEWANTIT!
NO!

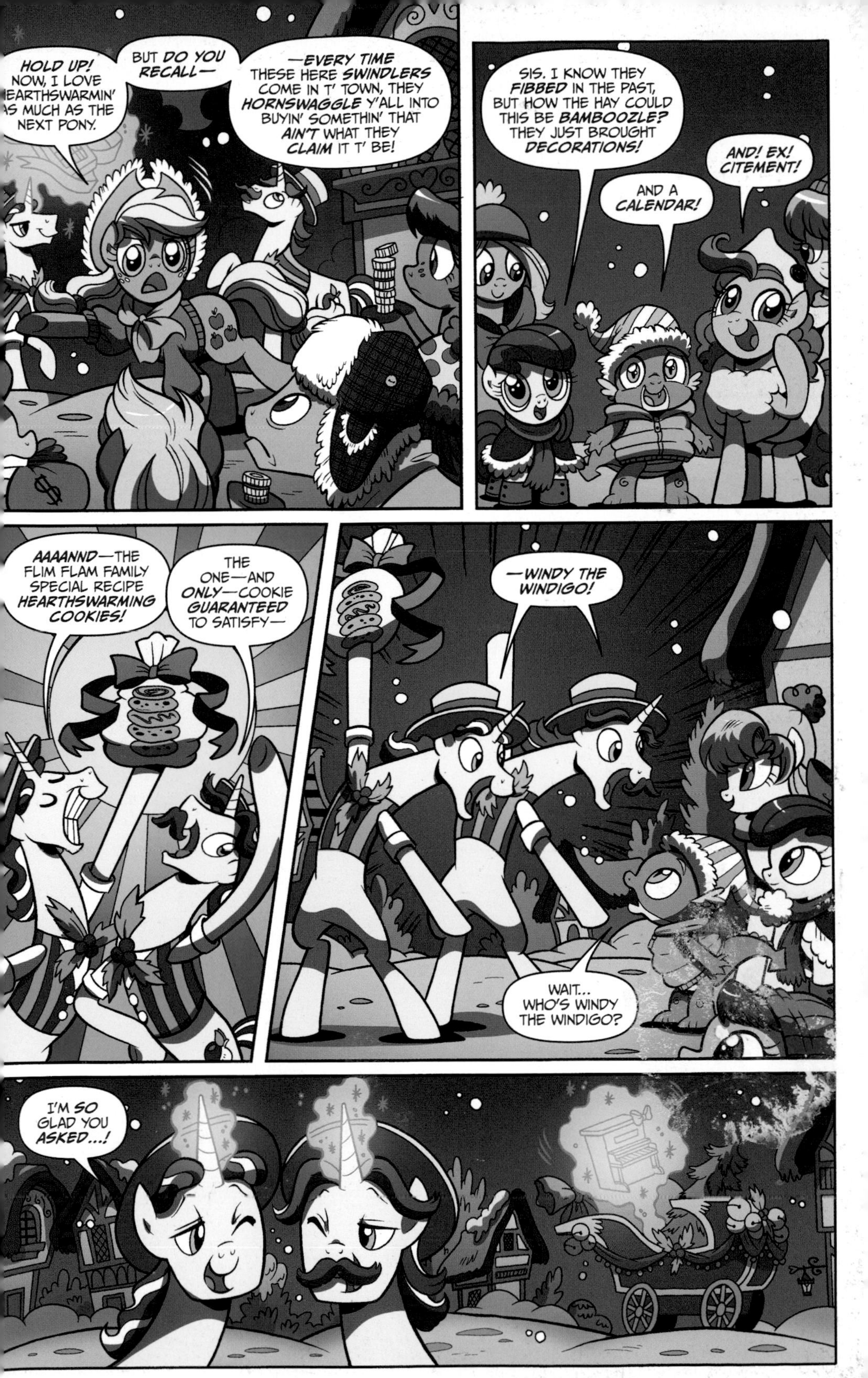
HOLD UP! NOW, I LOVE HEARTHSWARMIN' AS MUCH AS THE NEXT PONY.
BUT DO YOU RECALL—
—EVERY TIME THESE HERE SWINDLERS COME IN T' TOWN, THEY HORNSWAGGLE Y'ALL INTO BUYIN' SOMETHIN' THAT AIN'T WHAT THEY CLAIM IT T' BE!
SIS. I KNOW THEY FIBBED IN THE PAST, BUT HOW THE HAY COULD THIS BE BAMBOOZLE? THEY JUST BROUGHT DECORATIONS!
AND A CALENDAR!
AND! EX! CITEMENT!
AAAANND—THE FLIM FLAM FAMILY SPECIAL RECIPE HEARTHSWARMING COOKIES!
THE ONE—AND ONLY—COOKIE GUARANTEED TO SATISFY—
—WINDY THE WINDIGO!
WAIT... WHO'S WINDY THE WINDIGO?
I'M SO GLAD YOU ASKED...!

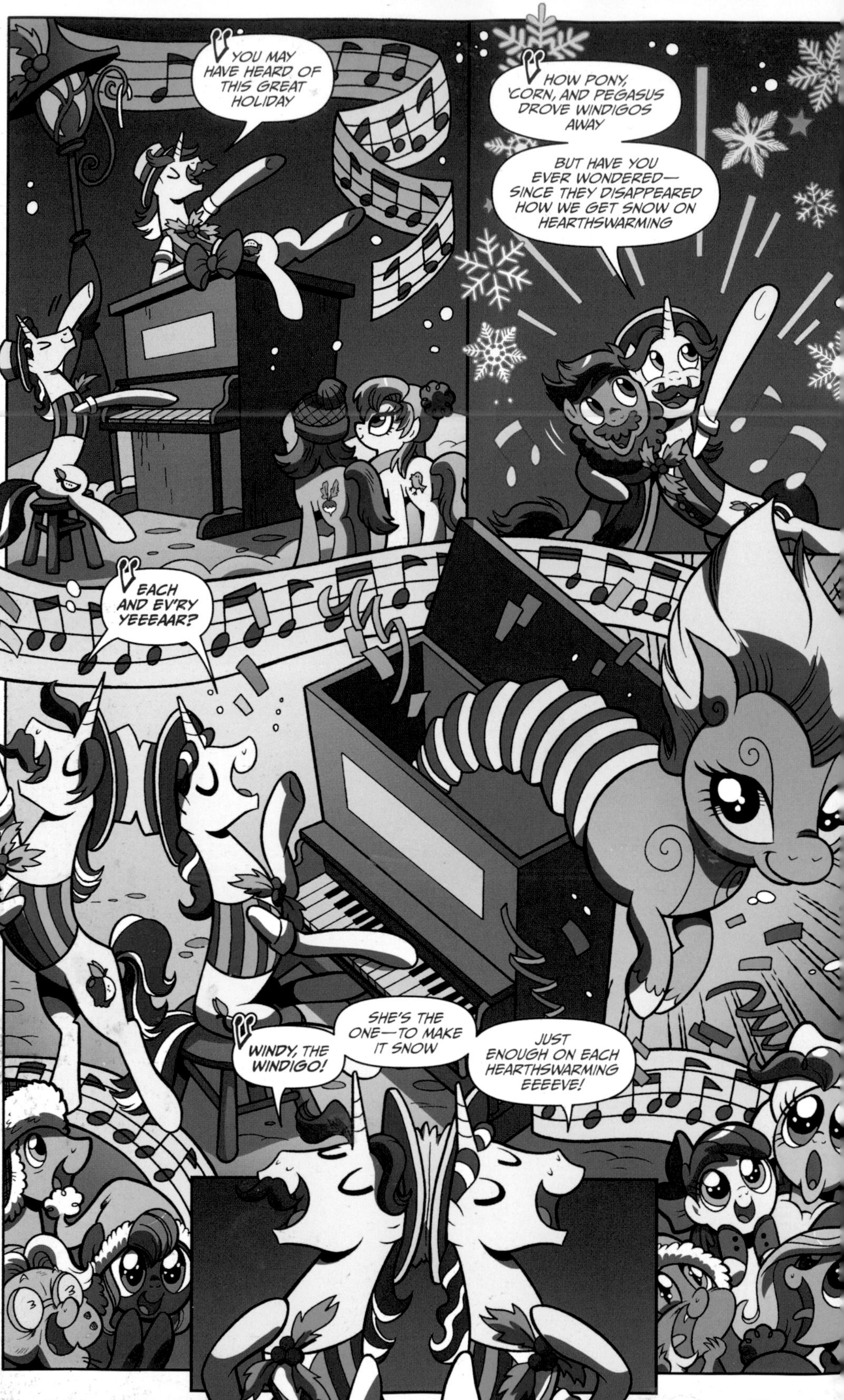
YOU MAY HAVE HEARD OF THIS GREAT HOLIDAY
HOW PONY, 'CORN, AND PEGASUS DROVE WINDIGOS AWAY
BUT HAVE YOU EVER WONDERED— SINCE THEY DISAPPEARED HOW WE GET SNOW ON HEARTHSWARMING
EACH AND EV'RY YEEEAAR?
WINDY, THE WINDIGO!
SHE'S THE ONE—TO MAKE IT SNOW
JUST ENOUGH ON EACH HEARTHSWARMING EEEEVE!

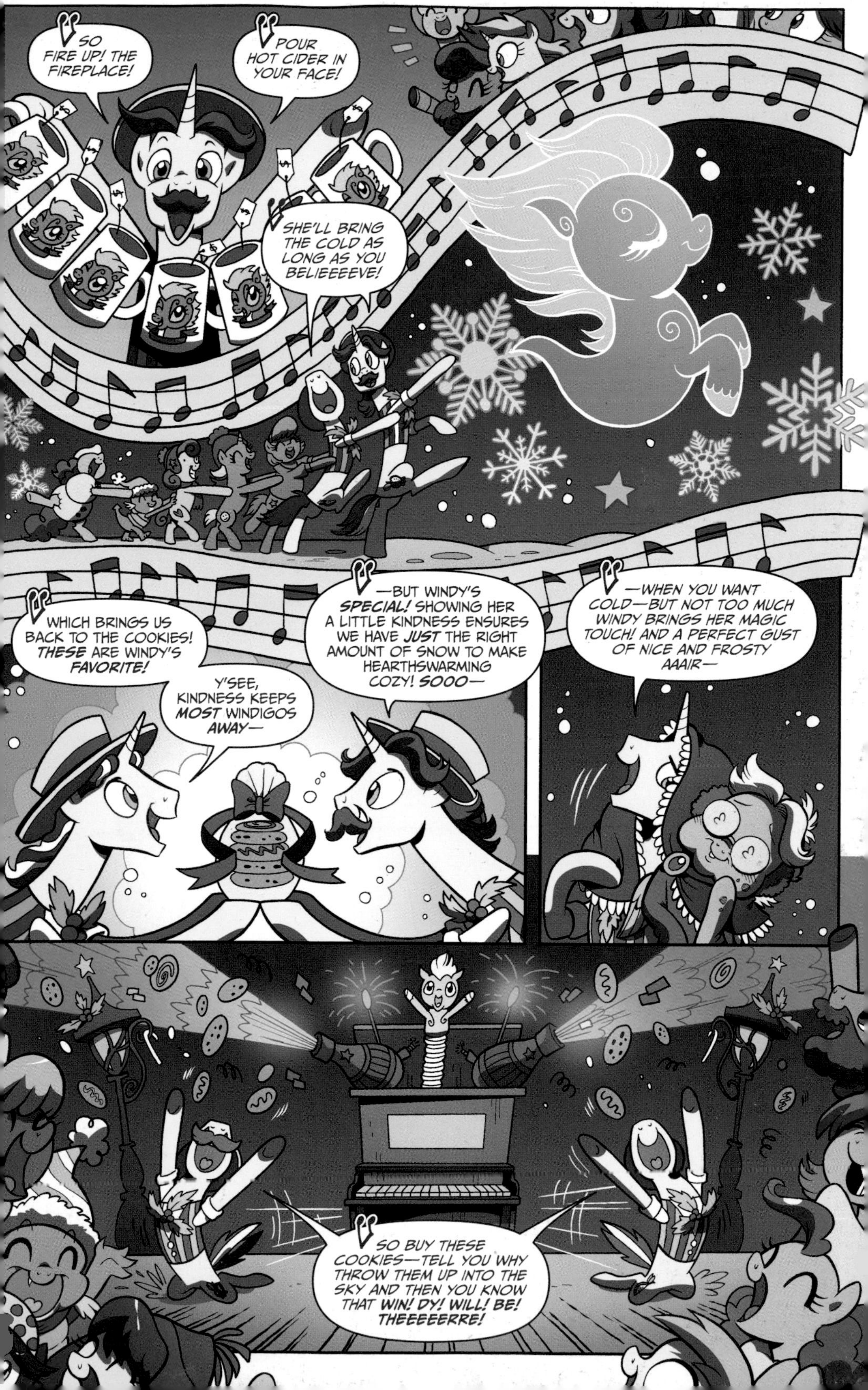

SO FIRE UP! THE FIREPLACE!
POUR HOT CIDER IN YOUR FACE!
SHE'LL BRING THE COLD AS LONG AS YOU BELIEEEEVE!
WHICH BRINGS US BACK TO THE COOKIES! THESE ARE WINDY'S FAVORITE!
Y'SEE, KINDNESS KEEPS MOST WINDIGOS AWAY—
—BUT WINDY'S SPECIAL! SHOWING HER A LITTLE KINDNESS ENSURES WE HAVE JUST THE RIGHT AMOUNT OF SNOW TO MAKE HEARTHSWARMING COZY! SOOO—
—WHEN YOU WANT COLD—BUT NOT TOO MUCH WINDY BRINGS HER MAGIC TOUCH! AND A PERFECT GUST OF NICE AND FROSTY AAAIR—
SO BUY THESE COOKIES—TELL YOU WHY THROW THEM UP INTO THE SKY AND THEN YOU KNOW THAT WIN! DY! WILL! BE! THEEEEERRE!

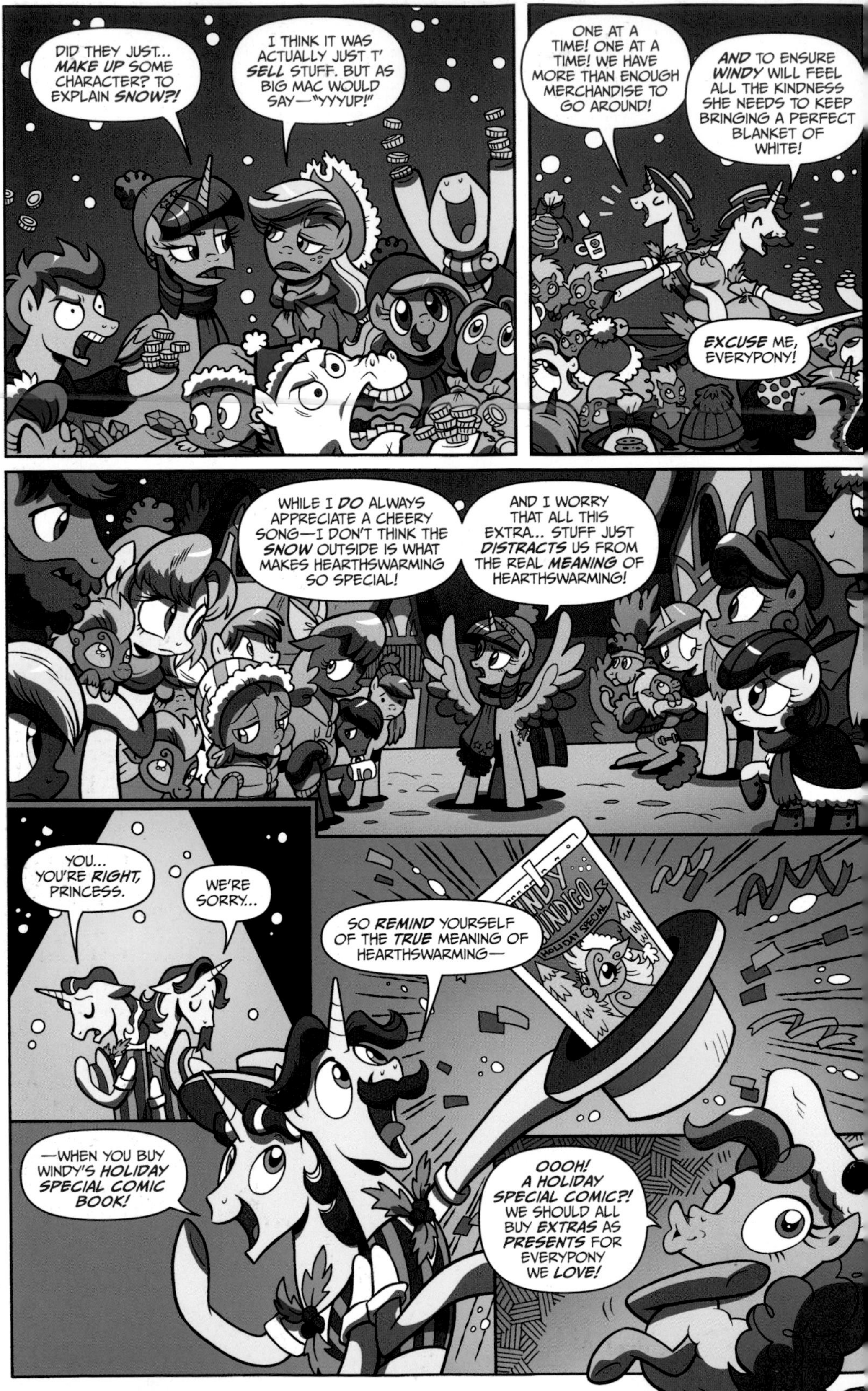

DID THEY JUST... MAKE UP SOME CHARACTER? TO EXPLAIN SNOW?!
I THINK IT WAS ACTUALLY JUST T' SELL STUFF. BUT AS BIG MAC WOULD SAY—"YYYUP!"
ONE AT A TIME! ONE AT A TIME! WE HAVE MORE THAN ENOUGH MERCHANDISE TO GO AROUND!
AND TO ENSURE WINDY WILL FEEL ALL THE KINDNESS SHE NEEDS TO KEEP BRINGING A PERFECT BLANKET OF WHITE!
EXCUSE ME, EVERYPONY!
WHILE I DO ALWAYS APPRECIATE A CHEERY SONG—I DON'T THINK THE SNOW OUTSIDE IS WHAT MAKES HEARTHSWARMING SO SPECIAL!
AND I WORRY THAT ALL THIS EXTRA... STUFF JUST DISTRACTS US FROM THE REAL MEANING OF HEARTHSWARMING!
YOU... YOU'RE RIGHT, PRINCESS.
WE'RE SORRY...
SO REMIND YOURSELF OF THE TRUE MEANING OF HEARTHSWARMING—
—WHEN YOU BUY WINDY'S HOLIDAY SPECIAL COMIC BOOK!
OOOH! A HOLIDAY SPECIAL COMIC?! WE SHOULD ALL BUY EXTRAS AS PRESENTS FOR EVERYPONY WE LOVE!

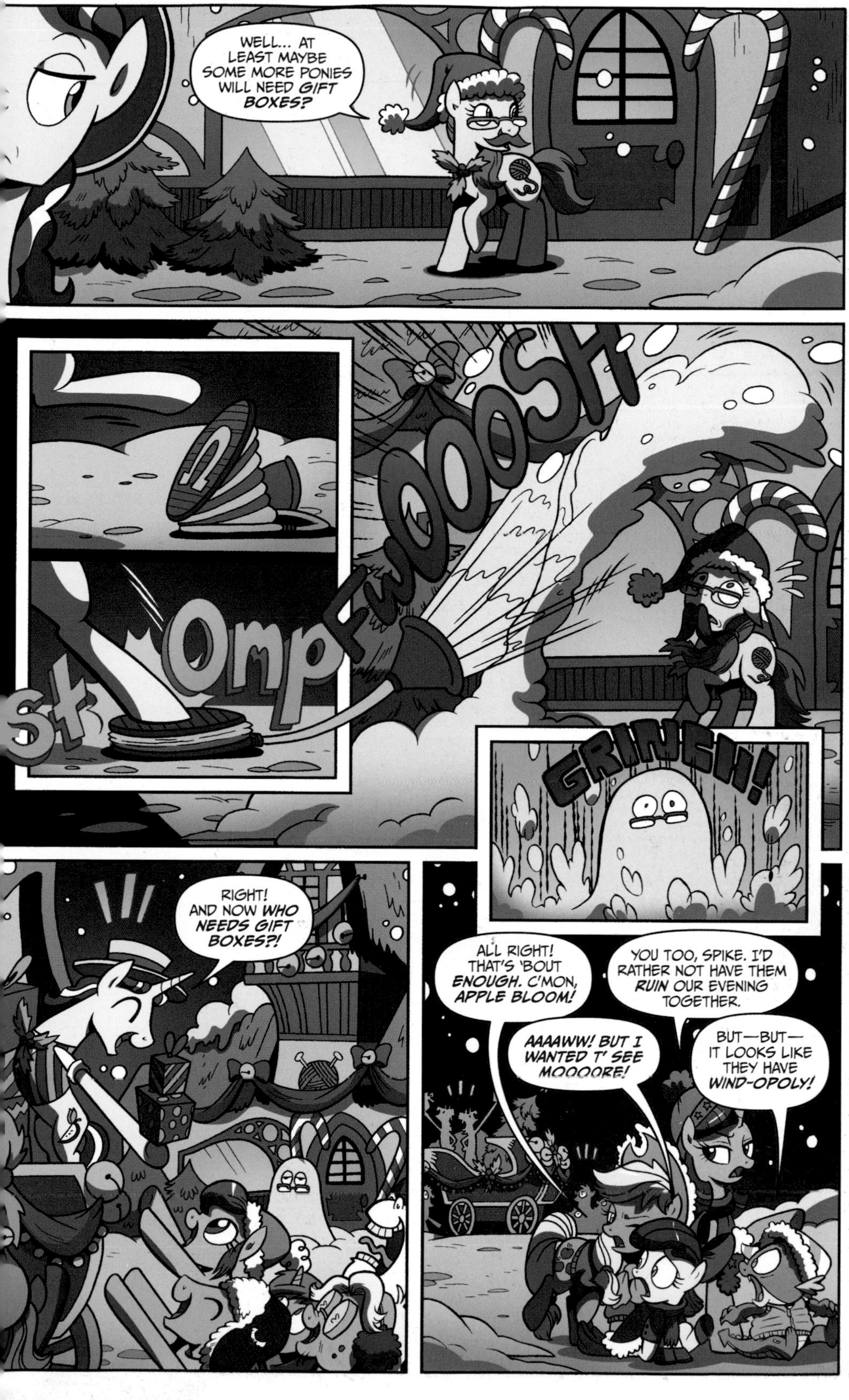
WELL... AT LEAST MAYBE SOME MORE PONIES WILL NEED GIFT BOXES?
StOmp
FWOOOOSH
GRINCH!
RIGHT! AND NOW WHO NEEDS GIFT BOXES?!
ALL RIGHT! THAT'S 'BOUT ENOUGH. C'MON, APPLE BLOOM!
AAAAWW! BUT I WANTED T' SEE MOOOORE!
YOU TOO, SPIKE. I'D RATHER NOT HAVE THEM RUIN OUR EVENING TOGETHER.
BUT—BUT— IT LOOKS LIKE THEY HAVE WIND-OPOLY!

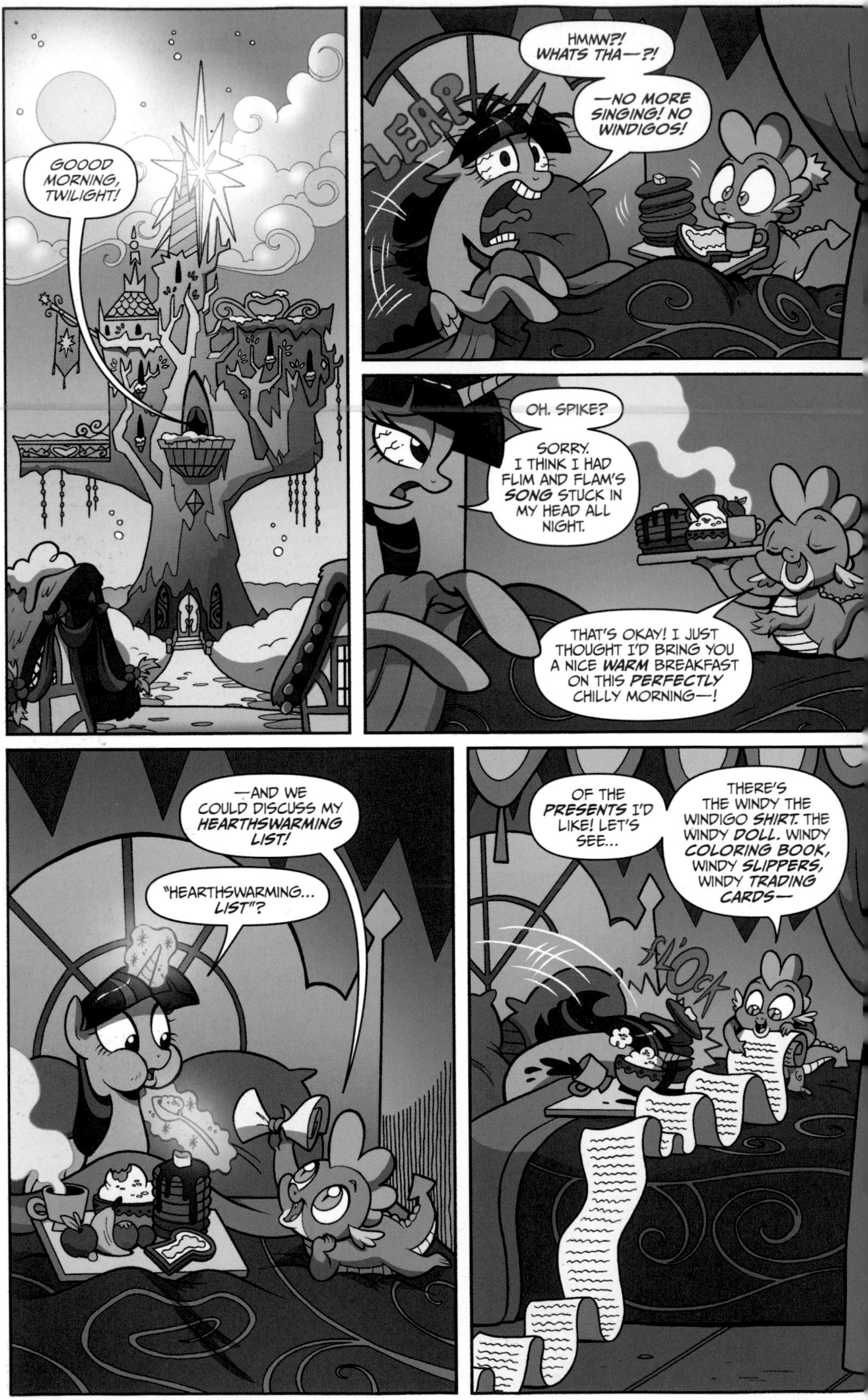
GOOOD MORNING, TWILIGHT!
LEAP
HMMN?! WHATS THA—?!
—NO MORE SINGING! NO WINDIGOS!
OH. SPIKE?
SORRY. I THINK I HAD FLIM AND FLAM'S SONG STUCK IN MY HEAD ALL NIGHT.
THAT'S OKAY! I JUST THOUGHT I'D BRING YOU A NICE WARM BREAKFAST ON THIS PERFECTLY CHILLY MORNING—!
—AND WE COULD DISCUSS MY HEARTHSWARMING LIST!
"HEARTHSWARMING... LIST"?
OF THE PRESENTS I'D LIKE! LET'S SEE...
THERE'S THE WINDY THE WINDIGO SHIRT. THE WINDY DOLL. WINDY COLORING BOOK, WINDY SLIPPERS, WINDY TRADING CARDS—
FLOCK

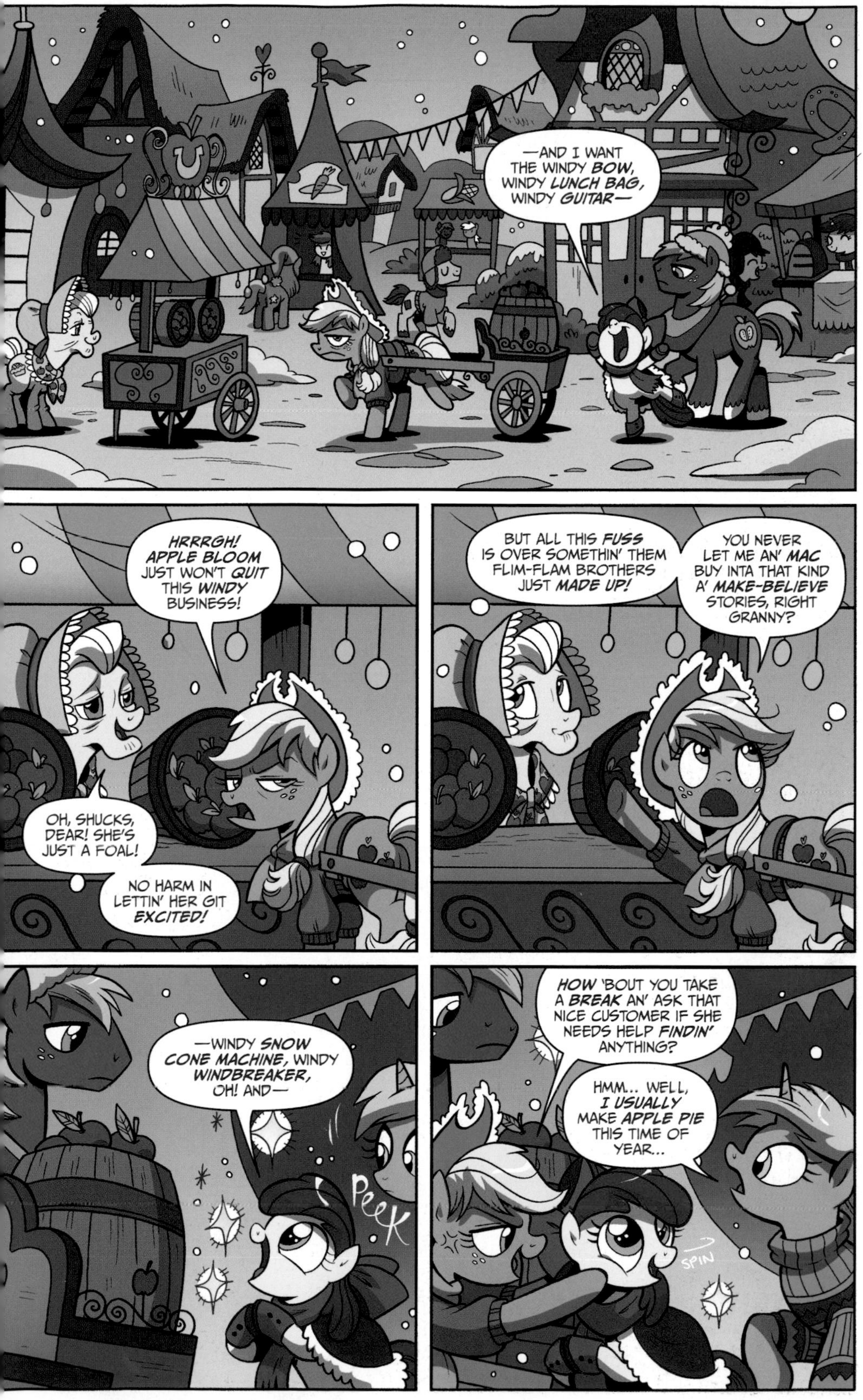
—AND I WANT THE WINDY BOW, WINDY LUNCH BAG, WINDY GUITAR—
HRRRGH! APPLE BLOOM JUST WON'T QUIT THIS WINDY BUSINESS!
OH, SHUCKS, DEAR! SHE'S JUST A FOAL!
NO HARM IN LETTIN' HER GIT EXCITED!
BUT ALL THIS FUSS IS OVER SOMETHIN' THEM FLIM-FLAM BROTHERS JUST MADE UP!
YOU NEVER LET ME AN' MAC BUY INTA THAT KIND A' MAKE-BELIEVE STORIES, RIGHT GRANNY?
—WINDY SNOW CONE MACHINE, WINDY WINDBREAKER, OH! AND—
PEEK
HOW 'BOUT YOU TAKE A BREAK AN' ASK THAT NICE CUSTOMER IF SHE NEEDS HELP FINDIN' ANYTHING?
HMM... WELL, I USUALLY MAKE APPLE PIE THIS TIME OF YEAR...
SPIN

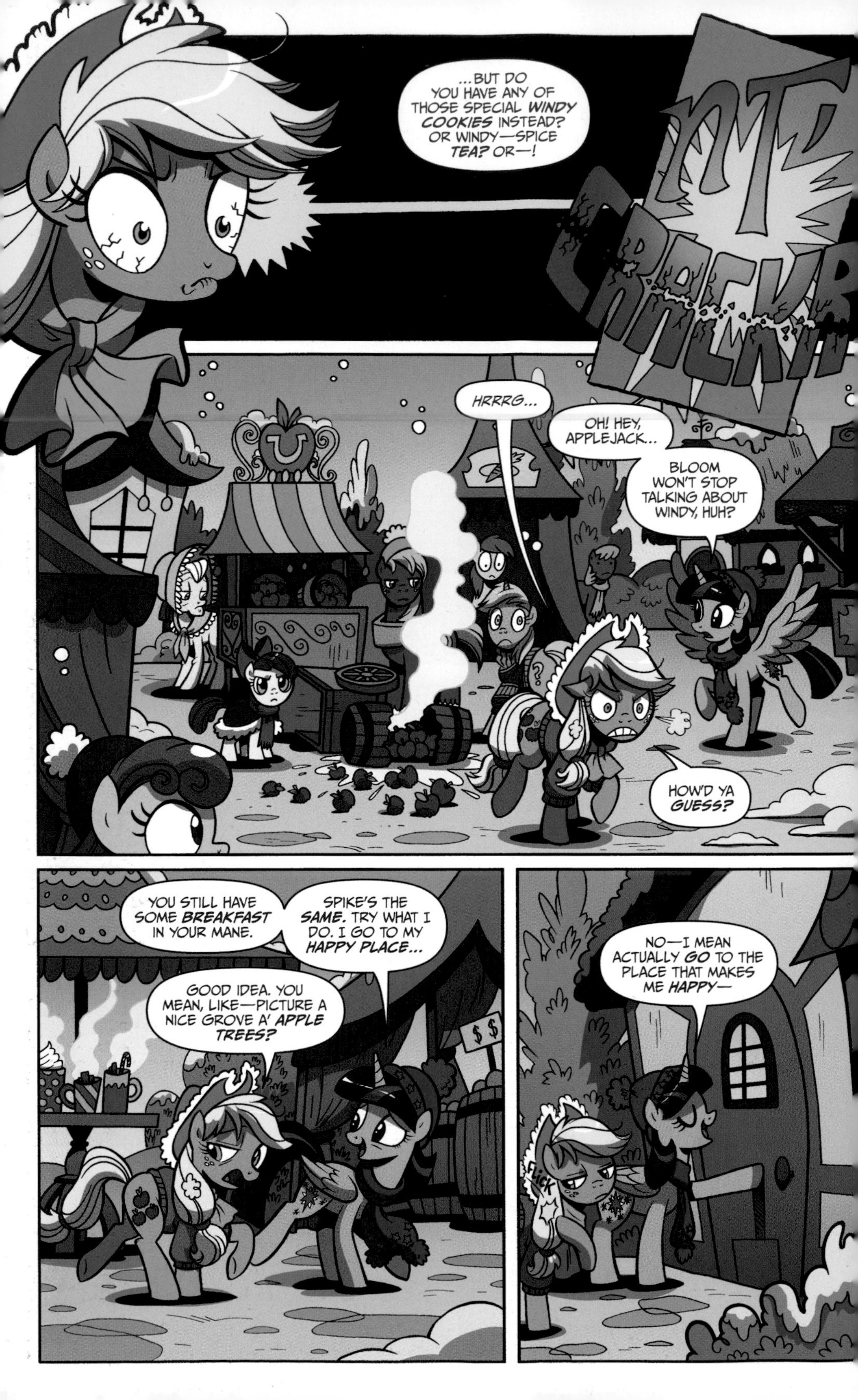
...BUT DO YOU HAVE ANY OF THOSE SPECIAL WINDY COOKIES INSTEAD? OR WINDY—SPICE TEA? OR—!
HRRRG...
OH! HEY, APPLEJACK...
BLOOM WON'T STOP TALKING ABOUT WINDY, HUH?
HOW'D YA GUESS?
YOU STILL HAVE SOME BREAKFAST IN YOUR MANE.
SPIKE'S THE SAME. TRY WHAT I DO. I GO TO MY HAPPY PLACE...
GOOD IDEA. YOU MEAN, LIKE—PICTURE A NICE GROVE A' APPLE TREES?
$ $
NO—I MEAN ACTUALLY GO TO THE PLACE THAT MAKES ME HAPPY—
FLICK

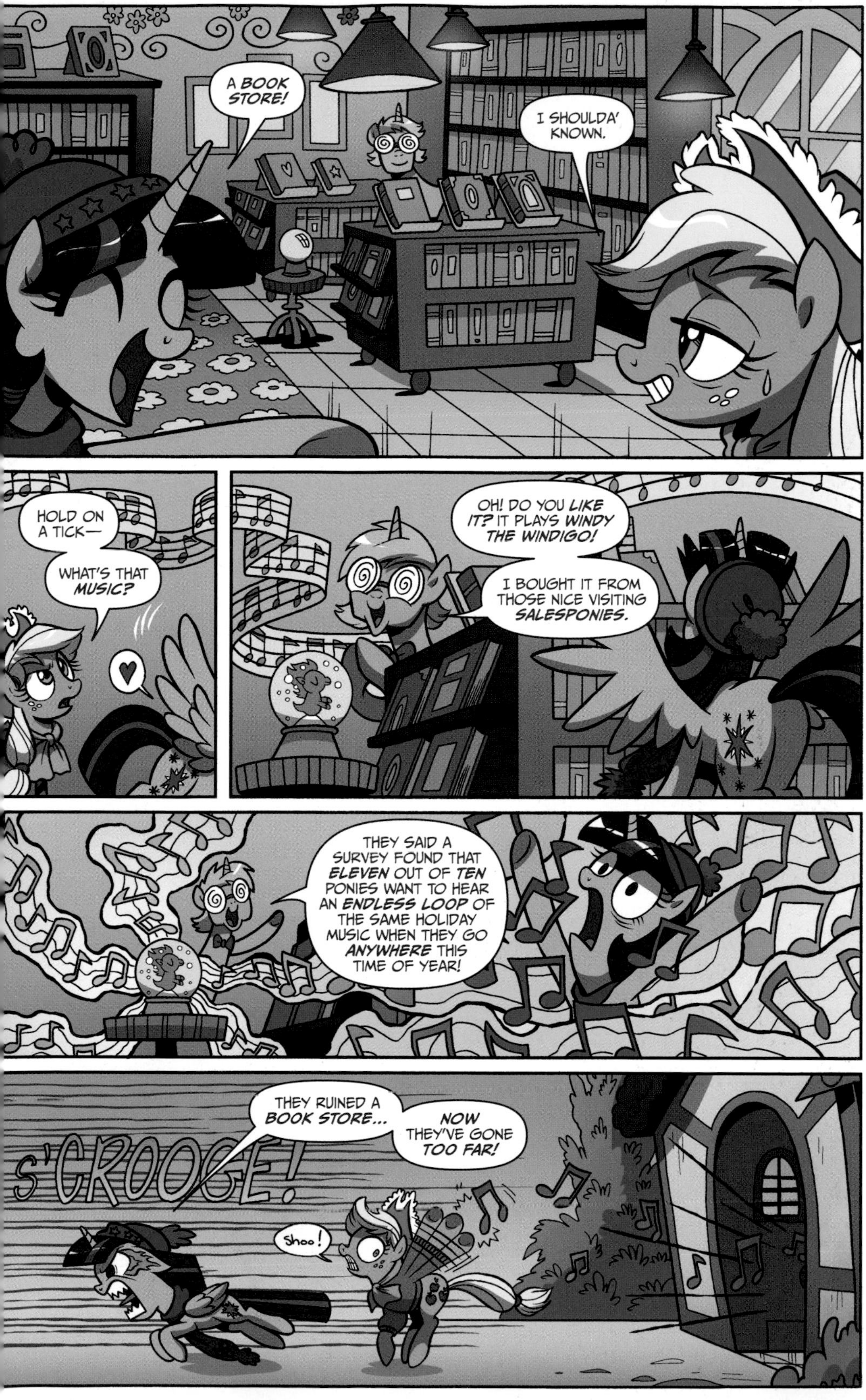

A BOOK STORE!
I SHOULDA' KNOWN.
HOLD ON A TICK—
WHAT'S THAT MUSIC?
OH! DO YOU LIKE IT? IT PLAYS WINDY THE WINDIGO!
I BOUGHT IT FROM THOSE NICE VISITING SALESPONIES.
THEY SAID A SURVEY FOUND THAT ELEVEN OUT OF TEN PONIES WANT TO HEAR AN ENDLESS LOOP OF THE SAME HOLIDAY MUSIC WHEN THEY GO ANYWHERE THIS TIME OF YEAR!
THEY RUINED A BOOK STORE...
NOW THEY'VE GONE TOO FAR!
S'CROOGE!
Shoo!

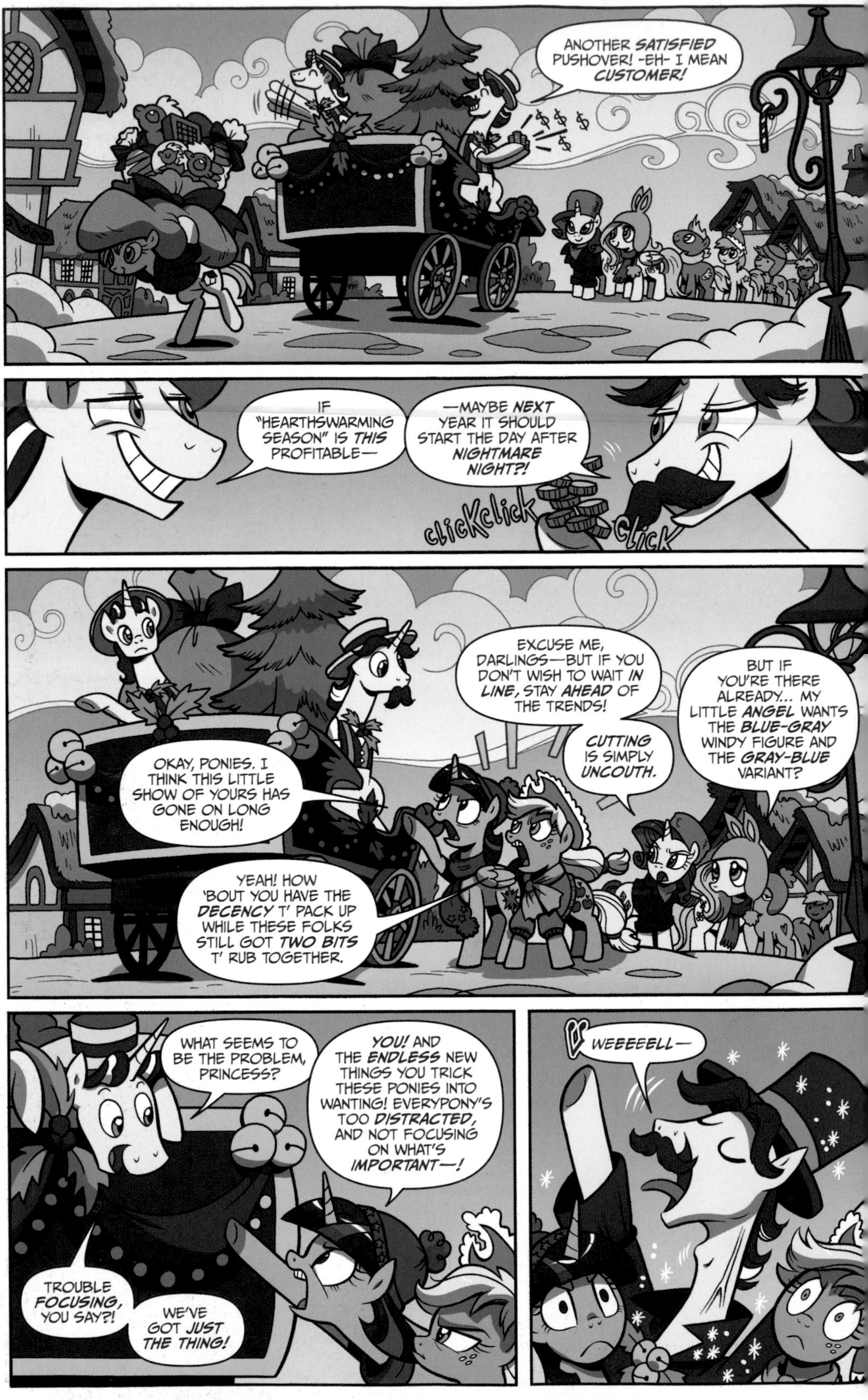
ANOTHER SATISFIED PUSHOVER! -EH- I MEAN CUSTOMER!
$ $ $ $
IF "HEARTHSWARMING SEASON" IS THIS PROFITABLE—
—MAYBE NEXT YEAR IT SHOULD START THE DAY AFTER NIGHTMARE NIGHT?!
clickclick
click
EXCUSE ME, DARLINGS—BUT IF YOU DON'T WISH TO WAIT IN LINE, STAY AHEAD OF THE TRENDS!
CUTTING IS SIMPLY UNCOUTH.
BUT IF YOU'RE THERE ALREADY... MY LITTLE ANGEL WANTS THE BLUE-GRAY WINDY FIGURE AND THE GRAY-BLUE VARIANT?
OKAY, PONIES. I THINK THIS LITTLE SHOW OF YOURS HAS GONE ON LONG ENOUGH!
YEAH! HOW 'BOUT YOU HAVE THE DECENCY T' PACK UP WHILE THESE FOLKS STILL GOT TWO BITS T' RUB TOGETHER.
WHAT SEEMS TO BE THE PROBLEM, PRINCESS?
YOU! AND THE ENDLESS NEW THINGS YOU TRICK THESE PONIES INTO WANTING! EVERYPONY'S TOO DISTRACTED, AND NOT FOCUSING ON WHAT'S IMPORTANT—!
TROUBLE FOCUSING, YOU SAY?!
WE'VE GOT JUST THE THING!
WEEEEELL—

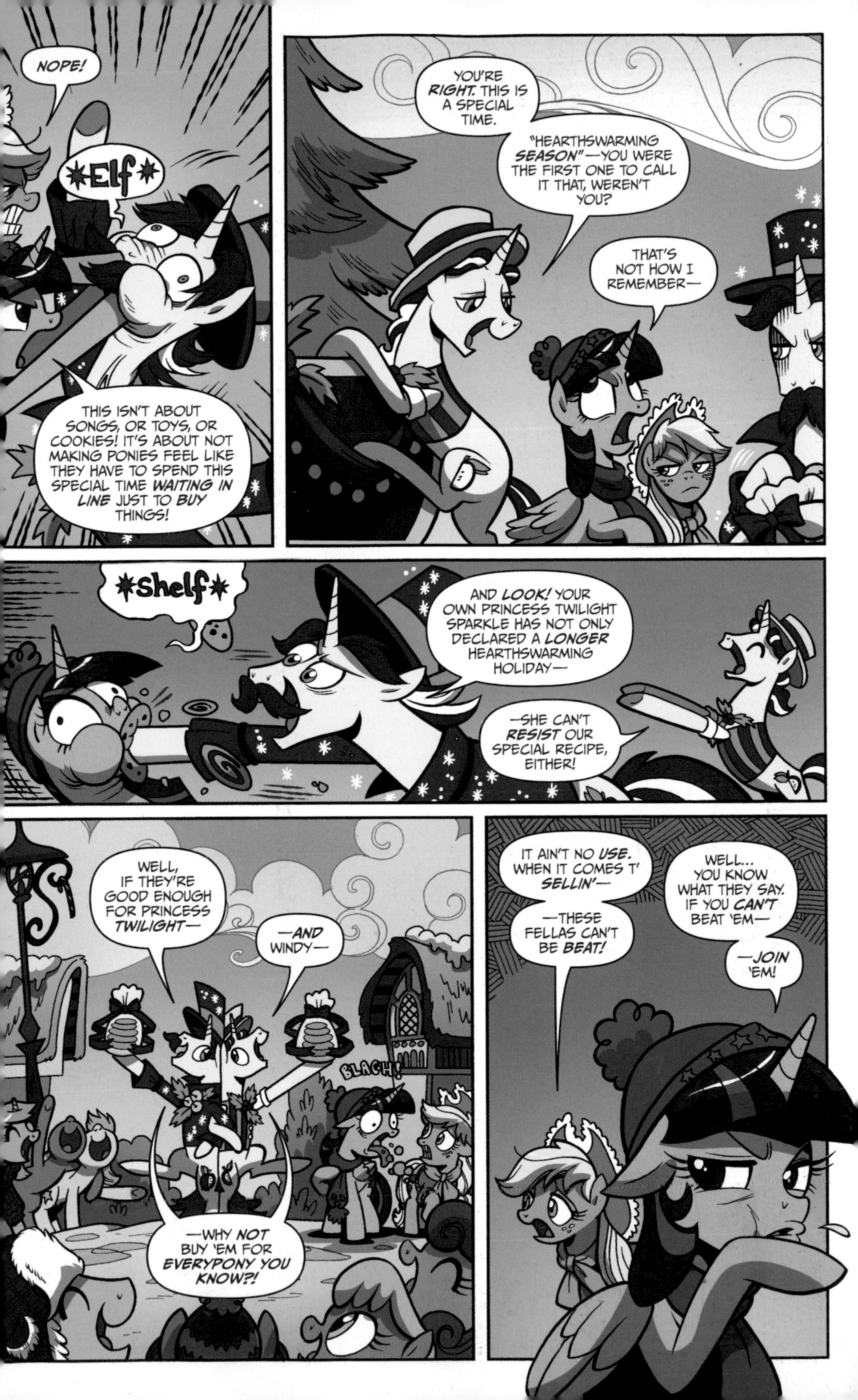
NOPE!
Elf
THIS ISN'T ABOUT SONGS, OR TOYS, OR COOKIES! IT'S ABOUT NOT MAKING PONIES FEEL LIKE THEY HAVE TO SPEND THIS SPECIAL TIME WAITING IN LINE JUST TO BUY THINGS!
YOU'RE RIGHT. THIS IS A SPECIAL TIME.
"HEARTHSWARMING SEASON"—YOU WERE THE FIRST ONE TO CALL IT THAT, WEREN'T YOU?
THAT'S NOT HOW I REMEMBER—
Shelf
AND LOOK! YOUR OWN PRINCESS TWILIGHT SPARKLE HAS NOT ONLY DECLARED A LONGER HEARTHSWARMING HOLIDAY—
—SHE CAN'T RESIST OUR SPECIAL RECIPE, EITHER!
WELL, IF THEY'RE GOOD ENOUGH FOR PRINCESS TWILIGHT—
—AND WINDY—
BLAGH!
—WHY NOT BUY 'EM FOR EVERYPONY YOU KNOW?!
IT AIN'T NO USE. WHEN IT COMES T' SELLIN'—
—THESE FELLAS CAN'T BE BEAT!
WELL... YOU KNOW WHAT THEY SAY. IF YOU CAN'T BEAT 'EM—
—JOIN 'EM!

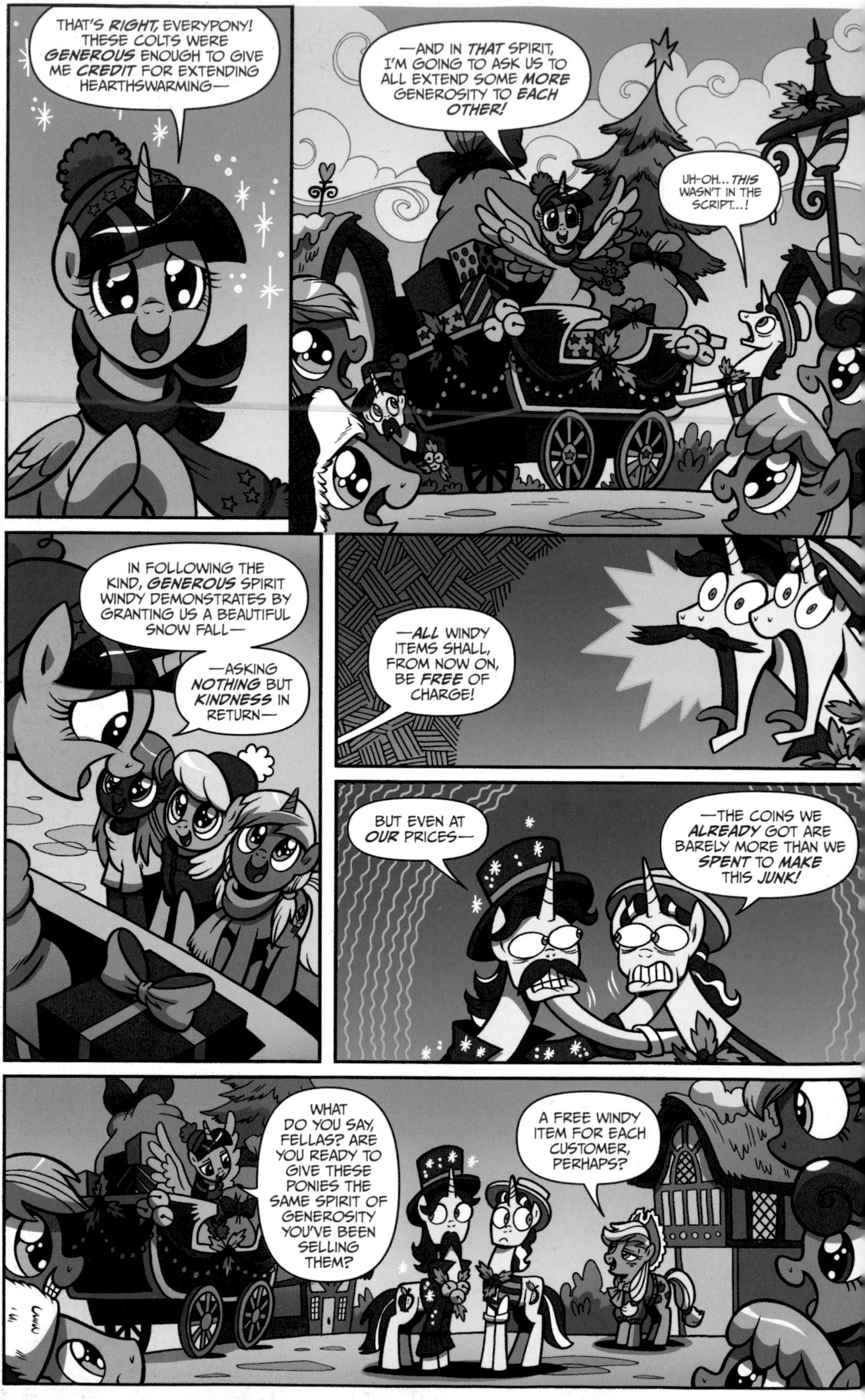
THAT'S RIGHT, EVERYPONY! THESE COLTS WERE GENEROUS ENOUGH TO GIVE ME CREDIT FOR EXTENDING HEARTHSWARMING—
—AND IN THAT SPIRIT, I'M GOING TO ASK US TO ALL EXTEND SOME MORE GENEROSITY TO EACH OTHER!
UH-OH... THIS WASN'T IN THE SCRIPT...!
IN FOLLOWING THE KIND, GENEROUS SPIRIT WINDY DEMONSTRATES BY GRANTING US A BEAUTIFUL SNOW FALL—
—ASKING NOTHING BUT KINDNESS IN RETURN—
—ALL WINDY ITEMS SHALL, FROM NOW ON, BE FREE OF CHARGE!
BUT EVEN AT OUR PRICES—
—THE COINS WE ALREADY GOT ARE BARELY MORE THAN WE SPENT TO MAKE THIS JUNK!
WHAT DO YOU SAY, FELLAS? ARE YOU READY TO GIVE THESE PONIES THE SAME SPIRIT OF GENEROSITY YOU'VE BEEN SELLING THEM?
A FREE WINDY ITEM FOR EACH CUSTOMER, PERHAPS?

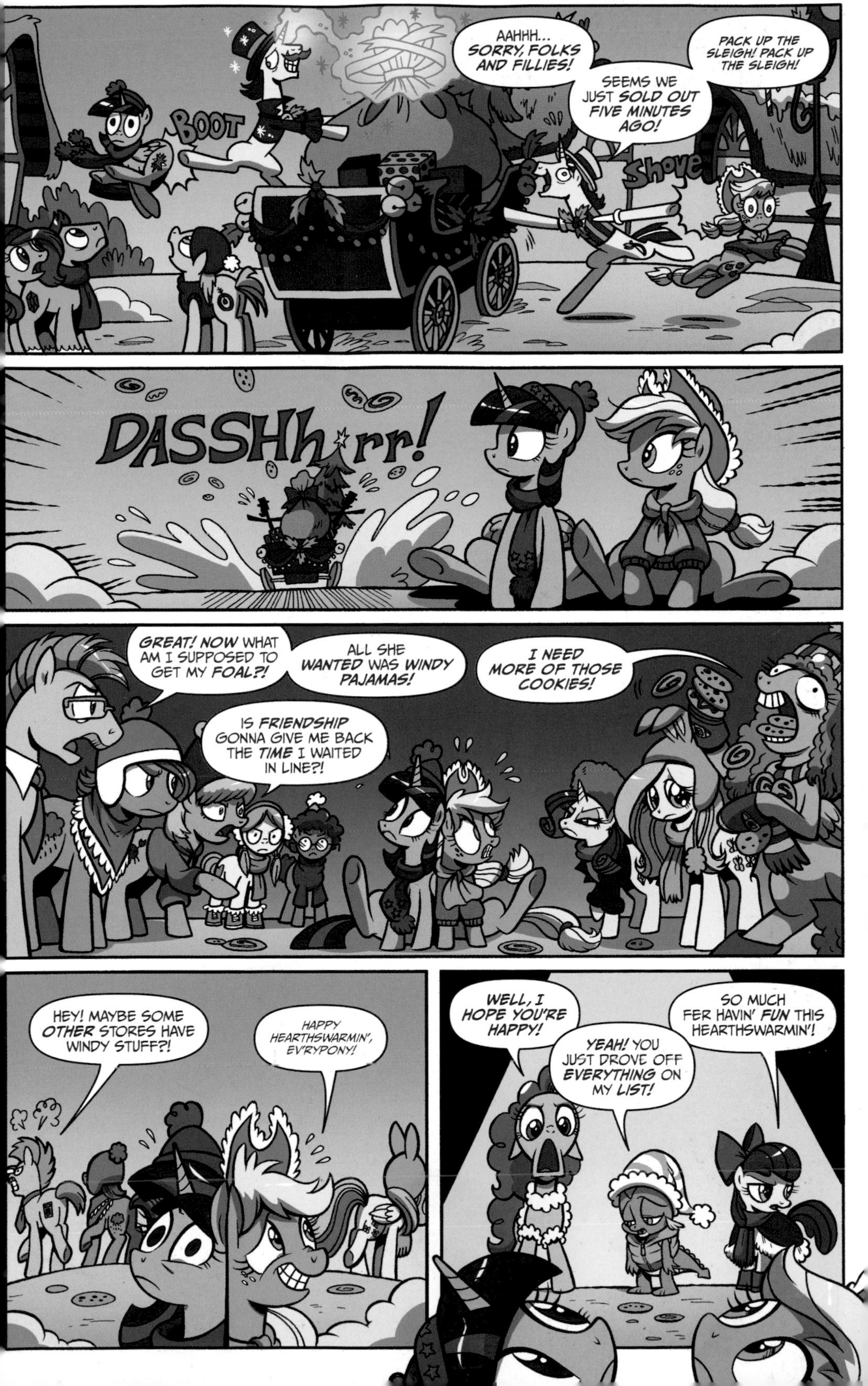
AAHHH... SORRY, FOLKS AND FILLIES!
SEEMS WE JUST SOLD OUT FIVE MINUTES AGO!
PACK UP THE SLEIGH! PACK UP THE SLEIGH!
BOOT
SHOVE
DASSHh rr!
GREAT! NOW WHAT AM I SUPPOSED TO GET MY FOAL?!
ALL SHE WANTED WAS WINDY PAJAMAS!
I NEED MORE OF THOSE COOKIES!
IS FRIENDSHIP GONNA GIVE ME BACK THE TIME I WAITED IN LINE?!
HEY! MAYBE SOME OTHER STORES HAVE WINDY STUFF?!
HAPPY HEARTHSWARMIN', EV'RYPONY!
WELL, I HOPE YOU'RE HAPPY!
YEAH! YOU JUST DROVE OFF EVERYTHING ON MY LIST!
SO MUCH FER HAVIN' FUN THIS HEARTHSWARMIN'!

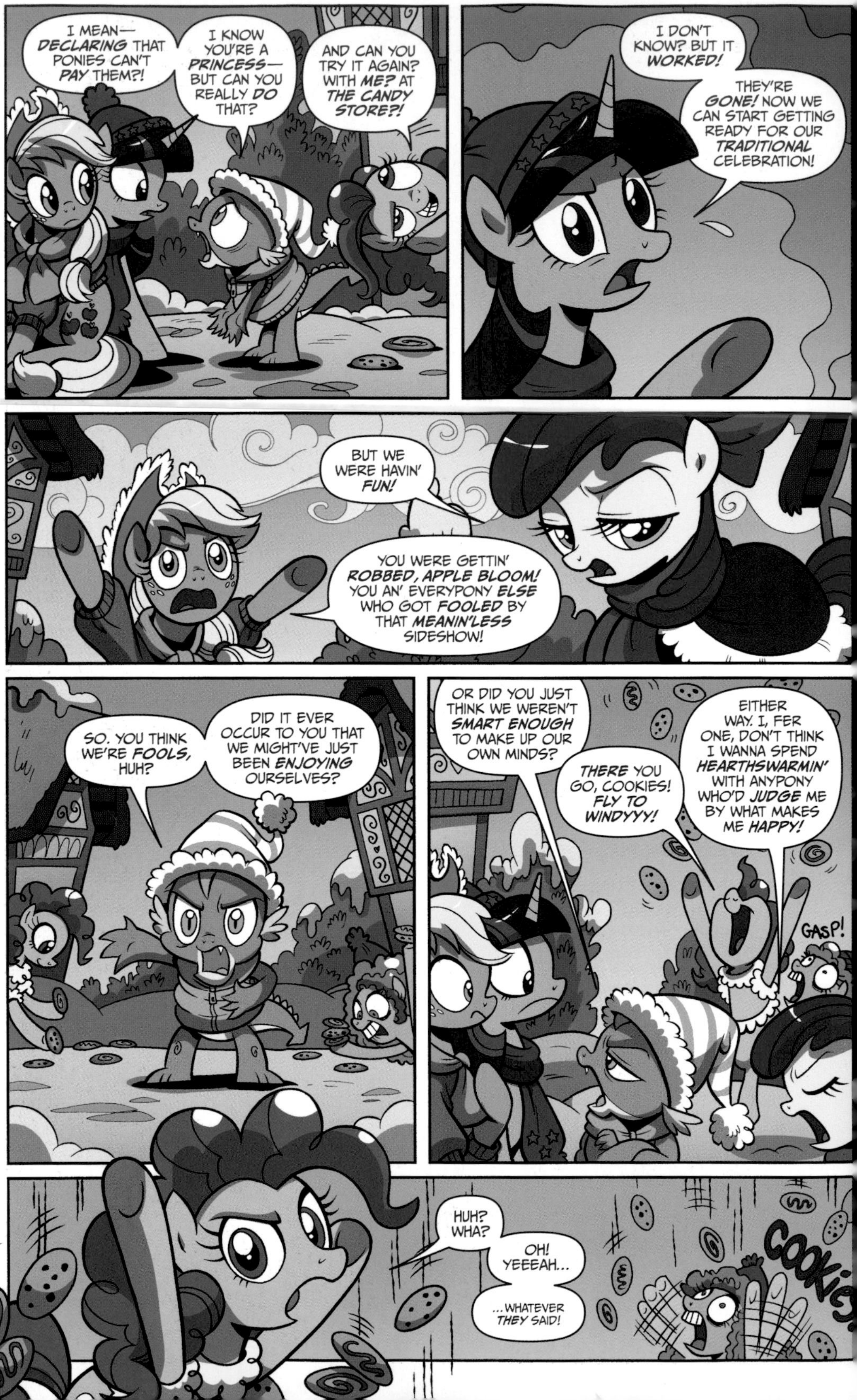
I MEAN— DECLARING THAT PONIES CAN'T PAY THEM?!
I KNOW YOU'RE A PRINCESS— BUT CAN YOU REALLY DO THAT?
AND CAN YOU TRY IT AGAIN? WITH ME? AT THE CANDY STORE?!
I DON'T KNOW? BUT IT WORKED!
THEY'RE GONE! NOW WE CAN START GETTING READY FOR OUR TRADITIONAL CELEBRATION!
BUT WE WERE HAVIN' FUN!
YOU WERE GETTIN' ROBBED, APPLE BLOOM! YOU AN' EVERYPONY ELSE WHO GOT FOOLED BY THAT MEANIN'LESS SIDESHOW!
SO. YOU THINK WE'RE FOOLS, HUH?
DID IT EVER OCCUR TO YOU THAT WE MIGHT'VE JUST BEEN ENJOYING OURSELVES?
OR DID YOU JUST THINK WE WEREN'T SMART ENOUGH TO MAKE UP OUR OWN MINDS?
THERE YOU GO, COOKIES! FLY TO WINDYYY!
EITHER WAY. I, FER ONE, DON'T THINK I WANNA SPEND HEARTHSWARMIN' WITH ANYPONY WHO'D JUDGE ME BY WHAT MAKES ME HAPPY!
GASP!
HUH? WHA?
OH! YEEEAH...
...WHATEVER THEY SAID!
COOKIE

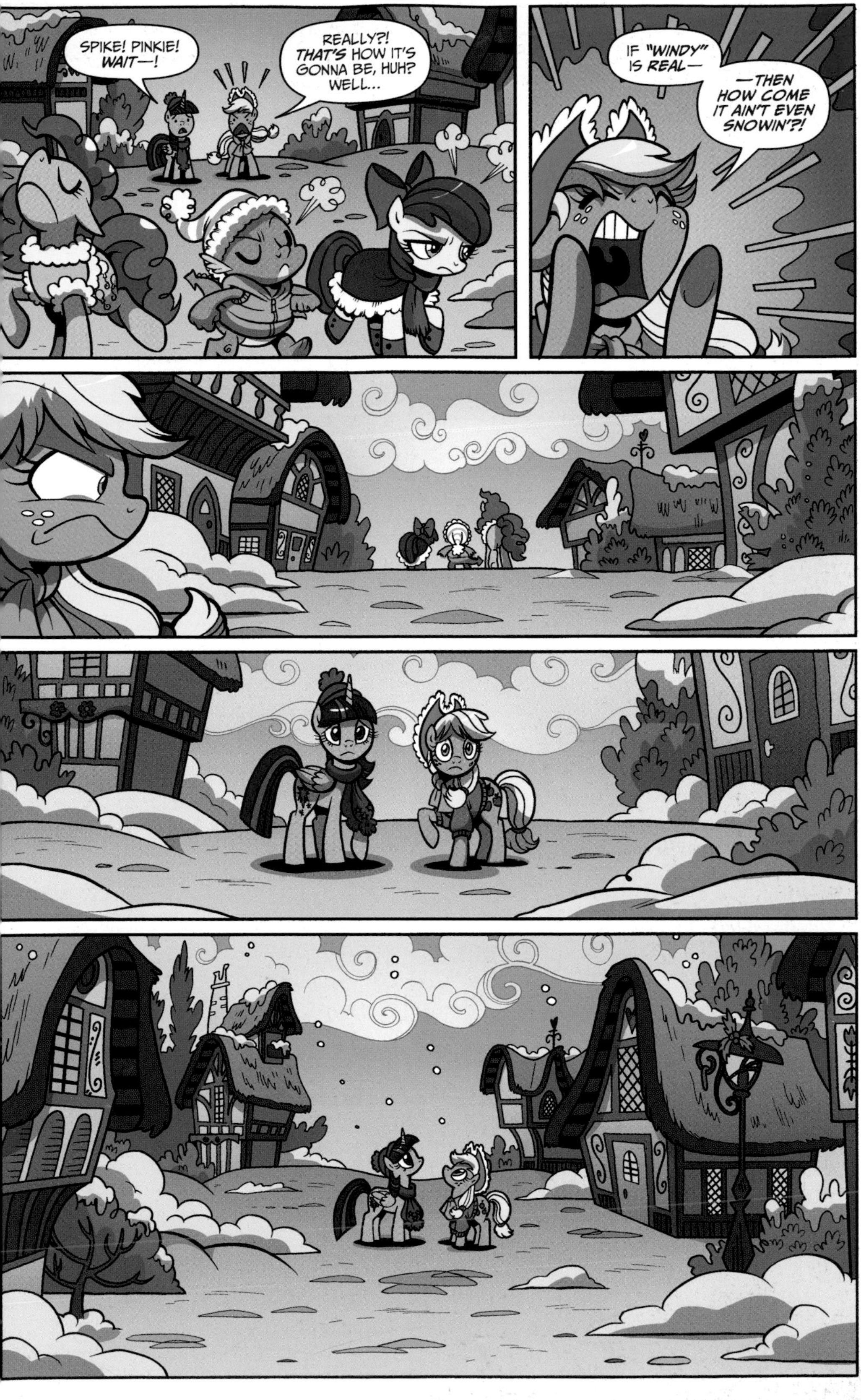
SPIKE! PINKIE! WAIT—!
REALLY?! THAT'S HOW IT'S GONNA BE, HUH? WELL...
IF "WINDY" IS REAL—
—THEN HOW COME IT AIN'T EVEN SNOWIN'?!

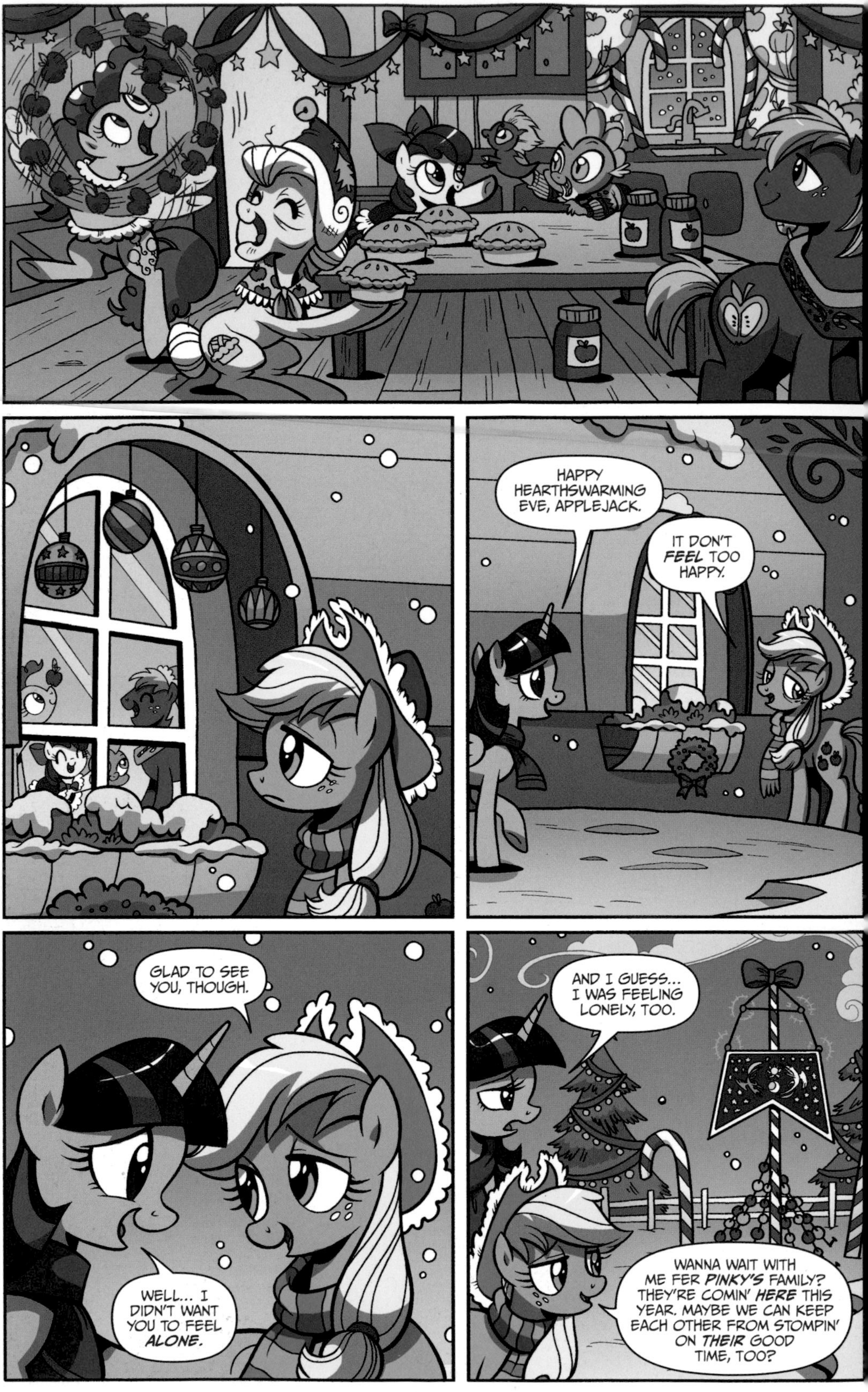
HAPPY HEARTHSWARMING EVE, APPLEJACK.
IT DON'T FEEL TOO HAPPY.
GLAD TO SEE YOU, THOUGH.
WELL... I DIDN'T WANT YOU TO FEEL ALONE.
AND I GUESS... I WAS FEELING LONELY, TOO.
WANNA WAIT WITH ME FER PINKY'S FAMILY? THEY'RE COMIN' HERE THIS YEAR. MAYBE WE CAN KEEP EACH OTHER FROM STOMPIN' ON THEIR GOOD TIME, TOO?

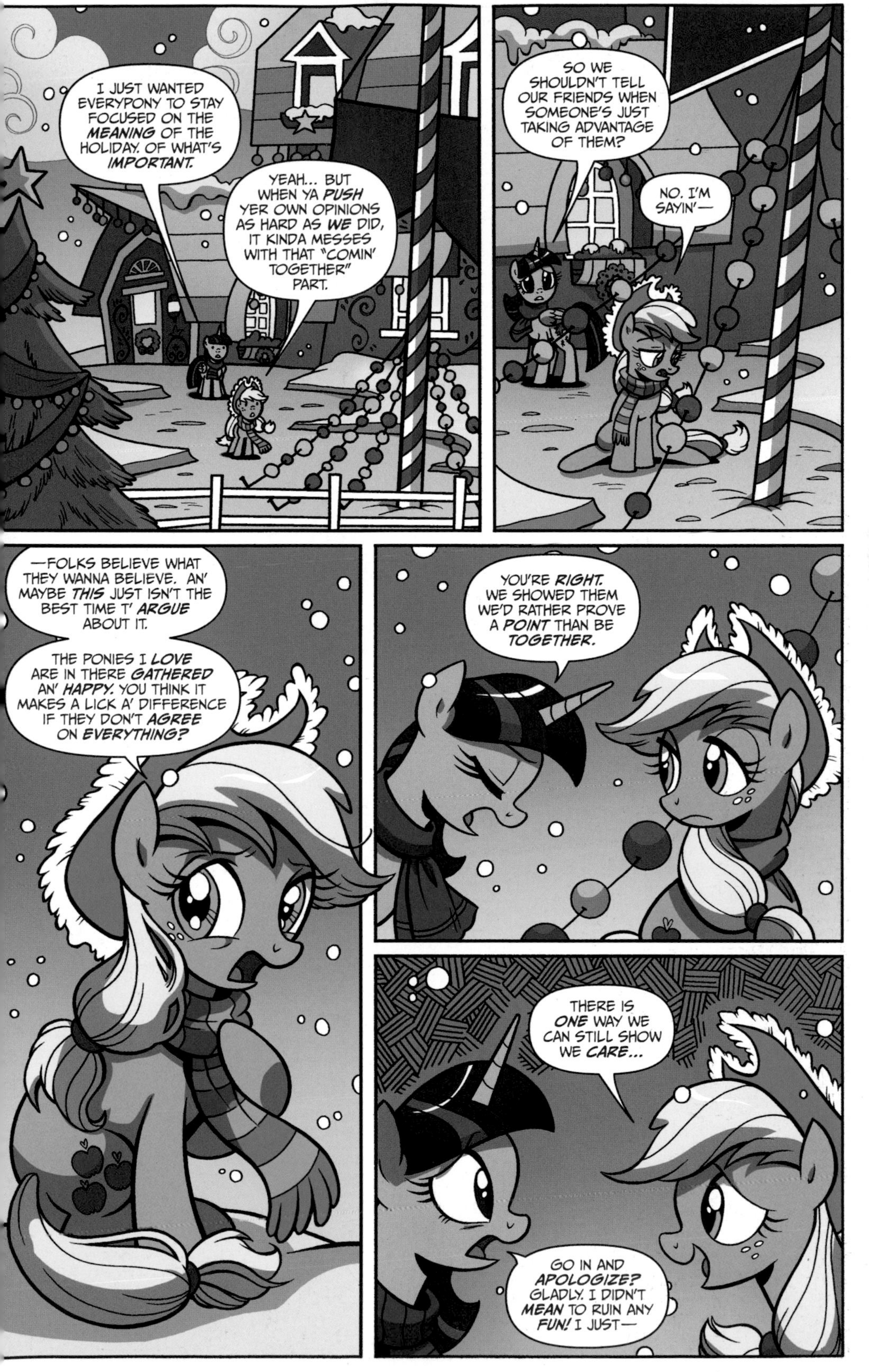
I JUST WANTED EVERYPONY TO STAY FOCUSED ON THE MEANING OF THE HOLIDAY. OF WHAT'S IMPORTANT.
YEAH... BUT WHEN YA PUSH YER OWN OPINIONS AS HARD AS WE DID, IT KINDA MESSES WITH THAT "COMIN' TOGETHER" PART.
SO WE SHOULDN'T TELL OUR FRIENDS WHEN SOMEONE'S JUST TAKING ADVANTAGE OF THEM?
NO. I'M SAYIN'—
—FOLKS BELIEVE WHAT THEY WANNA BELIEVE. AN' MAYBE THIS JUST ISN'T THE BEST TIME T' ARGUE ABOUT IT.
THE PONIES I LOVE ARE IN THERE GATHERED AN' HAPPY. YOU THINK IT MAKES A LICK A' DIFFERENCE IF THEY DON'T AGREE ON EVERYTHING?
YOU'RE RIGHT. WE SHOWED THEM WE'D RATHER PROVE A POINT THAN BE TOGETHER.
THERE IS ONE WAY WE CAN STILL SHOW WE CARE...
GO IN AND APOLOGIZE? GLADLY. I DIDN'T MEAN TO RUIN ANY FUN! I JUST—

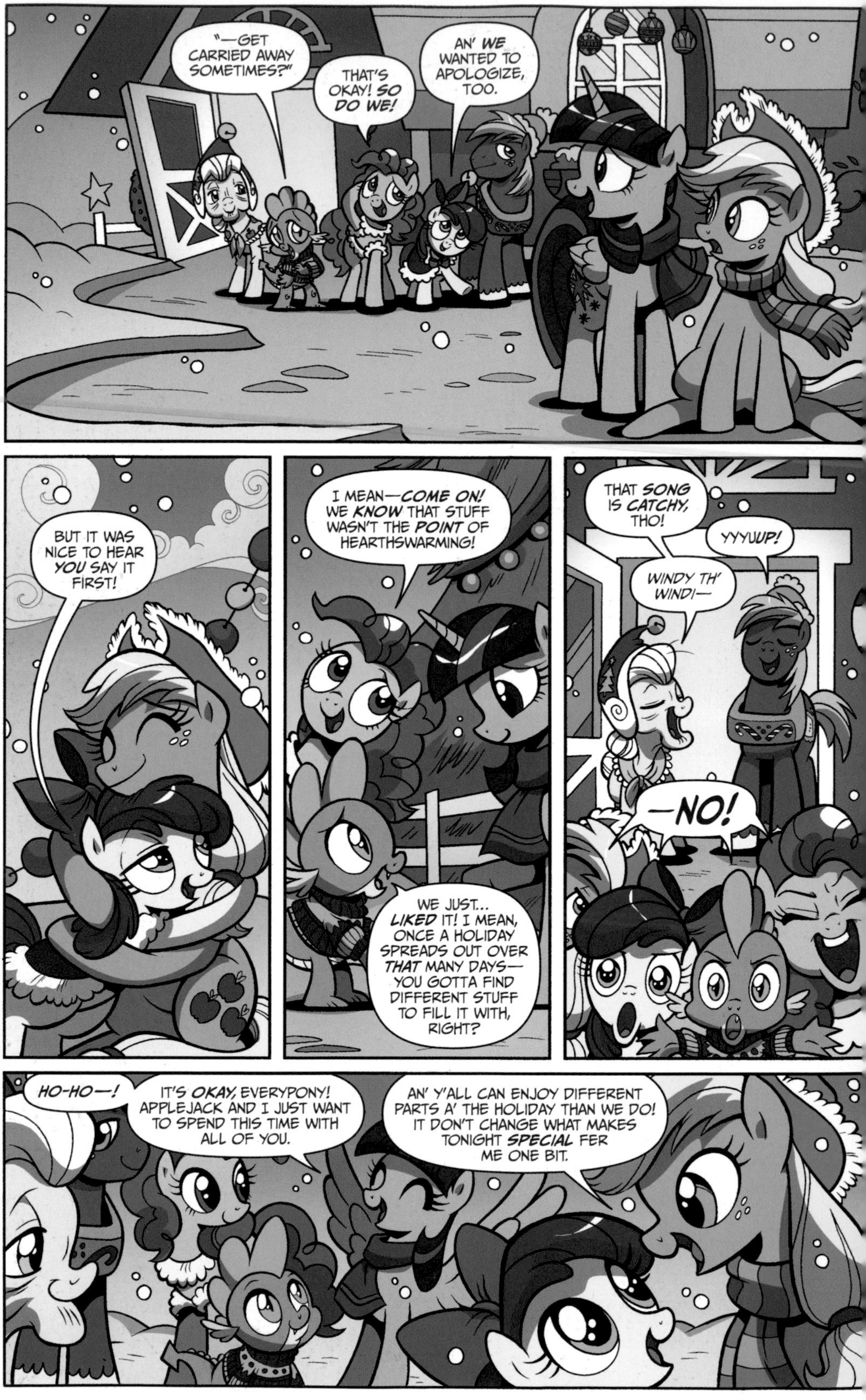
"—GET CARRIED AWAY SOMETIMES?"
THAT'S OKAY! SO DO WE!
AN' WE WANTED TO APOLOGIZE, TOO.
BUT IT WAS NICE TO HEAR YOU SAY IT FIRST!
I MEAN—COME ON! WE KNOW THAT STUFF WASN'T THE POINT OF HEARTHSWARMING!
WE JUST... LIKED IT! I MEAN, ONCE A HOLIDAY SPREADS OUT OVER THAT MANY DAYS—YOU GOTTA FIND DIFFERENT STUFF TO FILL IT WITH, RIGHT?
THAT SONG IS CATCHY, THO!
WINDY TH' WIND!—
YYYUUP!
—NO!
HO-HO—!
IT'S OKAY, EVERYPONY! APPLEJACK AND I JUST WANT TO SPEND THIS TIME WITH ALL OF YOU.
AN' Y'ALL CAN ENJOY DIFFERENT PARTS A' THE HOLIDAY THAN WE DO! IT DON'T CHANGE WHAT MAKES TONIGHT SPECIAL FER ME ONE BIT.

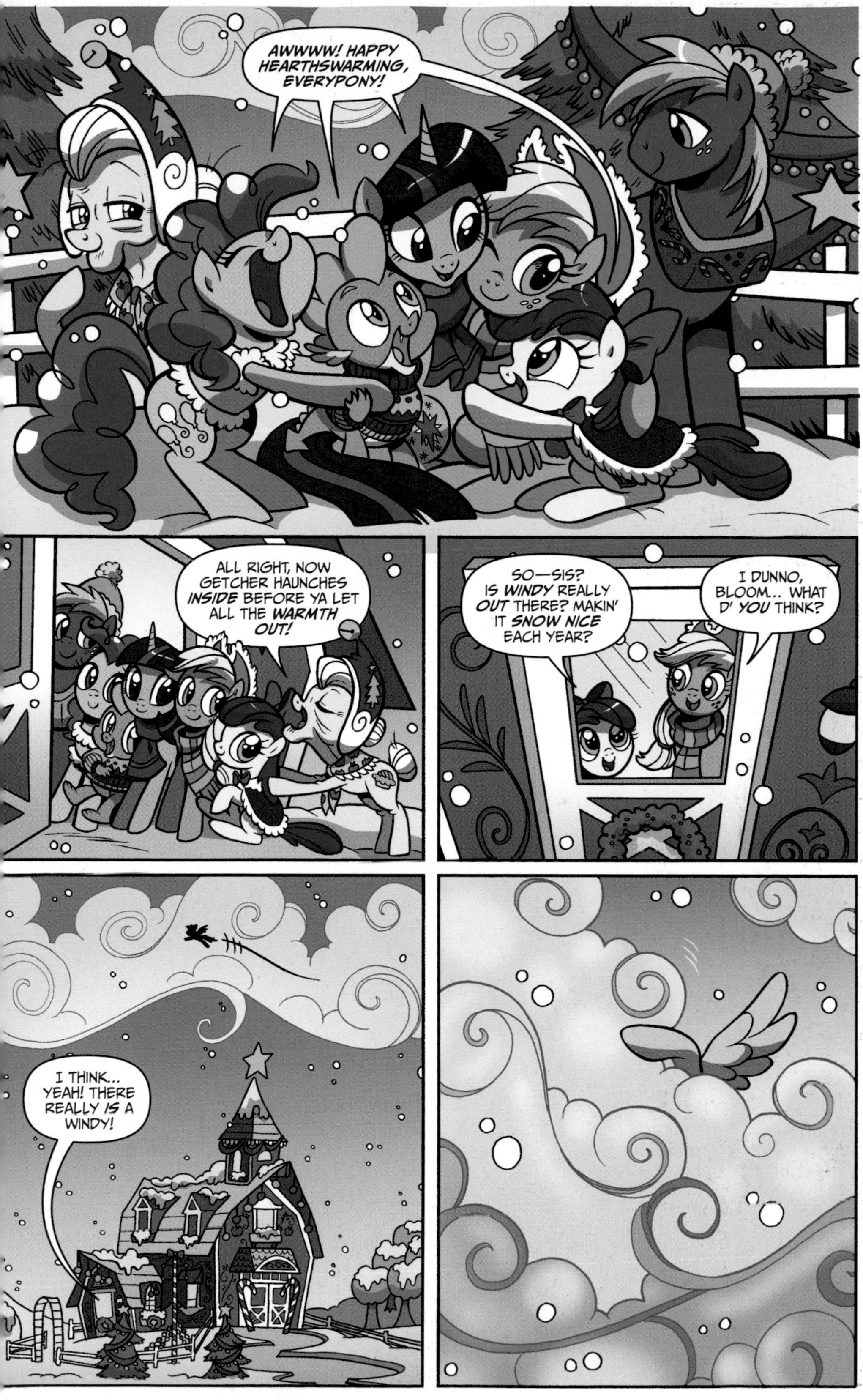
AWWWW! HAPPY HEARTHSWARMING, EVERYPONY!
ALL RIGHT, NOW GETCHER HAUNCHES INSIDE BEFORE YA LET ALL THE WARMTH OUT!
SO—SIS? IS WINDY REALLY OUT THERE? MAKIN' IT SNOW NICE EACH YEAR?
I DUNNO, BLOOM... WHAT D' YOU THINK?
I THINK... YEAH! THERE REALLY IS A WINDY!

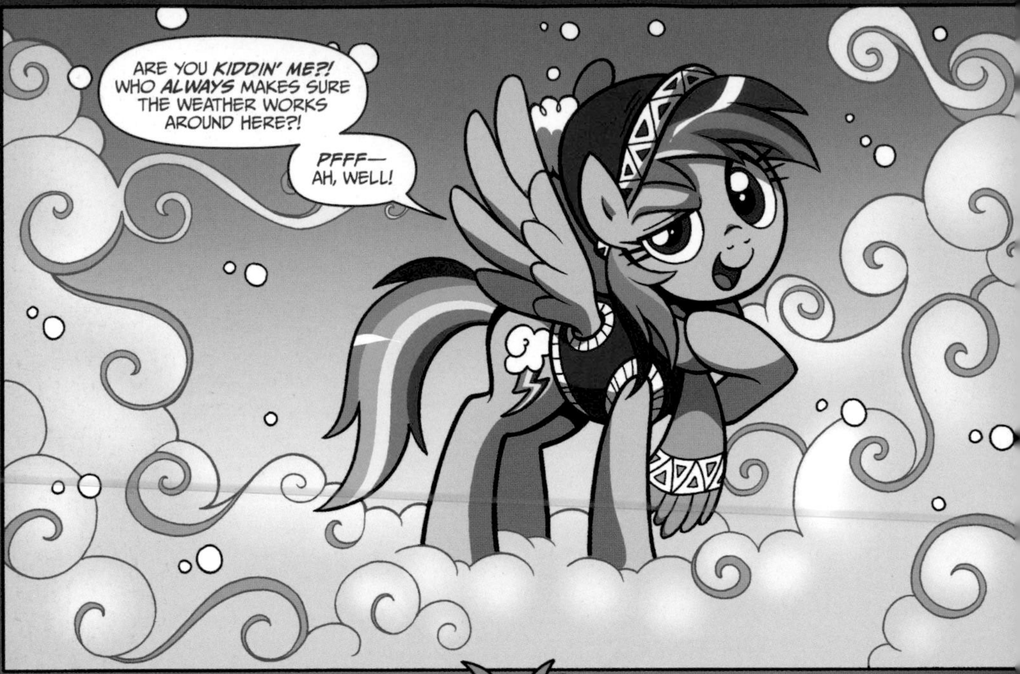
ARE YOU KIDDIN' ME?! WHO ALWAYS MAKES SURE THE WEATHER WORKS AROUND HERE?!
PFFF— AH, WELL!

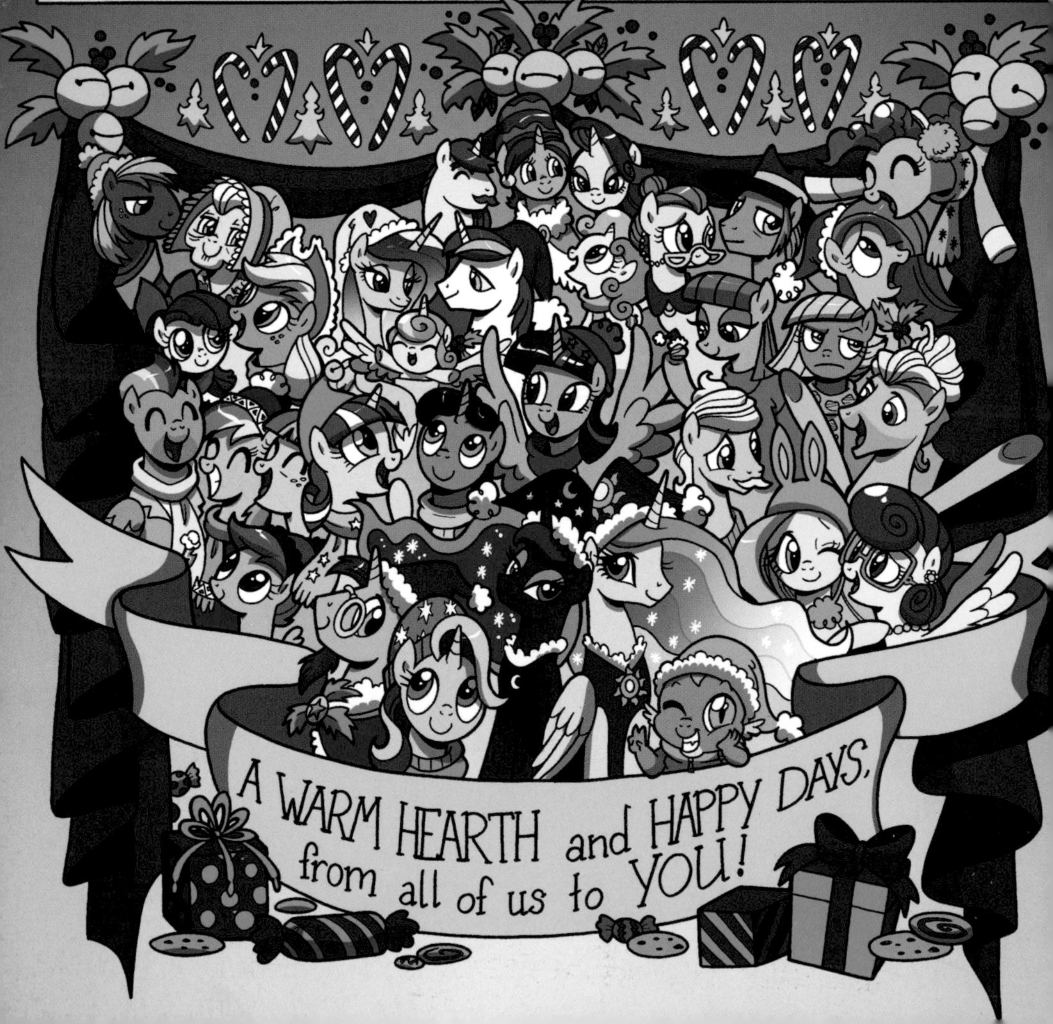
A WARM HEARTH and HAPPY DAYS, from all of us to YOU!

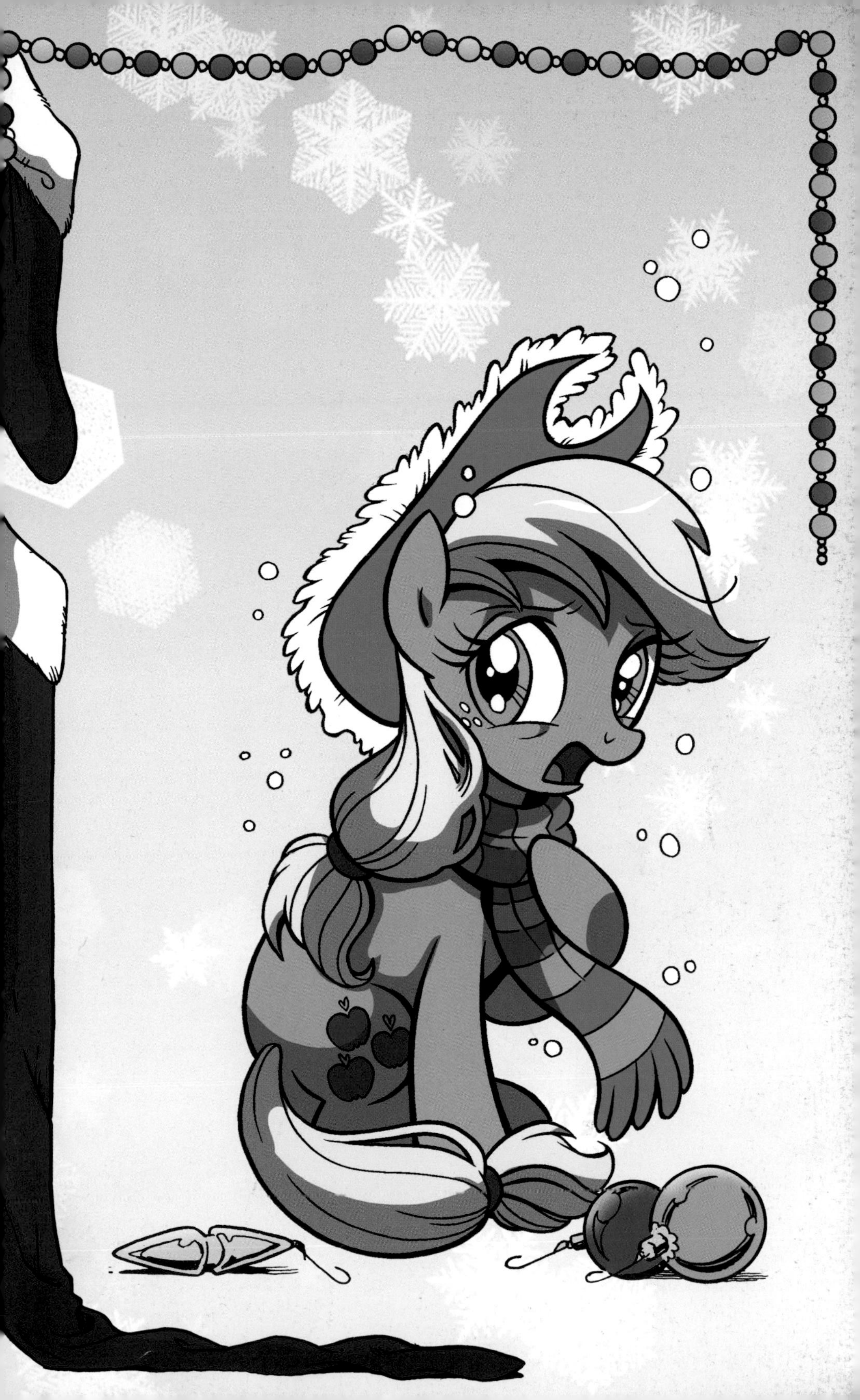

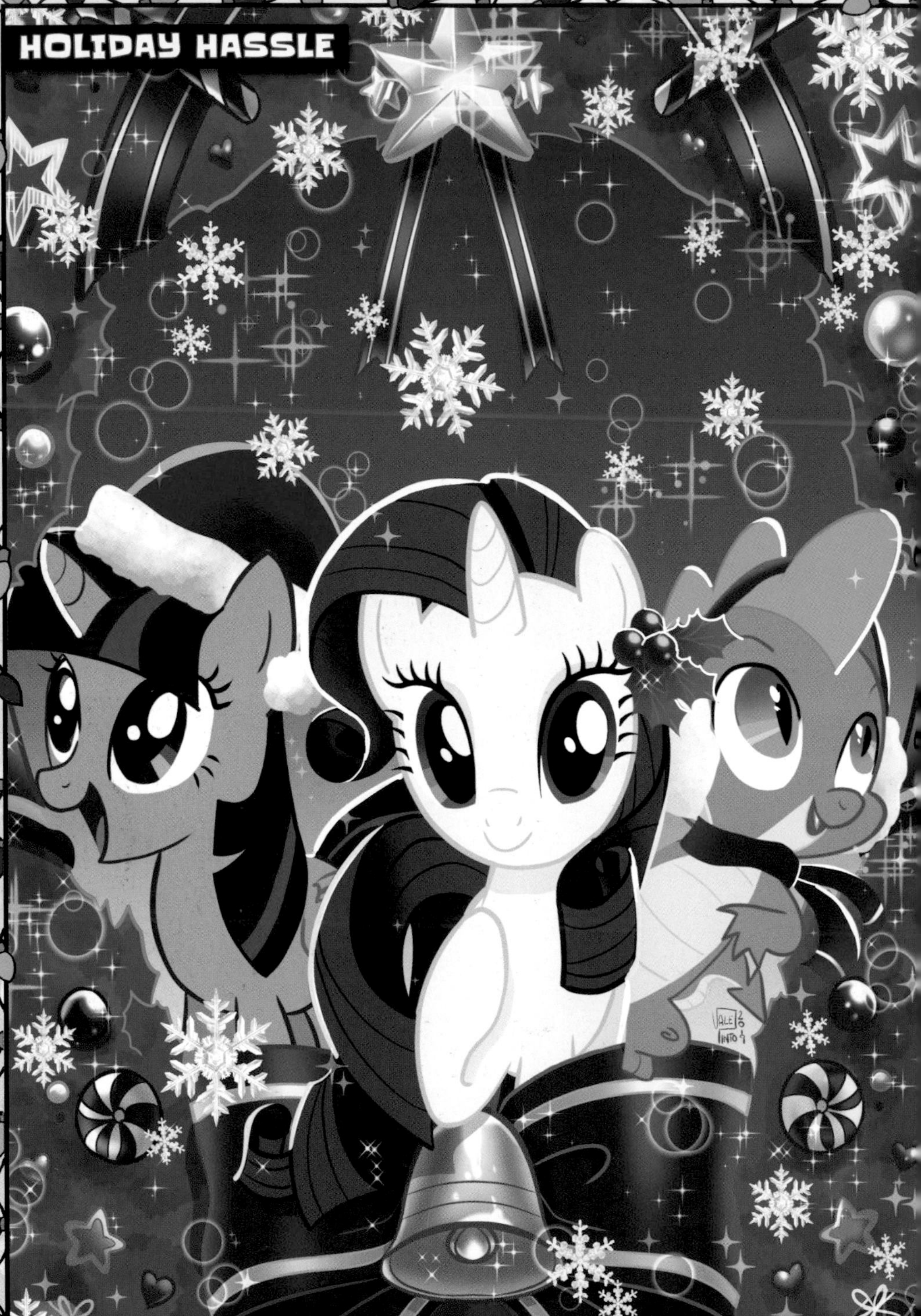
HOLIDAY HASSLE

ART BY Valentina Pinto

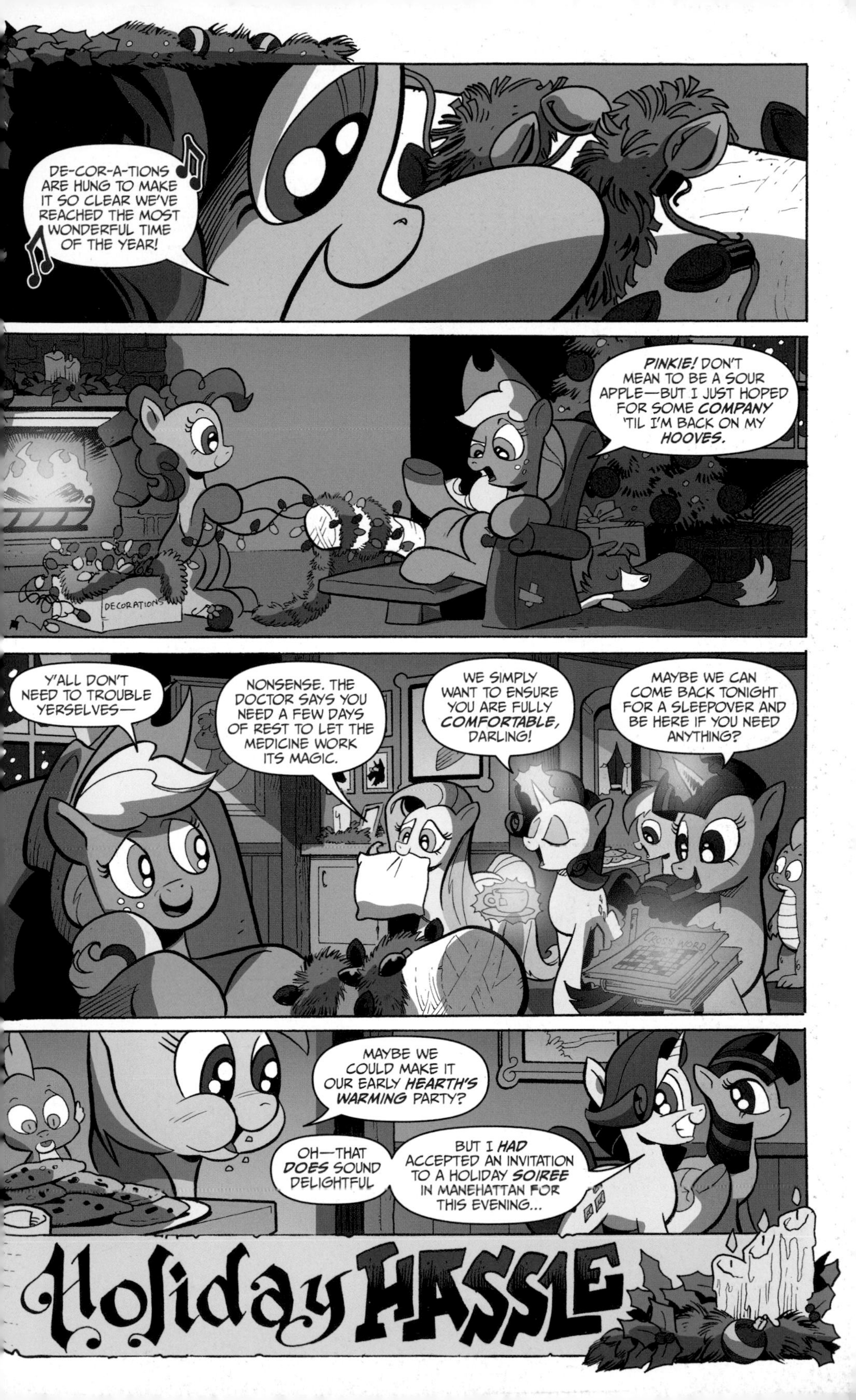
DE-COR-A-TIONS ARE HUNG TO MAKE IT SO CLEAR WE'VE REACHED THE MOST WONDERFUL TIME OF THE YEAR!
PINKIE! DON'T MEAN TO BE A SOUR APPLE—BUT I JUST HOPED FOR SOME COMPANY 'TIL I'M BACK ON MY HOOVES.
DECORATIONS
Y'ALL DON'T NEED TO TROUBLE YERSELVES—
NONSENSE. THE DOCTOR SAYS YOU NEED A FEW DAYS OF REST TO LET THE MEDICINE WORK ITS MAGIC.
WE SIMPLY WANT TO ENSURE YOU ARE FULLY COMFORTABLE, DARLING!
MAYBE WE CAN COME BACK TONIGHT FOR A SLEEPOVER AND BE HERE IF YOU NEED ANYTHING?
CROSS WORD
MAYBE WE COULD MAKE IT OUR EARLY HEARTH'S WARMING PARTY?
OH—THAT DOES SOUND DELIGHTFUL
BUT I HAD ACCEPTED AN INVITATION TO A HOLIDAY SOIREE IN MANEHATTAN FOR THIS EVENING...
Holiday HASSLE

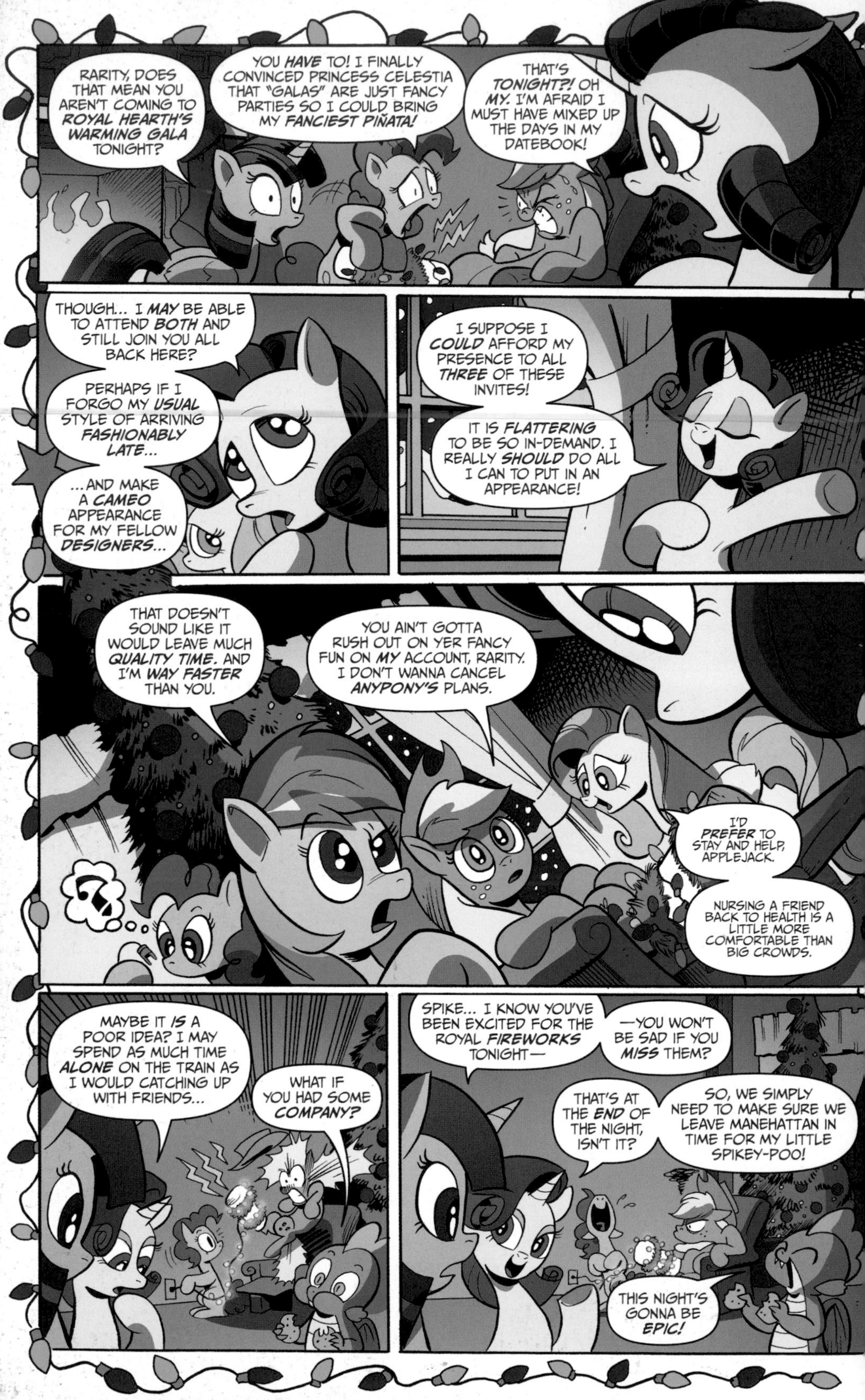
RARITY, DOES THAT MEAN YOU AREN'T COMING TO ROYAL HEARTH'S WARMING GALA TONIGHT?
YOU HAVE TO! I FINALLY CONVINCED PRINCESS CELESTIA THAT "GALAS" ARE JUST FANCY PARTIES SO I COULD BRING MY FANCIEST PIÑATA!
THAT'S TONIGHT?! OH MY. I'M AFRAID I MUST HAVE MIXED UP THE DAYS IN MY DATEBOOK!
THOUGH... I MAY BE ABLE TO ATTEND BOTH AND STILL JOIN YOU ALL BACK HERE?
PERHAPS IF I FORGO MY USUAL STYLE OF ARRIVING FASHIONABLY LATE...
...AND MAKE A CAMEO APPEARANCE FOR MY FELLOW DESIGNERS...
I SUPPOSE I COULD AFFORD MY PRESENCE TO ALL THREE OF THESE INVITES!
IT IS FLATTERING TO BE SO IN-DEMAND. I REALLY SHOULD DO ALL I CAN TO PUT IN AN APPEARANCE!
THAT DOESN'T SOUND LIKE IT WOULD LEAVE MUCH QUALITY TIME. AND I'M WAY FASTER THAN YOU.
YOU AIN'T GOTTA RUSH OUT ON YER FANCY FUN ON MY ACCOUNT, RARITY. I DON'T WANNA CANCEL ANYPONY'S PLANS.
I'D PREFER TO STAY AND HELP, APPLEJACK.
NURSING A FRIEND BACK TO HEALTH IS A LITTLE MORE COMFORTABLE THAN BIG CROWDS.
MAYBE IT IS A POOR IDEA? I MAY SPEND AS MUCH TIME ALONE ON THE TRAIN AS I WOULD CATCHING UP WITH FRIENDS...
WHAT IF YOU HAD SOME COMPANY?
SPIKE... I KNOW YOU'VE BEEN EXCITED FOR THE ROYAL FIREWORKS TONIGHT—
—YOU WON'T BE SAD IF YOU MISS THEM?
THAT'S AT THE END OF THE NIGHT, ISN'T IT?
SO, WE SIMPLY NEED TO MAKE SURE WE LEAVE MANEHATTAN IN TIME FOR MY LITTLE SPIKEY-POO!
THIS NIGHT'S GONNA BE EPIC!

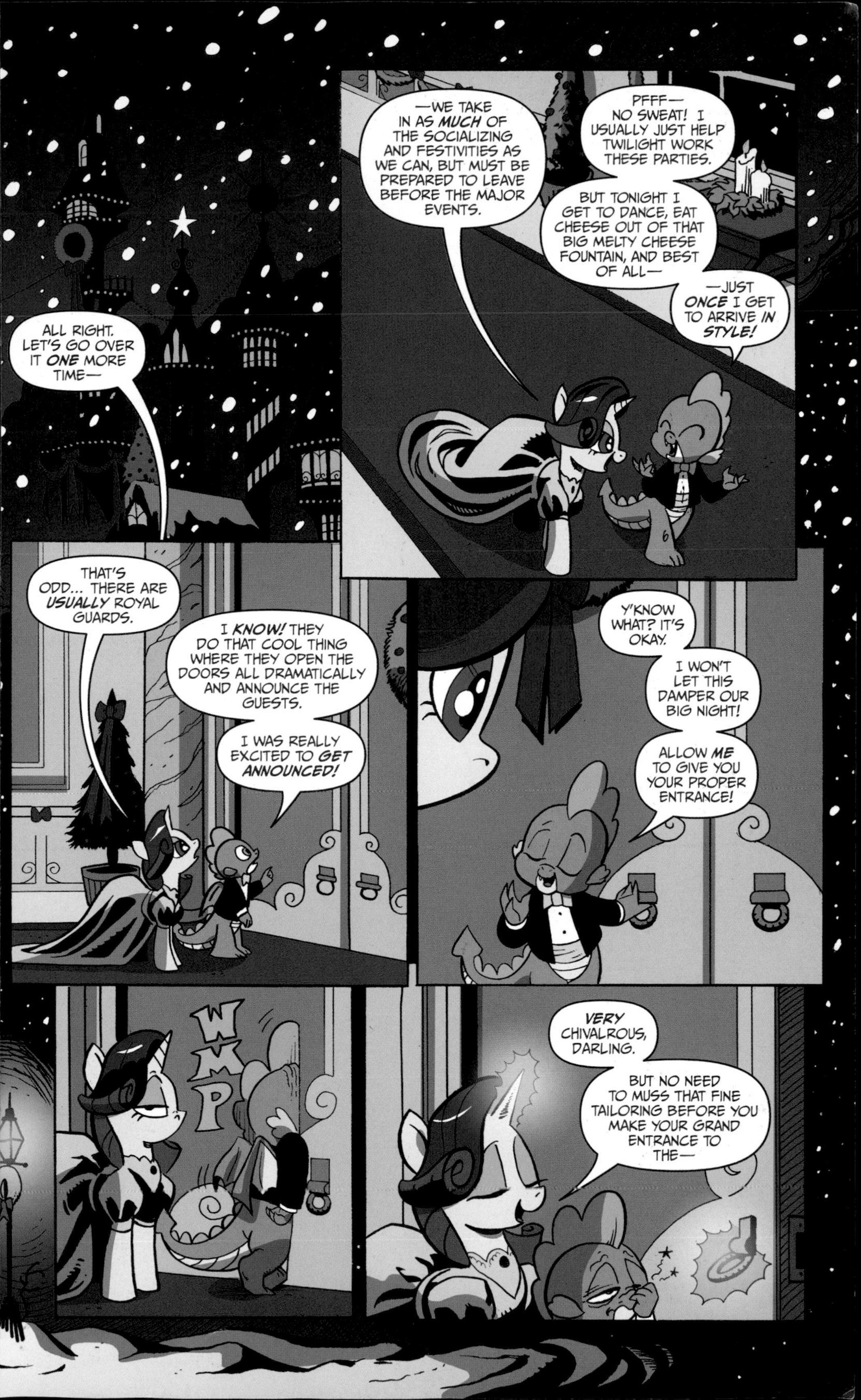
ALL RIGHT. LET'S GO OVER IT ONE MORE TIME—
—WE TAKE IN AS MUCH OF THE SOCIALIZING AND FESTIVITIES AS WE CAN, BUT MUST BE PREPARED TO LEAVE BEFORE THE MAJOR EVENTS.
PFFF— NO SWEAT! I USUALLY JUST HELP TWILIGHT WORK THESE PARTIES.
BUT TONIGHT I GET TO DANCE, EAT CHEESE OUT OF THAT BIG MELTY CHEESE FOUNTAIN, AND BEST OF ALL—
—JUST ONCE I GET TO ARRIVE IN STYLE!
THAT'S ODD... THERE ARE USUALLY ROYAL GUARDS.
I KNOW! THEY DO THAT COOL THING WHERE THEY OPEN THE DOORS ALL DRAMATICALLY AND ANNOUNCE THE GUESTS.
I WAS REALLY EXCITED TO GET ANNOUNCED!
Y'KNOW WHAT? IT'S OKAY.
I WON'T LET THIS DAMPER OUR BIG NIGHT!
ALLOW ME TO GIVE YOU YOUR PROPER ENTRANCE!
WMP
VERY CHIVALROUS, DARLING.
BUT NO NEED TO MUSS THAT FINE TAILORING BEFORE YOU MAKE YOUR GRAND ENTRANCE TO THE—

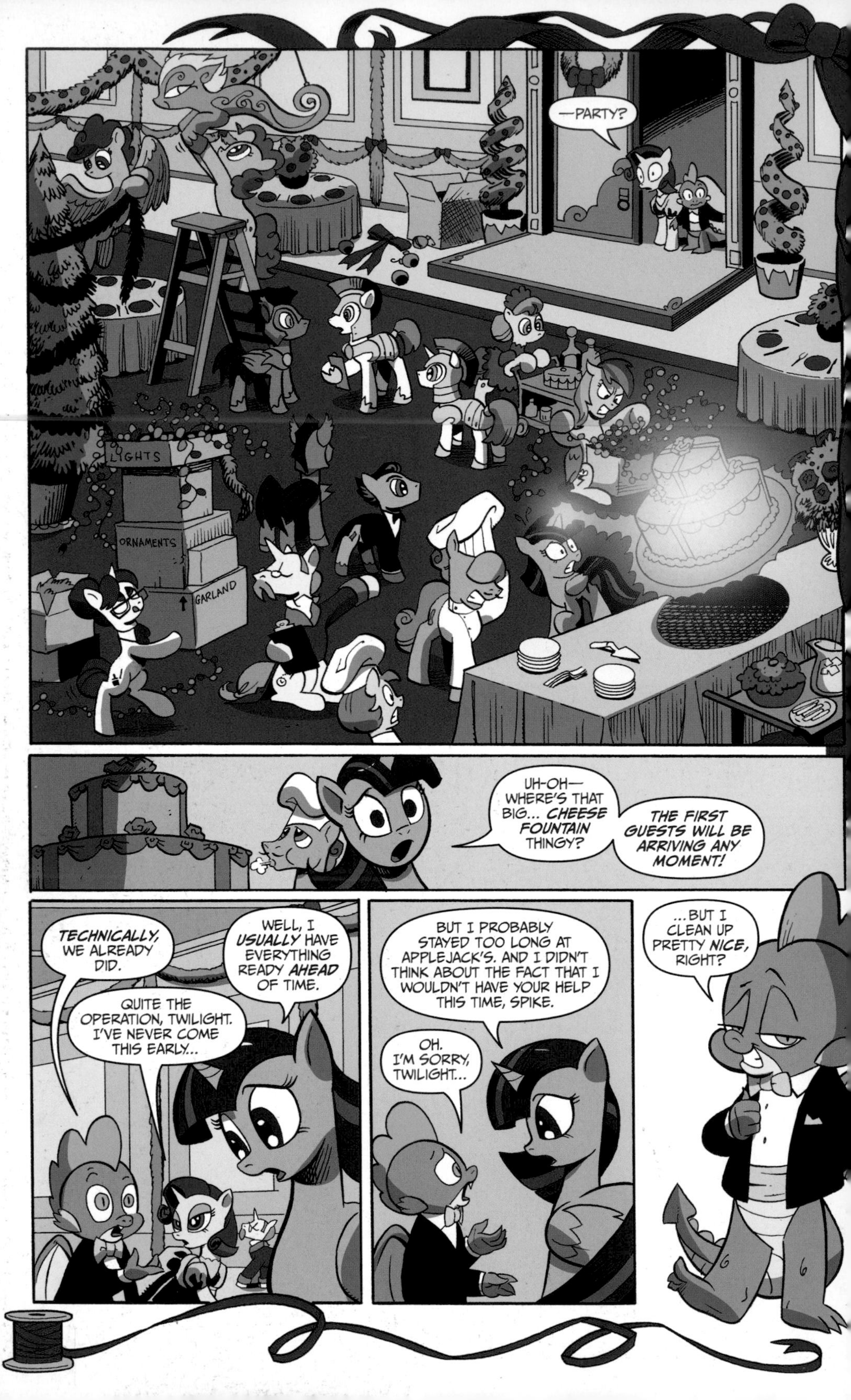
—PARTY?
LIGHTS
ORNAMENTS
GARLAND
UH-OH— WHERE'S THAT BIG... CHEESE FOUNTAIN THINGY?
THE FIRST GUESTS WILL BE ARRIVING ANY MOMENT!
TECHNICALLY, WE ALREADY DID.
WELL, I USUALLY HAVE EVERYTHING READY AHEAD OF TIME.
QUITE THE OPERATION, TWILIGHT. I'VE NEVER COME THIS EARLY...
BUT I PROBABLY STAYED TOO LONG AT APPLEJACK'S. AND I DIDN'T THINK ABOUT THE FACT THAT I WOULDN'T HAVE YOUR HELP THIS TIME, SPIKE.
OH. I'M SORRY, TWILIGHT...
...BUT I CLEAN UP PRETTY NICE, RIGHT?

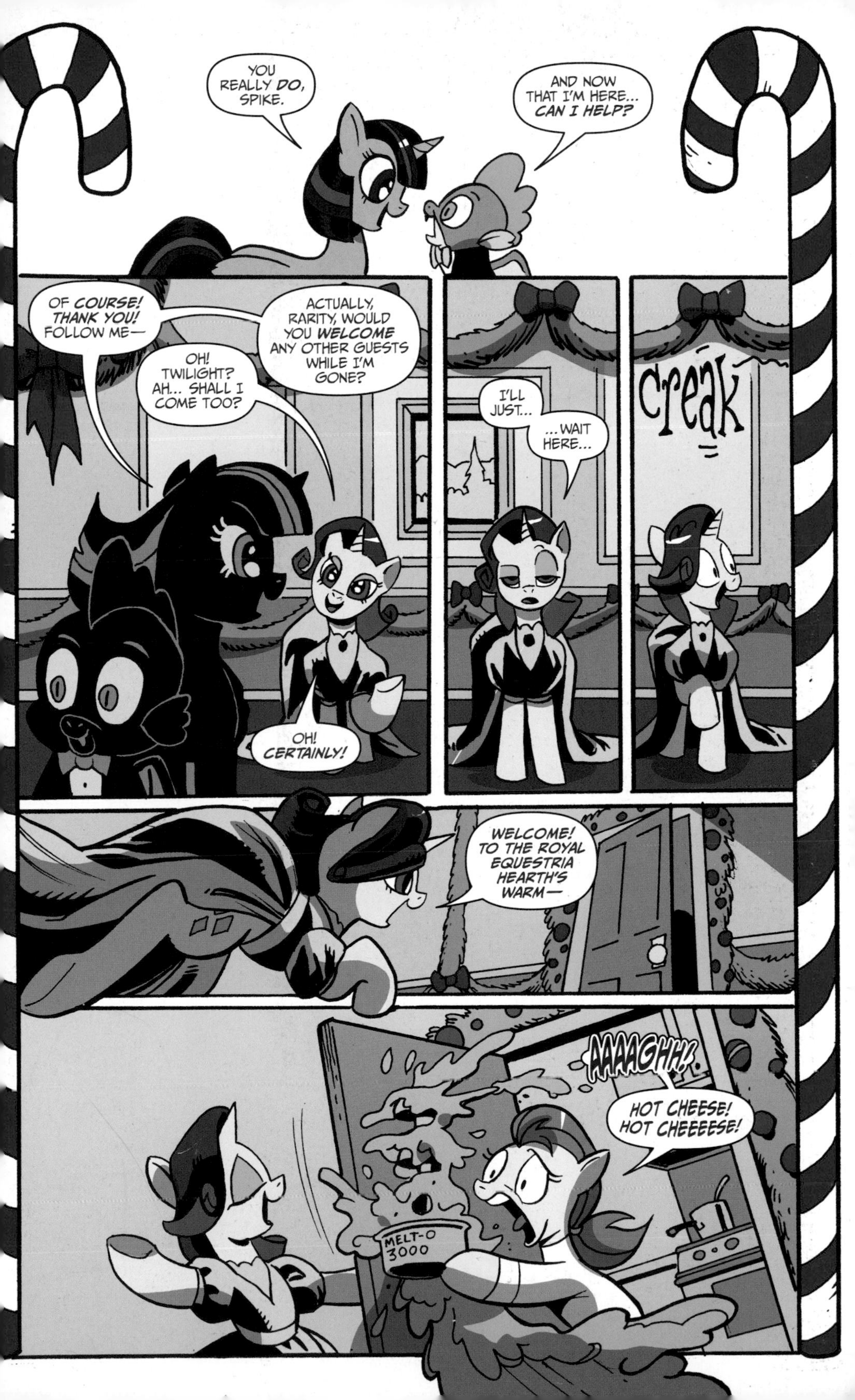
YOU REALLY DO, SPIKE.
AND NOW THAT I'M HERE... CAN I HELP?
OF COURSE! THANK YOU! FOLLOW ME—
ACTUALLY, RARITY, WOULD YOU WELCOME ANY OTHER GUESTS WHILE I'M GONE?
OH! TWILIGHT? AH... SHALL I COME TOO?
OH! CERTAINLY!
I'LL JUST...
...WAIT HERE...
creak
WELCOME! TO THE ROYAL EQUESTRIA HEARTH'S WARM—
AAAAGHH!
HOT CHEESE! HOT CHEEEESE!
MELT-O 3000

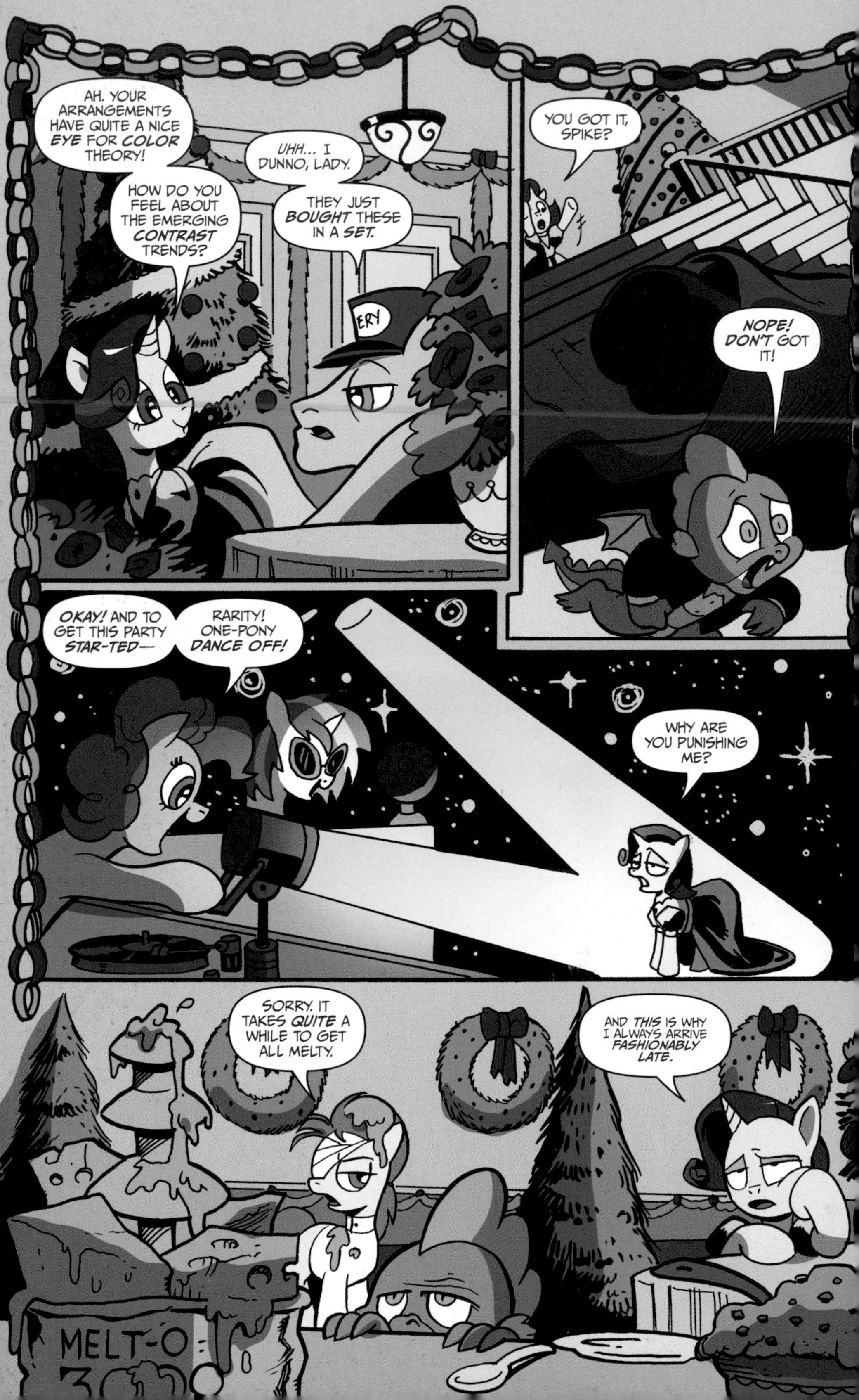
AH. YOUR ARRANGEMENTS HAVE QUITE A NICE EYE FOR COLOR THEORY!
HOW DO YOU FEEL ABOUT THE EMERGING CONTRAST TRENDS?
UHH... I DUNNO, LADY.
THEY JUST BOUGHT THESE IN A SET.
YOU GOT IT, SPIKE?
NOPE! DON'T GOT IT!
OKAY! AND TO GET THIS PARTY STAR-TED—
RARITY! ONE-PONY DANCE OFF!
WHY ARE YOU PUNISHING ME?
SORRY. IT TAKES QUITE A WHILE TO GET ALL MELTY.
AND THIS IS WHY I ALWAYS ARRIVE FASHIONABLY LATE.
MELT-O

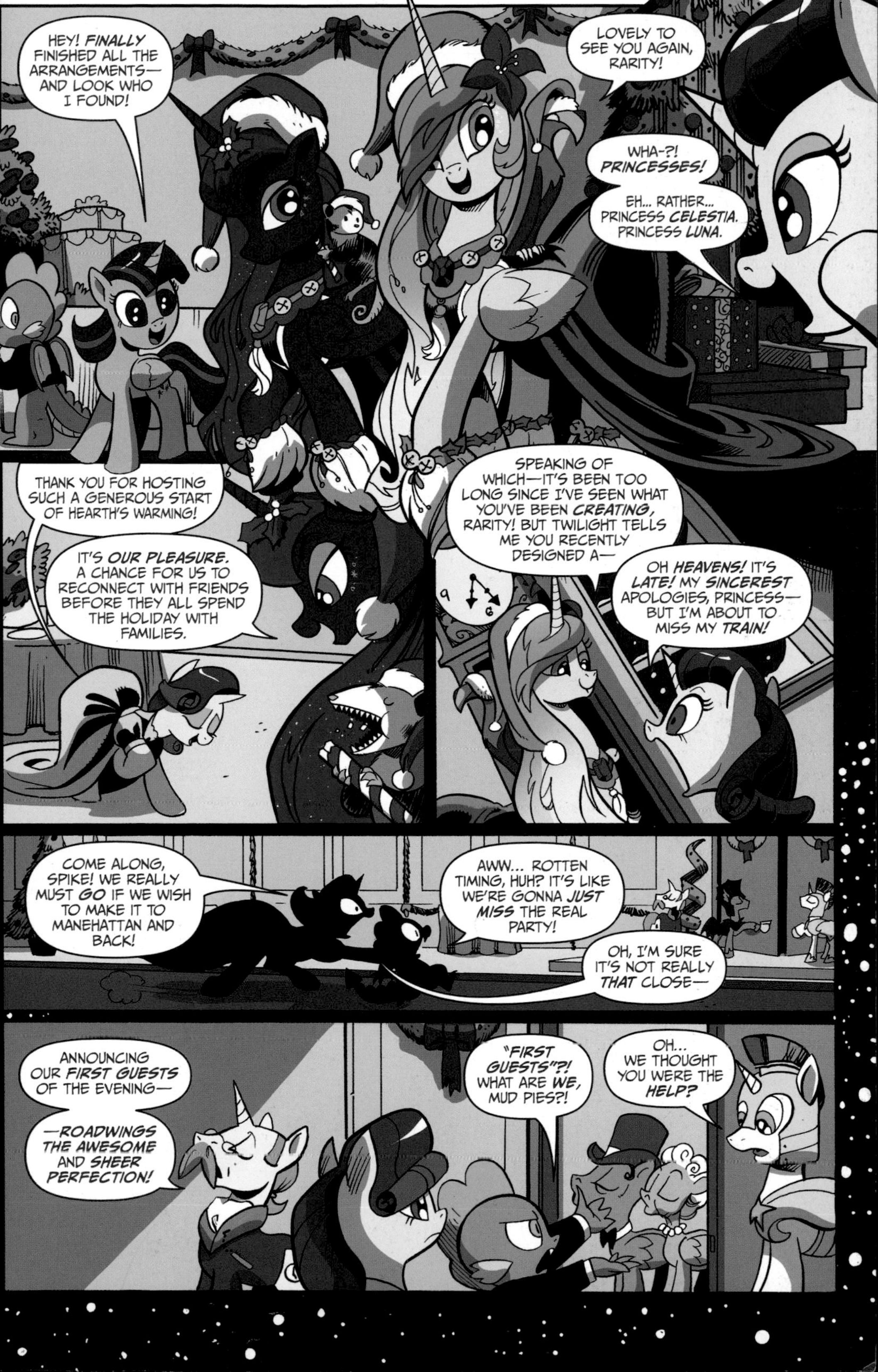

HEY! *FINALLY* FINISHED ALL THE ARRANGEMENTS— AND LOOK WHO I FOUND!
LOVELY TO SEE YOU AGAIN, RARITY!
WHA-?! *PRINCESSES!*
EH... RATHER... PRINCESS *CELESTIA.* PRINCESS *LUNA.*
THANK YOU FOR HOSTING SUCH A GENEROUS START OF HEARTH'S WARMING!
IT'S *OUR PLEASURE.* A CHANCE FOR US TO RECONNECT WITH FRIENDS BEFORE THEY ALL SPEND THE HOLIDAY WITH FAMILIES.
SPEAKING OF WHICH—IT'S BEEN TOO LONG SINCE I'VE SEEN WHAT YOU'VE BEEN *CREATING,* RARITY! BUT TWILIGHT TELLS ME YOU RECENTLY DESIGNED A—
OH *HEAVENS!* IT'S *LATE!* MY *SINCEREST* APOLOGIES, PRINCESS— BUT I'M ABOUT TO MISS MY *TRAIN!*
COME ALONG, SPIKE! WE REALLY MUST *GO* IF WE WISH TO MAKE IT TO MANEHATTAN AND BACK!
AWW... ROTTEN TIMING, HUH? IT'S LIKE WE'RE GONNA *JUST MISS* THE REAL PARTY!
OH, I'M SURE IT'S NOT REALLY *THAT* CLOSE—
ANNOUNCING OUR *FIRST GUESTS* OF THE EVENING—
—*ROADWINGS THE AWESOME* AND *SHEER PERFECTION!*
"*FIRST GUESTS*"?! WHAT ARE *WE,* MUD PIES?!
OH... WE THOUGHT YOU WERE THE *HELP?*

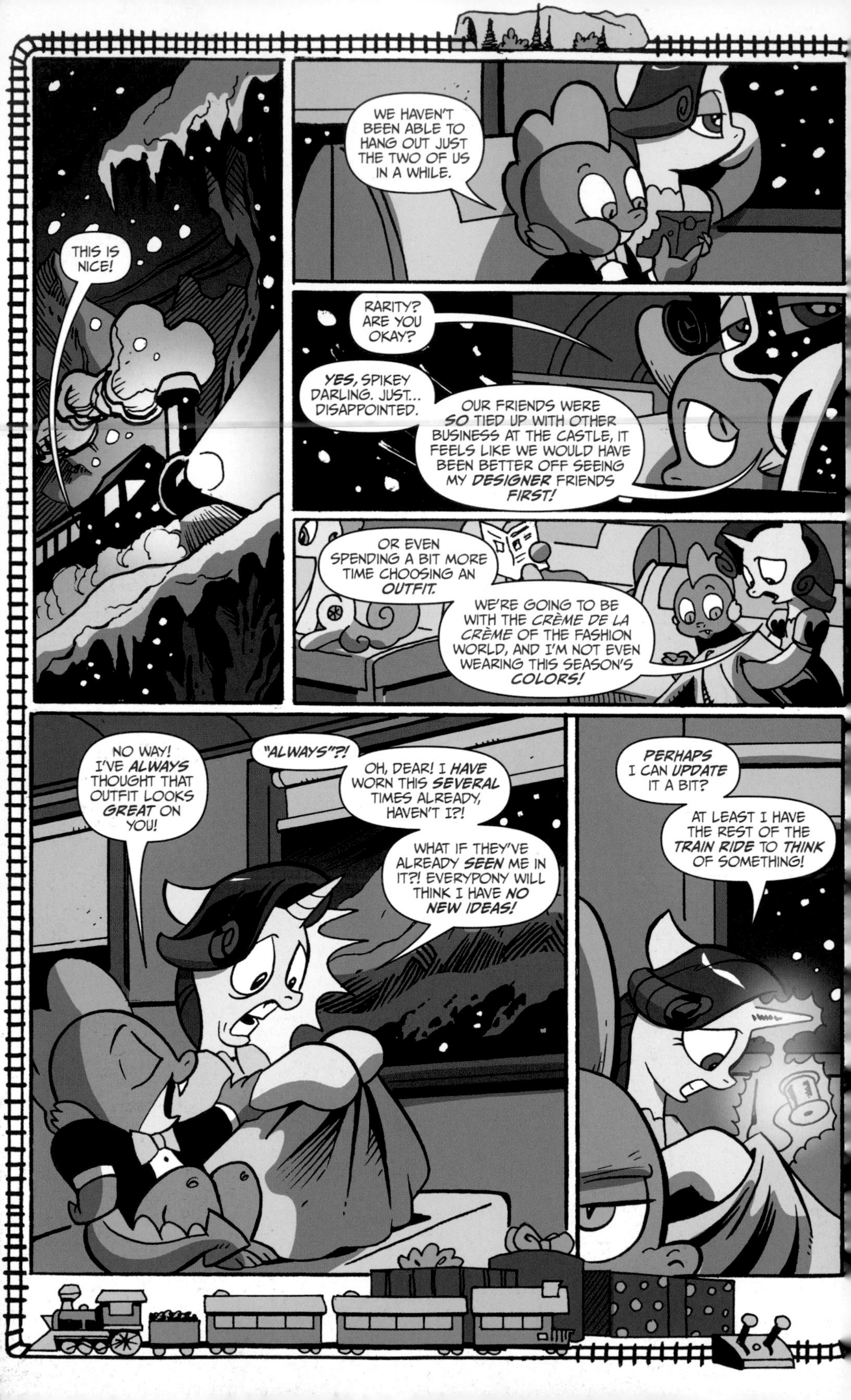
THIS IS NICE!
WE HAVEN'T BEEN ABLE TO HANG OUT JUST THE TWO OF US IN A WHILE.
RARITY? ARE YOU OKAY?
YES, SPIKEY DARLING. JUST... DISAPPOINTED.
OUR FRIENDS WERE SO TIED UP WITH OTHER BUSINESS AT THE CASTLE, IT FEELS LIKE WE WOULD HAVE BEEN BETTER OFF SEEING MY DESIGNER FRIENDS FIRST!
OR EVEN SPENDING A BIT MORE TIME CHOOSING AN OUTFIT.
WE'RE GOING TO BE WITH THE CRÈME DE LA CRÈME OF THE FASHION WORLD, AND I'M NOT EVEN WEARING THIS SEASON'S COLORS!
NO WAY! I'VE ALWAYS THOUGHT THAT OUTFIT LOOKS GREAT ON YOU!
"ALWAYS"?!
OH, DEAR! I HAVE WORN THIS SEVERAL TIMES ALREADY, HAVEN'T I?!
WHAT IF THEY'VE ALREADY SEEN ME IN IT?! EVERYPONY WILL THINK I HAVE NO NEW IDEAS!
PERHAPS I CAN UPDATE IT A BIT?
AT LEAST I HAVE THE REST OF THE TRAIN RIDE TO THINK OF SOMETHING!

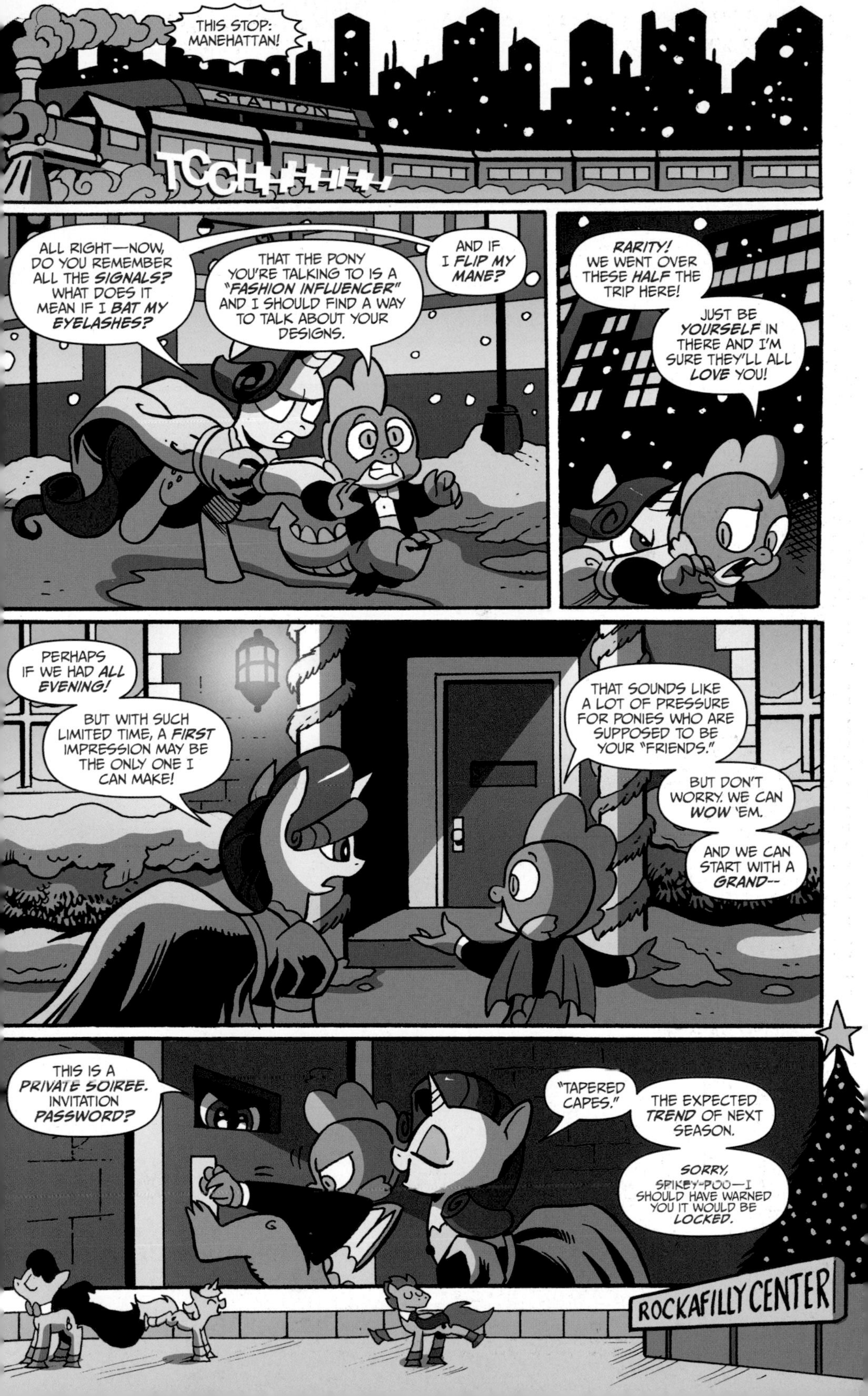
THIS STOP: MANEHATTAN!
STATION
TCCHHHHHHH!
ALL RIGHT—NOW, DO YOU REMEMBER ALL THE *SIGNALS?* WHAT DOES IT MEAN IF I *BAT MY EYELASHES?*
THAT THE PONY YOU'RE TALKING TO IS A *"FASHION INFLUENCER"* AND I SHOULD FIND A WAY TO TALK ABOUT YOUR DESIGNS.
AND IF I *FLIP MY MANE?*
RARITY! WE WENT OVER THESE *HALF* THE TRIP HERE!
JUST BE *YOURSELF* IN THERE AND I'M SURE THEY'LL ALL *LOVE* YOU!
PERHAPS IF WE HAD *ALL EVENING!*
BUT WITH SUCH LIMITED TIME, A *FIRST* IMPRESSION MAY BE THE ONLY ONE I CAN MAKE!
THAT SOUNDS LIKE A LOT OF PRESSURE FOR PONIES WHO ARE SUPPOSED TO BE YOUR "FRIENDS."
BUT DON'T WORRY. WE CAN *WOW* 'EM.
AND WE CAN START WITH A *GRAND--*
THIS IS A *PRIVATE SOIREE.* INVITATION *PASSWORD?*
"TAPERED CAPES."
THE EXPECTED *TREND* OF NEXT SEASON.
SORRY, SPIKEY-POO—I SHOULD HAVE WARNED YOU IT WOULD BE *LOCKED.*
ROCKAFILLY CENTER

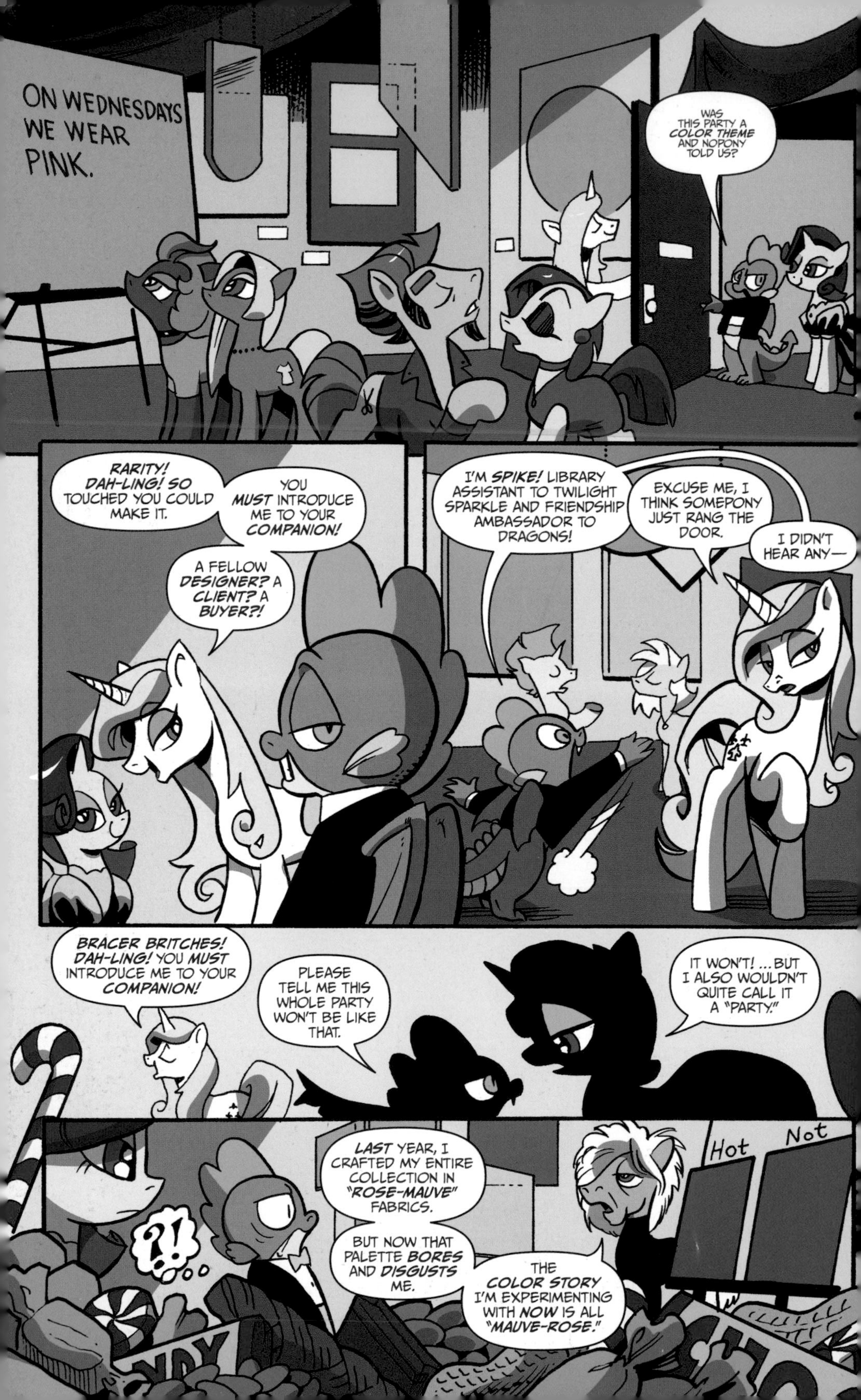

ON WEDNESDAYS WE WEAR PINK.
WAS THIS PARTY A COLOR THEME AND NOPONY TOLD US?
RARITY! DAH-LING! SO TOUCHED YOU COULD MAKE IT.
YOU MUST INTRODUCE ME TO YOUR COMPANION!
A FELLOW DESIGNER? A CLIENT? A BUYER?!
I'M SPIKE! LIBRARY ASSISTANT TO TWILIGHT SPARKLE AND FRIENDSHIP AMBASSADOR TO DRAGONS!
EXCUSE ME, I THINK SOMEPONY JUST RANG THE DOOR.
I DIDN'T HEAR ANY—
BRACER BRITCHES! DAH-LING! YOU MUST INTRODUCE ME TO YOUR COMPANION!
PLEASE TELL ME THIS WHOLE PARTY WON'T BE LIKE THAT.
IT WON'T! ...BUT I ALSO WOULDN'T QUITE CALL IT A "PARTY."
?!
Hot
Not
LAST YEAR, I CRAFTED MY ENTIRE COLLECTION IN "ROSE-MAUVE" FABRICS.
BUT NOW THAT PALETTE BORES AND DISGUSTS ME.
THE COLOR STORY I'M EXPERIMENTING WITH NOW IS ALL "MAUVE-ROSE."

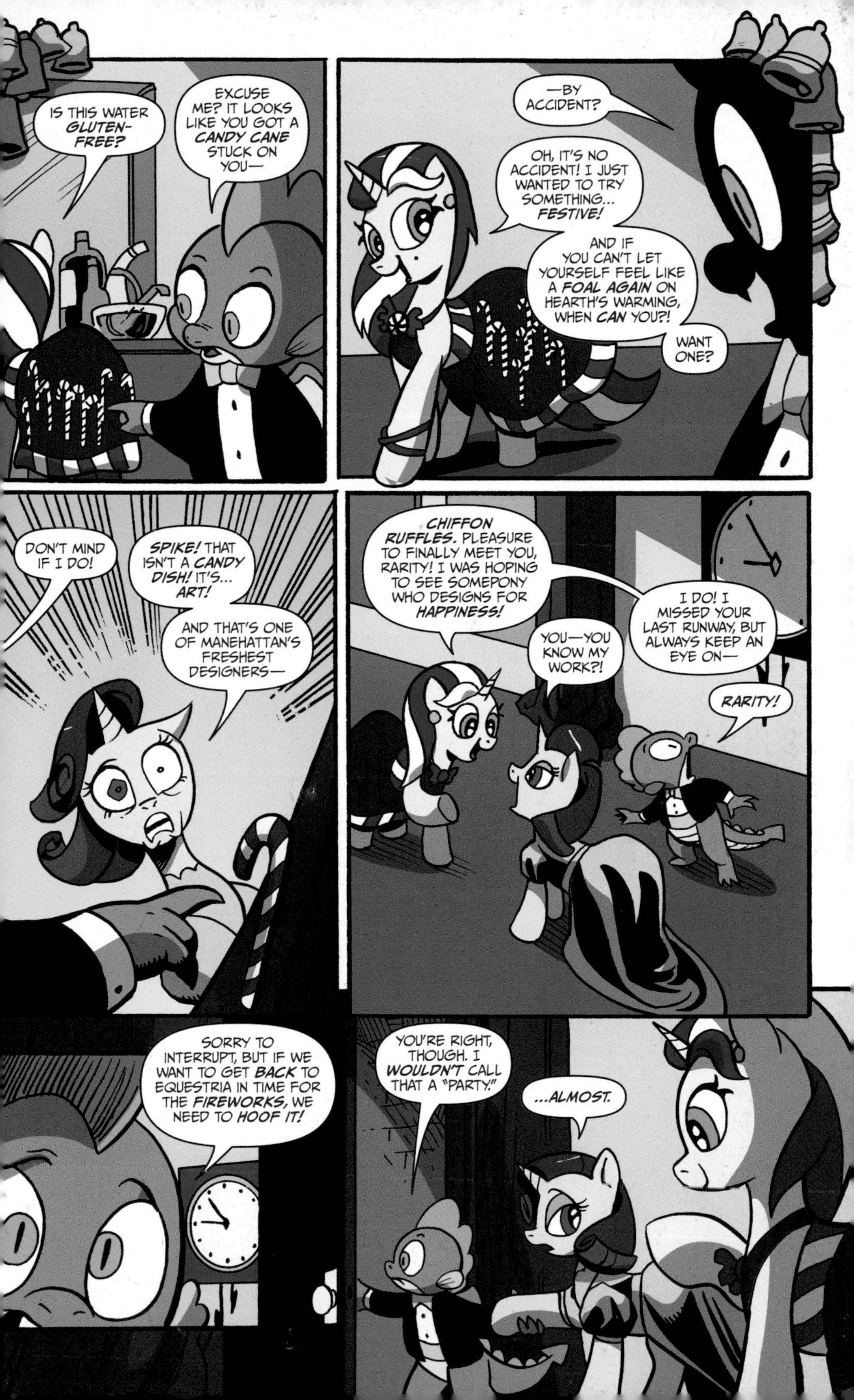
IS THIS WATER GLUTEN-FREE?
EXCUSE ME? IT LOOKS LIKE YOU GOT A CANDY CANE STUCK ON YOU—
—BY ACCIDENT?
OH, IT'S NO ACCIDENT! I JUST WANTED TO TRY SOMETHING... FESTIVE!
AND IF YOU CAN'T LET YOURSELF FEEL LIKE A FOAL AGAIN ON HEARTH'S WARMING, WHEN CAN YOU?!
WANT ONE?
DON'T MIND IF I DO!
SPIKE! THAT ISN'T A CANDY DISH! IT'S... ART!
AND THAT'S ONE OF MANEHATTAN'S FRESHEST DESIGNERS—
CHIFFON RUFFLES. PLEASURE TO FINALLY MEET YOU, RARITY! I WAS HOPING TO SEE SOMEPONY WHO DESIGNS FOR HAPPINESS!
YOU—YOU KNOW MY WORK?!
I DO! I MISSED YOUR LAST RUNWAY, BUT ALWAYS KEEP AN EYE ON—
RARITY!
SORRY TO INTERRUPT, BUT IF WE WANT TO GET BACK TO EQUESTRIA IN TIME FOR THE FIREWORKS, WE NEED TO HOOF IT!
YOU'RE RIGHT, THOUGH. I WOULDN'T CALL THAT A "PARTY."
...ALMOST.

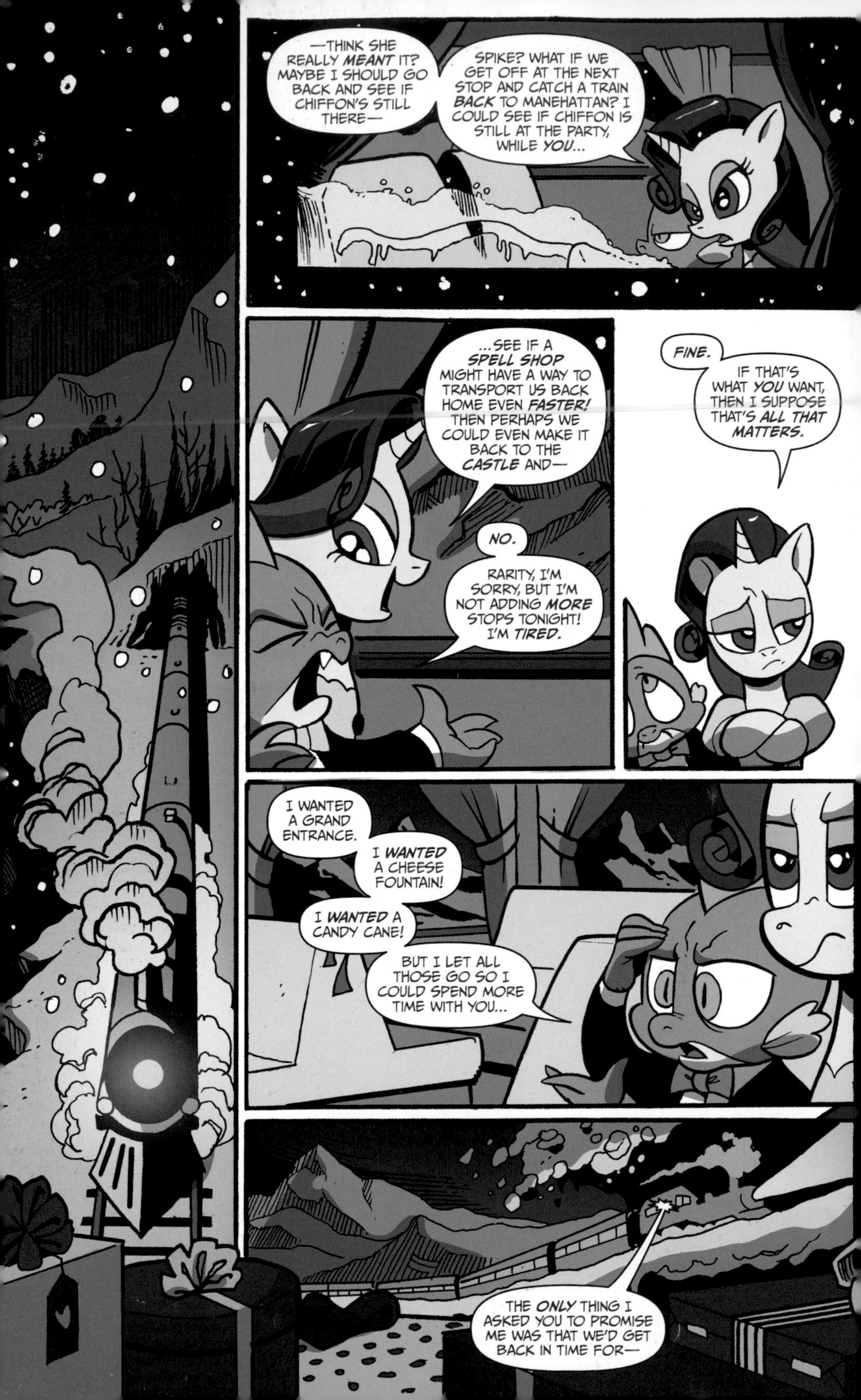
—THINK SHE REALLY *MEANT* IT? MAYBE I SHOULD GO BACK AND SEE IF CHIFFON'S STILL THERE—
SPIKE? WHAT IF WE GET OFF AT THE NEXT STOP AND CATCH A TRAIN *BACK* TO MANEHATTAN? I COULD SEE IF CHIFFON IS STILL AT THE PARTY, WHILE *YOU*...
...SEE IF A *SPELL SHOP* MIGHT HAVE A WAY TO TRANSPORT US BACK HOME EVEN *FASTER!* THEN PERHAPS WE COULD EVEN MAKE IT BACK TO THE *CASTLE* AND—
NO.
RARITY, I'M SORRY, BUT I'M NOT ADDING *MORE* STOPS TONIGHT! I'M *TIRED.*
FINE.
IF THAT'S WHAT *YOU* WANT, THEN I SUPPOSE THAT'S *ALL THAT MATTERS.*
I WANTED A GRAND ENTRANCE.
I *WANTED* A CHEESE FOUNTAIN!
I *WANTED* A CANDY CANE!
BUT I LET ALL THOSE GO SO I COULD SPEND MORE TIME WITH YOU...
THE *ONLY* THING I ASKED YOU TO PROMISE ME WAS THAT WE'D GET BACK IN TIME FOR—

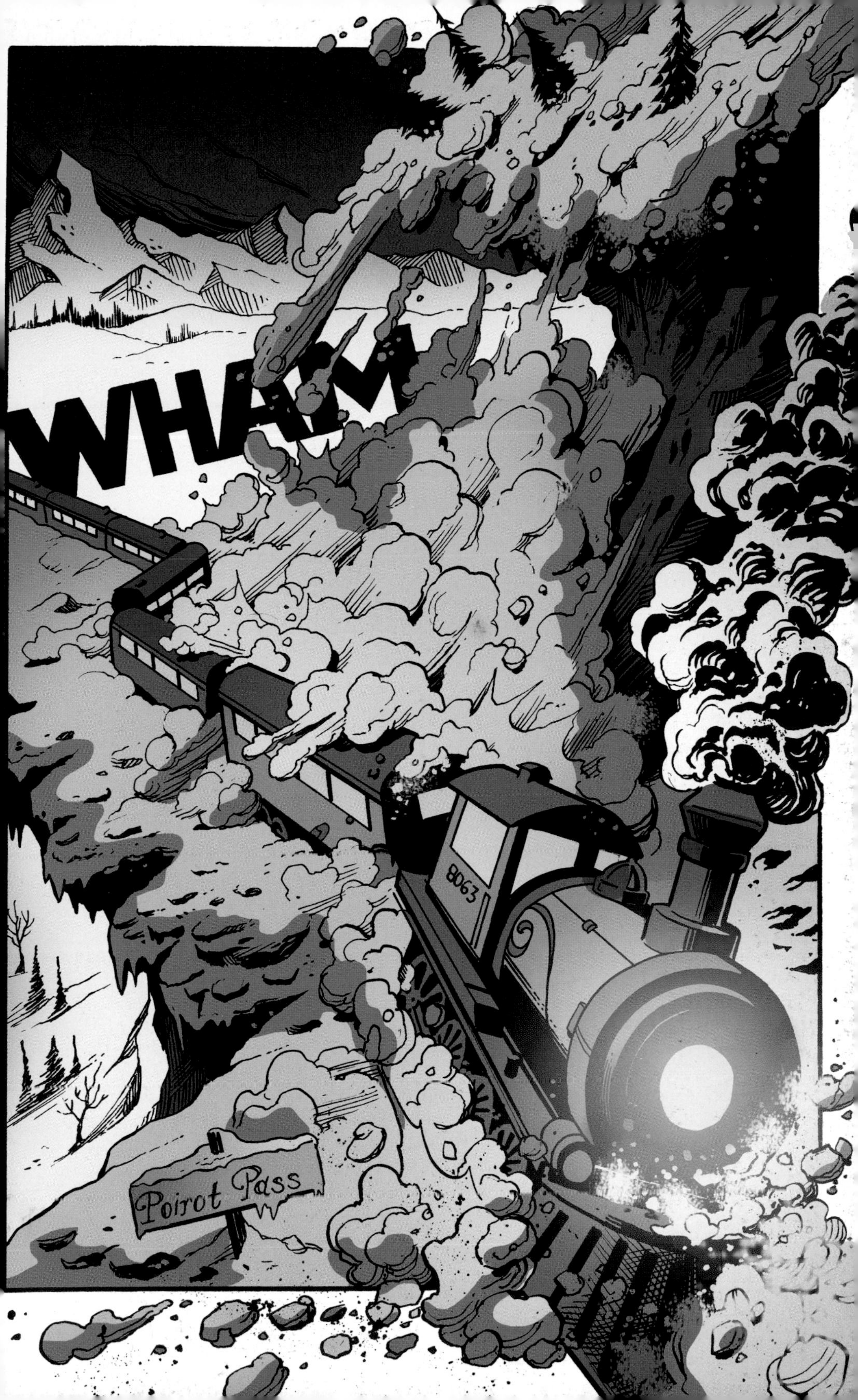
WHAM
8063
Poirot Pass

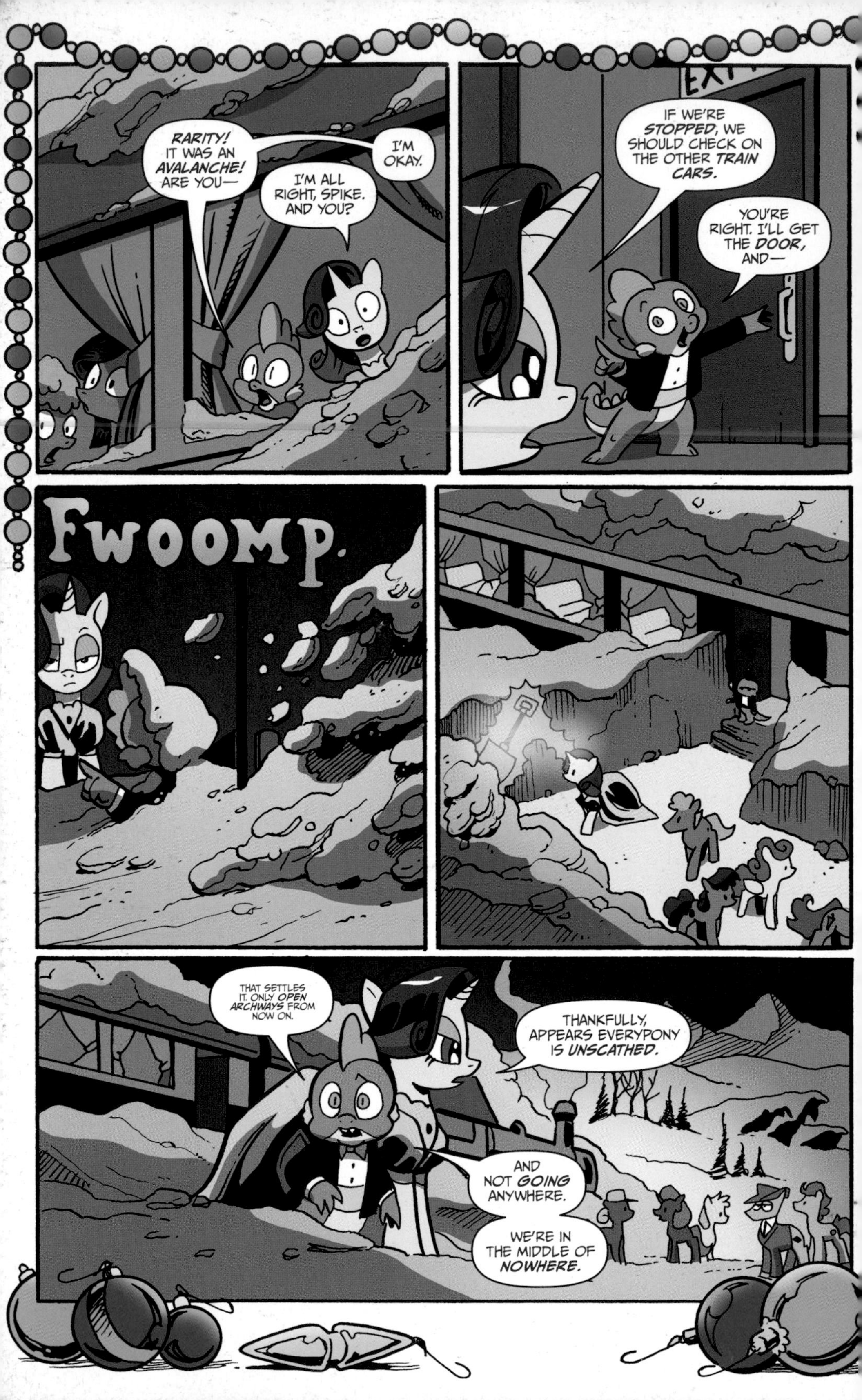
RARITY! IT WAS AN AVALANCHE! ARE YOU—
I'M OKAY.
I'M ALL RIGHT, SPIKE. AND YOU?
EXIT
IF WE'RE STOPPED, WE SHOULD CHECK ON THE OTHER TRAIN CARS.
YOU'RE RIGHT. I'LL GET THE DOOR, AND—
FWOOMP.
THAT SETTLES IT. ONLY OPEN ARCHWAYS FROM NOW ON.
THANKFULLY, APPEARS EVERYPONY IS UNSCATHED.
AND NOT GOING ANYWHERE.
WE'RE IN THE MIDDLE OF NOWHERE.

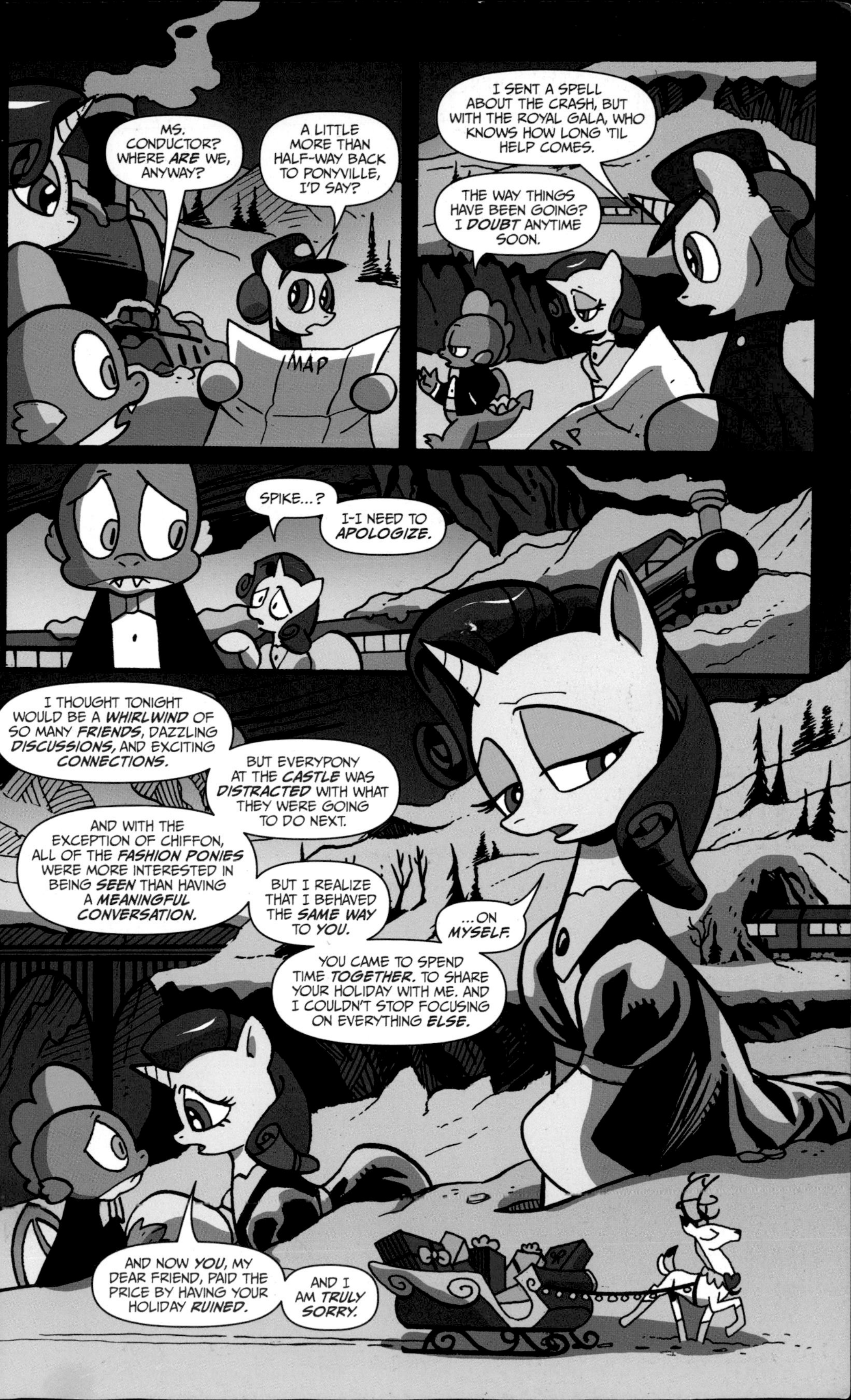
MS. CONDUCTOR? WHERE ARE WE, ANYWAY?
A LITTLE MORE THAN HALF-WAY BACK TO PONYVILLE, I'D SAY?
MAP
I SENT A SPELL ABOUT THE CRASH, BUT WITH THE ROYAL GALA, WHO KNOWS HOW LONG 'TIL HELP COMES.
THE WAY THINGS HAVE BEEN GOING? I DOUBT ANYTIME SOON.
SPIKE...?
I-I NEED TO APOLOGIZE.
I THOUGHT TONIGHT WOULD BE A WHIRLWIND OF SO MANY FRIENDS, DAZZLING DISCUSSIONS, AND EXCITING CONNECTIONS.
BUT EVERYPONY AT THE CASTLE WAS DISTRACTED WITH WHAT THEY WERE GOING TO DO NEXT.
AND WITH THE EXCEPTION OF CHIFFON, ALL OF THE FASHION PONIES WERE MORE INTERESTED IN BEING SEEN THAN HAVING A MEANINGFUL CONVERSATION.
BUT I REALIZE THAT I BEHAVED THE SAME WAY TO YOU.
...ON MYSELF.
YOU CAME TO SPEND TIME TOGETHER. TO SHARE YOUR HOLIDAY WITH ME. AND I COULDN'T STOP FOCUSING ON EVERYTHING ELSE.
AND NOW YOU, MY DEAR FRIEND, PAID THE PRICE BY HAVING YOUR HOLIDAY RUINED.
AND I AM TRULY SORRY.

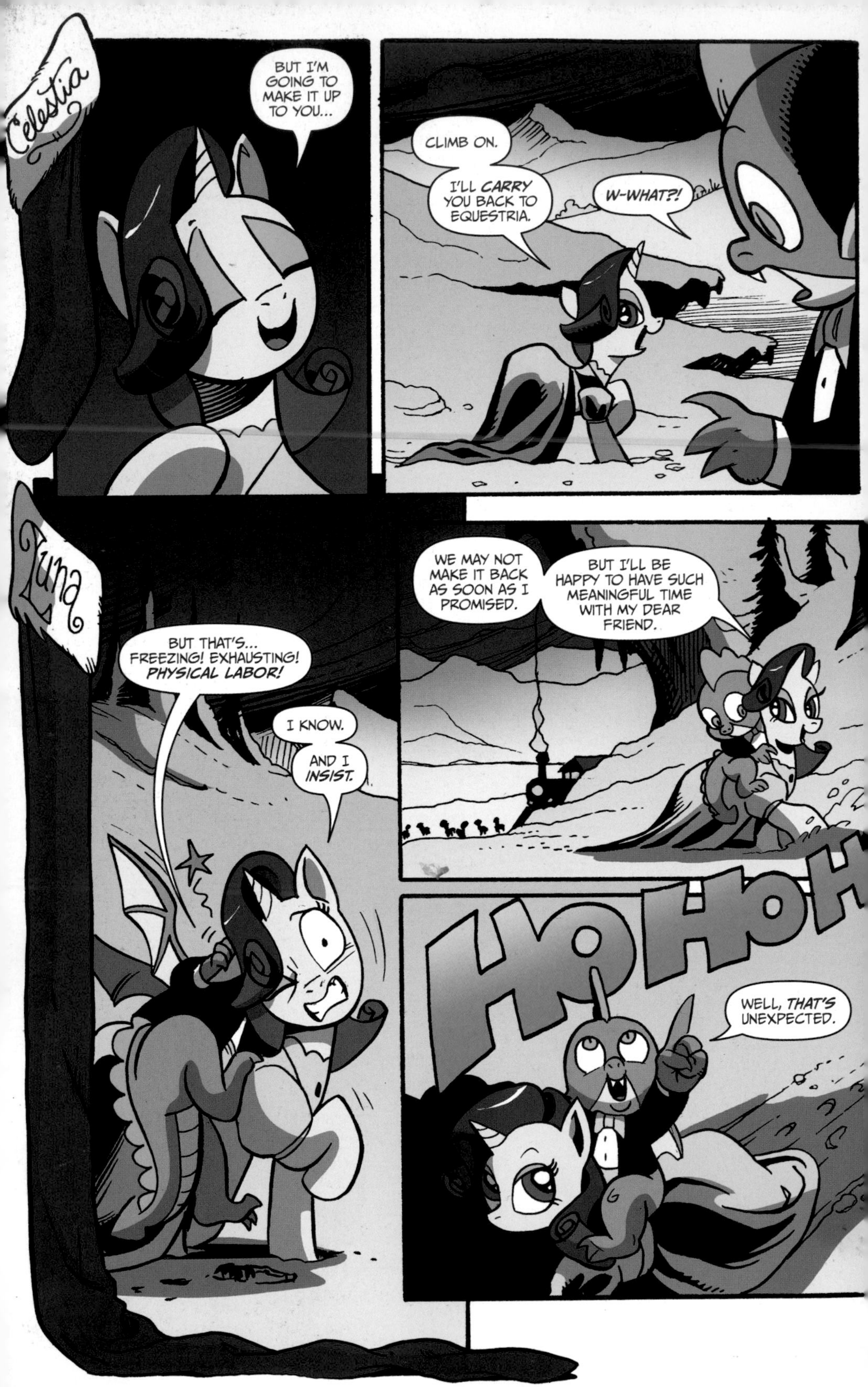
Celestia
BUT I'M GOING TO MAKE IT UP TO YOU...
CLIMB ON.
I'LL *CARRY* YOU BACK TO EQUESTRIA.
W-WHAT?!
Luna
BUT THAT'S... FREEZING! EXHAUSTING! *PHYSICAL LABOR!*
I KNOW.
AND I *INSIST.*
WE MAY NOT MAKE IT BACK AS SOON AS I PROMISED.
BUT I'LL BE HAPPY TO HAVE SUCH MEANINGFUL TIME WITH MY DEAR FRIEND.
HOHOHOH
WELL, *THAT'S* UNEXPECTED.

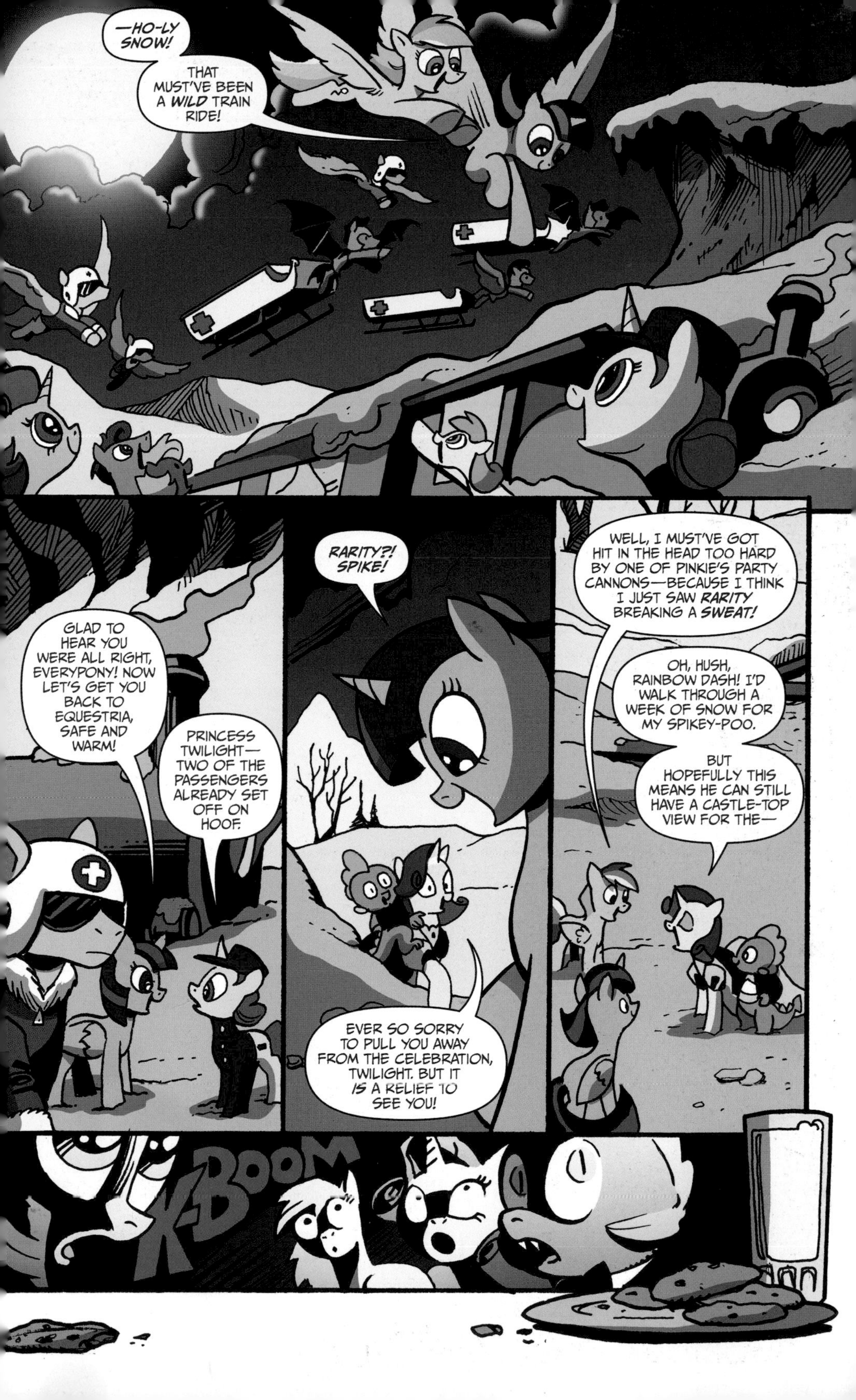
—HO-LY SNOW!
THAT MUST'VE BEEN A WILD TRAIN RIDE!
GLAD TO HEAR YOU WERE ALL RIGHT, EVERYPONY! NOW LET'S GET YOU BACK TO EQUESTRIA, SAFE AND WARM!
PRINCESS TWILIGHT— TWO OF THE PASSENGERS ALREADY SET OFF ON HOOF.
RARITY?! SPIKE!
EVER SO SORRY TO PULL YOU AWAY FROM THE CELEBRATION, TWILIGHT. BUT IT IS A RELIEF TO SEE YOU!
WELL, I MUST'VE GOT HIT IN THE HEAD TOO HARD BY ONE OF PINKIE'S PARTY CANNONS—BECAUSE I THINK I JUST SAW RARITY BREAKING A SWEAT!
OH, HUSH, RAINBOW DASH! I'D WALK THROUGH A WEEK OF SNOW FOR MY SPIKEY-POO.
BUT HOPEFULLY THIS MEANS HE CAN STILL HAVE A CASTLE-TOP VIEW FOR THE—
K-BOOM

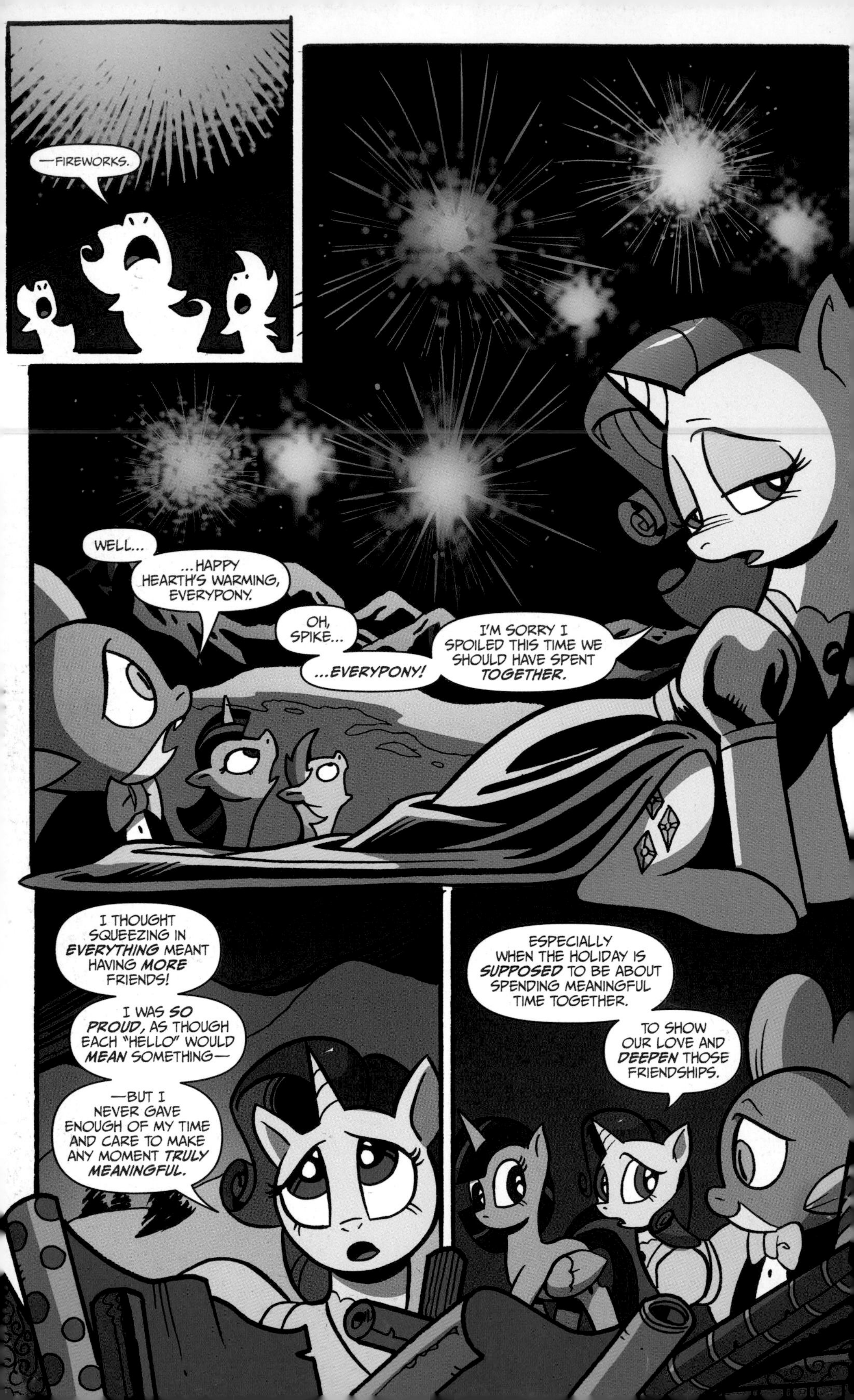
—FIREWORKS.
WELL...
...HAPPY HEARTH'S WARMING, EVERYPONY.
OH, SPIKE...
...EVERYPONY!
I'M SORRY I SPOILED THIS TIME WE SHOULD HAVE SPENT TOGETHER.
I THOUGHT SQUEEZING IN EVERYTHING MEANT HAVING MORE FRIENDS!
I WAS SO PROUD, AS THOUGH EACH "HELLO" WOULD MEAN SOMETHING—
—BUT I NEVER GAVE ENOUGH OF MY TIME AND CARE TO MAKE ANY MOMENT TRULY MEANINGFUL.
ESPECIALLY WHEN THE HOLIDAY IS SUPPOSED TO BE ABOUT SPENDING MEANINGFUL TIME TOGETHER.
TO SHOW OUR LOVE AND DEEPEN THOSE FRIENDSHIPS.

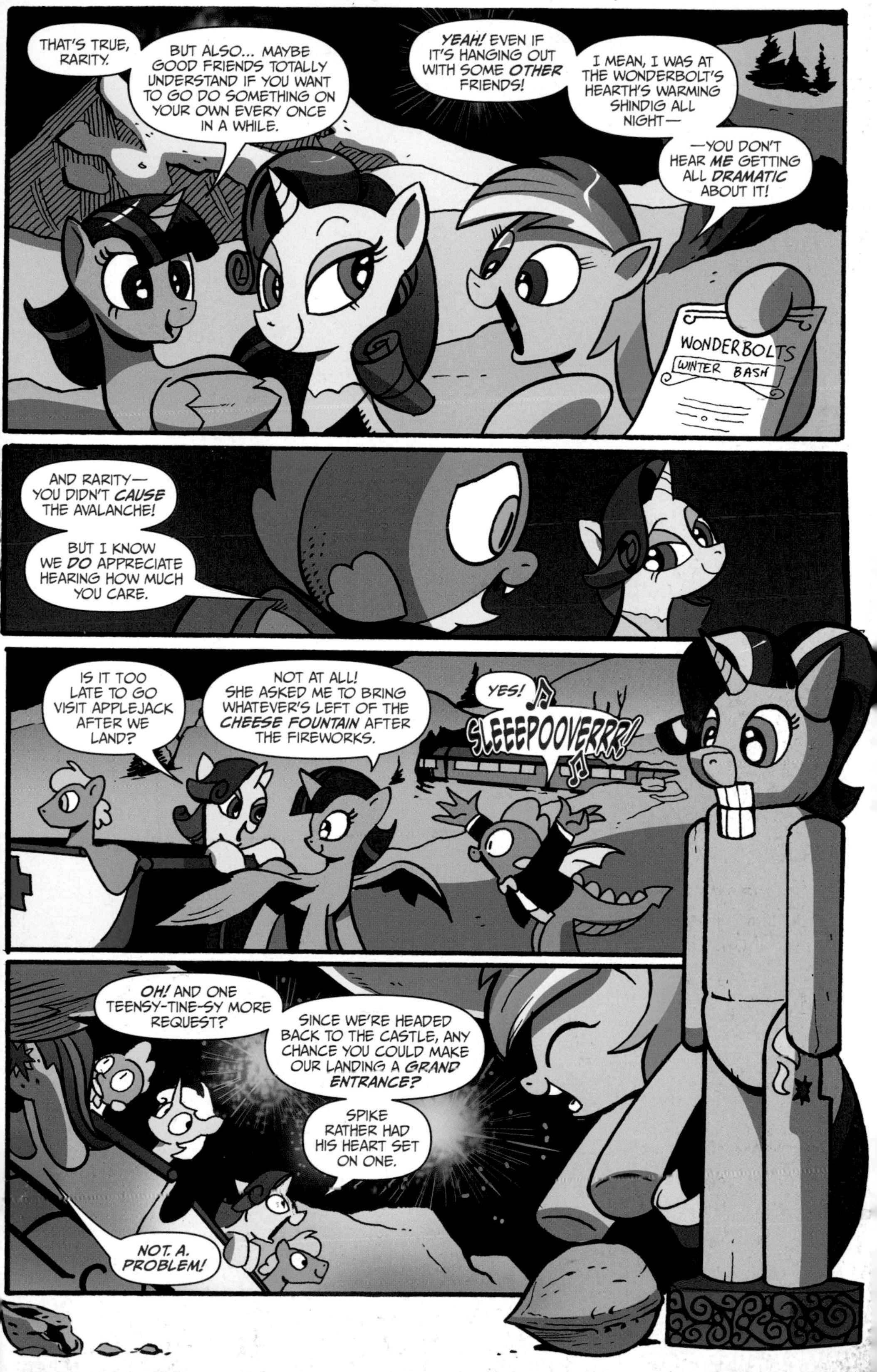
THAT'S TRUE, RARITY.
BUT ALSO... MAYBE GOOD FRIENDS TOTALLY UNDERSTAND IF YOU WANT TO GO DO SOMETHING ON YOUR OWN EVERY ONCE IN A WHILE.
YEAH! EVEN IF IT'S HANGING OUT WITH SOME OTHER FRIENDS!
I MEAN, I WAS AT THE WONDERBOLT'S HEARTH'S WARMING SHINDIG ALL NIGHT—
—YOU DON'T HEAR ME GETTING ALL DRAMATIC ABOUT IT!
WONDERBOLTS
WINTER BASH
AND RARITY— YOU DIDN'T CAUSE THE AVALANCHE!
BUT I KNOW WE DO APPRECIATE HEARING HOW MUCH YOU CARE.
IS IT TOO LATE TO GO VISIT APPLEJACK AFTER WE LAND?
NOT AT ALL! SHE ASKED ME TO BRING WHATEVER'S LEFT OF THE CHEESE FOUNTAIN AFTER THE FIREWORKS.
YES!
SLEEEPOOVERRR!
OH! AND ONE TEENSY-TINE-SY MORE REQUEST?
SINCE WE'RE HEADED BACK TO THE CASTLE, ANY CHANCE YOU COULD MAKE OUR LANDING A GRAND ENTRANCE?
SPIKE RATHER HAD HIS HEART SET ON ONE.
NOT. A. PROBLEM!

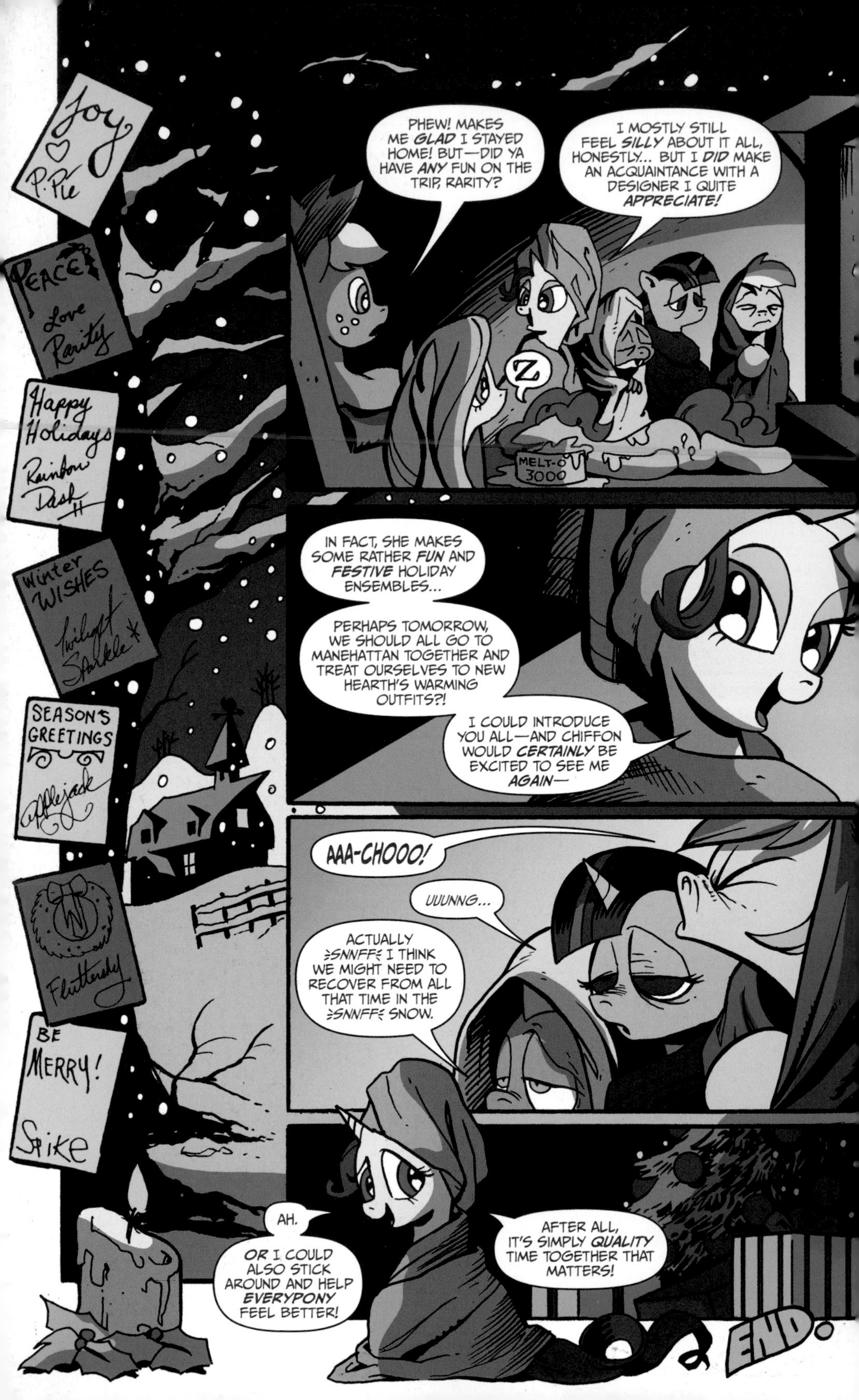
Joy ♡ P. Pie
Peace Love Rarity
Happy Holidays Rainbow Dash
Winter WISHES Twilight Sparkle
SEASON'S GREETINGS Applejack
Fluttershy
BE MERRY! Spike
PHEW! MAKES ME GLAD I STAYED HOME! BUT—DID YA HAVE ANY FUN ON THE TRIP, RARITY?
I MOSTLY STILL FEEL SILLY ABOUT IT ALL, HONESTLY... BUT I DID MAKE AN ACQUAINTANCE WITH A DESIGNER I QUITE APPRECIATE!
Z
MELT-O 3000
IN FACT, SHE MAKES SOME RATHER FUN AND FESTIVE HOLIDAY ENSEMBLES...
PERHAPS TOMORROW, WE SHOULD ALL GO TO MANEHATTAN TOGETHER AND TREAT OURSELVES TO NEW HEARTH'S WARMING OUTFITS?!
I COULD INTRODUCE YOU ALL—AND CHIFFON WOULD CERTAINLY BE EXCITED TO SEE ME AGAIN—
AAA-CHOOO!
UUUNNG...
ACTUALLY ≶SNNFF≷ I THINK WE MIGHT NEED TO RECOVER FROM ALL THAT TIME IN THE ≶SNNFF≷ SNOW.
AH.
OR I COULD ALSO STICK AROUND AND HELP EVERYPONY FEEL BETTER!
AFTER ALL, IT'S SIMPLY QUALITY TIME TOGETHER THAT MATTERS!
END.

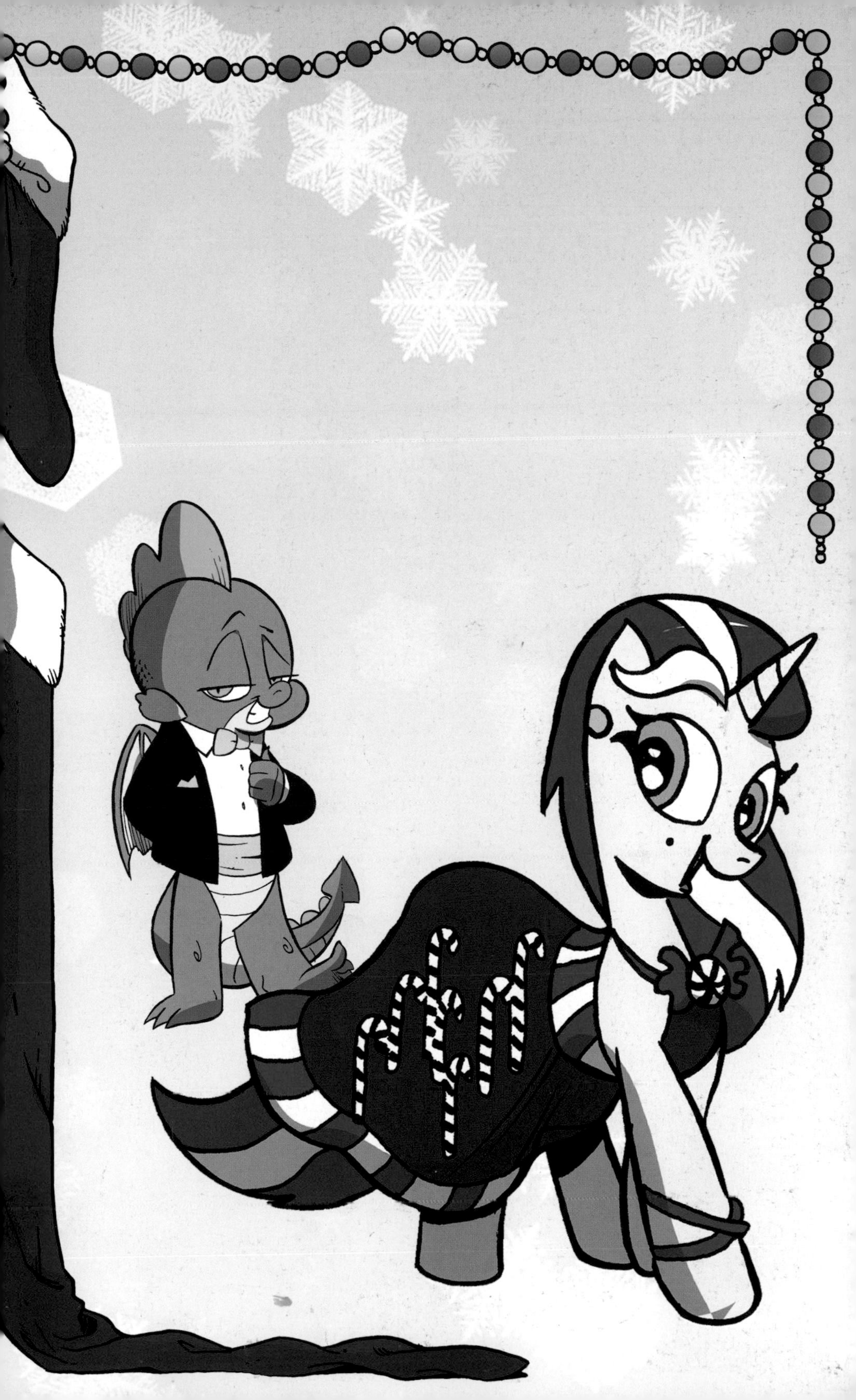

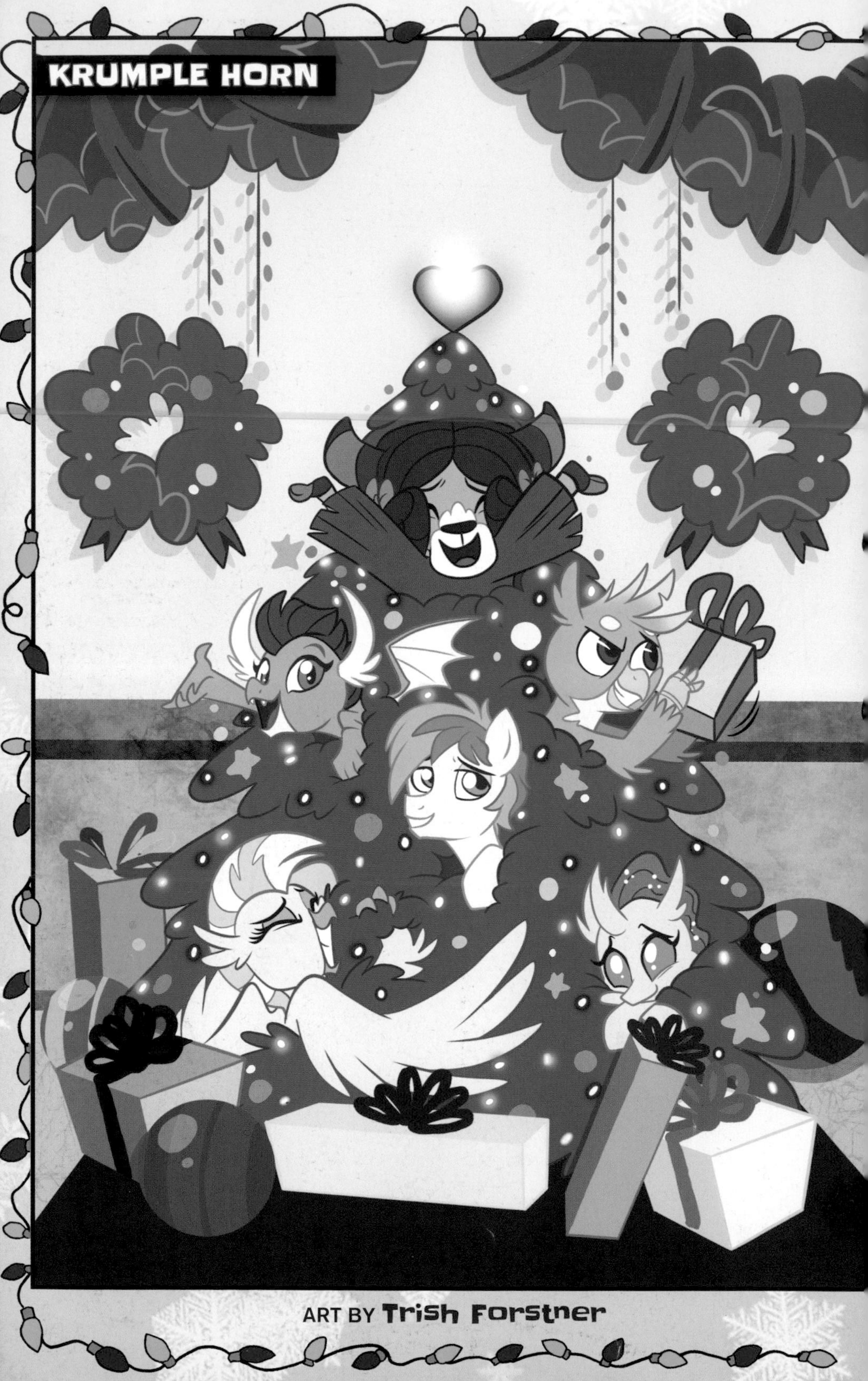
KRUMPLE HORN

ART BY Trish Forstner

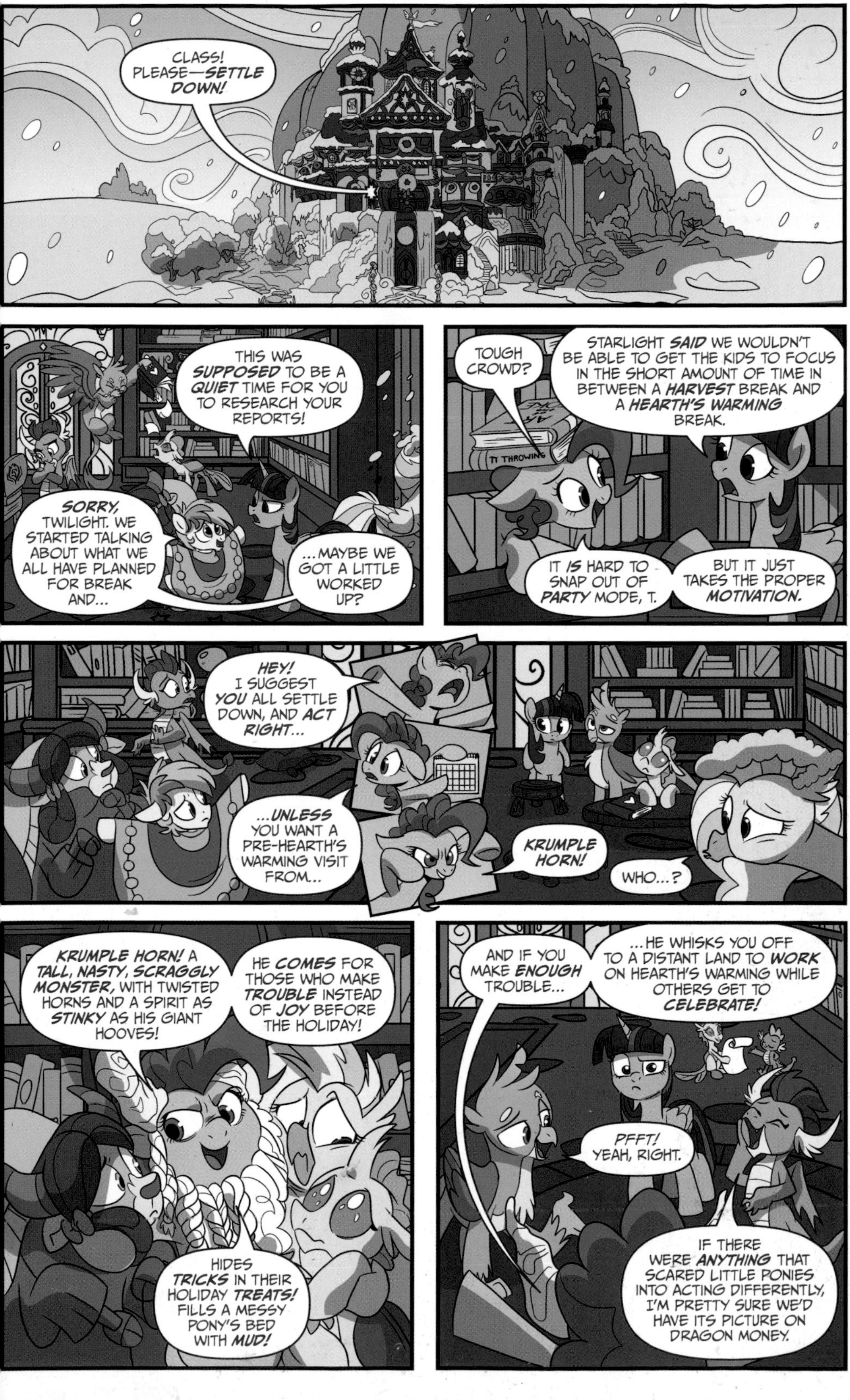
CLASS! PLEASE—SETTLE DOWN!
THIS WAS SUPPOSED TO BE A QUIET TIME FOR YOU TO RESEARCH YOUR REPORTS!
SORRY, TWILIGHT. WE STARTED TALKING ABOUT WHAT WE ALL HAVE PLANNED FOR BREAK AND...
...MAYBE WE GOT A LITTLE WORKED UP?
TOUGH CROWD?
STARLIGHT SAID WE WOULDN'T BE ABLE TO GET THE KIDS TO FOCUS IN THE SHORT AMOUNT OF TIME IN BETWEEN A HARVEST BREAK AND A HEARTH'S WARMING BREAK.
IT IS HARD TO SNAP OUT OF PARTY MODE, T.
BUT IT JUST TAKES THE PROPER MOTIVATION.
HEY! I SUGGEST YOU ALL SETTLE DOWN, AND ACT RIGHT...
...UNLESS YOU WANT A PRE-HEARTH'S WARMING VISIT FROM...
KRUMPLE HORN!
WHO...?
KRUMPLE HORN! A TALL, NASTY, SCRAGGLY MONSTER, WITH TWISTED HORNS AND A SPIRIT AS STINKY AS HIS GIANT HOOVES!
HE COMES FOR THOSE WHO MAKE TROUBLE INSTEAD OF JOY BEFORE THE HOLIDAY!
HIDES TRICKS IN THEIR HOLIDAY TREATS! FILLS A MESSY PONY'S BED WITH MUD!
AND IF YOU MAKE ENOUGH TROUBLE...
...HE WHISKS YOU OFF TO A DISTANT LAND TO WORK ON HEARTH'S WARMING WHILE OTHERS GET TO CELEBRATE!
PFFT! YEAH, RIGHT.
IF THERE WERE ANYTHING THAT SCARED LITTLE PONIES INTO ACTING DIFFERENTLY, I'M PRETTY SURE WE'D HAVE ITS PICTURE ON DRAGON MONEY.

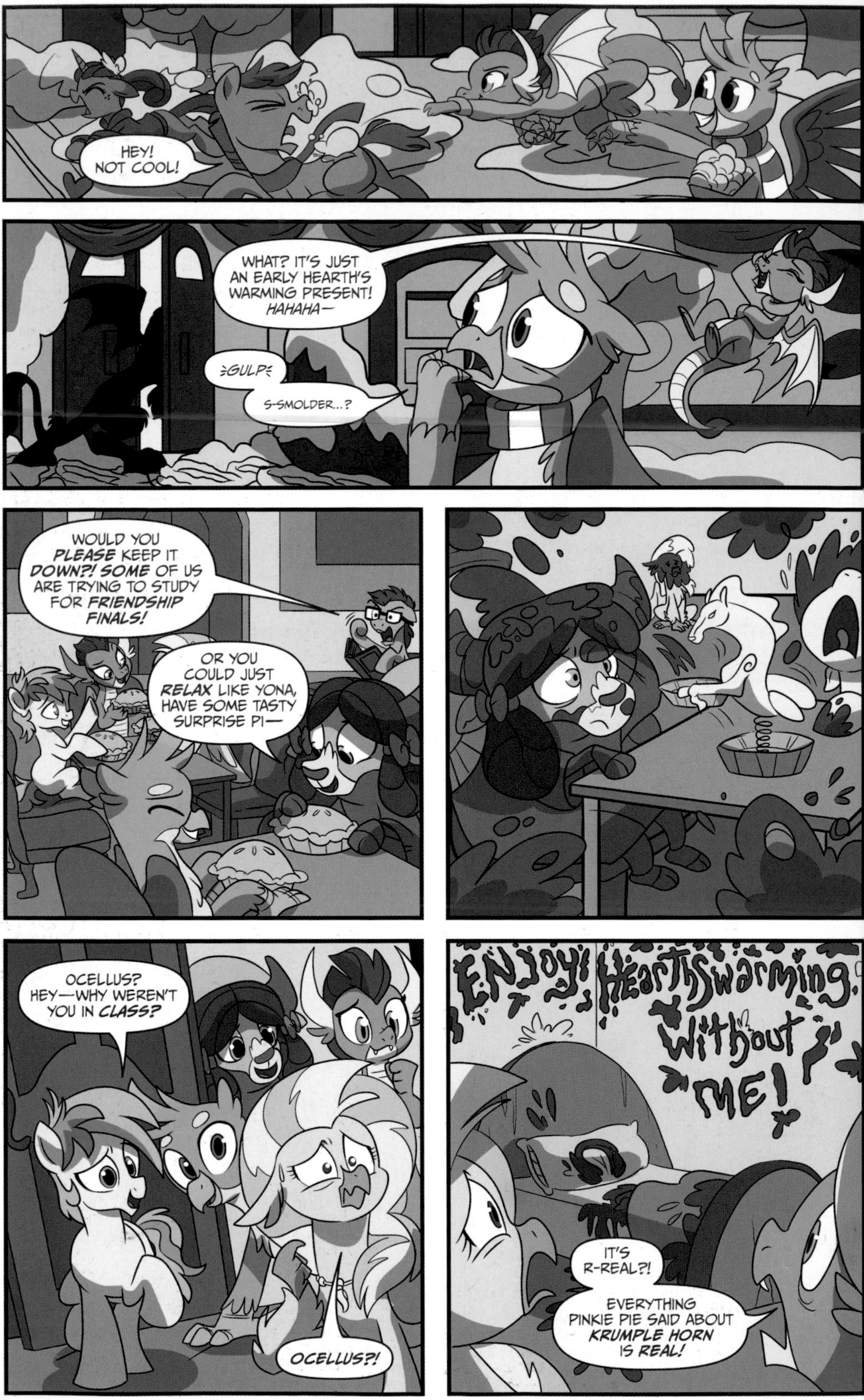
HEY!
NOT COOL!
WHAT? IT'S JUST AN EARLY HEARTH'S WARMING PRESENT! HAHAHA—
GULP
S-SMOLDER...?
WOULD YOU PLEASE KEEP IT DOWN?! SOME OF US ARE TRYING TO STUDY FOR FRIENDSHIP FINALS!
OR YOU COULD JUST RELAX LIKE YONA, HAVE SOME TASTY SURPRISE PI—
OCELLUS? HEY—WHY WEREN'T YOU IN CLASS?
OCELLUS?!
ENJOY HEARTHSWARMING WITHOUT ME!
IT'S R-REAL?!
EVERYTHING PINKIE PIE SAID ABOUT KRUMPLE HORN IS REAL!

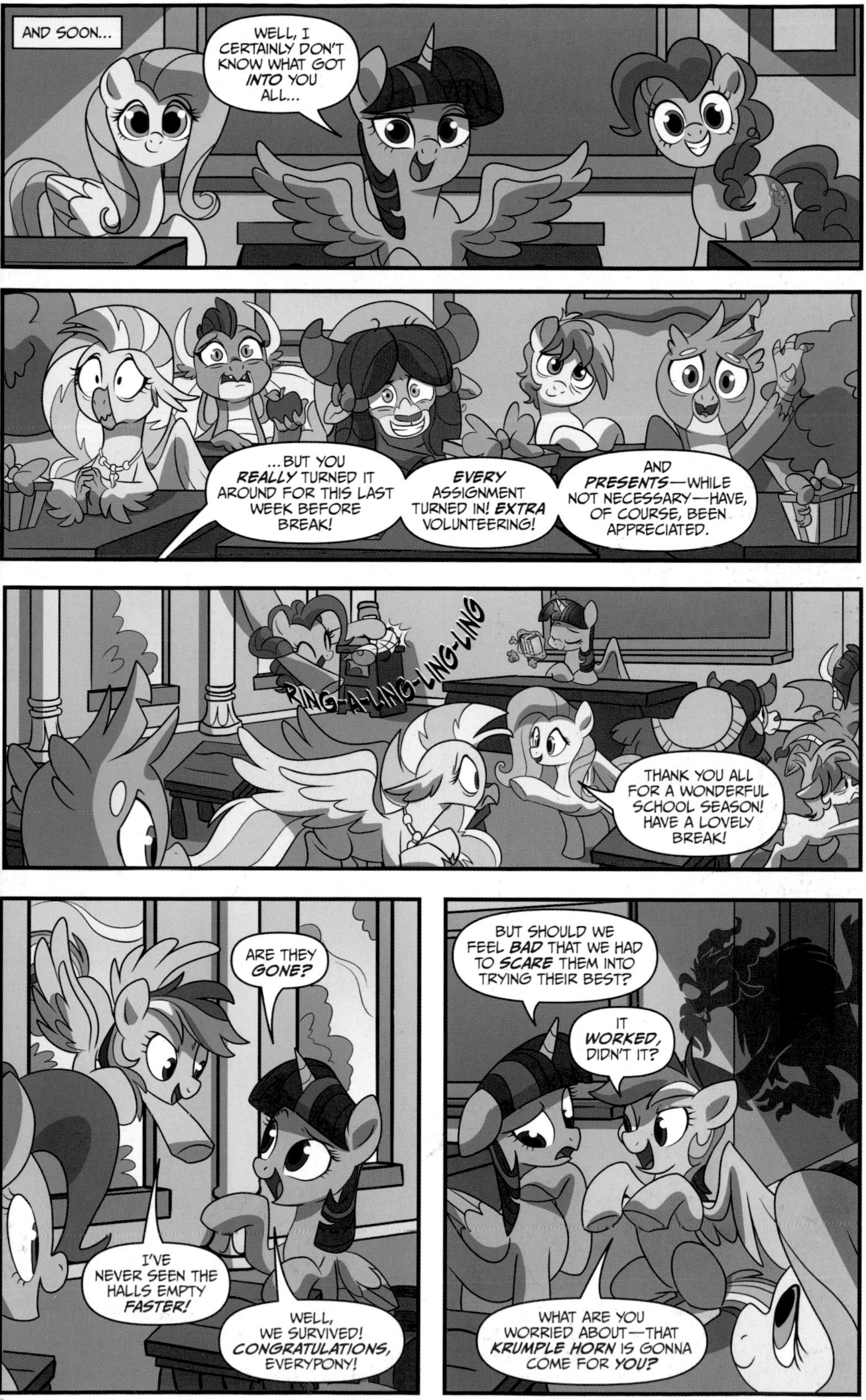
AND SOON...
WELL, I CERTAINLY DON'T KNOW WHAT GOT INTO YOU ALL...
...BUT YOU REALLY TURNED IT AROUND FOR THIS LAST WEEK BEFORE BREAK!
EVERY ASSIGNMENT TURNED IN! EXTRA VOLUNTEERING!
AND PRESENTS—WHILE NOT NECESSARY—HAVE, OF COURSE, BEEN APPRECIATED.
RING-A-LING-LING-LING
THANK YOU ALL FOR A WONDERFUL SCHOOL SEASON! HAVE A LOVELY BREAK!
ARE THEY GONE?
I'VE NEVER SEEN THE HALLS EMPTY FASTER!
WELL, WE SURVIVED! CONGRATULATIONS, EVERYPONY!
BUT SHOULD WE FEEL BAD THAT WE HAD TO SCARE THEM INTO TRYING THEIR BEST?
IT WORKED, DIDN'T IT?
WHAT ARE YOU WORRIED ABOUT—THAT KRUMPLE HORN IS GONNA COME FOR YOU?

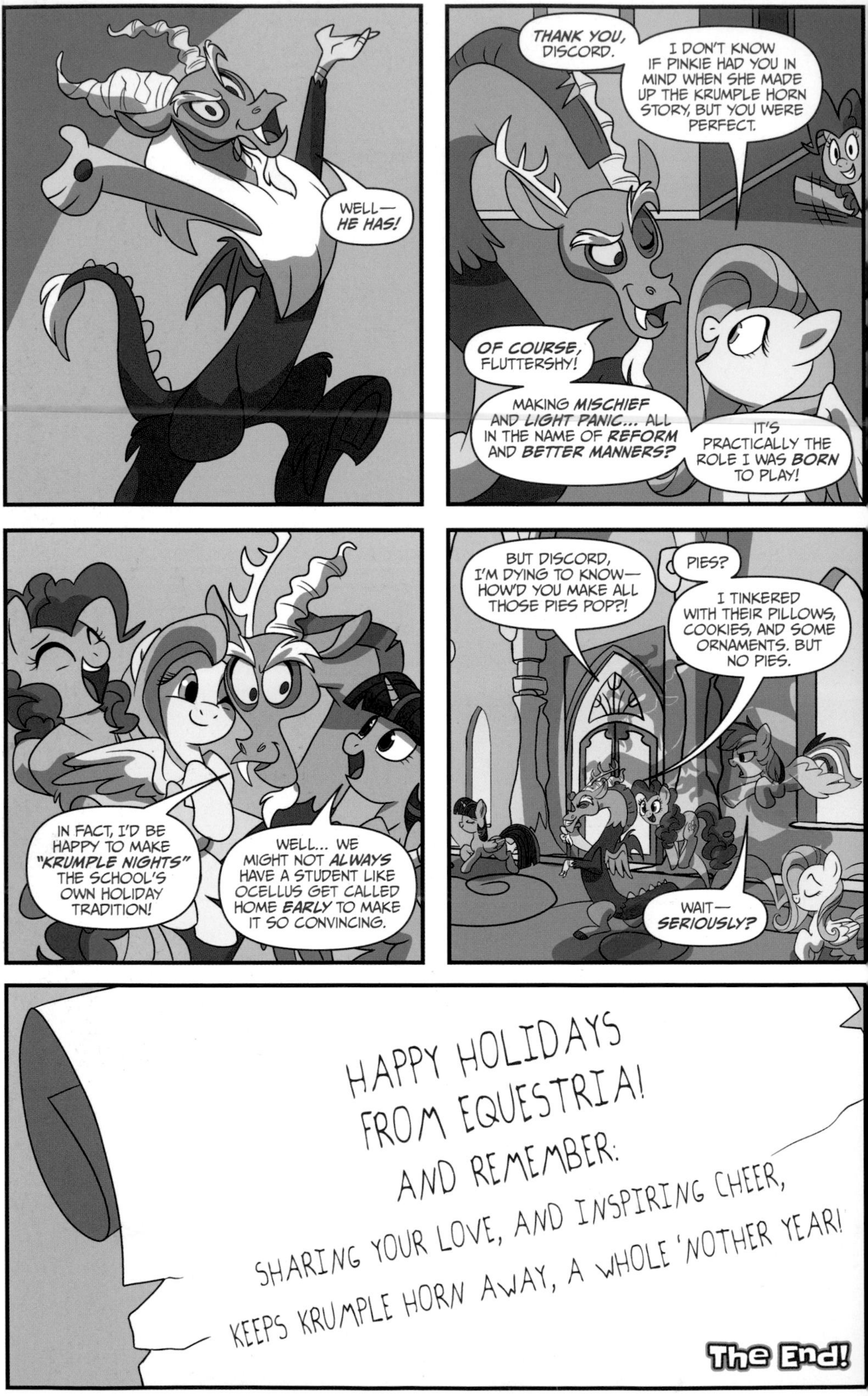
WELL—
HE HAS!
THANK YOU, DISCORD.
I DON'T KNOW IF PINKIE HAD YOU IN MIND WHEN SHE MADE UP THE KRUMPLE HORN STORY, BUT YOU WERE PERFECT.
OF COURSE, FLUTTERSHY!
MAKING MISCHIEF AND LIGHT PANIC... ALL IN THE NAME OF REFORM AND BETTER MANNERS?
IT'S PRACTICALLY THE ROLE I WAS BORN TO PLAY!
IN FACT, I'D BE HAPPY TO MAKE "KRUMPLE NIGHTS" THE SCHOOL'S OWN HOLIDAY TRADITION!
WELL... WE MIGHT NOT ALWAYS HAVE A STUDENT LIKE OCELLUS GET CALLED HOME EARLY TO MAKE IT SO CONVINCING.
BUT DISCORD, I'M DYING TO KNOW— HOW'D YOU MAKE ALL THOSE PIES POP?!
PIES?
I TINKERED WITH THEIR PILLOWS, COOKIES, AND SOME ORNAMENTS. BUT NO PIES.
WAIT— SERIOUSLY?
HAPPY HOLIDAYS FROM EQUESTRIA!
AND REMEMBER:
SHARING YOUR LOVE, AND INSPIRING CHEER,
KEEPS KRUMPLE HORN AWAY, A WHOLE 'NOTHER YEAR!
The End!

'Twas the
Night of Hearth's
Warming Eve

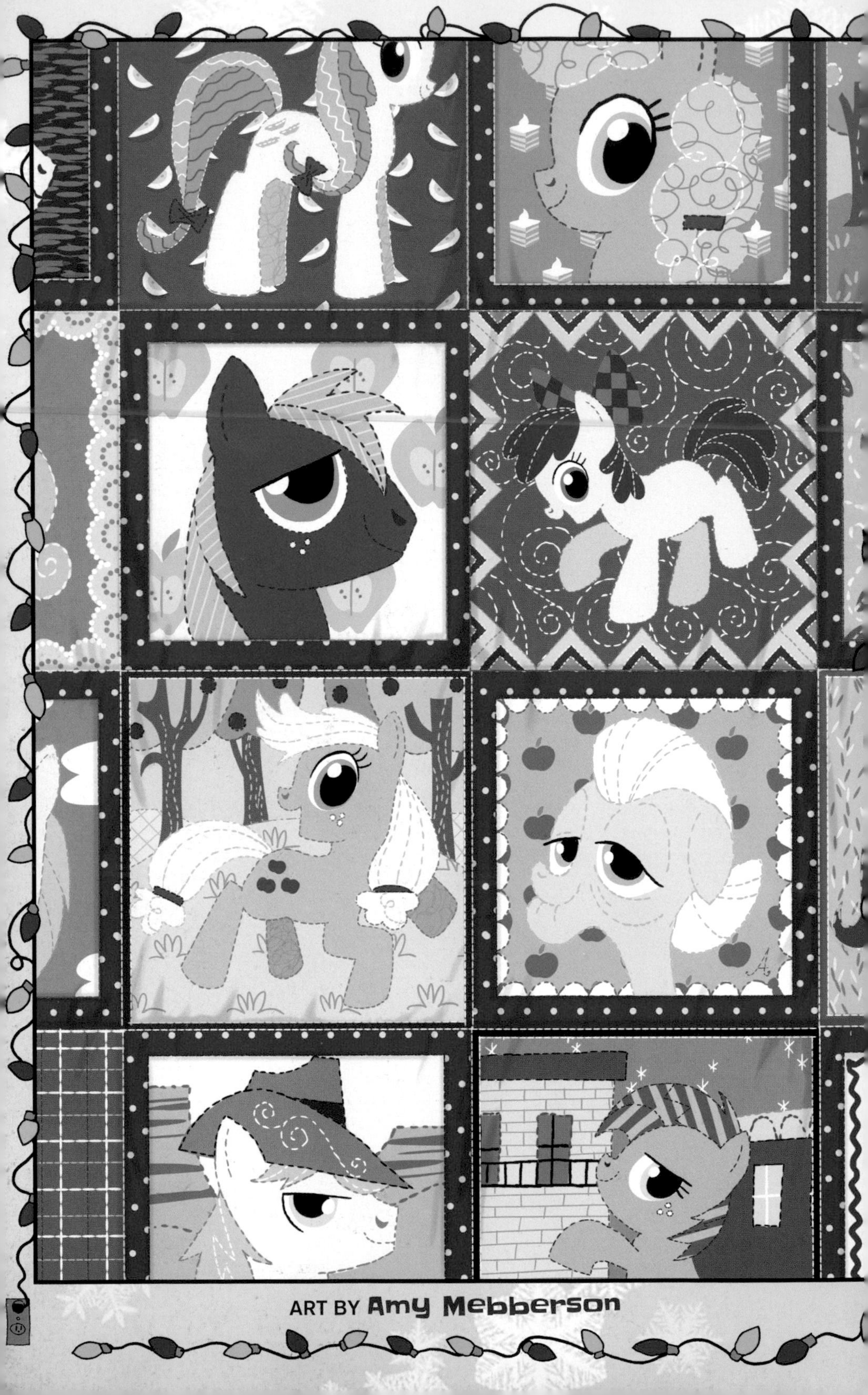

ART BY Amy Mebberson

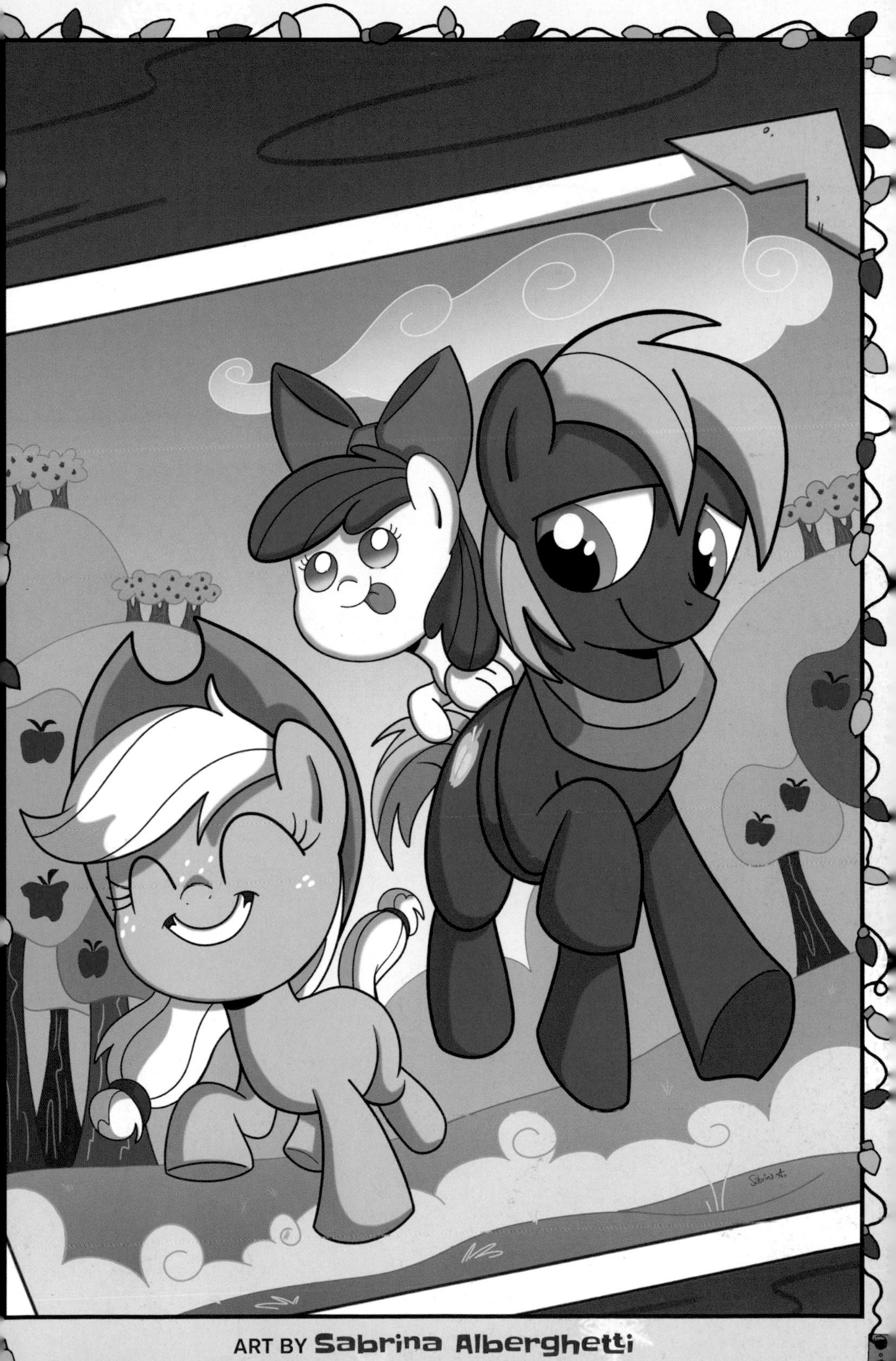
Sabrina A.

ART BY **Sabrina Alberghetti**

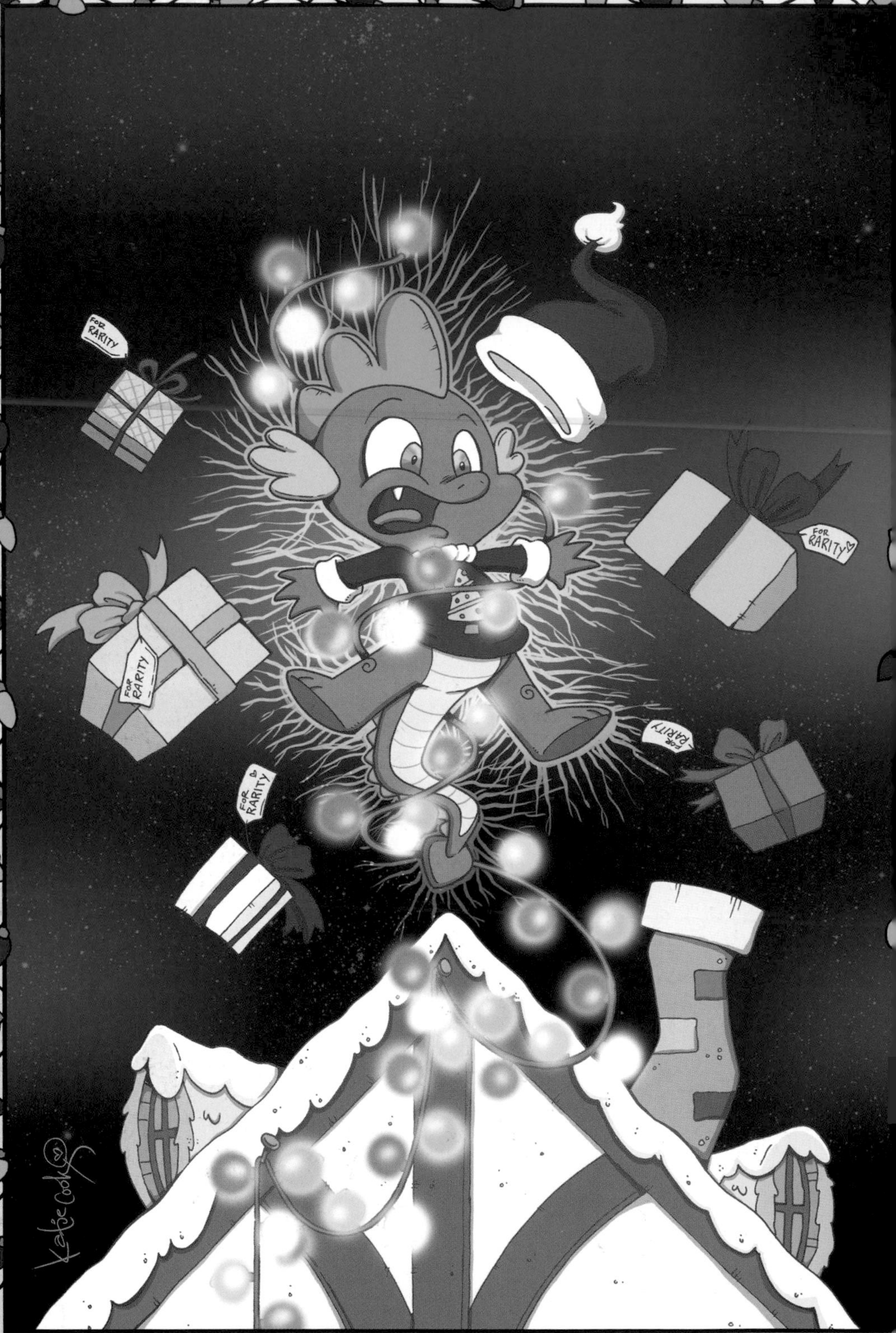
FOR RARITY
FOR RARITY
FOR RARITY
FOR RARITY
FOR RARITY
katie cook

ART BY Katie Cook

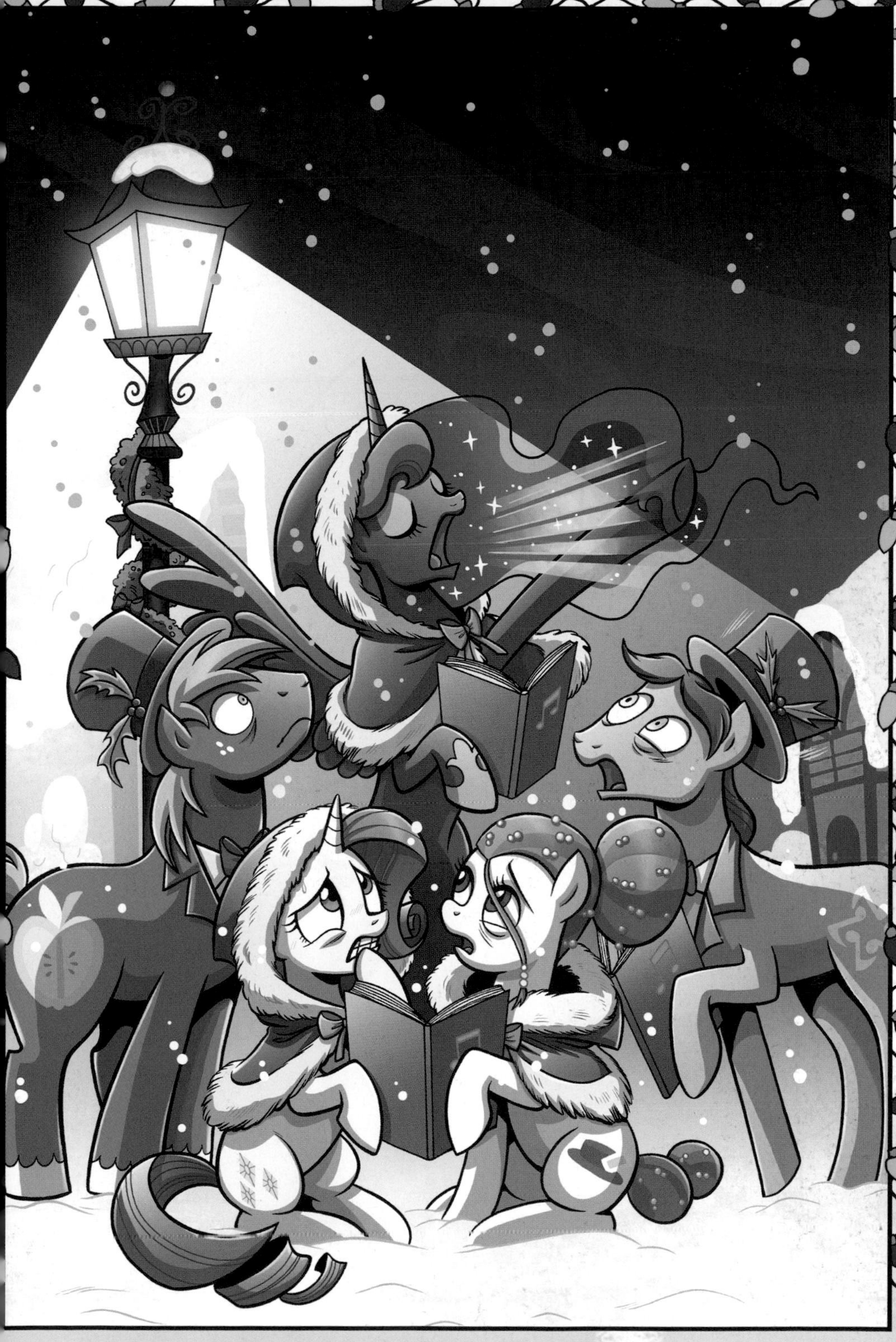

ART BY Brenda Hickey

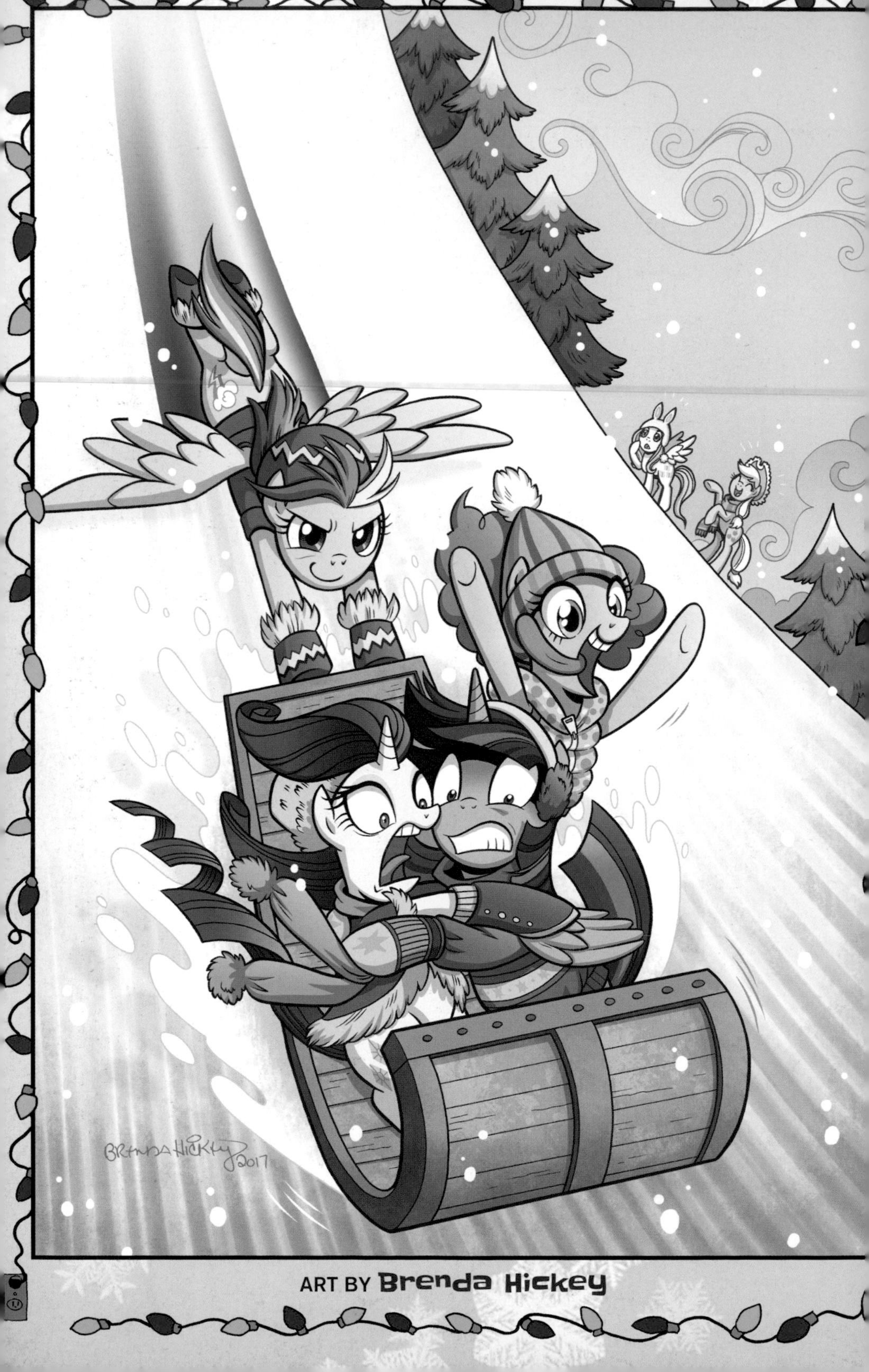
BRENDA HICKEY 2017

ART BY Brenda Hickey

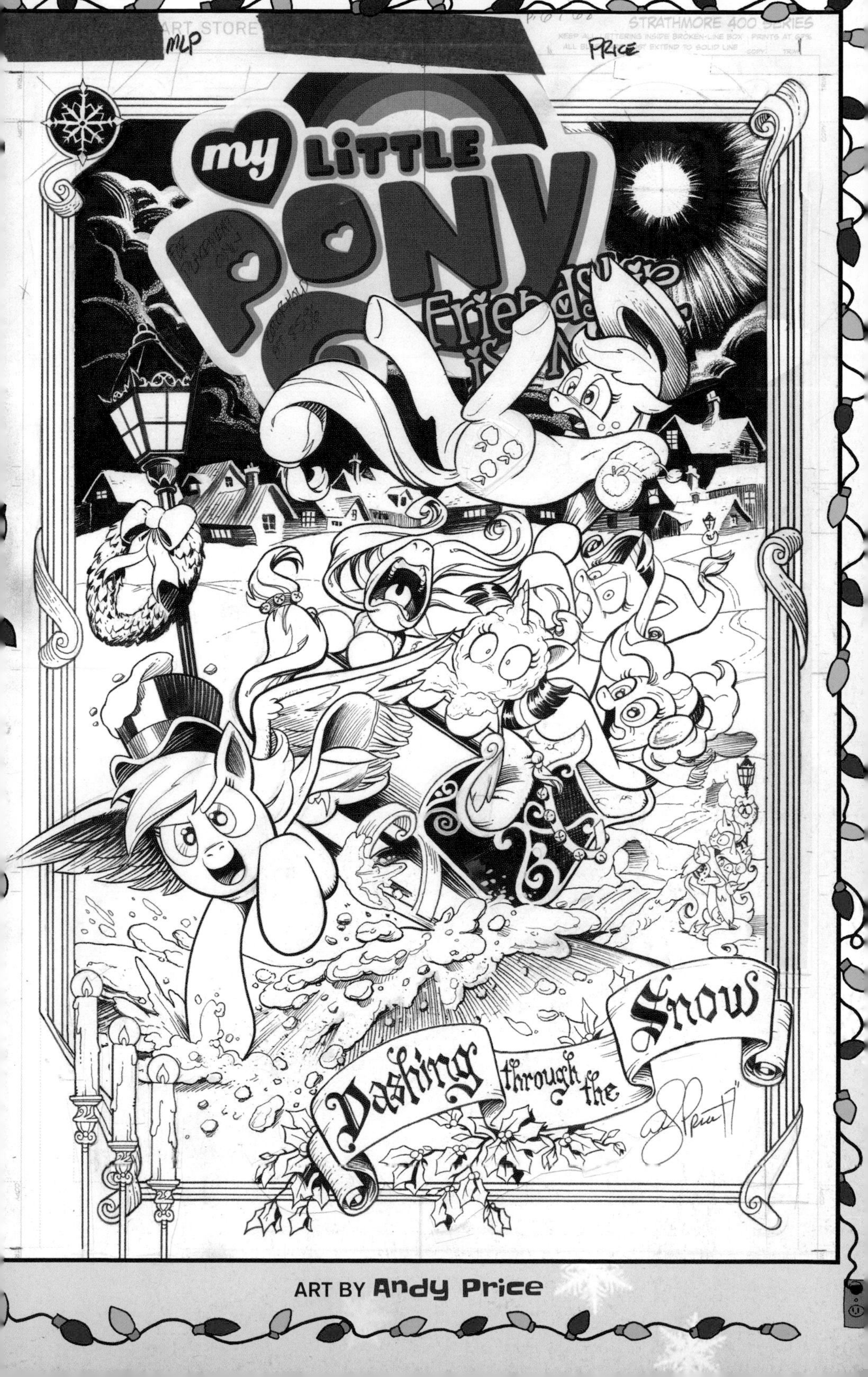
my LITTLE PONY
Dashing through the Snow

ART BY Andy Price

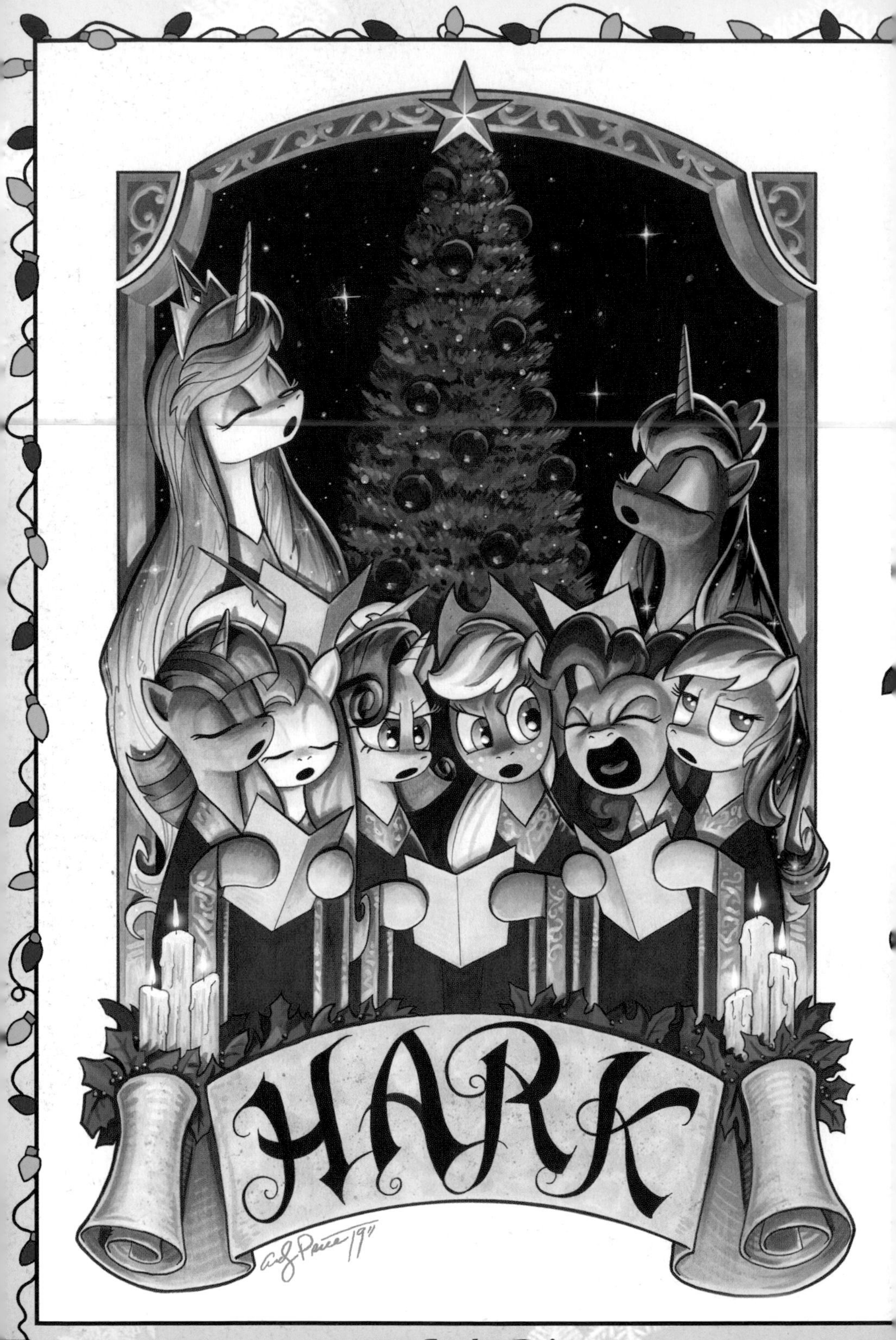
HARK
Andy Price '19

ART BY Andy Price

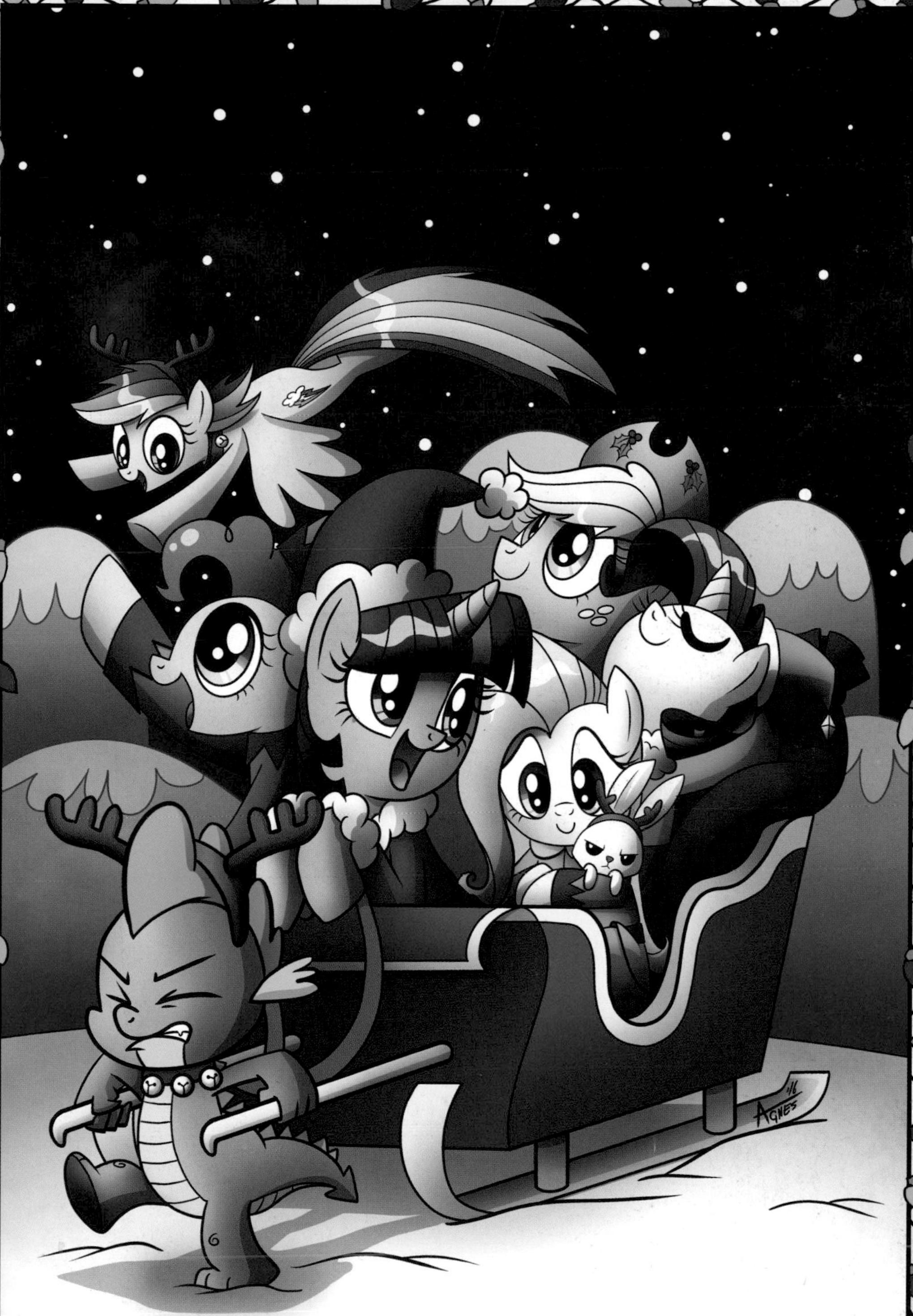
AGNES '16

ART BY Agnes Garbowska

The End.